PRAISE FOR THE LAD ...

"[A] history mystery in fine Victorian style! Anna Lee Huber's spirited debut mixes classic country-house mystery with a liberal dash of historical romance."

—*New York Times* bestselling author Julia Spencer-Fleming

"Riveting. . . . Huber deftly weaves together an original premise, an enigmatic heroine, and a compelling Highland setting."

—*New York Times* bestselling author Deanna Raybourn

"[A] fascinating heroine. . . . A thoroughly enjoyable read!"

—National bestselling author Victoria Thompson

"Reads like a cross between a Gothic novel and a mystery with a decidedly unusual heroine."

—*Kirkus Reviews*

"Includes all the ingredients of a romantic-suspense novel, starting with a proud and independent heroine. . . . Strong and lively characters as well as believable family dynamics, however, elevate this above stock genre fare."

—*Publishers Weekly*

"[A] clever heroine with a shocking past and a talent for detection."

—National bestselling author Carol K. Carr

"[Huber] designs her heroine as a woman who straddles the line between eighteenth-century behavior and twenty-first-century independence."

—New York Journal of Books

"[A] must read. . . . One of those rare books that will both shock and please readers."

—Fresh Fiction

"One of the best historical mysteries that I have read this year."

—Cozy Mystery Book Reviews

A FATAL
ILLUSION

ANNA LEE HUBER

BERKLEY PRIME CRIME
New York

BERKLEY PRIME CRIME
Published by Berkley
An imprint of Penguin Random House LLC
penguinrandomhouse.com

Library of Congress Cataloging-in-Publication Data

Names: Huber, Anna Lee, author.
Title: A fatal illusion / Anna Lee Huber.
Description: First edition. | New York: Berkley Prime Crime, 2023. |
Series: The Lady Darby mysteries
Identifiers: LCCN 2022056147 (print) | LCCN 2022056148 (ebook) |
ISBN 9780593198483 (trade paperback) | ISBN 9780593198490 (ebook)
Subjects: LCGFT: Detective and mystery fiction. | Novels.
Classification: LCC PS3608.U238 F38 2023 (print) |
LCC PS3608.U238 (ebook) | DDC 813/.6—dc23/eng/20221212
LC record available at https://lccn.loc.gov/2022056147
LC ebook record available at https://lccn.loc.gov/2022056148

First Edition: June 2023

Printed in the United States of America
2nd Printing

For my nieces and nephews—Andrea, Alexandra,
Angela, Liam, Amelia, Lilly, Aiden, Gavin, Reagan, Kendall,
Maddox, Nolan, Archie, Micah, and Clara.
May you always know how loved and cherished you are.

A Fatal
Illusion

CHAPTER I

Let me be that I am and seek not to alter me.

—WILLIAM SHAKESPEARE

"Wait, Kiera," my husband, Sebastian Gage, called as he guided his horse to the edge of the road. "It's best to let the coach go first down this hill."

I pulled up on Figg's reins, bringing the strawberry roan into line with Gage's chestnut gelding as our carriage lumbered over the crest of the ridge with our coachman skillfully handling the ribbons as it began its descent.

Though not as treacherous as it had once been, the slope leading down into the gorge was still quite formidable. I well remembered my first journey south on the Great North Road some ten or eleven years past, before a new road had been cut out of the limestone rock through which the River Went flowed. We'd clung to the walls of the coach as we'd been driven down the precipitous path into the narrow valley, and then been forced to walk alongside the carriage as we ascended in order to alleviate some of the burden for the horses as they toiled back up the other side. In the years since, I'd been exposed to some colorful curses by the coachmen of the passing mail and stagecoaches who regularly drove this route, all of whom despised the nuisance of this stretch of road as much as the rest of us.

My lips quirked at the sight of our coachman's lips moving as he passed, and I couldn't help but wonder what curse he was muttering to himself. But my amusement vanished when I recalled that my infant daughter was ensconced inside the carriage he'd been entrusted to drive, along with Emma's nanny, Mrs. Mackay, and my maid, Bree. Once the dust had settled from their passing, Gage and I urged our mounts to follow.

The sun shone hot on our backs as we left the shade of the old-growth forest behind us to navigate the steep, rutted road. I trusted in Figg's sure-footedness to manage the descent. There wasn't much more I could do, for it took most of my concentration to maintain my seat in the saddle. I might have remained in the carriage, but having spent nearly a week inside its confines on the road from the Highlands, I'd begun to relish any opportunity I could to escape. When we'd broken our journey in the Borders at Blakelaw House—my childhood home, which now belonged to my brother—I'd seized the chance to requisition the strawberry roan, who for all intents and purposes had always been mine, from the stables.

By all rights, I should have remained at Blakelaw House with our young child and the female members of our staff. At least, that's what any *normal* wife would have done. But I, and everyone around me, had long accepted I wasn't a typical gentlewoman, and I simply couldn't bear to wait in comfort while my husband faced what was before him.

The exact nature of what he was to confront wasn't yet known to us, but it soon would be—likely within the hour—and the evidence of that strain marked his handsome face. His strong jaw was tight, and his brow furrowed, and whenever I caught a glimpse of his pale blue eyes, I could see the fear lurking in their depths.

As if aware of my scrutiny, he pressed his hand to the breast of his deep green frock coat over the interior pocket, which contained the source of his distress. I'd watched him remove the letter often enough over the past six days, unfolding it to study the few short lines, as if perhaps, this time, the words would be different. But no matter how many times he read it, or how worn and pliant the paper became with use, the message never changed. His father had still been attacked along the Great North Road nine days ago.

It was impossible to know what we would discover once we reached Wentbridge. The letter Lord Gage's valet, Mr. Lembus, had penned to my husband had been short on details. Haste had clearly been his sole objective. That fact alone stirred the dread within me, as I knew it did Gage. For if his concern that word reach Gage promptly had not been so great, would he not have shared more? As such, the trepidation that we might arrive to find his father was already deceased was never far from either of our thoughts.

We could see little of what lay before us, for the carriage blocked the road, and the cuttings through the limestone soared twenty feet high on either side. Plants and vines had begun to take root in the crevices of the rock walls and along the verge of the road, and trees that had been trimmed back when the cutting was made had begun to gently arch over the lane in places, forming a tunnel. The air was thick with a swirling musk of damp from the vegetation and dust from passing coaches.

As we rounded a series of slight curves, the road began to level and the walls ended to afford us an expansive view of golden fields and brilliant blue skies. Several hundred feet farther along we spied the first stone cottages perched at the outskirts of the village. The carriage slowed, and Gage and I spurred our horses forward to overtake it now that we were no longer in danger of being bowled over by it on the steep incline.

Two riders waited at the edge of the road a short distance away, and my stomach dipped at the sight of the familiar figures. Gage had sent his half brother, Lord Henry Kerr, and his loyal valet, Anderley, ahead to do reconnaissance, as it were. For while Lembus's terse letter had said that Lord Gage had been taken to the village of Wentbridge, he hadn't told us exactly where. Perhaps because he didn't know where his employer would end up. By sending Henry and Anderley ahead of us to find out, we'd hoped to be spared from traveling back and forth across the village with a lumbering carriage and an infant in tow.

I searched the two men's faces as we approached, seeking any indication of what they'd uncovered—whether Lord Gage was alive or already deceased—but neither revealed more than a stoic resolve. Anderley's face habitually wore such an expression, so I found my eyes drawn toward Henry, who was not usually so adept at hiding his emotions. Though the prospect of facing his natural father for the first time in years, the father who had firmly stated he wanted nothing to do with him and then forbidden him to tell Gage—his half brother—of his existence, must be weighing on him heavily. That Gage now knew, and had confronted his father on the issue, albeit only in letters, simply increased the tension.

"Any word?" Gage asked as we drew our horses to a stop before them.

Anderley turned to Henry, perhaps feeling he should reveal their findings, and the pause made my heart stutter in my chest.

"He's alive," Henry finally declared.

Gage's relief was palpable as his head bowed and he inhaled a shuddering breath. I exhaled a breath of my own and reached for him, clasping his fingers tightly when he lifted his hand to mine. "Where is he?" he managed to ask after he'd composed himself.

"He's under the care of the local surgeon, a Dr. Josiah Barker, and apparently staying in his home. It's just a little farther along the road this way." Henry gestured in the direction we must travel.

Gage nodded to both men as the clatter of our carriage's wheels approached. "Lead on, then."

Henry and Anderley swung their thoroughbreds around and started up the road at an easy pace, but one that would not require our coachman to slow the carriage horses, and Gage and I fell in behind them. At first, I didn't speak, recognizing that my husband still needed another moment to gather himself. He'd been in more than half dread that we would learn his father was already deceased, and the discovery that he was not had staggered him. After all, their relationship had never been easy, particularly in the past few months. One could feel both profound relief and dread at the same time, just as one could love someone and still feel fiery anger, disappointment, and disgust. And those were only a handful of the complicated emotions his father provoked in us.

"At least the worst has not occurred," I ventured to say, trying to cast as positive a light on the situation as I could. "And the fact that he's survived this many days after his attack must be viewed as encouraging."

Gage's brow puckered. "Yes, but my father is a stubborn man. I fear he must be poor off, indeed, if he's condescended to stay in the home of a surgeon." We all knew that Lord Gage was nothing if not haughty.

"Maybe," I replied obliquely.

While it was true that most surgeons were considered below the dignity of gentlemen—getting their hands dirty as they did, setting bones and performing surgeries—their services *were* still needed. The physicians that the gentry and nobility traditionally relied upon for their medical needs could not be called upon to perform those less than genteel tasks. As such, on occasion a surgeon was required, and preferably one of an elevated status, such as my late husband, Sir Anthony Darby. Sir Anthony had already been wealthy and well connected when he was made sergeant surgeon to His Majesty, the late king George IV, who had then granted Sir Anthony a baronetcy for services rendered, further opening the door into that rarified world. There were other surgeons like he'd been. Though, the likelihood of a surgeon of such status being found in a small village in rural Yorkshire was rather miniscule.

"Whatever the case, we shall face it. And we shall face it together," I promised.

He turned his head to look at me, and I saw the strain it was causing him to remain composed. It was writ in the rigidity of his jaw and the way his skin stretched taut across his cheekbones. His solemn gaze shimmered with uncertainty, seeming to both beg me to say no more and plead with me to tell him what to do. Had I known the right words to say, I would have said them, but all I could do was remain at his side, to let him know he was not alone.

His throat worked as he swallowed, and a bead of sweat trickled down the side of his neck from his hairline, leaving a faint trail through the fine layer of dust coating our skin from the road. But better dirt than mud. We'd been fortunate in the weather thus far, enjoying a stretch of mostly dry, albeit warm, days, which had enabled us to travel more easily than a spell of rainy weather would have allowed.

We had yet to reach the heart of the village, which clustered about the River Went, but the number of cottages staggered along the roadside had increased. Henry and Anderley veered off on a narrow lane that appeared in a gap in the line of hedges bordering the road—one that all but obscured our view of anything to the east. Once beyond the hedgerow, the vista expanded, offering a sweeping view of a rolling, pastoral landscape beyond. While to our left stood a small, charming Georgian manor.

By no means was it as large or palatial as the homes of some of the nobility, but there was a graciousness to its simplicity, a pleasing aspect to its clean lines and tasteful landscaping. This was the home of a member of the gentry or a prosperous businessman, or, as it appeared, a surgeon of no small means, and certainly not a dwelling to be scoffed at by all but the most supercilious of individuals. I wasn't sure where Lord Gage fell on that spectrum.

Our approach up the short gravel drive must have been noted, for before any of us could dismount, the door was opened, and a rather distinguished-looking man emerged. He was dressed in sober gentleman's garments and stood with one hand propped beneath his dark coat on his hip. Gage assisted me in descending, and I could sense that he was bracing himself for what was to come as he concentrated on the task of guiding my right leg over the top pommel and lowering me to the ground. When his gaze lifted to mine, a mask of polite reserve had fallen over his features—the one he donned whenever he wished to hide his emotions from others. Pulling my arm through his, he guided me across the yard toward the man waiting, with Henry following us a few steps behind.

"You must be Mr. and Mrs. Gage," the man declared in a pleasing tenor pitch. I judged him to be approximately twoscore years of age, perhaps a little older, and he possessed a head of thick cinnamon brown hair which seemingly refused to be tamed, adding even more length to an already long, narrow face with an equally long, narrow nose. It was by no means an attractive set of features, but it was not unpleasant to behold either.

"We are," Gage confirmed.

"Then you must be searching for Lord Gage." He gave a little bow at the waist. "I am Josiah Barker. I've had the privilege of treating your father."

I couldn't help but search the surgeon's face for any sign of sarcasm, for given how difficult Lord Gage was to contend with when he was healthy, I could only imagine he was tenfold worse when he was injured and unwell. But from all appearances, he appeared to be in earnest.

He looked behind him toward the interior of his home, where a woman I suspected was his wife lingered—her gown was too fine to belong to a servant—and beyond her a tall man who may have been their butler. "Please, you are most welcome in our home." His regard drifted over our shoulders. "Your servants as well."

"Thank you," I said, just as I heard Emma fussing. I turned to beckon Mrs. Mackay forward, knowing it must be almost time for my daughter to nurse. Taking her into my arms, I cradled her close, noting her red cheeks and how she was sucking on her fist. She was a sweaty, unhappy baby.

Dr. and Mrs. Barker both took the sudden appearance of an infant in stride as we were ushered inside the entry hall, paneled in pale oak and boasting a staircase with handsome woodwork. Already it was cooler simply stepping out of the sun into the shade. Gage introduced Henry while through the doorway I noted the Barkers' servants assisting Anderley and our coachman with the horses. A maid also appeared to guide Bree and Mrs. Mackay around to the servant's entrance.

"You have come a long way, I gather, and are undoubtedly exhausted," Dr. Barker declared once the essential cordialities were shared. "So I will be brief."

He pressed his hands together before him, almost as if in prayer, gesturing with them as he made each point. I noted their elegance. Sir Anthony's hands had been large and rather crude. A stark comparison with these small and dexterous digits. Given the manner in which a surgeon often had to make fine, precise movements, I imagined Dr. Barker's hands were a great asset.

"Lord Gage, indeed, suffered numerous injuries during an attack along the highway some nine days ago, but he is recovering. I daresay he is out of the wood now, and should continue to improve at a good pace." He smiled softly at each of us in turn. "While I am sure you wish to verify that for yourself, he is at the moment resting. So why don't you take some time to wash the dust from your faces." His eyes dipped to Emma. "And see to the needs of your little one."

"Aye, please," Mrs. Barker urged, speaking for the first time. Her voice was a shade less genteel than that of her husband, but far from coarse, and her Yorkshire inflection was perfectly understandable. "I've had the maids bring fresh water and towels to thy rooms."

"Oh, but we don't mean to be an imposition," my husband replied, having noted the same wording I had. "We understand there are a number of inns in the village. I'm sure we can acquire a set of rooms at one of those."

"'Tis no imposition," Dr. Barker assured him. "I can only imagine how anxious you are to be near to your father. And a coaching inn is truly no place for an infant. Not with all the manner of people who pass through, and the illnesses they might carry." He turned to me in empathy. "What perturbations you must have suffered already on this journey." He nodded his head in finality. "No, no. You must stay here at Bowcliffe House. I insist."

Gage and I shared a look, recognizing that everything he had said was true. We *had* suffered great pangs of anxiety over Emma's well-being, especially with the cholera morbus still plaguing parts of the country. To decline such a generous invitation when it was the best solution would be not only be churlish, but foolish.

My husband extended his hand to the surgeon. "Then, with gratitude, we accept."

"Good, good," he answered, shaking Gage's hand. "Mrs. Barker will show you to your rooms."

I spared a glance at Henry then, wondering if perhaps we should have consulted with him before agreeing to stay, but truly there was no other answer we could give, and I could see in Henry's face that he'd accepted that. Though, that did not mean he was easy with this fact. After all, he must be as apprehensive, if not more, about seeing Lord Gage. The man who had all but told him flatly that he never cared to see him again.

Before I could say anything, Emma's dissatisfied grunts transformed into outright wails. Mrs. Barker turned to offer me a sympathetic smile as she reached the foot of the stairs. I wondered briefly if they had children, but then all my attention was recaptured by Emma as I tried to soothe her and keep her from waking her grandfather, who needed his rest if he was still recovering. Lord Gage would also, no doubt, be easier to contend with if he was well rested than cranky and overtired. In that, he and his infant granddaughter were very alike.

CHAPTER 2

I thanked Mrs. Barker hastily as she showed me into a room whose walls were painted a soft green and then settled into the cushioned bergère chair positioned near the window to see to Emma. The poor dear's cheeks were flushed, and not just with anger. I pulled the bonnet from her head, letting her golden curls—so like her father's—spring free, and loosened the swaddling wrapped around her so that her skin could breathe before opening my own plum riding jacket.

Once her immediate needs were met, I was able to take greater stock of my surroundings. The room was lovely and feminine, without being blatantly so. It was decorated in shades of green and creamy white, with eyelet curtains and a plush bed I wished I could sink into and fall asleep. Though, truth be told, I was tired enough that if I tipped my head back and allowed my eyes to close, I suspected I could fall asleep just as easily in this chair.

A yawn cracked my jaw and I blinked wide, turning toward the view outside my window. Perched at the front corner of the house, my room overlooked the drive as well as a short sweep of lawn leading to a verdant patch of trees. Just at the edge of my current vantage I could see a small section of what appeared to be a summerhouse of sorts, or a gazebo.

As I'd initially surmised, Dr. Barker was a prosperous surgeon. That, or he'd inherited his wealth. Perhaps a little of both. Which helped calm some of my lingering fears about Lord Gage, despite the fact we'd yet to see him or learn the extent of his injuries. Gage was right. His father was undoubtedly pretentious. But Dr. Barker's home was just grand enough that Lord Gage would not have protested about staying here, presuming he was well enough to even raise such objections.

However, Dr. Barker had said his patient was on the mend, and I had believed him. What reason would he have to lie? Unless he feared we would blame him for Lord Gage's failure to heal? I swiftly considered and then discarded this possibility. He must realize we would apprehend the truth of Lord Gage's status for ourselves soon enough. No, Lord Gage must be improving, though from how dire of a state he had been rendered, we still needed to ascertain. Given that fact, all terms were relative.

Regardless, I felt lighter as at least that darker fear lifted from my shoulders. Lord Gage would not die. Or at least, he wouldn't do so before Gage was able to see him. After all, a surgeon, no matter how skilled, was not God. Sometimes things happened that were out of any of our control. But for now, Lord Gage lived. He would meet his first grandchild, and Gage would be able to speak with him.

It would not be an easy conversation. I knew how much hurt and anger the revelations he'd learned about his father in March had caused my husband. A hurt and anger that scored deep into his history and had shattered the tentative peace he had begun to make with his father late last year. A hurt and anger that were even now etched into the furrows in Gage's brow when he entered my room from the adjoining chamber a short time later.

He'd changed into a deep blue frockcoat and buff trousers, and his hair was still damp at the temples from where he'd washed his face and neck. My own skin suddenly felt grimy in comparison.

"I had them bring the luggage into the dressing room through my chamber," he told me. "Miss McEvoy is waiting for you there now. If Emma is finished, why don't you let me take her while you rap on the door to let Miss McEvoy know you're ready for her."

It was evident he was anxious we be ready as soon as his father woke, and I could not blame him. So I passed him our daughter and moved to do just as he'd suggested. "Our rooms are connected, then, through the dressing room?"

"Yes, rather conveniently."

I cast a coy smile at him over my shoulder only to discover his attention was entirely devoted to Emma. Then he wasn't being flirtatious, but rather referring to our shared luggage. This discovery was a bit lowering, but then I scolded myself for imagining that Gage could possibly have anything else on his mind other than our pending interview with his father.

After a swift rap on the dressing room door, I continued to the washstand, pouring water from a beautiful white-and-blue ewer into a matching bowl.

My maid, Bree, came bustling through the door as I splashed the water onto my face. "The cornflower muslin, m'lady?" she asked, looking as neat and trim as ever despite the long journey as she held the gown up for my inspection and I patted my face dry with a towel.

"Yes, that will do."

She laid the dress and its accessories across the bed and then hastened forward to help me remove the gold-epaulette-trimmed jacket of my riding habit which fit snug about my shoulders. "I understand we're to stay here until Lord Gage is weel enough to travel?" she asked in her gentle Scottish brogue.

My eyes cut to Gage, who was now tickling our daughter beneath her chin, much to her delight. "For the time being, at least," I answered honestly, uncertain what the next few days would hold.

I could see the pucker forming in Bree's brow in the mirror hanging over the washstand as she unfastened my skirt. "Is something wrong?" I asked. "I thought you'd be happy to hear we'd be staying here rather than at a busy inn."

"Oh, I am. I am, m'lady," she assured me as the skirt dropped to my feet and I stepped from the confines only for her to whisk it away. "'Tis only . . ." She clamped her lips together for a moment, as if wishing she could take back her words, but then continued. "I doona think the staff here are happy aboot it."

"Perhaps they're worried we'll make more work for them, as we indeed shall," I conceded. "But not as much as they might fear."

"It's Lembus," Gage declared without preamble as Bree settled the cornflower gown down over my head. I turned to see he had Emma propped upright on his lap facing him. "He's adopted my father's worst tendencies, particularly when it comes to staff members of a lower rank, as he probably sees all the staff here being."

Our reflection in the mirror showed that Bree and I were both grimacing in the same manner. I could well imagine how such behavior had been received by Dr. Barker's staff, especially his upper servants.

"When Anderley is affecting his best imitation of a pompous Englishman," Gage continued, "like he did when you first met him, Miss McEvoy, he's emulating Lembus."

"I heard that," the valet called out through the wood of the dressing room door.

This startled a laugh out of me and an impish grin from Bree, highlighting her deep dimples.

"Aye, he was behavin' a might too high in the instep," she replied, raising her voice to ensure Anderley would hear her.

"Now, see here," he replied, his footsteps moving closer. "May I come through the door to defend myself?"

"No," Bree and I replied at once, and then grinned at each other, for the truth was, my gown was nearly buttoned and she just needed to see to my hair.

Anderley exhaled in exasperation before stomping away, and I pressed a hand to my mouth lest he hear me laughing at him.

"Clearly these walls are thin." Gage stood, moving toward the window with Emma draped over his shoulder, gnawing on her fist.

I waved my fingers at her as I sank down on the bench before the dressing table and she gave me a slobbery smile.

Bree sighed at the sight of the unruly mass of my chestnut hair slipping from its pins but knew better than to attempt a total repair. Instead, she did her best to make quick work of smoothing out the worst of the upheaval. She had just replaced the last pin when there was a knock at the door. My heart gave a tiny leap in my chest, and I turned to look at Gage, wondering if nerves also churned in his stomach.

A young maid with a gap between her front teeth stood in the corridor when Bree opened the door. "Dr. Barker said to tell thee tha' his lordship is awake."

"Please tell him we will be with them in a moment," I replied, starting to turn to ask Bree to take Emma to Mrs. Mackay when I spied the nurse already standing in the corridor behind the Barkers' maid.

"I figured you'd wish me to take the bairn noo," she explained as she stepped forward.

Gage crossed the room to pass Emma to her, and I caught an unpleasant whiff. "Yes, I'm afraid she needs to be seen to."

"Aye, fillin' our bellies tends to have that effect."

Before Mrs. Mackay could go, I reached out to detain her. "Will you bring her to Lord Gage's chamber in about ten minutes' time?" I felt Gage's eyes on my face, for I had not suggested this move to him first, but I kept my gaze steadily trained on Mrs. Mackay, on the remote chance he might object. We both knew Lord Gage was anxious to meet his granddaughter, and it seemed boorish not to allow him the opportunity to do so as soon as possible. Plus, I had a suspicion we might have need of her calming presence before this interview was over.

I could see in Mrs. Mackay's wrinkled face that she'd understood my unspoken thoughts. "Aye. Miss Emma is a natural peacemaker, isna' she. That is, when she's no' in a right stramash," she teased her. The nurse must have been informed of the state of affairs between Gage and his father by one of the other members of our staff. That, or she'd inferred a great deal from our general unease the past week and more. "Aye, I'll bring her to ye," she finished before turning to go, prattling to Emma as she went.

I looked up to find Gage eyeing me in wary affront. "Is that really wise?"

Sensing this was not a conversation for her ears, Bree hurried to the other side of the room to busy herself with the task of gathering up my discarded garments.

Even so, I edged a step closer, reaching up to smooth the already neat lapels of his Spanish blue coat. "I know we both understand that our daughter is not a pawn to be played between you and your father, no matter what he has done. She is not part of it." Some months prior to her even being conceived, I might have blackmailed Lord Gage into attending our wedding with the threat of denying him access to any future grandchildren, but I had known even then, as I knew now, that I would never go through with it. Not as long as his actions didn't harm them.

Gage's pale blue eyes still glittered with uncertainty, prodding me to continue delicately despite the specter I would be raising.

"Besides which, there is no guarantee that your father will not somehow take a turn for the worse. And how would we feel if we denied him the opportunity to meet his granddaughter— the very reason he was traveling this road north to Edinburgh— while we had the chance?"

He inhaled, seeming to find it more difficult than usual to fill his lungs, and then closed his eyes, nodding on a long sigh. "Of course. You're right."

The back of my eyes began to sting at the evidence of the pain and insecurity he was struggling with, but before I could find the words to offer him some sort of comfort, Henry appeared at our sides.

He had dressed with the utmost care in a coat of bottle green superfine and dark cravat. His auburn hair had been combed and restrained with a sweet-smelling pomade. When he tugged at the front of his coat not once, but twice, exposing his anxiety, any annoyance I might have felt at his untimely interruption was superseded by a pulse of deep affection. He was in no easier a position than Gage.

"Perhaps I shouldn't take part in this first interview." His voice was tight with nerves, and possibly a bit of trepidation. Something I could well understand. Lord Gage could be incredibly intimidating. During the days of Gage's and my engagement, it had taken all my courage to face his father and later stand up to him.

"Nonsense," Gage declared, his jaw hardening. "You're also his son. You have just as much a right to be there."

While I wasn't so certain Henry's suggestion didn't have merit, allowing us to soften Lord Gage to the idea that his second son was here before they confronted each other, I also knew that my father-in-law appreciated only strength. The slightest show of weakness would make his upper lip curl in disgust. Of course, the dichotomy of this was that he also resented any resistance to his orders. He expected his son to follow his directives without argument but would have also despised him for doing so. This had left Gage forever in an unwinnable situation. And I imagined the same treatment was in store for Henry.

"Come. Let's see how serious his injuries are," Gage said, pulling my arm through his and striding forward before Henry or I could contradict him. He led us around a turn in the corridor to a room near the rear of the house, and I realized he must have already been informed where his father was convalescing. I wondered for a moment whether Henry would follow, but after a brief moment of hesitation, he fell in step behind us.

Gage paused before the door, squaring his shoulders and arching his neck as if his cravat was too tight. His agitation hummed along the surface of his skin, and I reached across with my other hand to squeeze his upper arm in support. He nodded his head once sharply and then lifted his hand to rap twice before reaching for the handle.

My first impression was one of relief, for the chamber was filled with light and air, the windows partially opened to allow a breeze to lightly billow the curtains—one that was rife with the sweet scent of flowers from the garden below. So many physicians and other medical men insisted on keeping convalescence rooms dark and closed up, making them stuffy and confining, but clearly Dr. Barker understood the benefits of fresh air.

However, my relief was short-lived.

Lord Gage reclined against the pillows mounded behind him, evidently having insisted on receiving us sitting upright but not being quite equal to the task. His face was pale and his eyes sunken with dark circles surrounding them. Whatever his injuries, he looked as if he'd been ravaged by a fever at some point, likely from an infection. He had dropped at least a stone's worth of weight. His face was clean-shaven, and his gray hair carefully combed, but no amount of grooming could hide the marks of ill health.

The only part of his appearance that reassured me was the hard glitter of his silver eyes. As contradictory as it seemed, that cold stare consoled me, letting me know that my father-in-law had not yet given up the fight and that Emma would not lose the last grandparent she had left. Not yet.

"You certainly took your time in coming," he groused, his voice sounding rougher than usual, either from his infirmity or disuse.

Gage stiffened. "We were in Argyll, Father."

"What the devil were you doing in Argyll? And with my granddaughter." His scrutiny shifted to me and then toward the door. "Where is she?"

The moment he noticed Henry was more than obvious, for his face transformed into a ferocious scowl. One that seemed to startle Dr. Barker, standing by the opposite side of the bed.

"What is *he* doing here?" Lord Gage barked. "He has no place here."

"Of course he does. He's your son, isn't he?" Gage challenged. "You've admitted as much."

"He's Bowmont's son," Lord Gage retorted, speaking of the duke who'd claimed Henry and raised him as his own. "I already made it clear I want nothing to do with him. Just as I made it clear you were not to be told." His eyes narrowed. "Though, I suppose the fact that he and his mother disregarded my orders means I need not uphold my end of the bargain either."

My heart ached for Henry, hovering near the door and trying

to appear stoic while his father and brother argued about him almost as if he wasn't there. I knew how anxious he was that Lord Gage not follow through on his threat to reveal certain secrets about his mother, the Duchess of Bowmont, if they revealed the truth about Henry's paternity to Gage. Given the scandalous things already whispered about the duchess and all but publicly confirmed, such as the fact that the four youngest of her six children had not been fathered by the duke, I couldn't help but wonder about this secret Lord Gage held over them. What could be so shocking that they feared his exposing it?

My husband's expression turned thunderous. "If you do that, if you divulge whatever it is you've been threatening them with, then I shall simply have to disclose a secret or two of your own."

Dr. Barker's already wide eyes grew even larger at this pronouncement as his gaze darted back and forth between father and son.

But far from being cowed, Lord Gage seemed to be emboldened. "If you knew what I do, you would be singing a different tune." His shrewd glare shifted to his other son. "Wouldn't he, Lord Henry?" He tipped his head back, resting it on the pillows mounded behind him as he assessed the younger man. "Or don't you know your mother's secret either?"

His barb appeared to have hit its mark, for Henry looked distinctly uncomfortable, though the clamped line of his lips and flushed cheeks told me he wanted to defend his mother.

"Ah, such loyal sons," Lord Gage mocked. "At least, to their mothers.

"My mother deserved my loyalty," Gage snapped. "As she deserved *yours*."

"Still ever ready to play the white knight, aren't you," his father scoffed. "To rescue the maiden and leap to the damsel's defense." His eyes flicked toward me. "To marry them even. But you haven't always been correct, have you? They haven't all been worthy of your services."

Gage's face blanched, and I realized his father was referring to the young woman Gage had fallen in love with in Greece eleven years prior when he'd joined the Greeks' struggle for independence from the Ottoman Empire. The woman he had later learned had only pretended to love him in return so that he and his connections would continue to fund the militia commanded by her father. The woman who had berated him for refusing to take part in the massacre at Tripolitsa.

It was not something I could ever imagine my husband confiding in his father. He'd had a difficult enough time telling me. But perhaps I was wrong. Regardless, somehow Lord Gage had found out, and now he was throwing it in his son's face just so that he wouldn't have to admit to his own betrayal of his marriage vows.

"Enough," I ordered, stepping forward. "This is getting us nowhere. The fact of the matter is, I guessed. Something you should have realized someone would do sooner or later." I glanced between Lord Gage and Henry. "The likeness is striking enough, even if Henry possesses auburn hair rather than the golden blond you possessed in your youth and you are now somewhat diminished due to your injuries."

Lord Gage apparently didn't appreciate being reminded that he was no longer in his youth and did not appear at his best, for he glowered at me. Something I ignored.

"So no one broke their word." I could see in Henry's face that he was about to contradict this. "And had Henry and his mother tried to deny it, I wouldn't have believed them. Therefore, if you want to blame someone for telling Sebastian what he had every right to know, then blame me," I challenged my father-in-law. "For I wasn't about to keep such a secret from my husband."

I trusted Gage wouldn't mention that I'd caused enough damage by concealing it from him for over seven weeks in order to honor my promise to Henry that he be the one to tell him, or that Henry wouldn't muddy the waters by notifying Lord Gage that he had been the one to actually speak the words. The details didn't matter, because the point remained the same. Once I'd realized who Henry was, it was a foregone conclusion that sooner or later Gage would be informed.

"Now, I'm sure both of your sons share my desire to hear the extent of your injuries and treatment from Dr. Barker. After all, we did hasten all the way here to ensure your well-being. And hasten, we did," I reiterated, lest Lord Gage attempt to refute this with another snide remark. "I would prefer to hear it *before* your granddaughter joins us in a few moments. So if you wish to meet Emma, I suggest you keep a civil tongue in your head."

Having finished delivering this speech, I turned toward Dr. Barker, nodding for him to proceed, while my pulse continued to pound in my ears. No one could rile me quite like my father-in-law, and when he hurt or attacked Gage, and evidently now Henry, my anger doubled. I felt Gage's hand press warm against my spine—in comfort, in gratitude, in solidarity—maybe all three.

"Yes, well . . ." Dr. Barker's voice came out rather high, perhaps indicating he was reconsidering his invitation for us to stay here. He cleared his throat, allowing it to settle back into a lower register. "As you know—or perhaps *don't* know—his lordship was brought to me following an attack on the Great North Road. He was suffering from a bullet wound to the right thigh and multiple bruises and lacerations to his torso and limbs."

My hand lifted unconsciously to my throat as my regard dipped to Lord Gage's surly visage. "How serious?"

"He'd lost a great deal of blood, and the bullet proved difficult to extract," Dr. Barker admitted. "We worried for some time that he might not revive. But he regained his senses for about a day and a half. Long enough to ingest a few bowls of fortifying beef broth before he developed an infection. Had he not done that, I'm not sure he would have had the strength to withstand the fever."

Lord Gage suddenly appeared wanner than he had moments before, but I didn't know if that was because his vigor was fading or because I better understood how precarious his situation had been.

"But you said he's improving. That he's now out of the wood?" Gage pressed.

The surgeon nodded hesitantly. "But *only* if he continues to rest. Too much movement, too much *excitement*, could hinder his recovery." The sternness of his voice was reprimand enough. Obviously today's disagreement had been more provoking than he believed was safe for his patient.

Never mind that Lord Gage had started it. He was the injured party—at least physically—and still in a great deal of discomfort if not outright pain. I remembered how sore I'd been when I'd been merely clipped by a bullet two years past, and I could imagine how much worse it must be for him. As such, he should be excused for some of his cantankerous behavior. We, on the other hand, could claim no such defense despite the emotional injury Lord Gage had caused both of his sons.

"Lembus shared nothing about the extent of my father's injuries in his missive," Gage asserted solemnly, though I couldn't tell whether this was directed at Dr. Barker, Lord Gage, or as a reminder to himself. "It was very brief."

A thought occurred to me then. "What of Lembus?" I asked. "And the coachman? Were they also injured?"

Lord Gage's jaw hardened.

"A few bumps and scrapes. Nothing more," Dr. Barker replied. His gaze lowered to his patient. "But I'm afraid the footman was beyond my aid."

Gage and I both straightened in alarm.

He was the first to find his tongue. "Your footman was killed?"

The question had been directed at his father, who continued to stare at the mound of his feet at the end of the bed, but Dr. Barker answered. "Yes. He was also shot."

"Have the authorities been informed?"

"Yes. Our local magistrate is aware of the matter. The coroner's jury that took place soon after the incident found that the footman had been murdered and his lordship attacked by a person or persons as yet unknown, pending further investigation by the parish constable."

That was all well and good, and exactly as to be expected, but parish constables were not always known for their astuteness and diligence. One would hope that the fact that a nobleman had been attacked—a nobleman who was a particular friend of the king—and his footman *killed* would properly motivate the official, but that didn't mean their abilities were up to the task.

I turned to meet my husband's eye, and I could tell he was thinking the same thing I was, though neither of us spoke aloud. If justice was to be done, it might very well fall to us to pursue it.

CHAPTER 3

W hat happened, sir?" Gage asked, reverting to the formality that often colored his interactions with his father.

His father's gray eyes shifted to meet his, their depths chill like silvery moonlight on water, but he didn't speak.

"How did the attack occur?" he rephrased, moving a step nearer to the bed.

Before Lord Gage could reply—and I held doubts that he intended to, for his jaw was set at the same stubborn angle as his son's did when he had no intention of divulging something—there was a knock on the door. I nodded to Henry to open it as I approached, already anticipating who it was. As Mrs. Mackay passed Emma to me, she searched my face for some indication of how our interview was progressing. What she saw there evidently was not reassuring, for her lips curled in silent commiseration.

Emma gurgled with contentment, happy now that her belly was full and she was swaddled in dry linens. She reached for my chin as I moved toward the bed, and I couldn't help but smile.

My eyes lifted to Gage, curious to see if he wished to take her, but he stepped back, apparently satisfied to allow me the honor of introducing our daughter.

"My lord," I proclaimed, turning and dipping my arms as I neared him so that he could better see, "meet Emma Alana Charlotte Gage, your granddaughter."

What I had been expecting from my ruthless father-in-law, I wasn't sure, but it wasn't the warm flush of affection that washed over his hitherto stern visage or the glitter of almost reverence that lit his eyes. His expression brought everything within me to a standstill. It rattled me, for I had never seen anything remotely resembling genuine love reflected in his features. Not for his friends, not for Gage, and certainly not for me. Though he had shown a softer, more compassionate side to me briefly in London the previous autumn.

I was glad when he urged me to perch next to him on the bed for, leaned over as I was, his sudden transformation would have caused me to topple onto it anyway.

He offered her his finger, which Emma grasped, studying his face before giving him a toothless grin. One that her grandfather was helpless not to return.

The sight of them smiling at each other shifted something inside me, and the sensation wasn't altogether comfortable. Because for all the relief I felt in seeing Lord Gage so readily take a liking to his granddaughter when part of me had feared he would disapprove of my not producing first a grandson and future heir, there was also the jarring recollection of all the hurt he'd caused me and his son in the past, and the blunt realization that he wasn't incapable of warmth and affection after all. He'd simply chosen not to give it.

And if I was stunned, how much more so was Gage?

I looked up at him, unsurprised to see his features twisted

into an expression that defied description. There was astonishment and satisfaction and tenderness, yes, but also hurt and disillusionment and longing. The moment was bittersweet in every sense of the word.

"May I hold her?" The hesitance in Lord Gage's voice, and the fact that he'd actually asked and not demanded, stunned me even further.

After a quick look at Dr. Barker to ensure he didn't object, I carefully passed her over, settling Emma's head into the crook of his left elbow so as not to discomfort his wounded right leg.

Gage moved closer, resting his hand on my shoulder as we watched his father murmur gentle compliments to his granddaughter. Compliments that Emma appeared to be eating up, if all the cooing and grinning she was doing were any indication. I lifted my hand to lay it over top of my husband's, intertwining our fingers, and wishing this moment could have been enjoyed without the splinter of pain from Lord Gage's past behavior still lodged in my heart.

"She looks just like you did, Sebastian," his father said, never removing his eyes from her. "All golden curls and smiling charm. You had all the officers' wives eating out of your palm before you could even speak."

I looked up at my husband, having forgotten he'd spent the first three years of his life in a cottage outside Plymouth. That he hadn't moved with his mother to his grandfather's estate on Dartmoor until she had fallen ill. By the sight of his stricken expression, it was easy to guess that his father had never spoken to him of such things. When Gage was growing up, his father had always been away far more than he was present—off fighting Napoléon or manning the naval blockade for fifty weeks out of a year. And when he was there, Gage had once confessed to me, his father seemed to have only criticism for what he'd done wrong, trying to pack in a year's worth of instruction and discipline rather than love and attention.

It was then that I remembered Henry standing near the foot of the bed. He stood stiffly, staring at his father holding Emma in his arms, his face a rigid mask of repressed pain.

I opened my mouth to say something, though I didn't know what, but he turned and left the room. The sight of his natural father cooing over his new granddaughter and speaking fondly about his first son's infancy were apparently too much to bear. And who could blame him? Not when Lord Gage had so coldly rejected him just a few short minutes earlier.

I felt Gage's hand tighten around my shoulder, and I pressed my hand harder over his, knowing guilt was stirring within him. But Henry's pain was not his doing. That fault lay solely with his father. Yes, Henry deserved our empathy and support, but Gage's adopting unfounded feelings of guilt would do no one good, especially not Henry.

Lord Gage appeared to note his second son's disappearance as well, for a pleat formed between his brows—one that might have been caused by irritation or remorse. Perhaps he was not so indifferent to Henry after all. Or perhaps he was merely in pain. His rough and perpetually bronzed skin from all his years at sea was looking increasingly gray and haggard. He had rallied at the sight of Emma, but now he seemed to be fading again.

When his head fell back against his pillows while he still tried to retain the semblance of a smile for his granddaughter, I felt my first pulse of true alarm since our arrival. Lord Gage might be out of the wood, but he was far from well, and as Dr. Barker had cautioned, without great care, he could just as easily plunge back into the thick of it.

The surgeon stepped forward then. "I'm afraid I must insist we cut this visit short," he proclaimed, not unkindly. "His lordship needs his rest."

"Yes, of course," I murmured, taking Emma from Lord Gage's arms. "Later perhaps. Or tomorrow morning."

Lord Gage nodded his head weakly. "Yes, I should like that."

Pushing to my feet, I glanced anxiously at my husband, who had yet to speak since his father had taken hold of Emma.

"Get your rest, sir." Gage's voice firmed. "We shall take care of everything else."

His father didn't respond, his eyes already drifting shut. His teeth gritted against a twinge of pain, and then his features fell slack.

Dr. Barker dipped his head to us as we moved toward the door and then returned his attention to his patient.

I wasn't surprised to find Bree, Anderley, and Mrs. Mackay congregated before the door to my bedchamber, whispering, when we returned. Their voices fell silent, but they didn't bother to hide their curiosity and concern.

"He is recovering, but still very weak," Gage said in answer to their unspoken query. "I suspect it will be some days or even weeks before he can safely be moved."

The servants exchanged looks of equal parts misgiving and resolve.

"What of the attackers?" Anderley asked. "Have they been apprehended?"

"That is a question I shall have to put to the parish constable tomorrow." Gage's jaw set. "Particularly as we've just learned that this isn't merely a case of assault, but murder."

Bree gestured to the valet, her eyes a well of sympathy. "Anderley just told us he'd learned his lordship's footman had been killed. Tha' they had to bury him in the churchyard in Darrington."

"Lembus?" Gage surmised, correctly thinking the two valets might have exchanged words. They *were* familiar to each other.

"Yes." Anderley's face contorted into an unpleasant expression. "He had a number of things to say." Not all of which were complimentary to me and Gage, I suspected, as they were coming from Lord Gage's valet.

Gage's voice hardened. "Well, he can say them to my face, then, for I've a few questions of my own. Go find him and my father's coachman. I believe it's still Mr. Melton."

Anderley confirmed this.

"Beg a room from Mrs. Barker for us to use to speak with them."

He hurried off to do as instructed, and Gage turned to Bree, speaking in a low voice. "Miss McEvoy, I've a task for you, if you're willing."

"O' course," she replied, straightening to her full height.

"While Lembus is otherwise occupied, see what you can learn from the staff here." He arched a single eyebrow. "I imagine they're none too happy with my father and his staff's continued presence. Perhaps they would be willing to share anything they might know if they thought it might remove their unwanted guests sooner."

Bree's eyes twinkled. "Aye, I've already gathered they're none too fond o' Mr. Lembus. I'll see what I can do."

As she peeled away, Mrs. Mackay stepped forward. "I suppose ye wish me to take Miss Gage."

"Do the Barkers have any children?" I asked as I handed my daughter to her.

Her gentle smile turned sad. "Nay. And wi' a great big nursery on the floor above wi' no bairns to fill it."

Then there would be no governess or nursemaids for Mrs. Mackay to question. I thought back to the sympathetic look Mrs. Barker had offered me when Emma had begun fussing as she led us to our rooms, wondering if it had also been masking pain. Or perhaps relief? The world presumed all women desired children, but I'd learned to stop making such assumptions.

"Did you happen to see where Lord Henry went?" Gage queried before she could depart.

"Doon the stairs." Her solemn stare met his and then mine. "He seemed troubled."

Though she did not pose a question or speculate on the cause of his discontent, it was quite clear she'd guessed it. She didn't wait for a response, but moved off toward the second set of stairs with Emma.

"Should we look for him?" I murmured.

Gage's lips flattened and his brow creased as he peered off in the direction his half brother had gone. "Give him some time. If I were in his shoes, I would not want anyone prodding at the wound my father just delivered. Not so soon."

I nodded, wishing something could be done. Unfortunately, the outcome was entirely up to Lord Gage.

I'd feared just such a thing happening. That Henry hoped and wished for more than Lord Gage was willing to give. That Lord Gage was cold and cruel enough to reject him to his face. But they were grown men, responsible for their own actions, both good and bad.

I heaved a sigh and reached for Gage's arm as we moved in the direction of the stairs. "Well, our first meeting with your father went better . . . and worse than I expected." I looked up at my husband's somber features, wondering what he was thinking. "What did you . . . ?"

"Not now, Kiera," he snapped, cutting me off with more force than was necessary. A fact he realized, for he brought us to a stop near the base of the stairs, closing his eyes as he exhaled a long breath. "I apologize. I shouldn't have barked at you." His features rippled with tension as he tried and failed to suppress all evidence of his pain. "I'm just . . . I'm not ready to discuss any of this yet."

I pressed my hand to his upper arm. "You don't have to explain. I understand." His gaze met mine, and I tried to communicate with my eyes what I couldn't with my words in such a public place. That I knew today had been difficult for him. That seeing his father in such a feeble condition while still holding so much anger against him was disorienting and bewildering, and it had wreaked havoc on what was left of his self-composure and thrown his emotions into disarray. It would take time to untangle it all.

And untangle it he would have to, if he was to ever move past this and either reconcile with his father or cut ties forever. But at the same time, it wasn't something that could be wrestled with effectively when his feelings were still so raw. So for the time being, it was easier to focus on those things that could be quantified and physically confronted. Namely discovering the details of the attack.

Gage's arm tightened, the biceps bulging beneath my hand as he hugged me closer to his side, and his lips curled upward slightly at the corners in what I viewed to be an expression of gratitude. Had I not heard footsteps approaching, I would have arched up on my toes to press a kiss to his lips, but it wouldn't do to shock the Barkers' staff. Instead, I settled for tipping my head to the side to rest it on his shoulder as we continued down the steps.

Anderley stood in the corridor beside a door near the rear of the house, waiting to speak until we approached. "Mrs. Barker said we could use the morning room." He glanced over his shoulder, his eyebrows arching high. "Lembus is waiting inside, and Melton is being fetched from the stables as we speak."

What exactly he'd been communicating with his expression, I couldn't tell, but Gage seemed to understand. His valet noticed my inquiring look, flashing me a sudden grin, which only served to heighten my curiosity. Something he very well knew, if the impish glint in his eyes was any indication. I'd always thought of Anderley as a dark foil to my husband. They were both incredibly attractive, though I preferred Gage's golden good looks to Anderley's coal black hair and brown eyes. However, I could understand the manservant's appeal to other women, including Bree. That glint in his eyes all but promised the most delightful kind of mischief.

"Escort Melton in when he arrives," Gage directed him, before guiding me through the door.

True to its intention, the morning room's numerous windows looked out over the lawn to the east and the gardens to the north, so that sunlight could flood the room in the early hours of the day. But since it was summer, even in the late afternoon there was still ample light by which to see. It helped that the walls were painted in a soft shade of orange pink I associated with sunrises and sunsets. The furniture appeared to be of a more recent construction, and while I doubted the designer could be boasted of as being one of those who catered to the Quality, it was solid and well crafted. After all, not everyone could afford or wished to pay for a Hope or a Sheraton. The level of society to which the Barkers belonged—that of professionals, genteel tradesmen, and lesser gentry—had their own preferred designers and merchants, their own polite society stretching across rural England.

My father had been the grandson of a viscount and a duke, and my mother the daughter of a baron, but had my father not inherited substantial property from his mother, we could have easily fallen into the strata of provincial gentry. My first husband, Sir Anthony, had also just recently risen into the ranks of the nobility before I wed him. So I was quite familiar with the world in which the Barkers and their polite friends lived. In some ways, more familiar than I was with the beau monde, and the peers and royalty with whom I now associated as Gage's wife.

However, I did not have long to contemplate this before my

attention was drawn to the rather thin, dyspeptic-looking man who stood before the dormant stone hearth. It didn't take a great deal of imagination to realize this was Lord Gage's valet. After all, he had plainly perfected the disdainful glare he aimed at us from observing his employer. He was barely average in height, though his impeccable posture might have made him appear taller had Gage's six-foot-two-inch frame not towered over him.

Gage used that to his advantage, returning Lembus's scornful stare with one of his own. "My father might be allowed to greet me with such a sneer, but you certainly are not. I shall overlook it now because I am grateful you have taken such good care of him, but I warn you that I shall not be so lenient in the future. My father may encourage your contemptuous behavior toward those he deems less than him, but we both know he will not condone such treatment toward his heir *or* his daughter-in-law."

My husband was right. Lord Gage might deride us all he wished, but he would never allow such behavior from his staff, and it appeared from the manner in which Lembus's contempt faded to something much more muted, he realized it, too.

His point being made, Gage nodded to the armchair to the valet's left and guided me toward the saffron upholstered settee across from him. Once we were all settled, he eyed the other man. "Thank you for sending that message so swiftly. I only wish we had been closer when we received it."

"You weren't in Edinburgh, then?" he asked crisply, the derision he was struggling to conceal making his voice sound strangled.

Gage's lips pursed in annoyance before he responded. "No. About 150 miles northwest of the city, in Argyll."

Lembus made no response to this.

"Tell us what happened," Gage urged him. "Your letter was short on details." He held up his hand when the valet opened his mouth to argue. "Which is understandable given your haste to contact us. But my father was not well enough to provide us any more information, and you and Melton are perhaps more aware of the particulars anyway. So please, enlighten us."

A broad-shouldered man entered as he was speaking, clutching his hat before him. He was perhaps a decade older than Gage's five and thirty years, with a weathered face half hidden by a curling beard though his head was near bald. This was Mr. Melton, Lord Gage's coachman. Gage gestured for him to sit in the chair beside Lembus while Anderley moved to stand against the wall to our left, just inside the door.

"And start from the beginning," Gage continued, I supposed trusting Melton had heard at least part of what he'd been saying to Lembus. "You'd left London and were on your way to Edinburgh?"

"Yes," Lembus replied, straightening his deep brown coat. "His lordship was anxious to make good time. And we were doing so." He looked at the coachman uncertainly. "Until . . ."

"'Til a spoke broke on the left rear wheel, delayin' us by a few hours while 'twas fixed," Melton jumped in to explain. "When we reached the Blue Bell Inn here in Wentbridge there were still a few rooms that weren't bespoke, but his lordship insisted we press on to the White Swan in Ferrybridge, as planned."

The White Swan was one of the most famous and luxurious posting houses in northern England along the Great North Road. It also happened to be near the halfway point between London and Edinburgh along the route. As such, many people intentionally broke their journeys at Ferrybridge, and many more happened to pass through the waypoint's various inns because the stage between it and the next stop was seventeen miles. We ourselves had last paused at the White Swan on our trek southward to Wentbridge.

"So your last stop was at the Blue Bell?" Gage clarified.

"Aye," Melton continued, exchanging a look with Lembus.

"'Twas nearly full dark by tha' point, but there was a bright quarter moon. We'd just gained the top o' the hill and had begun to pick up speed when they came out o' the woods on either side o' the road, two on each side."

"Then there was four of them? Highwaymen?"

Melton nodded emphatically. "And 'twas clear we weren't the first carriage they'd waylaid. No' with how organized they were. The two at the front managed to grasp the lead horses' bridles and pull 'em to a stop before I could flick my lash at 'em more than twice. And before the poor lad could even lift the rifle to get off a shot."

Gage's hands flexed where he clasped them over his lap, the usual insouciance he affected when questioning witnesses or suspects having deserted him. "You're speaking of the footman? How was he killed?"

The coachman's already gruff voice grew rougher. "The blackguards at the front had pistols aimed at us and threatened to shoot if we moved. When their leader shot his lordship, it startled us, and Gregory began to lift the rifle in his lap. So they shot him in the head."

CHAPTER 4

I stifled a gasp, my stomach dipping at this discovery.

Melton shook his head, staring down at his feet. "He was just a lad. Not more than twenty. I don't know if 'twas instinct or foolishness that made him do it. But either way, it got him killed."

Gage's eyes shifted to Lembus. "Why did they shoot my father? Did he refuse to hand over his purse?"

Most highwaymen were after a passenger's valuables, and so long as the victim did not resist, death or injury was rare. Consequently, it was a logical assumption that he'd refused to give them his purse when they'd demanded it. Particularly given what we knew of Lord Gage's personality. I couldn't imagine him passing over anything that belonged to him lightly.

"No. They didn't even ask for it." Lembus's face contorted in perplexity. "That was what was so odd about it. They forced us from the carriage, and when your father offered them his purse, the man closest to him told him he'd take his black heart instead, and then shot him."

My skin flushed with residual fright, even knowing Lord Gage lay upstairs, recovering from his injuries. But I also couldn't help but be struck by the incongruity of the threat and its results.

"How close was the man standing to his lordship?" I asked Lembus, speaking for the first time. "Was he still on horseback?"

"Why, closer than I am to you," he answered. "He'd dismounted."

I frowned, turning to my husband to see if he was as confused. "Then was the gunman somehow thrown off balance, or did his lordship perhaps anticipate the bullet and try to dodge it?"

Lembus's brow furrowed. "No, my lady."

It was evident from all three men's faces that they didn't comprehend what I was attempting to ascertain, and I didn't bother to look at Anderley.

"Then how did Lord Gage end up shot in the leg?"

Lembus's expression was clearly copied from his employer, for it dripped with the scorn Lord Gage had so often exhibited when speaking to me. It left no doubt the valet thought I was an idiot. "The gunman lowered his weapon toward it and pulled the trigger."

My husband shifted position, finally grasping the point I was trying to make.

"He *lowered* the weapon? After he'd just said he'd take his heart instead."

Lembus's eyes widened, while Melton lifted a hand to scratch his beard.

"Why didn't he shoot him in the chest?" Gage demanded of his father's valet.

"I . . . I don't know," he stammered. "That's just what happened."

Gage scowled. "What transpired next?"

"His . . . his lordship dropped to the ground, and the man pulled out a cudgel, striking him with it repeatedly. I think he meant to hit him a great deal more, but the gunshot fired by one of his men—the shot that killed Gregory—seemed to unsettle him. He remounted, and they rode off into the night." He glanced warily at Melton, who sat in subdued silence. "There was nothing we could have done! Not without being shot and killed ourselves."

"I'm aware," Gage replied curtly. "I don't blame you. Had you both been injured, my father might have died along the side of the road before help arrived." He pushed to his feet, scraping his hand back from his forehead as he paced away from us and then returned. "I'm trying to understand. Wasn't my father carrying some kind of weapon?"

Lembus nodded. "Yes, two pistols. But the highwaymen anticipated such a thing and demanded he throw them to the ground before he descended."

My husband's gaze met mine. "Both?"

"Yes."

How had the highwaymen known for certain he carried two? Most men carried one, and Lord Gage would have lied about possessing two. He was no fool. But the gunmen had known better.

While Gage continued to grapple with this, I turned the other men's attention to a more obvious question.

"I know it was dark, and I imagine they were wearing garments to conceal their appearance, but did you notice anything distinguishing about them? Were they tall, or wearing a noteworthy hat, or holding their pistol with their left hand?"

Melton scratched his beard as he pondered the question. "None o' 'em seemed particularly tall to me, nor stocky neither.

And they wore cloths over their lower faces and hats pulled low on their heads."

I turned to Lembus, hoping the valet might have noted something distinctive about their clothing.

"They weren't gentlemen," he sneered. "I can tell you that. Their garments were merely serviceable." He tipped his head to the side. "Though the turf hat with the curled brim one of the men wore was somewhat unusual." He scoffed. "I suspect he stole it off another gentleman."

"We already told most o' this to the parish constable when he came around to ask us questions." Melton's eyes narrowed. "But I've been chewin' it over, and I think there *was* somethin' a bit off about the fellow what pointed his gun at me. 'Tis difficult to say for sure, but I think he may o' had two different-colored eyes. Couldn't make out the colors in the moonlight, but the one was darker 'an the other."

"Did you see anyone with that characteristic at the Blue Bell that night?" Gage interjected. "Has anyone seemed familiar since?"

Melton shook his head. "No' in the stable yard." He turned to look at Lembus, who might have entered the inn itself either with Lord Gage or on his behalf.

"I'm afraid not," the valet said. "And believe me, I've looked."

The coachman nodded. "Me, too." He eyed us both. "You *are* goin' to catch whoever did this, aren't ye?"

Lembus turned to us with the same stern expectation.

Whatever I might have thought about Lord Gage, it was apparent he inspired some sort of loyalty from his servants.

"Yes," Gage replied, his jaw hardening with resolve. "Yes, we are. I take it you're willing to help us."

Melton straightened. "Whatever you need."

Lembus nodded his agreement as well.

"Good. For now, simply keep your eyes and ears open." Gage's eyes slid toward Anderley. "You'd be surprised what you might learn."

I was more surprised to discover Henry standing beside my husband's valet. I'd not heard him enter, being too absorbed in the servants' testimonies.

Lembus and Melton rose from their seats, but Gage stayed them. "Before you go. I understand Gregory has been laid to rest in the churchyard in Darrington. But what of his family? Do either of you know if they've been notified? If anything has been done to ease their loss?"

Melton rolled the brim of his hat between his fingers. "Aye. Had a mother and several younger brothers and sisters he was helpin' to support."

Lembus chimed in. "His lordship instructed me to write Crabb." Lord Gage's butler at his town house in London. "To ask him to notify the family and see that they were paid Gregory's remaining wages as well as an additional sum to alleviate their burden."

The amount he named made my eyes widen, for it was more generous than I'd expected from such a hard man. If rationed, Gregory's family would not suffer from the loss of his income for at least another three years.

Gage thanked his father's servants and sent them on their way. Henry and Anderley joined us closer to the hearth.

"The men who attacked his lordship might have wished to make it appear like a simple highway robbery," Anderley remarked as he sank into the chair the coachman had vacated. "But it clearly was not."

"Not when they not only failed to demand his purse," Henry concurred, "but refused it and claimed to want to take his black heart instead."

A move that perhaps he agreed with after what had happened earlier.

I searched Henry's face for any indication of what he was thinking. It couldn't have been easy to confront his father's contempt and then listen to him ruminate on what a charmer his brother had been as an infant. I wouldn't blame him if his intentions toward the man who had sired him had changed. After all, he didn't *need* him. For all intents and purposes, the Duke of Bowmont was his father, and by all appearances, he'd been a good one. Gage and I were pleased to call him family and have him in our lives. But that didn't mean we had to include Lord Gage in our circle.

In truth, I wasn't certain what the results of this sojourn would be. It was obvious that Gage was determined to apprehend whoever had attacked his father and killed Gregory. His sense of honor and justice would demand it of him. But his relationship with his father had already been strained to the breaking point, and Lord Gage's reception of him did not bode well for a lasting reconciliation. The pain of his injuries could only partially be blamed for his belligerent reaction. Time would tell whether he would soften and offer his son the explanation for his past actions he was due. But I feared Lord Gage was too stubborn and controlling to show remorse, and Henry and Gage would both leave here more injured than before.

Henry's scrutiny shifted to meet mine before sliding away.

"I agree," Gage said, settling beside me again on the settee. "They plainly knew who my father was. This wasn't a simple incidence of being in the wrong place at the wrong time." His eyes narrowed in contemplation. "Which means they *must* have known he would pass that way."

"The Blue Bell. You think they took notice of him at the inn?" Anderley surmised.

"It makes the most sense." He leaned forward, gesturing with his hands. "They might have taken notice of him at an earlier stop, closer to London, but how could they have known he wouldn't stop for the night here in Wentbridge like his coachman assumed? And why would they have trailed him so long, waiting to hold him up?"

"Then you need to pay a visit to the Blue Bell," Henry said.

"As well as the parish constable, to see if he's made any progress tracking these supposed highwaymen down," Gage added crossly.

"The attack on your father might be irregular, but I don't think there's any doubt that these men have worked together in the past," I cautioned. "They knew how to waylay and ambush his carriage and subdue his servants swiftly and without much fuss. Their attack was coordinated, which indicates to me that they may have done it before."

"Mrs. Gage is right." Anderley extended his two index fingers together from his hands' clasped position. "Which should make it easier to track them down. There can't be many bands of highwaymen working with such expertise in the area."

I turned to gaze across the sweep of lawn toward the white summerhouse I'd been able to see only a small fraction of from my bedchamber window. "What I find most puzzling are the injuries Lord Gage suffered. Why did the attacker lower his gun to shoot him in the leg? If the goal was to kill him, to 'take his black heart,' as he said, then why didn't he shoot him in the chest?" I turned to ask the men. "Why *lower* the gun to wound him in a place that might not kill him? Or if the goal was to incapacitate him, why shoot him at all when they simply could have beat him?" I shook my head in bafflement. "But then why issue that threat? It doesn't make sense."

None of them spoke. Not until Anderley looked up from where he'd been staring at the rug to peer warily at Gage. "Maybe they weren't aiming for his leg."

It took me a moment to realize what he meant, though neither my husband nor his brother seemed surprised by the suggestion.

"Then, you think . . ." I began before breaking off, unwilling to speak the words. I swallowed. "Does that mean the man who shot him was someone he cuckolded?"

Gage shifted position, plainly uncomfortable with the idea. "Or a rival of some other kind, be it political, or personal, or even someone from his time in the Royal Navy. There are other reasons an attack might be directed at his manhood."

I nodded, trusting he was right. And if that *had* been the intention of the attack, I could only hope the motivation was something other than the obvious. Gage was already struggling to come to terms with his father's relationship with Henry's mother.

"What's to be done next?" Henry surprised me by being the one to ask. Given everything, I wouldn't have been shocked if he'd ridden away or refused to lift a finger to help, but here he was, outwardly eager to do his part. Though perhaps that was for his brother's sake more than his father's.

"We need to speak with the parish constable tomorrow, and I would also like to visit the Blue Bell Inn." Gage's expression darkened. "Another conversation with my father is also in order, to find out what, if anything, he knows, and whether he has any suspicions who his attackers are."

"I wonder if Dr. Barker or his wife might know more than they've said thus far," I remarked. "After all, if they've lived in this village for long, they must have heard rumors, if nothing else."

Gage nodded. "Whatever the case, I suppose the same advice I gave Lembus and Melton goes for the rest of us." He looked to each of us with grim determination. "Let's keep our eyes and ears open. *Someone* must know *something*. We just need to figure out who."

. . .

Idressed with care for dinner that evening. This was a prosperous surgeon's home in a small village in Yorkshire, not an earl's manor house or a London dinner party. A balance must be struck. My most elegant of dinner dresses would be too extravagant, and yet it simply would not do to insult them by arriving at the table underdressed. To that end, Bree and I selected a Parma violet gown with *à la reine* sleeves of blond net. It was simple, yet exquisitely cut. And rather than adorning myself with a more expensive necklace, I opted instead to wear the simple amethyst pendant that graced my neck most days, the one my mother had given me before she died.

When I entered the drawing room, I was pleased to discover I'd made the right choice. Mrs. Barker was dressed in a gown the shade of budding leaves, one that was not in the first stare of fashion, but which complemented her dark blond hair and warm brown eyes and had been cut perfectly for her petite figure. I estimated her age to be somewhere between a score and ten years and a score and fifteen, about a decade younger than her husband.

She smiled, perhaps relieved by the appearance of another woman, as I was the last to arrive. Gage, Henry, and Dr. Barker stood near the dormant hearth—the weather still being too warm for a fire—conversing on some subject. Being all dressed alike in dark evening attire, I couldn't help but note how much taller and broader of shoulder my husband and his brother were than the surgeon. When standing separately, Dr. Barker had seemed average in stature, but next to both of the other men his proportions seemed diminished somewhat. Although, to be fair, Gage's and Henry's statures were rather on the larger side.

But when Mrs. Barker approached, I noticed a guardedness lurking in the depths of her eyes, and I soon discovered why.

"Lady Darby, I hope thy maid was able to locate everything thou needed."

So she'd realized who I was, then. The infamous Lady Darby. Former wife of the late, great anatomist Sir Anthony Darby. The scandal that had erupted after the discovery that he'd forced me to utilize my artistic abilities to observe and sketch his dissections for the definitive anatomy textbook he was writing had been far-reaching. Particularly given the uproar over the recent discovery of Burke and Hare, a pair of men who had used the body-snatching trade to hide at least sixteen murders—selling their victims to the anatomists in Edinburgh. Because of them, the rumors that had followed the revelation of my involvement with my husband's work had been even more lurid.

In the past two years, my marriage to Sebastian Gage and assistance with his work as a gentleman inquiry agent had done much to repair my reputation, as well as my refusal to be cowed any longer, but there were still some who looked on me with either disdain or barely concealed horror and suspicion. Mrs. Barker appeared to be the latter. Given her husband's profession, this wasn't surprising. Though I did wonder what Dr. Barker himself made of me. In my experience, medical men either eyed me with hostility and contempt or viewed me with a mixture of curiosity and pity.

"She was," I told her, forcing a bright smile. "But please, call me Mrs. Gage. I much prefer it to the courtesy of my late husband's title," I explained. Given the fact that Sir Anthony's rank as a baronet outranked Gage's current status as a mere mister, much of society continued to call me by my first husband's title out of courtesy, not by right. I'd given up on correcting most of the beau monde on the matter, on trying to make them understand why I preferred to take the lower rank of my current husband's name, but I hoped Mrs. Barker would accede to my wishes.

Her gaze searched mine, compassion eclipsing her guardedness and making me think perhaps she understood too well. I couldn't help but look at Dr. Barker, alarmed he might be the man who had educated her on such things.

Her hands lifted to clasp mine where I held them before me, recapturing my attention. "My father." She smiled weakly. "His wasn't an easy temperament to live with."

I nodded, equal parts empathy and relief flooding me at this acknowledgment that she understood what it was like to fear a man's wrath, but that at least her suffering was in the past.

We turned, linking arms naturally as we strolled back toward the men. "I haven't had an opportunity yet to thank you for the care you've taken of my father-in-law. When we received word of his attack and injuries . . . well, I suppose you can imagine how alarmed my husband was. And us being so far away."

"'Twas our pleasure to be of service," she proclaimed, patting my arm. She looked affectionately toward her husband, raising her voice so that he would hear. "Truth be told, I think Dr. Barker's enjoyed his company."

The surgeon turned toward her with a chuckle, his face flushing. "Yes, it's been a long time since I've had a good jaw with a fellow military man."

My ears perked up at this interesting bit of information, but before I could ask him about it, the butler appeared to announce that dinner was ready.

Dr. Barker turned to me with a jovial expression. "Lady Darby . . ."

"She prefers Mrs. Gage," his wife interjected softly.

"Of course," he replied, taking this correction in stride, though I could see the questions forming in his mind he would be too polite to ask. "I believe, as host, I have the pleasure." He offered me his arm. "Shall we?"

I released Mrs. Barker's arm to take his, allowing him to lead me from the room as Lord Henry—the recognized son of a duke—took precedence over my husband and escorted our hostess.

"You must be relieved to escape the confines of your carriage after so many days travel," he murmured. "Though, it appears you are also a horsewoman."

"Yes, to both." I gave a light laugh. "And the latter helped to alleviate the former."

He grinned, but it was tempered, and I soon understood why. "I never met your first husband, Sir Anthony Darby," he informed me, his eyes trained forward. "But I was aware of his reputation."

This statement could have meant many things, but when his gaze shifted to meet mine, I could tell he wasn't expressing his admiration. His mouth was clamped into a thin line of disapproval, one that might have made me stiffen at the possibility that some of that censure was directed at me, except there was also a softness to his features that told me he didn't hold me at fault.

Something passed between us then, something in my experience that was rare, even between myself and men of longstanding acquaintance. Something I can describe only as an unspoken recognition of mutual regard and respect.

"And that is all we will say on the matter," he declared, turning away.

A peace settled over me, for I believed him. But it was tempered by a burgeoning curiosity about who exactly this man was.

CHAPTER 5

The dining room at Bowcliffe House, like the drawing room, was gracious and unpretentious. Its walls were papered in a small twining floral print, one whose colors were picked up in the wooden accents of the fireplace, the mauve of the upholstered dining chairs, and the goldenrod shade of the drapes. The window looked out upon the same sweep of the lawn as the morning room had, though the sky was now tinged with the deepening shades of blue that blurred the horizon to the east at twilight. Candles had been lit down the center of the table, displaying the spread of dishes to advantage.

Though we had arrived only a few short hours before, I was surprised to see guinea fowl set before us. It was doubtful that this had been their intended meal for the evening, but rather they had gone out of their way to prepare something special for our arrival. As such, I made certain to compliment the meal.

"Our neighbor, Mr. Fenton, is forever shooting things," Dr.

Barker remarked as he forked a bite of asparagus. "So we are well provisioned in that regard."

"Aye, but he also knows that by keeping thee in his good graces thou are less likely to complain when he sends for thee in the middle of the night because his mother-in-law is suffering from heart palpitations yet again, and that thou won't impose on them like that physician from Pontefract does," his wife pointed out.

"That is true," he conceded.

"Irrespective of the hunting, I imagine in the normal course of things, you don't see many bullet wounds here in Wentbridge," Gage remarked, taking a drink of his ginger beer.

"No, mostly farming mishaps and the odd laceration or broken bone from a carriage accident or a young lad taking a tumble. His lordship's injuries were the first I've seen of that sort since returning from Africa." He tilted his head to the side. "I take that back. Walker's lad shot himself in the foot a few years back. But that wasn't nearly so serious." His expression turned grave. "An inch or so farther to the left and your father would've bled out before I could do aught for him."

Gage's face had paled, and Henry appeared uncertain what to say, so I leapt into the void lest the silence make either of them more uncomfortable.

"What do you make of the fact that Lord Gage's attacker lowered his gun to shoot him in the leg rather than the chest?"

Dr. Barker's brow furrowed. "Well . . . perhaps he was a green lad and didn't know that a bullet through the leg could kill a man as surely as one through the heart. Maybe he thought it would convince him to hand over his purse."

I frowned. "But they didn't ask for his purse."

The surgeon's eyebrows arched in surprise, and he turned to look at his wife, who had lowered her utensils to the table. "They didn't?"

"No." I exchanged a glance with Gage. "According to Lord Gage's valet, he even offered it, but that doesn't appear to be what they were after, for they didn't take it."

"None of them told you this?" Gage's voice was tinged with the same confusion I felt.

Dr. Barker sat back in his chair, genuine bafflement seeming to make the pitch of his voice rise. "No, and I didn't ask. I was content to leave the questions to Mr. Robinson, our parish constable. I just assumed . . ." He broke off, his pale eyes flickering left and right as he revised his initial assessment.

Meanwhile, my attention had been captured by Mrs. Barker, who continued to stare down at her plate. A flush began to rise from my neck as I realized how much I'd discomfited her.

"I must apologize. This is hardly appropriate dinner conversation."

Mrs. Barker's gaze slowly lifted to meet mine.

"Please forgive me. It was impolite of me to mention it."

"No, no, Mrs. Gage," Dr. Barker contradicted. "If the fault is anyone's, it is mine. For I was the one to introduce the topic of his lordship's injuries."

"Aye, *please*, think no more o' it," Mrs. Barker hastened to assure me with a forced smile. "After all, I should be accustomed to it by now." She fixed her eyes fondly on her husband. "I've certainly been subjected to worse from Dr. Barker's military friends."

He chuckled. "I'm afraid so."

"You served as a surgeon with the Royal Navy, then?" Gage deduced, clarifying Dr. Barker's earlier comment about having enjoyed conversing with Lord Gage as a fellow military man.

He nodded as he swallowed a drink of ginger beer. "The army, actually. First at the Royal Military Hospital in Plymouth, and then in Cape Town, South Africa."

That would further explain Lord Gage's contentment in

staying here, not that in his condition he had any choice in the matter. Having served in the Royal Navy for a large portion of his life, he would naturally feel more comfortable with a fellow former military man.

"What brought you to Yorkshire?" Henry asked in a tone of voice that was perfectly polite, though his face didn't totally hide his bemusement that a man who had traveled so far afield would wish to settle here, of all places. "Were you born here?"

Dr. Barker's eyes were alive with humor. "No. I was born in Ireland, actually." He pushed away his plate, folding his hands over his stomach. "I enjoyed my time in South Africa, but after suffering a severe bout of illness, I decided it was time to retire from my military career and put the inheritance I'd received from my uncle to good use." His regard shifted to his wife. "I was traveling north to visit an old friend when I stopped in Wentbridge for the night. I decided to go for a walk to stretch my legs and stumbled upon something I liked." The glint in his eyes made it clear that "something" was Mrs. Barker. "And I never left."

She blushed under his regard, and I couldn't help but smile at their simple devotion to each other.

"And I'll leave it at that," he finished, sensing, as I was, how abashed his wife was with everyone's attention being directed at her.

"Why don't I cut this curd tart," she declared, as if to distract us, though her plate was still half-full. "'Tis one o' our cook's best dishes."

I felt Gage's regard resting on me while Mrs. Barker served Henry a slice of the lemon-scented tart and turned to find his features shadowed by something akin to regret. Perhaps he was thinking about how when two years prior he'd stumbled upon me at my brother-in-law's Highland castle, he'd run rather than confront the feelings that had developed between us during the course of our first investigation together. He'd confided in me later that I'd haunted his thoughts during the two months that followed before our next meeting. That he'd been forced to realize he could never truly escape me or the emotions I'd stirred in him.

While I was, of course, hurt at the time, I no longer regretted the path our courtship had taken. Truth be told, I had been no readier to accept the sentiments Gage roused in *me*. Had he not departed, had he not given us both the time and space to wrangle with our own longings and desires, who knew what would have happened, or how long it would have taken for us to come to our senses?

I tried to convey at least some of this in the look I returned to him, but there is only so much that can be said without words, and with a table between you around which sat three other people. In any case, I'd already noted how Henry was keeping his eyes on his plate, perhaps self-conscious of being the only bachelor present. Not wanting him to feel any more excluded than he already did—both with his natural father and two married couples—I deliberately addressed him and turned the subject.

But no matter how hard I tried, I could still sense that he'd withdrawn part of himself. It was an act I was intimately familiar with, for it had been one of the strategies I'd developed in order to survive my marriage to Sir Anthony. To withdraw that innermost part of myself and build a wall around it, attempting to preserve at least a small portion of who I truly was and shield it from harm in the way I hadn't been able to protect the rest of myself. As long as I could keep that fraction of myself safe, no matter how forcefully Sir Anthony strove to chip away at it, I'd believed I could survive.

The trouble was that I'd also withdrawn that part of myself from those who loved and cared for me. I'd become so good at shielding it, that even when the threat was over, I hadn't known how to allow anyone to scale its fortifications. And until I'd been able to do so, until I'd been willing to let those internal walls be breached, I couldn't truly heal.

I didn't want that for Henry.

So shortly after dinner, when he excused himself for the evening, I also made my excuses so I could follow him. I didn't have to struggle to find an explanation. I'd been stifling yawns for the last half hour. Our days of travel combined with our worry for Lord Gage and Emma's nocturnal feedings had exhausted me. I suspected Gage knew what I intended, but he didn't attempt to interfere, instead engaging Dr. and Mrs. Barker in a question that would keep them in the drawing room for at least a few more minutes.

Henry had just begun to climb the stairs when I called out for him to wait. He observed my approach warily but was too polite to ignore me.

"It has been quite a long day, hasn't it?" I observed breathlessly as I reached him.

"It has," he concurred, shifting his body toward the wall so that I might grasp the railing as we climbed.

"And a rather disorienting one as well," I added, hoping to gently broach the topic of Lord Gage's cruel behavior toward him.

However, Henry appeared to be already armored against this. "Kiera, I appreciate your concern. But if this is about what happened this afternoon, I would really rather not talk about it."

I peered up at his profile, so familiar—for at this angle he and Gage looked most alike, sharing similar facial structures—and yet not. His strong jawline was hard, showing his irritation with me for interfering. As I observed his rigid posture, his hands clasped firmly behind his back, the natural concern I'd been feeling which had sent me scurrying after him began to war with a sisterly instinct to tweak his nose in aggravation. Had he been my brother Trevor, I would have undoubtedly said something vexing by now, but it being Henry, I exerted more restraint.

"I'm behaving like Eleanor, aren't I?"

He turned to me in question, not having expected me to refer to his sister—the Duke and Duchess of Bowmont's daughter. Though, truth be told, she wasn't the duke's child either, or Lord Gage's for that matter. The duchess's four youngest children had all been sired by different fathers.

"Like an annoying little sister," I clarified. I tilted my head to the side "Though, I suppose in her case, she's an annoying older sister." My lips curled into a mischievous smile. "Either way, we sisters do tend to have a habit of thrusting our noses into our brothers' affairs."

He scoffed. "You've got nothing on Nell. You should just read some of her letters." He tried to maintain his scowl, but fondness tugged at the corners of his lips. "She's still trying to meddle all the way from Norfolk."

Where she had wed the Marquess of Marsdale a few short months ago, after her first marriage to the Earl of Helmswick had been declared invalid because of his having committed bigamy. The wedding had been a scandal of immense proportions, and one that Gage and I had already anticipated, as we had been two of the people who had brought Helmswick's bigamy to light during the course of a previous investigation, though we'd left it to Eleanor and her family to decide whether to conceal or reveal that fact. It had been a complicated situation, but Eleanor had chosen to escape her cruel first husband and wed the man she should have married in the first place. The man whose child she would soon deliver.

"What does she say?" I asked. My own letter from Lord Marsdale informing us of his nuptials had been rather brief and to the point, except for a few irreverent observations the rascal knew I would shake my head at.

His brow quirked in renewed impatience as he turned to look at me, letting me know that he was aware that this was yet another ploy to convince him to discuss his feelings. But this time, he willingly took the bait, perhaps hoping his brusqueness would deter me from pressing further. "That it's a waste of my time. That we already have a father."

I ruminated on this for a moment as we climbed the last few risers. "Is she aware of who her natural father is?"

Henry rounded on me, anger flashing in his eyes. An emotion that always made my heart stutter in unhappy remembrance. Though I didn't cower or retreat, my shoulders stiffened, and upon seeing this, his anger died as swiftly as it had flared to life. We stared at each other uncomfortably for a moment as I fought the embarrassment and shame that always rose in me when my body unwittingly betrayed my unfortunate past, and he struggled with whether it was better to say anything or not.

Ultimately, I chose to break the heavy silence. "I wasn't asking you to tell me who he is, simply whether Eleanor knows."

He swallowed. "Yes. We all know."

I nodded in recognition of what this meant. His two other brothers who had been born on the wrong side of the blanket were also aware of who their natural fathers were.

"And does she have any sort of relationship with him, albeit a private one?" If it had been public, I would have already known about it.

The look in his eyes was answer enough. "She corresponds with him and even visits him from time to time."

Recalling the rumor that Eleanor's father was some sort of member of royalty, my curiosity was understandably piqued, but I also knew it was none of my business. And also not pertinent to the point I was trying to make.

"Then I'm not sure it's fair for her to tell you it's a waste of time to pursue a relationship with your own natural father." I held up my hand to stop him from leaping to her defense. "Though I'm certain her intentions were to prevent you from being hurt."

Too late for that.

The pain he'd been suppressing all evening flashed across his face almost as if I'd said those words aloud, and he turned his head to the side, as if that might hide what he was thinking.

My chest constricted seeing him struggle. "All I wanted to say," I began hesitantly, "is that . . . I understand why you want to know your father, and that . . . I wish he were an easier man."

He turned to look at me then, his silvery gray eyes bright with unsaid things. Things that perhaps he'd never dared to let cross his lips. Things that perhaps he needed someone else to say.

"I know that he has hurt you."

His face collapsed into a deep scowl that I knew was meant to mask emotion as much as reveal anger.

"And I fear that he will hurt you again."

"If he does, that's my concern, not yours," he bit out.

I dipped my head in acknowledgment, though not agreement. "I cannot make you share your thoughts and feelings, and I won't try to. But I *do* want you to know that Sebastian and I are both here for you." I moved a step closer, pressing my hand to his chest over his heart. "Don't shut us out," I pleaded.

His gaze continued to hold mine, and his ferocious glower softened under my earnest regard. "I won't," he declared.

I lowered my hand. "Good night, Henry."

"Good night," he replied as I slowly walked away.

I didn't look back until I'd reached the door to my bedroom, but when I did, it was to find him staring down the corridor toward Lord Gage's chamber, pain etched like granite over his features.

CHAPTER 6

The following morning, after Gage, Emma, and I had all had breakfast, we paid another visit to Lord Gage, hoping to find him well rested and in a less contentious mood. The sight of Emma's drooling grin seemed to help. I perched beside my father-in-law on the bed, propping my daughter up so that he could better see her, partially reclined in bed as he was. While he crooned and chattered at her, I couldn't help but scour his features, attempting to work out the puzzle he presented.

A welcome bit of color had returned to his complexion, and I didn't detect lines of pain radiating from the sides of his mouth as I had yesterday. Though the laudanum that I suspected was the cause of his constricted pupils might be helping that. However, nothing explained to me how the cold, scornful, ruthless man I'd come to know had transformed into this doting, gibbering grandfather. Yes, Emma was adorable—and perhaps more pertinently, his flesh and blood—but I'd never seen him show such warmth or affection toward his more immediate family.

The most regard I'd ever seen him show his son was a firm handshake on our wedding day—a ceremony I'd had to blackmail him into attending.

Unfortunately, my scrutiny didn't go unnoticed.

"Normally, I'm flattered when a young woman stares at me so," Lord Gage remarked wryly, his eyes lifting to meet mine. "But I don't detect admiration in your eyes, my dear, but rather perplexity and, dare I say, censure?" He tsked, returning his attention to Emma. "Is my behavior unbecoming?" he mocked.

A flush stung my cheeks at being caught out thusly. I could only be glad Dr. Barker was not present, having been called to attend another patient. However, I refused to be cowed, as he'd intended.

"Some might say so," I replied, adjusting Emma in my arms. "After all, many believe children are a woman's purview, not a man's."

He looked at me, seeming genuinely curious to hear what I would say.

"But I happen to find it rather sweet that you are so taken with Emma."

His guardedness subsided, but I wasn't finished.

"I only find it baffling that you are so unfeeling to others."

Lord Gage's eyes narrowed, flicking to Gage, who sat in a chair next to the bed, and then back to me. "And by others, I take it you mean my son and yourself."

"And Henry."

His jaw hardened.

Had Henry been present, I wouldn't have had the nerve to broach such a delicate subject, not when my father-in-law's reaction could wound Henry even worse than it had the day before. But his taunting had riled me, and so I refused to play his game by ignoring the issue entirely.

However, he declined to address it, instead turning his barbs toward Gage. "I wasn't aware that a grown man needed coddling."

My temper sparked at this cruel remark. "There is a vast difference between coddling and a simple display of warmth and courtesy, and you know it."

Emma's eyes widened and her lower lip began to quiver, making me regret having let him rile me. I pulled her close, bouncing her lightly to soothe her lest she think I was angry at *her*. Pivoting, I rose to my feet, needing to put a bit of space between myself and the cause of my fury. Gage squeezed my arm as I passed, offering *me* a bit of comfort when I should have been comforting *him*.

"Tell me about the attack?" Gage urged his father while I paced with Emma.

He heaved a sigh, as if we'd asked him to recite the Magna Carta, but then reluctantly began to tell his side of the tale. He had little to add to what his servants had already told us except a description of the horse that the man who had shot him had been riding—a black or chestnut steed with a white star marking above his eyes. The highwaymen had been wearing masks, but their horses had been wholly uncovered.

We hadn't thought to ask about their horses. I felt a surge of anticipation at this discovery. Perhaps we wouldn't be able to identify the men by their appearance, but we might be able to identify them by their horses. We would have to ask Melton and Lembus if they recalled anything about the other highwaymen's mounts. The coachman being a horseman himself must have noted something.

"How old would you say your attacker was? The one who spoke to you?" Gage queried.

Lord Gage's brow creased in annoyance.

"Just a rough estimate," he prodded. "Was he a young lad? An older man?"

"Definitely not young. I would estimate he was at least a score and five years of age, likely a decade or more beyond that. But no more than fifty. He moved too nimbly."

Then that ruled out Dr. Barker's theory that he'd been a green lad, though it didn't preclude the possibility that the man was unfamiliar with how much damage a bullet to the leg could cause.

Gage studied his father, perhaps wondering like I was why he was taking umbrage at so many of his questions. Did he resent not being able to conduct the inquiry himself? Or was it because the pain-dulling effects of the laudanum he'd taken were beginning to wear off? Perhaps his discomfort was returning.

"What of the people you encountered during your stop at the Blue Bell?" Gage asked in an even voice, lest it rile him. "Could any of them have been your attackers?"

He regarded him for a moment. "Is that where you think I became their target?"

"It makes the most sense, doesn't it?"

Lord Gage considered this and then nodded. "It does." He grimaced as he pushed against the mattress, trying to raise himself higher on the pillows mounded behind him. Gage rose to help, but he waved him back down. "Though I'm sorry to say, I can't recall anyone I encountered there. We weren't there above half an hour, and Lembus handled procuring me a private parlor to dine in." He rubbed his hand over his forehead, ruffling his gray hair. "I was tired and intent on reaching Ferrybridge. I didn't pay as much attention to my surroundings as I should have."

It was the closest I'd ever heard Lord Gage come to directly conceding he'd made any sort of error, and based on the resulting silence, I suspected his son was similarly affected by his admission. Or perhaps Gage was struck by how more and more wan and fatigued his father appeared the longer our conversation continued. We had been warned not to tire him, and so

Gage leaned forward, propping his elbows on his knees, to ask one final pointed question.

"Do you have any idea who might have attacked you, sir?"

Lord Gage stilled his fretful movements and turned to look into his son's earnest face.

"It seems obvious these men weren't simple highwaymen after a wealthy man's purse. So it stands to reason they were sent after you for a specific reason. Do you know what that was? Do you know who might have sent them after you?"

These questions might have seemed counter to our theory that Lord Gage had become their target at the Blue Bell, but we also had to entertain the possibility that the attackers had been lying in wait at the inn specifically for him. They might have known his carriage was likely to stop there before the steep ascent out of Wentbridge. Given the relative isolation of the stretch of road to the north, it seemed an ideal place to plan an ambush.

Lord Gage chuckled mirthlessly. "Do you have a pen and paper?"

"To write a name?" Gage asked in evident confusion.

"To write an entire *list* of them." He made a derisive sound at the back of his throat. "A man of my origins in my line of work doesn't reach my position without making a few enemies, son."

Gage turned his head to meet my gaze, his eyes dipping to where Emma was cradled in my arms, chewing on her fist. "Are you speaking of your work as an inquiry agent or politics?"

"Both," he snapped, but after a glance at his granddaughter he softened his tone. "But to reach this far north into Yorkshire, it's more likely a political rival. Someone who resents my sway with members of both parties, or even the king himself."

Lord Gage had served under King William IV as a midshipman on the HMS *Pegasus* when His Majesty was still just a younger son with no expectations of one day inheriting the

Crown. This connection, as well as his own daring and proficiency, had served Lord Gage well as he'd risen up the ranks of the Royal Navy. His prowess and wealth had increased with each daring raid, each captured ship, and made him something of a war hero, though nowhere near the status of Nelson or Wellington. So when he'd retired from the navy, he'd already amassed a sizable fortune and possessed a number of highly placed friends, despite his relatively low social rank as the second son of a minor baronet from Cornwall. He'd then proceeded to prove himself useful in assisting the king—then George IV—and his royal brothers and high-status friends whenever they found themselves in troubling circumstances, and his renown and influence had continued to grow. So much so that when William became king, he was granted a title for his services.

That was how Gage had first found himself in the role of gentleman inquiry agent, assisting his father. A task at which my husband had thrived, as consequently had I when I'd begun to assist him. We had much to be grateful to Lord Gage for in setting us on this path—a path it was highly unlikely we would ever have stumbled upon ourselves—but that didn't mean we were obliged to follow in his footsteps. Gage and I had deliberately chosen a different track than his father's. One that would undoubtedly bring us less clout and prestige, but that was hopefully fairer and more just, and nonetheless held its own rewards in our knowing we'd done our best to help others and see that justice was done regardless of the person's status.

As such, our sway in politics was minimal compared with Gage's father's. Gage was also quite firmly a Whig in most of his views, though he didn't often voice them aloud. Lord Gage, on the other hand, was more of a vicar of Bray, preferring to play both sides, though he was more of a Tory in mind-set. This pretense and the connections my father-in-law flouted brought him distinction, but also made him a target.

"Then let's narrow the field," Gage finally replied. "Who do you know that might wish you ill and would also be familiar with or have influence in this area?"

His father's mouth flattened in displeasure. "There is one person I can think of. Lord Portis."

I was not familiar with the Earl of Portis, but I was aware of his reputation as a stalwart and ruthless Tory. Given the recent passage of the Reform Act, which the Tories had vehemently opposed, I recognized his frame of mind might not be the most charitable, but that didn't explain why he would want Lord Gage either injured or dead.

"He's fallen out of favor with His Majesty," Lord Gage informed us. "And he happens to blame me rather than his own pigheadedness and unruly tongue."

"Why would he blame you?" I pressed.

He exhaled in annoyance. "Because I have the ear of the king, and so anytime His Majesty does something counter to someone's wishes, it's easier for them to blame *me* for planting the idea in his brain rather than the sovereign himself."

I supposed I could understand that logic, though it reduced the king to little more than a puppet whose strings were tugged on by various masters. An analogy I doubted His Majesty would appreciate.

Gage frowned. "But isn't Portis's estate near Bristol?" Two hundred miles away.

"Yes, but his brother resides just south of here, at Skelbrooke Hall."

"And you think his brother arranged this attack on you?" I asked, struggling to keep my skepticism from my voice.

"Butler served in the army for a number of years. I shouldn't be surprised if he cultivated relationships with a number of unsavory persons."

This seemed like some sort of prejudicial remark Royal Navy

men might use against their counterparts in the army rather than a viable assumption. Gage's expression echoed my doubt on this point, but he didn't argue. "We shall pay this Mr. Butler a visit," he declared, pushing to his feet.

His father tipped his head back deeper into the pillows and closed his eyes. "Even if it turns out not to be Butler and Portis, they're good acquaintances to cultivate for the future."

A pucker formed between Gage's brows, plainly wondering as I was how his father could be accusing them of attempting to murder him in one breath and then encouraging his heir to nurture a relationship with them in the next.

"When it comes to politics, there's a fine line between enemy and ally," his father replied to this unspoken query without even opening his eyes. "You'll learn that soon enough."

It was apparent Gage didn't know how to respond to that, so for the moment, he ignored it. "We'll report back later."

Lord Gage's face was slack, making me wonder if he'd already fallen asleep, so we slipped quietly from the room.

Just like the previous afternoon, we found our staff gathered in the corridor outside our bedchambers waiting for us, except this time Henry was with them. Gage looked about in frustration. "Let's not make it quite so obvious we're all working together," he grumbled in a low voice, urging the men along before him toward his bedchamber.

Bree flushed at his gentle scolding and opened the door to my room, waiting for me to step inside.

But first I passed Emma to Mrs. Mackay. "I believe she's ready for her nap."

"Aye, m'lady," she replied dutifully, though I could tell she must be disappointed to be left out of the pending conversations.

"And I'll send Bree up to you when we're finished."

Her dark blue eyes met mine, grasping the unspoken meaning of those words—that she would relay to her what she'd missed. "Aye, m'lady."

Amused by her eagerness, I couldn't entirely repress the smile that curled the corners of my lips as she turned toward the stairs. Some might say we'd turned all our servants into inquisitive ghouls, involving them in our investigations as we did, but I felt we were merely encouraging their natural curiosity and desire to help. Not to mention allowing them to utilize their brains in ways other than the most mundane.

Bree looked as if she was biting back a grin of her own when I turned to look at her, though color still rode high in her cheeks. I pressed a hand to her upper arm in reassurance as I passed.

While Bree helped me to change from my morning dress into my wheat brown carriage dress with swirled stripes of mahogany embroidery and forest green–trimmed dagged pelerine capelet, I reiterated what Lord Gage had told us. "I'm sure Mr. Gage is going to ask Anderley to speak to Melton and Lembus about the attackers' horses, and whether they remembered anything else of pertinence. While I would like you to continue acquainting yourself with the Barkers' staff and learning whatever you can."

She finished adjusting the last pin in my hair and set my periwinkle-trimmed bonnet over my curls. I could still smell the lavender that had been packed alongside my clothes in their trunks and boxes. Bree's whisky brown eyes sparkled with anticipation in the reflection of the mirror. "I *have* learned something, m'lady. Or at least, I think I have."

I swiveled on the bench to face her. "Yes?"

She pressed her hands together before her as if to restrain her excitement. "Did ye ken that this area is purportedly the real haunt o' Robin Hood? That the village of Wentbridge lies at the northernmost edge o' the vale of Barnsdale, and the forest of

Barnsdale is the *real* Sherwood Forest o' legend. 'Tis supposedly mentioned as such in the earliest ballad aboot Robin Hood."

I was aware of a monument just south of here along the Great North Road, not far from the Barnsdale Bar toll bar, that was dedicated to Robin Hood, but I'd never really given the matter much thought until now.

"Given the fact that Robin Hood led essentially a merry band of highwaymen, and Lord Gage was accosted by highwaymen, the connection seems noteworthy." I frowned. "Though Robin Hood's legend is popular because he allegedly robbed from the rich and gave to the poor, not murdered people. So what does that make Lord Gage? The Sheriff of Nottingham?"

Tipping my head to the side, I contemplated the matter a moment further before brushing it aside. There were highwaymen at work in various parts of the country on isolated, well-traveled roads. As such, there were bound to be some who prowled the same haunts where Robin Hood may or may not have once roved, so searching for a direct correlation was likely futile.

"The Barkers' staff told you this?" I asked.

"Aye. Became quite animated by it. Seems an association they're proud o'."

That was understandable, for it gave their village a certain notoriety that not many others could claim.

She narrowed her eyes, crossing her arms over her chest. "But I can also tell there's something they're no' tellin' me. One o' the maids started to say more, but the others hushed her before she could."

"Then keep at them. See if you can contrive a way to speak with this maid alone. Or . . ." I paused before continuing. "If you're comfortable with it, ask Anderley to try using his charm."

This had been a point of contention between the pair in the past, especially when Anderley and Bree had begun courting in January. Their relationship had been unsettled, and so after three months they'd mutually agreed to end it. But when Bree had nearly been killed by poison a few short weeks ago, the strength of Anderley's feelings for her had been made evident—to us and perhaps even himself. As such, I would not have been surprised to discover they'd resumed their courtship. That is, if they could resolve the differences that had beleaguered their relationship the first time.

One of those differences had been Anderley's flirtatious nature with other women—lighthearted even as it was—when he was attempting to extract information from them for an inquiry, and Bree's jealousy and mistrust. Knowing that, I was wary of raising the issue, though it was something that needed to be addressed between them sooner rather than later.

But contrary to my expectations, she seemed to already be considering this option. "If my friendliness fails, 'tis good to keep in mind."

I said no more, leaving the matter in her more than capable hands.

CHAPTER 7

We located Mr. Robinson, the parish constable, in a modest home about five hundred feet south of the Blue Bell Inn along the Great North Road. Much of rural Britain had yet to establish any sort of formal police like the great metropolises had. In fact, London itself had instituted their New Police just three years prior. As such, most of Britain was still regulated by the old system of peacekeeping, with appointed individuals to the roles of local magistrate, sheriff, undersheriff, and parish constable, helped along by special constables and the local militia or yeomanry if necessary. But not all of these positions were exactly coveted. The position of parish constable, in particular, was not a popular one. So those appointed the duty often paid a deputy to take their place in carrying out the day-to-day tasks.

Wentbridge's constable was just such a deputy.

He seemed rather agitated to be receiving us in his front parlor, which smelled strongly of old pipe smoke, as well as backflow from a partially clogged flue. Fortunately, the day was warm, so the window had been propped open to allow a breeze to flow through the dimly lit chamber, the better to hide the shabbiness of some of the furnishings. It was a respectable home, but not a very prosperous one.

"Thee could've summoned me to Dr. Barker's. I would've gladly come," Mr. Robinson declared for the second time as Gage and I perched on the settee across from him.

I'd thought Henry would be joining us, but Gage had asked him to ride north with Melton to examine the place where his father had been attacked. It was doubtful any evidence would remain, but it needed to be searched nonetheless.

"I appreciate that," Gage replied. "But we had other calls to make, so we thought we'd spare you the trouble."

The constable nodded, appearing ill at ease, which did not bode well for our hopes of his having anything useful to report. He was a tall man and broad of shoulder. The type you expected to be good with his fists. Which may have been why he'd been hired by the appointed constable as his deputy. His hair was an indeterminate shade of dark blond or light brown curling against the collar of his coat.

"We understand you've been investigating the attack on my father, Lord Gage, and the murder of his footman," Gage continued. "Have you been able to make any headway?"

"Not as much as I'd hoped," he confessed. "The trouble is no one wants to speak out against 'em. No' when I suspect at least half the parish is reapin' the benefit of their trade."

Gage and I both frowned in confusion.

"The benefits?" he questioned. "But as far as I'm aware, they didn't take anything from my father?"

Mr. Robinson dipped his head in more of a gesture than a nod. "Aye, and that's the first."

Gage and I shared a look of dawning understanding.

"Then this isn't an isolated occurrence, but rather an established band of highwaymen who have robbed people along this stretch of road before," my husband surmised.

The constable pounded a fist against his leg. "Aye, they've been plaguin' the road from Doncaster to Ferrybridge for more than a year now, robbin' wealthy coaches an' frighten' travelers."

"Just like Robin Hood allegedly roved the Barnsdale Forest some five hundred years ago," I observed, making the connection between what Bree had told me and what Mr. Robinson had just said.

He pointed at me. "Exactly. Or so they'd like us to believe."

But Gage wasn't so much interested in that connection as enraged at the constable's apparent ineptitude. "Then why on earth haven't they already been caught?" His eyes glittered with fury.

"We've tried." The constable lifted his hands in defense. "We've taken out patrols multiple times and tried to set traps to ambush 'em, but someone always tells 'em we're comin'."

"Are you sure that someone isn't you?" Gage charged with a surprising lack of finesse.

Mr. Robinson straightened, his shoulders suddenly bristling with the muscles his ill-fitting coat had partially hidden. "I take offense at that, Mr. Gage. 'Appen as not an' maybe I'm not a particularly clever man, but I *am* an honest one."

I pressed a hand to Gage's arm, lest he make another undiplomatic remark. "Please excuse him, Mr. Robinson. I'm sure you can appreciate how anxious my husband is for his father's health and upset that someone attacked him so viciously and killed Gregory Reed, his footman."

The constable deflated a bit at this conciliatory remark. "Aye. I can understand that. And thee should know, this is the first they've killed anyone. Never even injured anyone before, 'cept a single blow to keep one man in line."

And there was a significant difference between a simple thief and a violent one. Had Lord Gage been confronted by the former, he would have been relieved of his purse, but not his footman's and nearly his own life.

"Then their attack on my father was an anomaly," Gage commented, having reined in his own temper. "It was irregular, uncommon. Different from their normal mode of operation," he clarified, upon seeing Mr. Robinson's quizzical expression.

"Aye." His eyes narrowed in mistrust. "Thou's father's manservant claims his lordship didn't threaten 'em. Even offered up his purse willingly."

"As does my father," Gage confirmed. "And though it would make more sense for the attackers to have shot him if he'd refused or endangered them in some way, I believe him."

"Lord Gage isn't the type of man to deny defending himself," I elaborated. "He's more likely to boast about it."

The constable subsided deeper into his chair with a nod. "Then I can't account for this . . . anomaly, as thee called it."

Gage's brow furrowed in consternation. "You said you've had trouble convincing anyone to speak out against them? That you suspect half the parish is receiving money from them."

"At least. And in the neighborin' parishes as well." His expression turned solemn. "Times are lean. There's many that need the help, and not many to give it."

Gage finished his thought. "So they welcome it wherever they can get it."

"Aye."

"What else is known about them?" Gage queried after a moment of consideration. "Even though much of the local populace is refusing to help you apprehend them, a few details must have slipped out or been deduced."

Mr. Robinson's eyebrows arched. "Such as where they coordinate themselves and make camp? Aye, we've raided any number o' suggested sites, includin' the Sayles Plantation and the church of St. Mary Magdalene—where Robin Hood is said to have wed Maid Marian. But if they were ever there, they're long gone before we arrive."

"What of the Blue Bell?"

"The inn?" He exhaled a long breath through his lips. "Aye. T'wouldn't surprise me to hear they're patrons."

"It would be a convenient place to stable their horses."

The constable appeared doubtful. "Aye, but a conspicuous one. I've received any number o' horse descriptions from those who've been robbed, but I've never been able to match 'em to a steed in town, includin' at the Blue Bell."

I was relieved to hear he'd asked for descriptions of the highwaymen's horses and searched for them, for it further proved Mr. Robinson wasn't incompetent, simply hampered by uncooperative villagers and few resources. Though it seemed he'd made good use of those resources he *had* been granted. From the manner in which Gage's rigid jaw softened, I suspected he was harboring similar thoughts about the constable he'd only moments earlier accused of duplicity.

"Do you suspect these highwaymen are switching horses between robberies?" he asked.

"Must be. Or else some o' the witnesses made up their descriptions out o' whole cloth." Mr. Robinson rolled his shoulders, as if not entirely comfortable sitting in the chair he occupied. "But I've been circulatin' the description his lordship's servants gave me o' his attacker's horses anyway. 'Specially that one with the white star above its eyes. 'Tis distinctive. 'Appen we'll get lucky."

"What of the highwaymen?" I interjected. "I presume they always wore masks, but did any of the other victims notice anything about them?"

He shook his head. "Nowt. Least nowt worth repeatin'."

"What do you mean?"

"Most o' the robberies happened in the dark, so how a lady could tell that one man was wearin' a shirt o' Prussian blue—no' just any blue, mind ye, but Prussian blue—I can't fathom. Not that such a detail does us much good." A sneer curled his lip. "And I'll spare thee the litany o' heights I've heard, but suffice it to say, our highwaymen range from four and a half feet tall to over seven feet."

Evidently, these witnesses were not as reliable as one hoped. But the constable had given us much to think on nonetheless. Particularly about this gang of highwaymen who fancied themselves to be like Robin Hood and his merry band of outlaws.

Gage had risen to his feet, and I followed suit. "Well, add the possibility that one of the highwaymen has two different-colored eyes to your queries. After giving it some thought, my father's coachman feels fairly certain the ruffian closest to him possessed that distinctive feature."

Mr. Robinson appeared to give this some consideration.

Gage offered him his hand. "We won't take up any more of your time, but please keep us apprised if you learn anything more, and we'll do the same."

"Thou are intent on investigatin' thyselves, then?" His gaze flickered back and forth between us. "Not that I'm surprised. After all, thy reputations do proceed thee. But if thou are, take care where thee treads and who thee riles. Not all will take kindly to the questions o' an outsider. 'Specially about those they consider to be their own."

It wasn't a threat but a warning, and one delivered with good intentions. But I still felt as if a chill breeze had blown across the back of my neck.

"We'll keep that in mind," Gage assured him.

The constable scrutinized us both once more before turning to escort us to the door.

When we emerged into the sunlit front garden, I wasn't as surprised as I might have been to discover about half a dozen villagers lurking nearby. I supposed by now they had all heard that the son and daughter-in-law of the injured baron convalescing at Dr. Barker's house had arrived. Just as they had likely known about the surgeon's houseguest within twenty-four hours of the attack. After all, I'd grown up in a small village. I knew how quickly news spread. The more scandalous the incident, the swifter the gossip flew. Even those who were gentry or minor nobility, and therefore somewhat set apart, still gleaned the details from their servants.

As such, our carriage had been observed by unseen eyes from the moment we'd departed Bowcliffe House, and those eyes had remained fixed on it while we were inside the constable's home. A few brave souls had ventured closer, tending their own gardens, or leaning against a fence post to speak to a neighbor, or standing by the roadside to scrape something from a horse's hoof with a stick, but all the while their eyes remained focused on us. Even when a coach rumbled past, hurtling south down the Great North Road and leaving a swirling trail of dust in its wake, they all but ignored it.

I lifted the dagged pelerine capelet which draped over the shoulders of my carriage gown to cover my nose and mouth and turned way, lest I inhale the dirt. Apparently, Mr. Robinson was accustomed to it, for he scarcely flinched as the cloud of debris enveloped us. He raised his arm to holler at the man caring for his steed along the verge of the road and beckoned him closer.

The man lowered his horse's hoof, eyeing us all stonily. For a moment I thought he would ignore the constable's request. But then he straightened, tossing the stick he'd been using aside, and grasped the dappled mare's reins to lead her toward us. His clothes were that of a laborer. They were worn but well mended, making me suspect he had someone to look after him, possibly a wife. His beard was grizzled, though his face was unlined.

"Tom, thou art at the Blue Bell most nights," the constable declared. "Do thee recall seeing the lord who was attacked near the top o' the cutting at the inn as he passed through?"

Tom's leer shifted to us, scrutinizing us as he scratched his chin. "Can't rightly recall if I do."

Mr. Robinson's brow furrowed. "Thou can't recall if thou saw his lordship?"

He shrugged one shoulder, turning back to his horse. "That neither."

His determinedly lackadaisical responses did little to convince us he was telling the truth, but then I suspected that was the point. That, and irritating the constable. His eyes cut to him periodically, as if judging his effect on the man.

"Thou doesn't remember a baron passing through the Blue Bell?" Mr. Robinson scoffed.

"Lots o' lords pass through the Blue Bell on their way to and from the north. I don't mark 'em *all*."

"'Appen. But how many o' those lords are then attacked. *That* I would mark."

"'Appen that's it," Tom conceded. "But I keep myself to myself." His hard stare shifted to Gage. "I've nowt to tell thee." By which it was clear he meant he had nothing he *would* tell us, not that he actually knew nothing. What wasn't clear was whether he knew something worth reporting in the first place or he was simply intent on making us feel unwelcome. Either way, with this parting shot, he turned and walked away, leading his desultory horse.

All the constable could do was grunt in a sort of begrudging acceptance laced with aggravation. If this was the type of reception we would receive from most of the villagers, we had our work cut out for us, indeed.

Mr. Robinson turned to look at us and then at his neighbors still observing us from their gardens and front walks. "Maybe I should introduce thee at the Blue Bell. At the least, it might ease their suspicions about thee not bein' from around here, considerin' they're used to me askin' questions."

I deferred to Gage on this matter, curious to hear how he would respond. On the one hand, Mr. Robinson was correct. We *were* strangers, and an introduction might smooth the way. However, our appearance with the constable—the most visible representative of the law within the parish—might just as easily set their backs up against us and make it *more* difficult to gather any worthwhile information from them. But I supposed, given his neighbors' intense scrutiny and Tom's uncooperative answers, our conference with the constable was already known.

Gage seemed to realize this as well. "Yes, I would appreciate that."

Mr. Robinson gestured for us to proceed with him in the direction of the Blue Bell, some three buildings to the north. Gage nodded to our coachman, who would follow with the carriage.

I pasted a smile on my face as we neared the front garden of the neighbor directly to Mr. Robinson's right, but the forbidding expression she aimed at me froze the words on my lips. Gage was not as quickly intimidated, offering her a warm greeting, but rather than thaw under his charms as most did, the older woman turned her back on us and walked away.

"My apologies about that," the constable's voice rumbled from behind us. "But I did warn thee the villagers are rather clear in their allegiance."

He was right. He had. Though neither Gage nor I had taken

him at his word. It was no wonder he hadn't been able to capture the band of highwaymen plaguing this stretch of the Great North Road. Not if the villagers closed ranks around them.

I was reminded rather uncomfortably of our somewhat reluctant alliance with Bonnie Brock Kincaid, the leader of the largest criminal gang in Edinburgh. He was also viewed by the lower denizens of that city as a sort of Robin Hood figure, which had made it almost impossible thus far for the city police to apprehend him. And the few times that they had, the charges against him never stuck, for someone else was always at the ready to step in and take the blame to protect him. Those citizens were content to live under his rule because they believed they benefited from it, and because his code of honor was one they could comprehend when so often the actual rule of law seemed either counter to their interests or was twisted to suit those of wealth and power. At least, with Bonnie Brock, they knew where they were and could call that fair.

However, Bonnie Brock's intentions were not exactly noble, and he would be the first to admit that. He was a thief, a smuggler, a liar, a violent offender, and a murderer. The few worthy acts he'd committed—including rescuing me and Gage from the squalid vaults underneath the city—didn't erase all the terrible things he'd done. It simply meant that he wasn't irredeemably coldhearted. Though our tentative friendship and his saving me from giving birth in the dank, cold, dark underground world in which we'd been trapped understandably complicated my feelings toward him.

These villagers' blind faith in their local highwaymen and the good they believed they did them was not much different from Edinburgh's allegiance to Bonnie Brock. And yet we'd aligned ourselves with Bonnie Brock more than once, albeit reluctantly, overlooking some of the crimes he'd committed in the past in order to capture other murderers who'd preyed on the innocent or endangered the city. Did that not make us as guilty as these Yorkshiremen?

It was an uneasy thought. Particularly now that we were on the other side of the equation. We'd given little thought to the families of Bonnie Brock's victims because it was all too easy to imagine those victims had been rival gang members or other scurrilous individuals, killed in a brawl in which they were as much the aggressor. But we didn't know that to be fact. Truth be known, I'd long feared the opposite, given the swift and casual violence I'd witnessed. What if some of the blood on his hands was not drawn in self-defense? What if he was as guilty as these highwaymen appeared to be, and yet we'd conveniently ignored it for the sake of the justice we happened to be pursuing?

This conundrum left me with a bitter taste in my mouth as we rounded a patch of birch trees to approach the inn. The Blue Bell was an attractive enough building, formed of whitewashed wood and stone, and backed by the picturesque slopes of the forested Went Valley. The carriage yard seemed scarcely large enough for a busy coaching inn in such a prominent location along the Great North Road, but then it wasn't the only inn in town. I supposed if the Blue Bell was too congested, coachmen could carry on to the Bay Horse farther along the road. Perhaps some people even preferred it.

At this hour, there were only two carriages in the adjacent yard. One whose occupants could be seen scampering back into its confines as we entered the inn. Wide wooden planks worn with age covered the floor, while low wooden beams propped up the ceiling. I thought for a moment my husband, who stood over six feet, would be forced to stoop, but his head cleared the distance with only a few inches to spare. The room smelled of smoke, onions, and stale ale—not the most enticing of aromas, but not unexpected in such an establishment.

Only about a half a dozen occupants filled the room at the

scattered tables, sitting in the drowsy sunlight filtering through the windows overlooking the road and each nursing a glass of porter or hunched over a plate of food. Mr. Robinson led us toward a round, rosy-cheeked fellow who stood chuckling with one of his patrons, who boasted a red naeve along the side of his neck below his ear. The round man's eyes creased merrily at the corners, and his belly shook with each chortle. He turned to look at us as we approached, and while his smile didn't dim, I noted how the joviality faded from the depths of his heavy-lidded dark eyes.

"Robinson!" he exclaimed. "'Ow do?"

"Oh, nobbut middlin'," the constable replied, nodding to the patron before addressing the innkeeper again. "Have ye a moment?"

"Aye," he affirmed, leading us away from the now curious onlooker. We drew to a stop near the long bar, its top worn smooth and gleaming with age—far enough away that the inn's other occupants couldn't hear us, but within their line of sight. "What can I do for thee?"

"'Tis about his lordship who was attacked on the road north some ten nights past."

The innkeeper nodded. "Aye. Thee must be his kin," he told Gage.

"Yes." My husband extended his hand to him in courtesy. "Sebastian Gage."

"Billy Fryston," he replied, taking his hand to shake it even as he shook his head. "'Tis a sad business."

"As I understand it, my father stopped here before setting off toward Ferrybridge," Gage remarked evenly, though I could tell that he was studying the man closely.

"Aye, 'tis true. Though I'm afraid I didn't share more than a dozen words with his lordship. Showed him into a private parlor, and that's about all. Mainly dealt with his manservant."

Which corroborated what both Lord Gage and Lembus had told us, and seemed true to the behavior I would expect from Gage's father. But if that was the case, it offered very little opportunity for anyone in the inn to have discovered who Lord Gage was or that he carried two pistols.

As such, Gage continued to prod around the point. "Was it crowded that night? Did his lordship request such privacy?"

The question had been posed smoothly enough, but it was evident from the slight pause before Mr. Fryston's answer that he was at least suspicious of why he was asking. "His lordship wished for privacy," he replied, answering just one of the questions.

Gage tilted his head, attempting a more direct tack. "Then he didn't interact with any of your patrons?"

"Not that I noticed."

The innkeeper's expression was difficult to read. By all appearances, he seemed like he was being open and honest, but there was a passivity to the edges of his features that warned me otherwise. Perhaps it was his bushy beard, for it hid much of his lower face, but I was wary it was more than that. There had also been a false note in his voice, a flatness that signaled obstruction.

His gaze cut toward something over our shoulders, and his head gave an almost imperceptible shake, but when I glanced behind me to see whom he'd been signaling to, I caught only a glimpse of a dark coat disappearing behind a door that shut after them. When I turned back, I found Fryston staring at me, a sharp glint of challenge in his eyes—one that told me his amiable demeanor was not all that it seemed. Had I not been as confident in my own perceptions as I'd become, I might have doubted what I'd seen, for in the next moment all trace of that defiance had vanished to be replaced by an affable grin. But I knew what I'd observed, and his ability to mask it so swiftly and thoroughly only heightened my suspicions.

"Did any travelers pass through here that evening—or any of the days before it—that roused your suspicions?" Gage pressed. "Did anyone seem not as they should be?"

"I'm afraid not. Least, none that I noticed," Mr. Fryston replied. "It may no' look like it now, but I run a busy establishment. At peak times there's always people comin' and goin'. 'Twould be impossible for me to remember 'em all." He chuckled mirthlessly at the prospect.

We could hardly dispute this assertion, for it was probably true. But that didn't mean someone on his staff hadn't noticed.

"Would you mind if we posed the same questions to your employees? I would send my manservant to do it, so as not to disturb the running of your inn more than necessary," Gage added when the man didn't appear pleased by the prospect. In any event, Anderley was likely to get more information from the staff than we ever could.

A slight furrow formed in his brow, but he nodded his assent. "Aye. I'll ask 'em to cooperate."

And meanwhile warn them to watch what they say. I couldn't help but entertain the thought.

Gage seemed to eye him askance. "And may we examine the livestock in your stable?"

Mr. Fryston looked to Mr. Robinson. "O' course, if thou need to do so again. Though the horses thee will find there now will not be the same as were there then. But if thee thinks it will help, then thou are welcome to it."

He was right. This was a coaching inn, and as such the horses were traded in and out frequently as carriages passed through, swapping out the steeds at each stage in order to make the journey quicker. And those who had lodged here or merely taken their ease on the evening of the attack on Lord Gage would now be long gone. As such, it was probably a waste of time, but they needed to be examined regardless.

I turned to study the patrons seated at the tables, finding half of them studying us in return with expressions none too friendly, while the other half were absorbed in their meals. It would be fruitless to ask any of them what they might know. The first half were clearly mistrustful of us and unlikely to reveal anything of use, while the second were passing travelers with nothing to do with the matter.

My scrutiny trailed about the stone walls of the room. I only wished we had some excuse to search the rest of the establishment without rousing further suspicions. For something was definitely going on here. Something that Mr. Fryston didn't wish for us to find out about. Whether it had anything to do with the attack on Lord Gage, I didn't know, but Fryston and the Blue Bell warranted further investigation.

Gage had just begun to draw my arm through his to lead me from the inn when a subtle movement out of the corner of my eye drew my attention. There, in the shadows created by a heavy beam near the far corner of the room, stood Tom. Even at such a distance I could feel the hatred in his narrow-eyed gaze. It burned like a hot iron and was far more vehement than our prodding questions justified. Which meant that, to him, the matter was far more personal than it first seemed.

CHAPTER 8

I waited outside while Gage and Mr. Robinson searched the stables, content to watch the carriages and patrons come and go while concealed behind the door to our own conveyance. The sun beat down warm on the black lacquer coach, but a soft breeze scented by the flowering broom shrub bordering the stable yard billowed through the windows, cooling my cheeks. Even so, I learned nothing of use. Nothing more than we already knew, in any case. A number of narrowed sets of eyes cut in the direction of the stables as the men to whom they belonged strode away from the inn. None approached, but it was evident our presence was unwanted.

I heard my husband and the constable returning before I saw them and leaned out as Gage was taking his leave of the other man. "Excuse me," I called before Mr. Robinson could take another step across the yard. "Mr. Robinson, may I ask you a question?"

His gaze flitted to Gage in surprise before returning to me as he moved closer. "O' course."

My husband opened the door of the carriage so I wouldn't have to speak through the window.

"What can you tell us about that fellow you questioned outside your home? I believe you said his name was Tom?" I had been contemplating the man—and his obvious animosity—and had been unable to come up with any satisfactory answers.

"Aye, Tom Hutchinson. Worked as a linen weaver 'til a few years ago. Now he takes whatever work he can find."

I could sense Gage's curiosity, though he didn't question aloud why I was asking after the man, having realized some time ago that my intuitions often bore merit.

"Has he ever been in trouble with the law?"

Mr. Robinson shifted his feet, propping his hands on his hips beneath his jacket, clearly trying to puzzle out why I was asking. "He didn't move to my patch 'til about four years ago, but some ten or twelve years ago he got himself in trouble when he lived down in Barnsley. Arrested for taking part in the Grange Moor Rising. But they let him go without pressin' charges, and accordin' to my colleague in Barnsley, he hasn't been in trouble since." His brow furrowed. "Why do thee ask?"

"He just seemed unhappy about our asking questions."

The constable nodded. "Apparently, he lost a brother some years ago to violence, and the matter was never investigated to his satisfaction. As a result, he's not keen on assistin' the authorities."

I supposed it made sense then that he would resent me and Gage, and our inquiry into Lord Gage's attack. After all, not everyone was so fortunate in their rank or connections. It came as no surprise to anyone that a crime against a wealthy nobleman would receive more interest and effort in resolving it than the killing of a weaver. It wasn't right, but it was a fact of life.

As such, I couldn't blame Tom Hutchinson for resenting us if that was his reason. Had our situations been reversed, I imagined I would have felt similarly. And perhaps that was all there was to it. But I couldn't help but feel wary of the man all the same.

"I wouldn't let him bother thee," Mr. Robinson assured me in a gentle tone. "He might be angry at the likes of me, but he'll come to realize he can't begrudge the likes of thee for wishin' to bring justice to your own loved ones."

I wasn't so sure about that. We were an easy target for his fury at the injustices of the world, especially since we would be moving on once Lord Gage was recovered enough to travel. His rage for what we represented would not be an easy thing to relinquish. But I recognized Mr. Robinson's comment for the kindness and reassurance he meant, so I simply offered him a grateful smile and allowed him to carry on his way.

Gage climbed inside our carriage to sit beside me before he rapped the ceiling to tell our coachman to drive on to Bowcliffe House across the river. He turned to me as the carriage rounded the yard and then gathered speed as we pulled onto the Great North Road. "Why the interest in Tom Hutchison? I would have thought Mr. Fryston the innkeeper would have piqued your suspicions more."

"Oh, he did," I confirmed, settling deeper into the squabs. "But then I noticed Tom lurking in the corner of the inn, and if looks alone could kill, we would no longer be breathing."

He straightened in alarm and glanced back in the direction of the inn. "When was this?"

"As we were leaving," I answered calmly. "It was obvious he didn't wish to be seen, and I thought drawing attention to him might cause more harm than good."

Gage seemed to be ruminating on this point, which allowed me time to ask the question nettling at me.

"What is the Grange Moor Rising?"

He turned his head to look at me, but I wasn't sure he was actually seeing me, still being lost in his own thoughts.

"The reason Mr. Hutchinson was arrested in Barnsley?" I prodded.

A deep furrow formed in his brow. "It was part of larger rebellion that took place across the West Riding of Yorkshire in the spring of 1820. Reformists, mostly weavers, who were angry at the economic hardships they faced and the failure of the government to act in their favor. They organized a number of protests that were supposed to take place simultaneously and capture several lightly defended towns, which they hoped would spur a wider uprising. Grange Moor was one of their planned meeting places."

"I take it they were unsuccessful," I deduced, given the fact I'd never even heard of the revolt.

"Most of them dispersed on their own when they saw the lack of support, but a handful were arrested, and a few were made examples of."

I didn't ask further questions, understanding what that meant. They'd either been executed or transported to Van Diemen's Land.

But given the fact that this had all happened twelve years prior, I didn't see how it could have bearing on current matters except for explaining Hutchinson's hatred of authority. That was, unless he'd vented that hatred directly on Lord Gage and his lordship's footman, Gregory, had paid the ultimate price for it.

"Do you think Hutchinson could be one of the attackers?" I asked aloud, though I could read from my husband's rigid jaw and taut expression that he was already contemplating the same thing.

"He could be. Though we have no proof that's the case." His gaze drifted toward the window, stark with misgiving. "Motive does not mean guilt." He sounded as if he was speaking to himself as much as me. "After all, as his son and sole heir—who also happens to be furious with him and his past indiscretions—I have as much motive as anyone."

I reached out to take his hand where it rested on the seat beside me, lifting it to my lap. "Gage. Sebastian," I murmured when after a few seconds the first did not capture his attention. "Look at me."

Slowly his head turned, and I cradled his jaw with the opposite hand, forcing his eyes to meet mine. Their pale blue depths were clouded with pain and anguish. "He could have died," he managed to choke out, an acknowledgment of all the worries he'd carried with him since receiving Lembus's letter but had been too terrified to voice. "He could have died, and I . . . I . . ."

He couldn't seem to finish the thought, but I knew what he was trying to communicate.

"But he didn't," I told him, my skin flushing with the intensity of my own emotions. I grasped his chin more firmly, looking him straight in the eye. "He *didn't.*"

I felt his Adam's apple move up and down as he swallowed.

"And you have every right to be outraged at what he's done." I shook my head gently. "Your anger didn't almost kill him. Your refusal to brush aside the hurt he's caused you as if it were a mere trifle did not bring about this attack either." I exhaled, struggling to control the tumult within, wishing I could wrap him in a cocoon of my arms and shield him from all the pain his relationship with his father so often wrought. "But . . ." I forced the word out. "Now that you know he has survived, you need to make the most of this opportunity to reconcile. For your sake. For his sake. For Emma. And for Henry."

I lowered my hand, trusting he wouldn't turn away. "That doesn't mean it's possible." I closed my eyes against a wave of my own frustration at my father-in-law. "Heaven knows your father is the stubbornest, most selfish man alive." I blinked up at Gage. "But you have to try." My hand fell to his chest just below the folds of his cravat. "What I wouldn't give to have just five minutes more with my father. To let him know I'm well. To introduce him to you and his granddaughter." My throat tightened until I felt I might choke on my next words, though they needed to be said. "To tell him I forgive him for arranging my marriage to Sir Anthony."

Gage wrapped his arms around me, tucking my head beneath his chin as he pulled me into his embrace. "He knows, Kiera," he whispered against my bonnet. "He knows."

I nodded against the superfine fabric of his deep charcoal coat, blinking back the tears that threatened.

"But I take your point," he continued a few moments later.

I lifted my head to look up at him, and he trailed the back of his hand over my cheek.

"I will try."

There was no need for a response, and he soon bent his head to press his mouth to mine to prevent one in any case. By necessity it was brief, for we were already pulling into the Barkers' drive, but it made my toes curl within their kid boots and my chest tingle with warmth nonetheless.

"Has Lord Henry returned?" Gage asked the Barkers' butler as we entered the house.

"Aye, sir."

Gage nodded but didn't say more, though I could tell by the way his eyes caught mine what he intended.

"Will you please send our maid and valet up to us?" I requested.

"Of course." The butler bowed at the waist and departed while we began to climb the stairs.

"Ten quid we find them already waiting for us," my husband muttered under his breath.

A smile quirked my lips. "Twenty."

He grinned outright, for we both knew our staff's insatiable curiosity rivaled only our own, and I felt a rush of release at this much-needed moment of shared levity after the heavy emotions we'd confronted in the carriage. It lessened the weight on my heart.

True to expectations, I found Bree already bustling about my bedchamber and had to repress a burst of amusement lest she think I'd suddenly lost all sense. She swiveled to face me, her hands clasped eagerly before her. That she wished to question me about what we'd learned was obvious, but she directed her attention to those tasks that needed to be completed first. "Did ye wish to change, my lady?"

"Yes, but first come with me," I urged, crossing to the dressing room door. I passed through the space filled with our clothes and belongings, rapping lightly on the door on the opposite side before entering. Gage's twinkling gaze met mine as I was greeted by the sight of not only Anderley but also Henry already present in his bedchamber.

"This is developing into rather a bad habit," I quipped.

During our most recent inquiry at Barbreck Manor, the five of us had taken to conferring surreptitiously in the bedchamber assigned to Gage. It was undoubtedly inappropriate, but given the fact that Gage actually slept in my chamber and there was no other space in the house where we could be certain of our privacy, it had proven to be the best solution all around. The same proved true here.

"Yes, I can just see the broadsheets hanging in the shop windows in London should a caricaturist get wind of it," Gage teased along with me.

"Just as long as they capture my dashing good looks," Anderley replied, arching his chin and straightening his cravat.

Bree and I both laughed, which only made him preen more.

Apparently, we all needed a bit of leavening. I sank down onto the camelback sofa positioned near one of the tall windows flanked by matching goldenrod-shaded drapes, hoping that by doing so the others would join me. Bree hovered for only a moment before lowering herself to perch on the edge of the cushion next to me. Then one by one, the men followed our cue.

Gage flopped down in one of the bergère chairs opposite us, turning to his half brother, who soon took occupation of its twin. "Did you and Melton find anything of interest at the site of the attack?"

Henry grimaced in disappointment. "Nothing more than trampled dirt at the verge of the road, and a pair of overgrown paths leading into the forest on either side."

"Is that where Melton believes they dispersed after the attack?"

"He says they retreated down the road toward Wentbridge, but after a matter of a few seconds the sound of their hoofbeats stopped, and he's fairly certain they peeled off into the woods."

"Going both directions?" Anderley queried, having carried over the chair from the writing desk in the corner.

Henry shrugged. "He couldn't say."

Gage nodded, his brow lowering as he considered this information. "Then they knew the layout of the land, which makes it unlikely they followed my father for any distance before striking."

Henry's fingers brushed over the ecru upholstery on the arm of the chair, his eyes narrowed on the twine-patterned rug, though it was clear his thoughts were back at the roadside. "The forest along that stretch of road is dense and thick with foliage. Had Melton not been certain of the place where they'd been forced to halt, I'm not sure we would have found those paths. As it was, we only located them because we were scouring the road for clues and found the place where they must have lain in wait for Lord Gage's coach to happen by." His eyes lifted to Gage. "Maybe in winter it would be easier to spot, but now, at the height of summer?" He shook his head. "They had to have known exactly what they were looking for to find it in the dark."

Gage looked to each of us in turn. "Then I think we're all agreed that these attackers must have a local connection. Either they live here themselves or they often operate in the area."

"Miss McEvoy has learned something pertinent to that," Anderley remarked, his dark eyes encouraging Bree to speak.

"Aye." She turned to focus on me, crinkling the jonquil muslin of her skirts in her fists where they draped over her lap. "Remember I told ye I'd learned aboot Robin Hood's alleged connection to Wentbridge, and how Barnsdale Forest is supposedly the real Sherwood Forest o' legend." She turned to include the others, leaning so far forward that I feared she might fall flat on her face. "Weel, I offered to help that maid I told ye aboot wi' some o' her chores, and *she* told me that they've their very own merry band of highwaymen, robbin' from the rich who pass along the highway to give to the poor."

My eyes met Gage's. "Mr. Robinson, the parish constable, told us the same."

Bree's shoulders deflated at not being first to inform us of this piece of information.

"But was she able to tell you how they operate? How do they pass the money along to the poor? How do they know who needs it?"

"She says those who need it will simply find it ootside their door wi' a small piece o' foolscap attached wi' a simple arrow drawn on it."

"A fitting symbol for Robin Hood," Henry remarked somewhat dryly.

Bree nodded, her loosely restrained strawberry blond curls bouncing in her enthusiasm. "She didna ken how exactly they ken who needed it, but I dinna think it would be verra hard for them to figure oot given the way gossip spreads in a small village."

"True." I narrowed my eyes in thought. "But I'm also wondering if they've tasked a few members of the community to uncover such information. Or if they *themselves* might be in positions to learn such things."

"Such as a minister," Anderley suggested.

Henry tilted his head. "The legendary Robin Hood *did* have Friar Tuck."

Anderley's eyebrows arched. "Or a surgeon."

It was something to consider. After all, medical men being called out to homes to treat the ill sometimes saw things that the patients otherwise kept hidden.

"Yes, but I don't gain the impression from Dr. Barker that he knows any more than he's already told us," Gage said after a moment of contemplation. "What of you?" he asked me.

"I agree. His answers have been straightforward. Though . . ." I hesitated, uncertain whether I wished to continue. But now that I'd already spoken, I could hardly take back my words. Not with everyone staring at me in anticipation. "I *do* sense that he and his wife are keeping something from us. But that could be any number of things—many of which have nothing to do with the attack on your father and his staff."

I could tell by the look on Gage's face that this was something we would address privately later, but for now he let it pass without comment. "In any case, the point still stands. Perhaps not everyone knows who these highwaymen are, but it's reasonable to assume at least a few people do." He propped one booted ankle over the opposite knee. "The question is, can we sniff out who they are, and will they tell us anything?"

Anderley shrugged. "It's worth a try."

I turned back to Bree. "Did the maid tell you what the staff's opinion is of the attack on Lord Gage and his servants? Does it not alarm them that these highwaymen turned violent and murdered someone? A fellow servant, even."

She seemed to struggle to keep her whisky brown eyes locked with mine, allowing me to guess what her answer would be. "They believe that Lord Gage brought it on himself. That he resisted and maybe even attacked them first, and so they must've been defendin' themselves." Her gaze darted to Gage and then back to me. "They dinna want to believe differently."

CHAPTER 9

It's to be expected," I spoke into the silence that had fallen, hoping to ease the forbidding expression from Gage's face. None of this was easy for him to hear. "After all, by all reports, thus far these highwaymen haven't resorted to violence beyond a single shove, and given the benefit the community seems to derive from their actions, it's been easy for them to justify their loyalty and their silence. They won't want to concede they might be wrong about them. So they adjust the narrative to fit the story they've already been telling themselves."

Henry leaned forward, bracing his elbows on his spread knees. "Couple that with the fact that their new Robin Hood is opposed to the excesses and undoubtedly the perceived corruption of the wealthy, and it's easy for them to imagine that their chosen narrative is the truth anyway." He peered warily at Gage's brooding face. "That the lord who was attacked is lying and was eager for vengeance."

"Yes, but we *do* believe Lord Gage is telling the truth, correct?"

Anderley asked, looking to each of us in turn. "That he wouldn't bother denying he attacked first, particularly given the fact that the law would see it as his right to defend himself." He scowled. "So why *did* the highwaymen attack him? Why did they alter their usual method?"

"And why *didn't* they ask for his purse?" I added, following his line of questioning. "If they're merely a band of merry highwaymen robbing from the rich to give to the poor, why didn't they even attempt to collect Lord Gage's coin?"

We all looked to Gage, I supposed all of us wanting him to make the logical deduction, given this was about his father. Even Henry, who seemed to recognize that the impact could never be the same for him. Not when he'd always had the duke caring for him as his father, regardless of their blood relation.

Gage heaved a deep sigh, scraping a hand back through his golden hair. "The obvious conclusion, the one we've already drawn, is that their intention in stopping him from the very beginning was to attack him rather than rob him. But as to why specifically they altered their usual method . . . ?" He shook his head. "I don't know."

"They must have recognized him," I ventured. "They must have realized who he was and, for whatever reason, possessed some sort of personal vendetta against him. That's the only thing that makes sense."

Gage's expression turned sour. "Which makes it less likely that the cause is some political rivalry or petty aristocratic quarrel." Clearly, he was thinking of what his father had told us about Lord Portis and his brother who lived nearby.

"Yes, but we should speak to Mr. Butler all the same. He may know something worthwhile." My voice tightened with frustration. "And unlike the villagers, be more receptive to speaking with us."

"I take it your visit to the parish constable and the Blue Bell was not as productive as you'd hoped," Henry said.

"Mr. Robinson was cooperative enough," Gage replied, his gaze seeking out mine as if in confirmation. "He seems to be doing what he can to investigate these highway robberies and the attack on my father and his staff. The trouble is, he has no power to make the villagers tell him what they know."

"*Do* they know anything?" Anderley asked.

Gage scoffed. "Oh, yes. At least some of them certainly do. And the majority of the rest seem content to mind their tongues on the chance that they might also."

"There may be someone willing to talk," I argued, but without any real force. "Just because Mr. Robinson's neighbors were somewhat hostile, and the patrons at the Blue Bell seemed to eye us with dislike, doesn't mean everyone will." I nodded to Bree. "Miss McEvoy convinced one of the maids here to confide what she knows."

"Aye, but . . . I ken there's much more she's still no' sayin'."

I turned to her in query.

"When I tried to prod her for more information, she denied she ken anythin' more, but I could tell that wasna true. No' by the way her eyes got so big and panicked when she realized how much she'd already said."

"Then keep at her," Gage directed. "Perhaps, in time, she'll let more slip." He pinned his valet with a more direct stare. "Anderley, I need you to go to the Blue Bell and interview the staff. The proprietor, Mr. Fryston, knows you're coming."

Anderley straightened. "What am I to ask?"

"Ostensibly you're there to discover if any of them noticed anyone suspicious lurking about the premises around the time Lord Gage stopped there before journeying on, but I suspect they'll already have been warned to tell you they didn't see anything whether they did or not. So do some poking about. See what you can see. Learn what you can learn. But have a care," he warned sternly. "This Fryston fellow is no fool. He undoubtedly expects as much."

"You suspect something havey-cavey is going on there, then?" Anderley remarked, utilizing a bit of slang he'd likely learned from his time living as a peddler on the streets of London.

"Yes. Though I cannot tell you precisely what it is, or whether it has anything to do with these highwaymen or the attack on my father." Gage looked to me, but I had nothing more to add other than my agreement that Fryston had wished to keep something concealed from us. Something that had to do with closed doors and Tom Hutchinson's simmering glare.

I heard rather than saw Bree's swift inhalation, and when I turned to look at her, I could see the agitation rippling through her poker-straight posture. Even the knuckles of her fingers clasped together in her lap were turning white. From the way she was sneaking glances at Anderley, I realized she was concerned for him, for his safety. But this extreme reaction seemed out of character. After all, Anderley had been assigned far more dangerous tasks in the past and yet she'd scarcely batted an eyelash. What was different about this one?

"Perhaps I should go with him," Henry suggested. A twist of auburn hair had fallen over his brow, much as Gage's was prone to do, and he brushed it aside. "To guard his flank, so to speak."

What Anderley thought of this suggestion I couldn't tell, for his face was a mask of careful indifference, but Bree's fingers flexed in her lap as if anxious for us to grasp the merit of this proposal.

Unfortunately, Gage had different concerns in mind.

"No, I need you to remain here. Kiera and I will be setting

out for Skelbrooke Hall later, and I need someone to remain here I can trust."

The gravity with which he spoke these words startled me. "Do you anticipate trouble?"

His gaze met mine steadily, and I could tell he was shuffling and discarding his words, not wishing to unduly alarm me. "Not necessarily. But until this point, these highwaymen have believed they've eluded the consequences of their crimes. However, they've only had to contend with the local officials, some of whom may be rather indifferent to their capture. Now that we're here and we've been witnessed asking questions rather than simply collecting my father and continuing on our way, the same cannot be said. They *might* . . ." he emphasized the word ". . . decide their best course of action is to try to threaten or intimidate us into leaving."

What he didn't say, though I recognized the implication, was that they might also decide to finish the job by killing Lord Gage or even attempt to silence those remaining witnesses who might have noticed anything incriminating.

"I realize that Lembus and Melton and even the Barkers are here to look after my father, but I only trust each of them to a certain extent." Gage addressed his brother. "I want someone here who I know I can rely on absolutely. Someone who can be trusted to look after our interests as well."

Henry squared his shoulders, and his chin came up, as if demonstrating this trust in him would not be misplaced. His desire for his brother's approval and Gage's display of faith in him made my heart warm despite the chill I felt at the idea that someone might come here to do further harm to Lord Gage, his servants, or, most disturbing, Emma.

But I also knew Gage. I was well acquainted with his strong protective instinct. I'd butted against it often enough in the past. If he believed there was genuine cause for concern for our daughter, he would never leave her behind, even in the more than capable hands of Mrs. Mackay and the rest of our staff.

"You can depend on me," Henry told him solemnly. "I will ensure everyone under this roof remains safe."

"And I'll be vigilant," Anderley promised. His eyes slid to Bree, telling me he wasn't oblivious to her worry. "Even more than I usually am." An impish spark lit the depths of his dark eyes, revealing he hadn't lost his mischievous streak entirely.

Bree's cheeks flushed, and her eyes narrowed at him.

Or perhaps he merely intended to rile her. I couldn't deny that an irritated Bree was an improvement over an agitated one.

"Stop by the Bay Horse Inn as well, if there's time," Gage instructed. "See what they might know."

A rap at the door interrupted him before he could issue any more orders. We all looked at each other guiltily, a fact that later struck me as humorous. By unspoken command, Bree and I moved toward the dressing room door so that we wouldn't all be discovered colluding together. Then we would never convince the Barkers' staff to confide in us.

Bree followed my direction, pausing just on the other side of the door and turning her ear toward the wall shared with Gage's bedchamber. But while we could hear the soft murmur of voices, we couldn't make out what they were saying. I shrugged, carrying on to my chamber, where it seemed we'd only just arrived when a rap sounded on *my* door. I fully expected to see Mrs. Mackay and Emma on the other side when Bree opened it, but instead Gage stood there pensively.

"What is it?" I asked, immediately sobering.

"Father is asking for me. Though, of course, he didn't say why." His voice was terse, and I could tell he was struggling to repress his own worry.

I reached out to touch his elbow. "Do you want me to come with you?"

"No, I don't know that there's any cause for concern. And you must have Emma to see to. I simply . . ." His words seemed to fail him for a moment. ". . . wanted you to know."

His palpable insecurity tugged at my heart. "Of course."

"I'll send word if this changes our plans for later this afternoon." With a swift kiss to my brow, he was gone, leaving me staring after him as he strode purposely down the corridor.

I stepped back, turning to close the door, when I spied Henry standing beside a console table in the corridor, watching Gage as well. His expression in that moment was laid open like a book, allowing me to see the naked longing and pain he felt. That he was forlorn he'd not been included in his natural father's summons was evident, just as was his chagrin when his gaze shifted to meet mine.

Heat stung my cheeks at the realization I'd intruded on his unguarded moment, imagining the discomfort it must cause Henry to know I'd seen it. But rather than hurry away as I'd expected, his eyes remained locked with mine. A deep inhale made his broad shoulders rise and fall, and then he nodded, acknowledging me and what I'd seen. I nodded back, hoping he knew he had nothing to fear from me.

He turned to go, and I slowly closed the door, torn by Henry's dilemma and wishing there was something I could do about it. But I couldn't even influence Lord Gage in my *own* favor, *or* Gage's. Not without blackmailing him. How could I ever hope to persuade him to put his hard-heartedness aside when it came to his second son?

I pivoted to cross the room, finding Bree standing before the dressing table, shuffling the few jars and items lined up along its top even though they had already been neat and orderly. In the reflection of the mirror, I could see the deep furrow between her eyes, but before I could address it, she gestured toward the morning dress draped over the bed.

"I've pressed the challis morning dress with floral bouquets. Will that do?"

"Yes." I swiveled so that she could reach the buttons at the back of my carriage dress while I untied the pelerine at my throat and began to unfasten the gown's matching belt. "But leave this laid out. I shall need it again later."

"Aye, m'lady."

Her head was bowed as she worked, so I could no longer read her expression, but I could tell by the twitchiness of her movements that something was still bothering her. "You seemed concerned at the prospect of Anderley venturing to the Blue Bell on his own," I remarked evenly, not wanting my curiosity to alarm her.

Even so, her hands momentarily stilled before resuming their work. "Aye, weel, he'll have no help should somethin' go wrong."

"That's true. But Anderley knows how to take care of himself," I attempted to reassure her. "He won't do anything reckless."

She didn't respond to this, but her lips clamped into a thin line as if she wanted to. She swept away the carriage dress and then settled the challis gown over my head.

"In any case, I don't actually anticipate trouble," I continued once I was no longer smothered by fabric. "Not when we know where he is, and the parish constable himself heard us ask if our manservant could be sent over to question the staff. Fryston knows suspicion would fall on him if something happened to Anderley, and he doesn't want the authorities looking too closely at his inn."

But rather than console her, this seemed to unsettle her more.

I turned to face her, taking hold of her hands. I was alarmed to feel that they trembled slightly. "Bree, what is it? What has you so agitated?"

She closed her eyes, shaking her head. "It's naught but foolishness."

"What is?" I squeezed her hands more tightly, compelling her to look at me.

"You'll think me ridiculous."

"I doubt that. You've always been quite sensible."

Except when it came to some superstitions. Then her Scots upbringing sometimes got the best of her. But then, the same could be said for me.

Still, she hesitated. "'Tis only . . . when I went to visit my family at Hogmanay . . ."

I nodded encouragingly, recalling how she'd taken leave to travel to Kirkcudbright for a week around the New Year.

She peered up at me from beneath her lashes. "My brother, he told me a story aboot a wayside inn along a lonely stretch o' moor. How some o' the guest rooms were rigged wi' trapdoors so that in the middle o' the night, after they fell asleep, the unsuspectin' traveler would plummet to his death." She spoke the last in a whisper.

My eyebrows arched. "And they were never caught?"

She shook her head and then paused as if giving the matter more thought. "I suppose eventually. Or else how would my brother have ken aboot it."

"Or he read the story in a book and only intended to scare you," I suggested gently.

Bree flushed, lowering her head.

"My brother used to tell me similar terrifying tales, often before we set out on a journey. Stories he'd read in one periodical or another or heard from his friends. Stories about trapdoors, and pits filled with bones, and bloodthirsty innkeepers carving up their victims to use their fat to make candles."

Her eyes widened and she shuddered.

I nodded. "Trevor was forbidden from attending the races with his friends after our father found out about that one." I tilted my head. "And you were about to set out on a journey of your own, returning to Blakelaw House on the mail coach."

She frowned. "Aye, maybe he meant to scare me. But that doesna mean it's no' true."

"Maybe. But there are always flaws to the supposed infallibility of these alleged plots. Wouldn't someone have noticed all the travelers who went missing at that particular inn? Wouldn't at least one of the alleged victims have noticed the trapdoor? And I don't think you can actually make a candle from human fat." This was meant to reassure her, but it didn't appear as if it was working.

I tilted my head, recalling something from our own journey here. "Is that why you fell asleep so often in the carriage? You were sitting up awake all night?"

Her expression turned sheepish.

"Oh, Bree."

"I was just bein' cautious," she replied defensively, urging me to turn around so she could finish doing up my buttons. "Some of it *could* be true!"

I didn't attempt to argue this point, recognizing it would do no good. Not when she was already embarrassed. Instead, I sought to comfort her with logic. "Well, Anderley has no reason to enter the guest rooms, so he shouldn't encounter any trapdoors or other such things."

At first, she didn't respond, and I thought she wished for me to drop the matter. Until she muttered under breath, almost so that I couldn't hear her, "No matter what ye say, I willna breathe easy 'til he's returned."

I waited until she'd finished twitching my dress into place and I'd settled on the bench for her to adjust my hair before I spoke again. It was true, one of the reasons I'd waited to reply was so that I could see her reaction to what I had to say in the reflection of the mirror. But I was also questioning whether I should be saying anything at all.

Given the unfair balance of power in our relationships with our staff, Gage and I had resolved it was best not to pry into our servants' personal lives. However, I had already broken this rule at least twice. First, when I couldn't remain silent in the face of Bree's evident unhappiness, and later when she had understandably been out of sorts after being poisoned and had been unfairly taking it out on Anderley.

"Things have changed between you and Anderley, haven't they?" I dared to remark.

I knew they'd changed for Anderley. I'd seen it in his eyes when he'd carried her back to Barbreck after she'd fallen ill from the poison. He'd been stricken by abject terror and panic, and whether he'd dared to admit it to himself before that moment, I knew then that he unquestionably loved her.

Bree's face contorted into one of uncertainty, and her hands tightened abruptly, tugging harder on the tresses she was securing with a pin than I knew she'd intended. For a moment I thought she might not respond, but then she murmured, "He wishes them to."

"But what do you wish?" I prompted when she didn't continue.

"I . . . I dinna ken." Her voice ached with insecurity and hope, and a whole host of unspoken things. Things that perhaps she wasn't yet ready to scratch the surface of. Knowing a bit of her past, I had a fair guess what some of them were. But it wasn't my right to probe them. Not unless she invited it. That would be stepping a shade too far.

So instead, I returned to the heart of the matter, the issue that had ended their romantic relationship four months ago.

"Has he told you how he feels?"

A light flush spread up her neck and into her freckled cheeks. "Aye."

I hid a smile, my heart warming at the pleasure evident in that simple word.

"And have you come to any understanding on his flirtatious nature?"

Her gaze lifted to meet mine in the reflection of the mirror before returning to my chestnut tresses. "No' officially. But . . . I've noticed a change in him. He's still Anderley." Her lips curled briefly before falling into more sober lines. "But he's more considerate o' my feelings. And I . . . I've realized that I dinna want him to change who he is." Her brow furrowed as she considered her words. "That just because he's flirtatious doesna mean he's unfaithful. That he's no' my father, and it's unfair to tar him wi' the same brush."

None of this was truly new to me. I'd already suspected that Bree had come to terms with the fact that her mistrust of Anderley stemmed from her father's infidelity to her mother. It was evident in the way she'd been able to tease him about charming information out of the maids—though he'd never been one to mislead them about his intentions, merely smile and tease, and perhaps harmlessly flatter. Just as Anderley's restrained reactions to the females who crossed his path and his recognition that he must allow Bree to complete her investigative assignments as she saw fit and wait for her to ask for his help if needed indicated his willingness to do what he could to ease her fears and demonstrate his respect for her. But it was good to hear her admit it.

They had both learned a great deal in the months since they had amicably ended their relationship. Though I believed Bree's poisoning had certainly spurred matters along. At least, for Anderley.

Much like I had been when I met Gage, Anderley was wary

of betrayal and had been hesitant to let others get close to him. Given the harsh treatment he'd received from the padrone master his Italian parents had sold him to—believing he would be taught a trade and given a better life, not forced to beg and peddle on the streets, treated as little more than a slave—it was to be expected. But Bree's near death had made him confront the depths of his feelings, and so he now checked those impulses he'd cultivated in order to survive, no longer attempting to beguile and charm the casual acquaintances he crossed paths with. It was a skill he'd long possessed, identifying which persona to adopt in which circumstance based on others' reaction to and expectations of him. Only now he had someone else's feelings to consider rather than merely his own.

However, I shared none of this with her, knowing she didn't need to hear it. Nor did I contradict her, for it sounded like things had already changed between them whether she realized it or not. Instead, I simply offered her an encouraging smile. "That's good to hear."

"It is," she agreed, smiling softly to herself.

I elected not to interrupt her musings, for these were undeniably more enjoyable than her worries over Anderley's safety. I just hoped Bree wouldn't require as drastic a prod as Anderley in order to admit how she felt. Of the pair of them, she was supposed to be the most openhearted, but it appeared he still had some convincing to do.

CHAPTER 10

After seeing to Emma's needs, I laid her on a blanket on the floor with her favorite ragdoll while I enjoyed my own repast of soup and bread, which I'd asked Bree to bring to me on a tray. Then I settled at the fruitwood writing desk to pen a few missives. I'd yet to send word to my sister Alana and brother Trevor that we had arrived safely, as well as update them on the status of Lord Gage's health. My family and friends at Barbreck Manor, from where we'd departed in a rush after receiving Lembus's letter, would also be anxious to hear from us.

However, I didn't allow myself to dwell over the details. I knew Emma would entertain herself for only so long by chewing on and cooing to her doll and practicing her rolling. Besides, the warm sunlight shining through the windows was beckoning to me. I recalled the lovely garden I'd spied through the morning room's windows and decided to venture out to explore it. After many days trapped within the confines of our carriage, and the unsettling discoveries since our arrival, a good ramble through the flowers would do me a world of good.

I could have passed Emma back into the care of Mrs. Mackay, but I chose to take her with me. The day was a fine one, and I suspected she would enjoy the colorful plants and their fragrant blossoms as much as I would. I lifted Emma, nibbling her little ears to make her giggle, and then snatched up the blanket to take with us on the chance we would find a lovely spot in which to recline.

I glanced at Gage's bedchamber door as I strode toward the stairs, wondering if he was still closeted with his father. He had not sought me out, but that didn't mean he was still in Lord Gage's presence. In fact, I found it difficult to imagine he was, given how quickly my father-in-law had tired from company the evening before while he was still recovering. But perhaps he'd sent his son on an errand. Or perhaps Gage needed some time to himself to untangle the complicated coil of emotions his father aroused in him. I'd found myself in desire of a private space in which I could vent my emotions a time or two after confronting Lord Gage, so I could empathize.

I stepped out onto the terrace overlooking the gardens and inhaled a deep breath rife with the heavenly perfume of living things. The rosebushes spanned by trellises to my left had already been deadheaded, but the paths elsewhere were lined with a profusion of peachy pink alstroemerias, magenta dahlias, scarlet zinnias, and orange tithonias. I began to pick my way through the floral wonderland, pausing to show Emma each bloom. She was particularly taken with the pale periwinkle love-in-a-mist and their intricate blossoms.

For myself, I was delighted to discover a portion of the garden near the farthest corner had been given over to wildflowers, allowing them to bloom in a riot of color as nature had intended.

Brilliant blue clustered bellflowers grew next to lavender rock-roses, orchids, salad burnet, yellow-wort, and betony. And hovering among the petals were dozens of butterflies—marbled white and orange with black spots fluttering from plant to plant. Emma watched them with intense fascination, as if unable to believe her eyes.

I tipped my head back to feel the sun directly on my skin and smiled, feeling the weight of the last week slip free from my shoulders, if only briefly. Perhaps it was time for us to find a country home of our own, somewhere I could cultivate a garden such as this. Though, truth be told, if I had a garden like this of my own and an art studio to create my paintings, I might never leave it.

Opening my eyes, I blinked against the brightness before lowering my head to shield my face once again with the brim of my blue watered-silk capote. I turned to survey the landscape, confronted with the stone wall separating the property from the Great North Road on one side and the long stretch of lawn leading to the forest I'd seen from my window on the other. Just ahead, I spied Mrs. Barker standing at the edge of the wildflowers. She'd been hidden by the wavering stalks grown waist high and the trunk of the tall shade tree in the corner. Her back was to me, and I couldn't tell what she was looking at, but I decided it would be rude not to approach.

In any case, Emma chose that moment to give a squeal of delight, ending any possibility of stealth. Mrs. Barker startled, pressing a hand to her chest. Clearly, she'd not realized we were close by. With one last look toward the field of waving amber field grasses spreading toward the northeast, she turned to greet us as we strolled nearer.

"We have been enjoying your garden," I told her with a smile. "I must compliment you, for it is absolutely lovely."

She blushed. "Oh, well, thank thee. I'm sure it cannot compare with those at some o' the greater homes. But I do love it," she murmured.

It was true, it could not compete with the larger cultivated spaces of many of the greater homes, but it did not need to. In any case, it had not been planted in order to impress, but rather to suit Mrs. Barker's whims and desires, and that made all the difference.

"Well, I would much rather wander through your blossoms any day." I allowed my gaze to trail over the speckled carpet of flowers. "They are not only pleasing to the nose and eye, but also . . . soothing." A thought occurred to me then. "I wonder if they would also help my father-in-law."

"Thou could ask Dr. Barker. 'Tis worth a try."

I nodded. "Perhaps I'll do that."

Emma lurched, recalling my attention as she reached for something. A willow warbler had just landed on a branch of the oak tree overhead.

I shifted her in my arms so that she had a better view. "Yes, do you see the bird?" I asked her as it began to sing. Her legs kicked in excited appreciation, and I laughed. "You like that, do you?"

"What a darling," Mrs. Barker remarked, thoroughly charmed.

I wondered again about her lack of children but did not ask. Even so, she must have sensed my curiosity, for she looked up from touching Emma's foot to offer me a sad smile. "Mr. Barker is unable to have children. An illness took that ability from him."

"How sad," I replied, uncertain how to respond to the complicated mixture of emotions that rippled across her features. Had she known about this before she wed Mr. Barker, or was his illness a more recent development? I recalled Dr. Barker informing us of an illness he'd suffered in South Africa. How it had been one of the reasons he'd elected to retire from the army.

But perhaps he hadn't known it had affected his fertility. Or maybe he had, and she'd married him anyway.

She nodded, smiling softly at my daughter. "Some things are just not meant to be." A pained expression flashed across her face as she murmured this platitude, letting me know she didn't really believe it. But it was a convenient excuse if one wanted to turn the subject. As such, I politely took her cue.

"Have you lived here all your life, then? In Wentbridge?"

The warbler had flown away, so we began to stroll back toward the cottage, the soft breeze lightly ruffling the hairs peeking out from our bonnets.

"Nay. I grew up in Monk Bretton, south o' Wakefield."

I nodded, though I didn't know where that was.

"My father claimed our roots there went back so far our ancestors were writ in the Domesday Book." The resulting report from the great survey of most of England and Wales ordered by William the Conqueror in 1085 which listed all landholdings. It was the earliest such public record of its kind in all of Britain. "'Appen that's true, but even if it's not, the Harringtons had lived there a long time. And so had my husband's people."

Her face flushed and then paled when I looked at her in confusion, for I distinctly recalled Dr. Barker telling us he'd come from Ireland.

"My *first* husband," she stammered in clarification.

Her reaction told me that she'd not intended to tell me this, but absorbed in her retelling, her words had slipped out before she could stop them.

"He died before we were wed even six months." I could hear the grief those words still caused her, as if they scraped across her heart. "The child I was carrying died a month later." This last statement was spoken so quietly I had to strain to hear it, but it stabbed my eardrums like the loudest thunder crash.

"He must have been a good man," I managed to respond. He had to have been for her to be mourning him still.

"I've met none better."

Her simple reply might have been viewed as an insult to her current husband, but I didn't think that was her intent. Once again, I suspected she'd spoken without thinking. An acknowledgment of all she'd lost, all she'd never have again. Some widows did not wed their soulmates, as Coleridge called them, the second time around like I had. Some women wed them first, when they were young, and then had the rest of their lives to mourn their loss.

It was something I was still contemplating several hours later when Gage and I set out for Skelbrooke Hall. Neither of us spoke as we passed over the Went bridge and through the village, both consumed by our own thoughts. But as the verdant fields on either side of the stone walls bordering the road began to stretch into the distance, I was pulled from my own self-absorption by the sight of the tight furrow in my husband's brow. I removed my kid leather glove and slid my hand into his, where it rested in his lap so that we were skin to skin, pulse to pulse.

He turned from the window to look at me, and I curled my fingers to brush them lightly over his palm before lacing them with his. His hand squeezed mine, and the lines of his face softened.

"What did your father want?" I asked, curious what had kept him occupied a good portion of the afternoon. Upon seeing how his teeth gritted, I wished I could take back my query.

"He wanted me to write a number of letters for him."

I didn't withhold my surprise. "Isn't that something Lembus could have done?"

"Yes, but he insisted the messages were too confidential. And that I needed to establish a better rapport with the men he was addressing."

"I see." I studied his taut features, reading between the lines to grasp the cause of his agitation. "So it wasn't the content of the missives that was so critical, but rather his forcing you to interact with the intended recipients."

"Yes. My father is determined I take his place in the world, when he passes." A small tic in his jaw told me that last remark had not been so easily made. "And he seems intent on grooming me for it now."

"But that's not the life you wish to lead," I replied. "Is it?"

"It is not," he bit out. "But of course, that won't deter Father. He's always been rather good at ignoring what I want when it's counter to whatever he's decided is good for me."

I couldn't fault him his resentment on this point. He had confided in me once that the only time his father had acceded to his wishes when he was young was when he had failed in his bid to see Gage join the Royal Navy as a young gentleman at the ripe old age of eleven. Though the only reason Gage had escaped this fate had been because his perpetually ill mother had begged his father not to take him from her. The second time he'd majorly rebelled against his father's plans had been to wed me rather than the socially and politically advantageous darling of the ton his father had chosen for him.

This had been part of the reason for Lord Gage's initial antagonism toward me, though he had since made some peace with his son's decision. It helped that the matter couldn't be undone. At least, not without a tremendous scandal. Something he would view as infinitely worse than simply accepting our marriage.

"But this isn't something he can force," I pointed out. "He can't make you embrace his political ideals any more than he can make you connive to be the throne's righthand man."

"That won't stop him from trying."

I clasped his hand tighter, trying to pour what little comfort I could into that gesture. "Were you able to talk about your mother? About Henry?"

He shook his head. "Every time I tried to raise the issue, he would turn the subject." The corner of his lip curled scornfully. "That or he suddenly found himself feeling weak or in pain."

This brought a scowl to my face. There was no doubt Lord Gage was still recovering from his attack and the subsequent infection and fever, but to hear that he was also manipulating the matter angered me.

"He doesn't honestly think he can avoid discussing them indefinitely, does he?" I asked.

"This is my father. Nothing surprises me anymore."

His voice was hollow with bitterness, and it tore at something inside me.

"Yes, but this isn't something he can just brush aside. He has hurt you terribly. He's hurt Henry terribly." My voice rose along with my fury. "We're not all going to just ignore that and pretend it never happened. For heaven's sake, he won't even *speak* to his second son!"

Gage released my hand to wrap his arm around me, pulling me close. My broad-brimmed bonnet with its various bows and feathers made it impossible for me to rest my head on his shoulder as I would have liked, but I still derived comfort from his body pressed against my side. I breathed deep, tempering my anger before I looked up into his face. His features had actually gentled rather than hardened, and affection warmed his eyes.

"This is why I love you," he murmured, lifting his opposite hand to touch my cheek. "Well, one of the reasons." His eyebrows arched. "And exactly why my father didn't wish me to marry you."

"You mean Lady Felicity wouldn't have taken umbrage on your behalf?" I attempted to quip, referencing the young lady his father had wanted to be his son's bride.

He scoffed. "She is far more likely to have taken Father's side, urging me to conceal and ignore Henry's existence as my brother lest there be a scandal, and conniving with my father to coax me into the Tory fold and to embrace their political ambitions as my own."

"But that would have made you miserable." The very thought of his being forced to live a life he hated made my heart clench. "Do you truly think she would have had so little care for what you wanted?"

"She would have seen it as doing what was necessary for my own, and *her* own, good. Never mind my happiness. Just like my father. Two peas in a pod, the pair of them." He frowned. "At one point, I wondered why Father didn't marry her himself. Yes, the age difference would have been significant, but when has that ever stopped noblemen in the past?"

I touched his face, bringing him back from the grim place his thoughts had gone. The light had dimmed in his eyes, and I wanted more than anything to rekindle it. Arching my chin, I leaned closer. "Then I'm glad I took pity on you and married you to save you from such a draconian fate."

A glint of challenge sparked in his pale blue irises, just as I'd hoped. "Took pity on me, did you?"

I shrugged one shoulder coyly, pressing my thumb to the cleft in his chin. "You seemed so lost without me. Like a little lamb."

His arm tightened around me. "A little lamb, was I?" he countered with a decidedly wolfish grin.

My answering laughter was smothered as his head dipped and his mouth captured mine. By the time our lips parted, my bonnet had been knocked askew, our breathing was rather rapid, and he had thoroughly made his point. But I was quite content to be set in my place when the act of doing so was so delightful. And when it recalled Gage from the unhappy contemplations into which his father's betrayal and continued disapproval drove him.

"I stand corrected," I conceded. "A wolf in sheep's clothing, then."

He chuckled. "But you are right about one thing," he murmured, his eyes intent on mine. "I would be lost without you. You gave me back myself. The parts that I had been hiding or missing since my mother died, since I'd discovered she was murdered, since I'd witnessed the worst of what humanity can be at Tripolitsa. Since I'd begun to give in to my father's demands and wishes, too uncaring to fight it."

"But you fought against his plans for you to marry Lady Felicity," I pointed out.

"I ran away from them," he countered in chagrin. "There is a difference." His calloused fingers brushed over my skin, leaving a tingling wake. "But then I met you. And *you* changed everything."

Tears stung the back of my eyes and my heart expanded, pressing against my chest until I thought I might burst with my love for him. "Just as you changed everything for me."

Saving me from my self-imposed exile. Not only seeing but also accepting me for who I was, and loving me because of it. Which in turn helped *me* to accept who I was, and allowed me to heal from all the pain Sir Anthony had caused me, both during our marriage and the scandal that erupted after his death and the discovery of my involvement with the illustrations for his definitive anatomy textbook. Not that those wounds were fully healed. I didn't know if they ever would be. But I had come a long way in the two years since I had met Gage, and I knew my life would look very different if we hadn't met. For one, Emma wouldn't have been born, and I couldn't bear to imagine that.

He pressed a kiss sweet with promise to my lips. "We are a well-matched pair." His regard shifted to the view outside my window over my shoulder, a wistful smile playing across his mouth. "I only wish my father could see the worthiness in me that you do."

I came very close to hating my father-in-law in that moment.

Only the fact that Gage would not want that, and that Lord Gage so clearly adored his granddaughter, kept me from descending into loathing. Even so, if he'd been seated before me then, I'm not sure I could have been held responsible for my actions.

But the most troubling fact of all was that it was not in my power to make this better. I could not force Lord Gage to alter his treatment of Gage. Just as I could not force him to accept Henry.

But I could dash well try.

CHAPTER 11

The village of Skelbrooke stood six miles south of Went-bridge, a short distance down a narrow lane cutting west through the golden fields away from the Great North Road. In the heart of the hamlet's single street lined with stone houses stood the round-topped gate piers leading to Skelbrooke Hall. A small gatehouse perched to the left of the piers, overlooking the drive, its walls built with the same mottled sandstone which seemed to be utilized in all construction in the area—be it homes or fences. Our coachman slowed as he entered the open gates, but when no one emerged to question us, we carried on toward the manor.

The drive on either side was lined with hedges and trees, some of which arched overhead, almost forming a tunnel. Their leaves rustled together in the wind, rising and falling like the sound of waves along the shore. I leaned closer to the window and closed my eyes, feeling the play of light and shadow across my eyelids as the late-afternoon sunshine filtered through the leaves. It was unexpectedly peaceful, and I couldn't help but envision Skelbrooke Hall's inhabitants inhaling a deep breath of the verdant forest and allowing their worries to slip from their shoulders as they traversed this lane.

As such, I wasn't as surprised as I might have been by the informal appearance of the gentleman who exited the front doors and descended the stairs to greet us, almost as if he'd witnessed our approach, though that was impossible. We hadn't emerged from the trees to be given our first glimpse of the house until we'd been nearly upon it. A small circular drive with a fountain at its center was all that stood between the forest and the sandstone edifice of the modest three-story country house. It had been constructed five bays wide with large quoins at the corners and an immense fanlight fitted above the blue double doors flanked by Doric columns.

One might have been excused for mistaking the man for a servant, for he strode up to the door of our carriage and opened it before we'd even come to a complete stop, but for the fact he was so obviously not a member of the staff. For one, his walnut brown hair was much too long, brushing his cheekbones on either side of his face rather than being cut short or restrained by a queue, and dark bristles had begun to show along his jaw below his side whiskers. His clothing also was not up to scratch, being both too well tailored and too carelessly donned. His cravat was loosely tied, and the waistcoat a gentleman would normally wear with such an ensemble was nonexistent.

But the clearest indicator was the broad grin that flashed across his face, revealing white teeth in a sun-bronzed face and a roguish glint in his green eyes as he offered me his hand. No footman would dare be so forward.

"Welcome to Skelbrooke Hall."

I allowed him to draw me from the confines of the carriage, admittedly feeling a little flustered by his attention. He was just so startlingly vital. A trait I usually associated with Gage, but in this regard the man before us outshone him. Though, to be fair, my husband's vigor had been rather diminished by days of travel and his worry for his father. I was intimately aware he'd not slept well since receiving the news of Lord Gage's attack, tossing and turning long into the night.

Gage swiftly followed me, stepping down onto the gravel drive beside us before I could find my tongue or withdraw my hand from the other man's grasp.

"I apologize for our unexpected visit," Gage remarked, drawing the man's scrutiny away from me. A small pleat in his brow told me my dumbfounded silence hadn't gone unnoticed. I pulled my hand from the man's fingers.

"There's no need," he said. "Whatever your reason, I'm sure it's a good one." He clasped his hands behind his back, straightening into a courteous posture equal to any gentleman's, before he bowed at the waist. "Allow me to introduce myself. Robert Butler, at your service."

"Sebastian Gage," my husband replied, unbending enough to offer Mr. Butler his hand. "And my wife."

Butler accepted his proffered hand, though his gaze returned to me, bright with intrigue. "Ah, the legendary Lady Darby." He tilted his head in consideration. "Though I suspect you prefer Mrs. Gage now, don't you, in spite of what the societal sticklers might say."

Whether that meant he knew something of my late husband's ill temperament or he was merely aware of the gossip that my and Gage's marriage was a love match, I didn't know. He could have simply wished to flatter my husband.

Whatever the case, he seemed determined to charm us, gesturing toward the open door behind him. "You are very welcome to my home. Why don't we adjourn to the drawing room?"

He offered me his arm, as any good host would do, and I wavered only a moment before accepting.

"Thank you," I told him, speaking for the first time as Gage fell in step behind us. It seemed as though it devolved to me to carry the conversation as we mounted the pair of wide stairs leading to the entrance. "It's absolutely lovely here," I remarked in perfect earnest. "Like a breath of fresh air or a cool drink of water on a sweltering day."

He turned to me with interest. "That's exactly how I feel." It was obvious from his scrutiny of me that others had not ascribed the same sentiment to the place—it being so far from anything society would deem noteworthy. He offered a light laugh as we stepped into the entry hall tiled in black and white checkerboard squares. "I suppose you can understand then why I prefer Skelbrooke to London or even York."

"Yes, indeed." I peered over my shoulder at Gage. "It makes one begin to long for a country house of one's own."

"Are you looking?" Butler asked.

"It's something we've discussed but haven't begun in earnest," Gage answered for us.

Butler nodded, guiding us toward the open door to the left. "I was fortunate in that I was granted the use of this property, so I don't envy your search."

A stone-faced footman emerged from the shadows beyond the turned staircase with delicate openwork panels. He was the first servant we'd caught even a glimpse of since passing through the gates, despite the fact Skelbrooke was large enough to require a dozen servants if not more, depending on the size of the stables and any attached farm. Under normal circumstances, we should have spied at least a handful—a gatekeeper to admit us, groomsmen or stable hands to assist with the carriage and horses, and a butler or footman to welcome us and announce us to their master. But Skelbrooke Hall seemed all but deserted save for Mr. Butler and this footman who stood stalwartly against the wall, never looking at us.

Perhaps the estate wasn't allotted a large enough income to afford a full complement of staff. After all, as the second son, Mr. Butler would be almost exclusively dependent on his older brother, Lord Portis, for his income. He'd said he'd been granted the use of Skelbrooke Hall, so I assumed that meant it was entailed to the Earl of Portis's estate. The British aristocracy liked to keep their wealth and land concentrated in the hands of but a few, so by the laws of the peerage the eldest son inherited the lot while younger sons were often allowed to live in and manage their lesser properties. Only properties that were not entailed to the estate could be given outright to someone who was not the titleholder, as had been the case with my father.

James St. Mawr had been but the first son of the *second* son of a viscount, but his mother had been the daughter of a duke. Blakelaw House—an unentailed property she'd inherited from her own mother—had been part of her dowry when my grandparents wed, and upon her death, it had been given to my father. But it sounded as if Mr. Butler had not been so fortunate, though he didn't seem to begrudge the fact.

The drawing room we entered was small by many standards, but elegant in its own right, if a trifle cold. I suspected it was little used. I'd not asked, but I'd gained the sense that Mr. Butler was not married, so he was not likely to receive many callers. And without a wife and family, it lacked many of the small touches which made a house a home. The focal point of the room was the keyed arch over the fireplace. Its graceful curves drew one's eye to the plaster festoons and floral drops along the upper walls and ceiling. A tall mirror on the wall facing the window was also plastered with a surround of decorative swans. Curiously, the mirror seemed to have been knocked askew. That or it had purposely been hung at its strange angle.

Given the fact my eye kept being drawn to it, I opted to sit with it at my back on the Hepplewhite sofa so my attention wouldn't wander. Gage soon joined me there while Mr. Butler opted for the coordinating chair positioned perpendicular to us.

"How is your father?" he asked as we arranged ourselves. "Yes, I heard what happened," he responded in some wryness to our evident surprise. "I suspect by now many in London already know, given how rapidly gossip spreads."

Gage nodded in recognition of this. "He is recovering. But it was a near thing for a time."

"I'm glad to hear it. Though I can only surmise it is the reason for your call."

My husband sank deeper into the cushions, by all appearances entirely at ease, though I knew better. When Gage seemed at his most relaxed was when he was most intent. It was a ploy he often used when interviewing witnesses and suspects. "What makes you say that?"

"Well, that *is* why you are here in the West Riding, is it not? To come to your father's aid. And my brother, Lord Portis, is well known to butt heads with Lord Gage." His voice wasn't accusatory, just matter-of-fact. "Given that your reputations as inquiry agents proceed you, I assume you're investigating his attack. So it stands to reason you've come to question me about it."

I didn't know quite how to view this speech, and it seemed that neither did Gage.

"His footman was also killed," he stated rather bluntly, his usual finesse deserting him. But perhaps that had been intentional.

Butler tipped his head back, though I couldn't tell whether this was because he was startled by his response or the manner in which it had been delivered. "Now, *that* information has not spread so widely, has it? But it makes it all worse, does it not?" He frowned, turning to the side. "Murder, not just assault."

I tilted my head, wishing I were better acquainted with the man before us. As it was, I couldn't tell whether he was generally this forthright, or if he was attempting to run circles around us with his words. Part of me wanted to believe he was as straightforward as he seemed, but another part of me was wary of such candor. Sometimes blatant honesty could hide as much as it concealed, allowing one to remain on the offensive and in control rather than forced to defend. As such, I knew we needed to formulate our questions with care.

"Did Lord Portis know Lord Gage was traveling north?" I asked.

Butler paused, making me suspect he was giving his answer as much consideration as I'd given to how I worded the question. "He did not inform *me* that he knew, but I don't imagine Lord Gage's plans were any great secret. My brother undoubtedly could have learned of his intentions."

"Were *you* aware my father was traveling along the Great North Road through Yorkshire ten days ago?" Gage interjected more pointedly.

"I was not," he answered. "At least, not until the day following his attack."

"Then your brother didn't ask you to do anything to waylay him? Or to deliver him a message, be it verbal or nonverbal?"

Butler might have justifiably been insulted by this insinuation, or at least irritated, but he remained unruffled, not even flickering an eyelash. "No. And if you require further assurance, I can confidently state I have not laid eyes on Lord Gage for at least three years. And neither have any of my servants. We run in very different circles now."

I took that to be a reference to their shared military past. Albeit Lord Gage's had been in the Royal Navy, while Mr. Butler had served in the army.

"Forgive me," I murmured, still trying to puzzle the man out. "But you don't seem offended by our asking."

His lips quirked. "And I take it most people are?" When I didn't join him in his amusement, he inhaled a sobering breath and laced his fingers across his lap. "I am not offended because were I in your shoes, I would be asking the same questions. I'm well aware of my brother's vitriol toward your father. It only stands to reason that you should be suspicious of the fact the brother of your father's enemy resides so close to the place where your father was attacked."

Gage's posture mirrored that of our host, and the pair of them sat quietly assessing each other for several moments while I attempted to peel back the thin layer of guise I sensed coloring his words. But was that pretense purely the formal charade all gentlepeople performed for one another or something more?

"Can anyone vouch for your whereabouts on the night in question?" Gage asked.

"My staff," he replied, as the footman I'd seen in the corridor entered carrying a tea tray. "But I assume that's not what you had in mind." He indicated the mahogany card table to my right, its base ornamented with a gilded angel figure and four claw legs.

I watched the footman as he withdrew, curious how he'd come to be employed here. He didn't fit the traditional mold. For one, he was far from handsome, with a mottled scar on one side of his face, and his stature was smaller than typical. I also detected a certain amount of surliness in his demeanor that made him rather off-putting yet difficult to ignore.

"Mrs. Gage, will you pour?" our host requested, pulling me from my silent inspection.

I slid forward to lift the teapot as Gage replied to his previous statement.

"I'm afraid not. One's staff tends to be quite loyal to their employer."

"Ah, but then I am not their employer, am I?"

"No, but if you *were* behind the attack, it was probably at the behest of their employer, so the result is the same." His eyebrows arched in emphasis. "Then none of your neighbors saw you?" Gage queried as he accepted the cup of tea I passed to him.

I turned to Mr. Butler.

"Just one sugar," he replied to my unspoken query before answering Gage. "It's doubtful. I kept to the house after nightfall. After all, I didn't know I would require proof of my whereabouts," he muttered dryly. Apparently even *his* sympathy had its limits.

"Then would you allow us to search your stables?"

The forwardness of this request made me falter as I leaned over to hand Butler his teacup. Butler might not have been able to prove he had nothing to do with Lord Gage's attack, but we also had no proof that he did. Nothing beyond Lord Gage's idle speculation. Butler had been obliging in allowing us to interrogate him, but he was also a gentleman. One who would be in his rights to take offense at being questioned so pointedly without even a shred of evidence to suggest his guilt.

Had Gage asked if we could be given a tour of his stables, we might have been able to carry on pretending there wasn't some ulterior motive. But as stated, there was no ambiguity. Gage had all but made a blatant accusation.

This unsettled me, for normally my husband was far more subtle and nuanced, but when I turned to look at him, his expression was implacable. He clearly did not trust Butler, and he clearly didn't care if he knew it.

In response, Butler's amiable demeanor underwent a startling transformation. His eyes narrowed into cold slits, and the muscular frame I'd suspected lay beneath his carelessly donned garments straightened and expanded.

I suddenly felt as if we were in a very precarious position. My gaze flicked toward the door, stiffening when I caught sight of the footman still lurking in the shadows in the corridor beyond. After all, we were on Mr. Butler's turf, and just because we hadn't seen any other members of his staff didn't mean they didn't exist. Even now, they could be gathered outside the door, waiting to intervene.

With his eyes locked in combat with our host, Gage seemed oblivious to this fact.

My hands fisted in my skirts, anxious to smooth matters over. "Perhaps we might be given a tour of your lovely property."

Butler was the first to break eye contact, his stare sliding sideways to meet mine. Seeming to sense my distress, his stance eased slightly. However, Gage remained resolute. Having thrown down the gauntlet, maybe he felt he couldn't now soften his posture. After all, this was an attack on his *father* he was investigating, not to mention the murder of his father's footman. No matter what my husband might insist to the contrary, it was evident his emotions were engaged, possibly to his detriment and mine.

Butler took a slow drink of his tea, scrutinizing us over the rim. "Given what has happened to your father, you are understandably . . ." He seemed to choose his words with care. "Distraught." He arched a single eyebrow. "So I will overlook your vulgar insinuation that I have been dishonest. I will even allow you to search my stables for whatever it is you are looking for."

Gage's shoulders began to relax, letting me know he hadn't been quite so oblivious to the misstep he'd made.

But our host wasn't finished.

"However," he declared, relaxing deeper into his chair as he propped one booted foot over the opposite knee. He again lifted his teacup to his mouth, finishing his statement before he took another drink. "Mrs. Gage must remain here with me while you do so."

My heart leapt in alarm even as Gage's scowl grew fierce.

"It is the price you will have to pay for my trust." His eyes narrowed. "Unless you *meant* to provoke me?"

I realized then that Mr. Butler had neatly backed us into a corner. If Gage refused his offer, then he was, indeed, insinuating he was untrustworthy, which would force Butler to demand satisfaction. But if Gage agreed, it would allow them both to preserve their dignity. Gage would prevail in his bid to view the stables while Butler would not be forced to concede to the implied insult to his honor.

In this scenario, I was the only potential loser. Though given the alternative—seeing my husband challenged to a duel or attacked outright—I could stomach the solution. Though Gage was going to receive a very stern talking-to when this was over.

Inhaling a bracing breath, I pasted on a false smile. "Go on," I told my husband before nodding to our host. "Mr. Butler and I shall simply finish our tea." Never mind the fact I hadn't even poured myself any.

My husband's eyes searched mine—both asking if that was what I wished him to do and apologizing for placing me in this situation. However, the deed was already done. He couldn't refuse now. When his gaze dipped briefly to where my reticule rested in my lap, I knew he was thinking of the Hewson percussion pistol I kept tucked inside, perhaps reassured that I wouldn't be completely defenseless should Butler take it into his head to be ungentlemanly. That seemed unlikely, but I had to admit I was also consoled by its weighty presence.

"Clarkson," Mr. Butler called, and the footman returned to the drawing room. *Not* that he'd gone far. "Escort Mr. Gage to the stables, and ask O'Leary to show him whatever he wishes to see."

Clarkson nodded once before turning on his heel, without waiting to see if Gage would follow.

"I'll return shortly," my husband promised as he hastened from the room to catch up with the footman.

CHAPTER 12

The thud of his footsteps receded down the corridor, and then silence fell, broken only by the ormolu clock on the mantel. Finding myself alone with Mr. Butler, I didn't quite know how to react. A significant portion of my sangfroid seemed to have abandoned me, and I suspected if I attempted to pour myself a cup of tea I would end up spilling it into my lap.

For his part, he seemed perfectly content sitting there staring at me. His smirk made my already smoldering temper spark, and I forced myself to look away, lest I say something I regretted. There were few paintings gracing the walls of the room, as the plasterwork was as much a work of art as the canvases, but one in particular caught my eye.

"I assure you, the tea isn't poisoned," Butler drawled as I pushed to my feet, slipping the cord of my reticule around my wrist to take it with me. "As your husband can attest."

"I'm not thirsty," I replied absently as I skirted the furniture to stand before the portrait of a woman peering coquettishly over her shoulder, holding a letter and a bouquet of flowers. A small white dog perched on the bench behind her. I recognized the artist almost immediately as Fragonard. The warm pastoral shades of his colors, the playful composition, and the late eighteenth-century style of her gown all pointed to the Frenchman.

"You have a fondness for art."

I startled at the sound of his voice so close to my ear and turned to find him standing just beyond my shoulder.

I shuffled a step away and attempted to resume my study of the painting.

But Butler was not so easily deterred. "Ah, but how could I have forgotten. You are purported to be a brilliant portrait artist in your own right."

I did not rise to his bait, deciding any commentary on my part was unnecessary and would only encourage him. My eyes traced the brushstrokes on the sleeves of the subject's gown, seeking to analyze how Fragonard had made the fabric appear to shimmer.

"Perhaps I should have you paint my portrait."

I nearly rolled my eyes at this hackneyed remark. Obviously, the man was not lacking in self-consequence. "I'm not accepting portrait commissions anymore."

"I see. I suppose such a thing simply isn't done once a gentlewoman marries."

I glowered at him, annoyed by his not unjustified assumption that upon my marriage I'd been required to cease my artistic ambitions. "No, because aristocrats and capitalists already have enough portraits of themselves hanging on their walls."

Far from being affronted, a muscle twitched in his cheek, indicating he was suppressing a smile. "Is that so?"

I sighed, realizing I couldn't leave it at that. "I've decided it would be more worth my time to paint portraits of the people society is content to ignore. Of those who are all around us every day, but yet we refuse to see. I hope to exhibit them one day in London or Edinburgh."

When he didn't respond, especially after he'd been so intent on pestering me moments before, I turned away, deciding I'd succeeded in shocking him. If so, he wouldn't be the first. A number of the Quality had expressed their outrage when I'd informed them I was refusing their commissions in order to paint a street sweeper or a scullery maid. But his voice when next he spoke didn't sound offended.

"That's . . . astonishing."

I turned my head to meet his stare, wondering what exactly he'd expected of me for him to be so astounded by my confession. Given my macabre past, he could as easily have anticipated I was a ghoul and a fiend as a vapid society matron.

"And Mr. Gage supports this?"

I frowned at him quizzically. "Yes."

"But I can't imagine Lord Gage does."

That was it, then. We'd been tarnished by a more immediate connection.

"I think you'll find there's a great deal we don't see eye to eye with Lord Gage about. Or Lord Portis either, for that matter," I added, unable to keep the mockery out of my voice. For all that Lord Gage and Lord Portis were professed enemies, they held similar views. So Mr. Butler judging us by our association was rather like the pot calling the kettle black.

But rather than be abashed at his mistake, he merely grinned. "Then we are alike in that regard. So you can see why it is impossible I should take offense on my brother's behalf and attack Lord Gage." A furrow formed between his brows. "My brother's dispute with him is childish."

I had been harboring a similar thought. After all, even if he had agreed with his brother, it was a great leap to suppose he would harm Lord Gage because of it. However, I neither agreed nor disagreed with Butler's remark. Sadly, men had committed violence for stupider reasons, and I didn't know him well enough to judge how rash or foolish he was. Experience had taught me prudence. Especially after our last inquiry.

"Do you know of anyone *else* who might have wished to harm Lord Gage? Anyone with the ability, that is," I amended, for my father-in-law had already admitted he had a long list of people who wished him ill, but most of them could not have arranged his attack.

"In Yorkshire?" He shook his head. "I'm afraid not."

I turned back toward the portrait of the lady with her love note, prepared to allow the matter to drop, but then another thought occurred to me. "What of this gang of highwaymen we've heard so much about? As I understand it, they prowl this part of the Great North Road, fancying themselves a contemporary Robin Hood—robbing from the rich to give to the poor." I watched his face, curious what his reaction would be. "What do you know of them?"

"Of course, I've heard mention of them. But if you're asking whether I've ever been robbed by them, the answer is no. Though I don't know if that's by luck or design."

I nodded, beginning to turn away yet again when he continued.

"I thought they were supposed to be a peaceable lot." He tipped his head to the side. "Well, peaceable by comparison. They *are* highwaymen." He frowned. "But if they were the ones who attacked Lord Gage, why did they change? Why did they decide to shoot Lord Gage and kill his footman?" He looked to me. "Did they resist?"

"Not according to Lord Gage, and he's not the type to deny defending himself. According to him and his valet, the highwaymen didn't even ask for his purse, and they complied with their other orders." I crossed my arms over my chest. "Though,

I admit, the footman's murder does appear to have been unintentional. When the lad heard the shot fired at Lord Gage, he began to raise the rifle across his lap, and they killed him for it."

Butler lifted his hand to his chin, striding several paces away before turning back. "Forgive me, but does all this not strike you as odd?"

I waited for him to elaborate.

"Why would a group of highwaymen whose aim, for the past year or more that they've been at work, seems to have been to help the struggling people of this district suddenly alter their strategy so drastically? And in a way that that will only hurt the people they profess to want to help." He seemed genuinely perplexed. "I mean, not only did they not ask for the victim's purse, but they shot and attacked the man. A baron! And killed his footman when their plan began to go sideways."

I paused to consider what he was saying, somewhat surprised by his willingness to give the matter such deep thought when moments before I'd feared he was about to demand satisfaction from Gage for the insult to his honor. "I admit I also question the stark inconsistency of their actions in this incident. But is it not more absurd to think there are two *different* groups of highwaymen at work? Two different groups with experience at making ambushes and slipping away without being caught."

"Actually, I think the very existence and success of the first gang makes the second gang more likely."

"How so?"

He swiveled to stare out the window past the fountain toward the lane down which we'd come. "Well, by now they'll have heard enough about the first gang of highwaymen to know that their method of waylaying coaches works, and how they go about it." He looked back at me. "They'll also have realized that, were they to copy their methods, others would assume the first gang of highwaymen is to blame. Because . . . how could there be two such groups?" His last comment might have been said with mockery, but he had tempered his voice, effectively making his point.

I crossed the room to stand on the opposite side of the window frame, filtering his logic through the known facts and considerations. "It does appear that they targeted Lord Gage, and if that's the case, then they may have emulated the highwaymen for the very reason it might cover their tracks."

His green eyes sparked with intrigue. "And if they targeted Lord Gage, then they must have known about his and his son's reputations as inquiry agents. That neither Gage would let the matter go unsolved or unpunished. So they would need all the tricks they could muster to avoid capture."

There was merit in what he was suggesting, and it would explain away many of the discrepancies we had been confronted with. However, we could not discard the possibility that the same gang of highwaymen wasn't responsible for it all so quickly. There were also viable reasons they might be one and the same. Either way, it all came back to the simple fact that *someone* had a vendetta against Lord Gage. One they were determined to go to great lengths to carry out. The trouble was, I feared we might never uncover precisely what that vendetta was, and without it we would never be able to figure out who the real culprit was.

"I would look into Lord Gage's past," he observed, almost as if he'd read my thoughts. His eyes narrowed as if he were peering back through the pages of time. "Perhaps he has some previous connection to Wentbridge or someone who now lives in the area."

"That's easier said than done," I replied grudgingly. "Lord Gage is professing ignorance of any such connection, and the villagers are being wholly uncooperative out of loyalty to the gang of Robin Hood highwaymen."

"Times are lean, Mrs. Gage," he explained measuredly. "In the past decade, it's become harder and harder to find employment.

And those who do have seen their wages cut or not increased commensurate with the price of goods. What was a good wage twenty years ago now scarcely provides a subsistence. So you can't really blame them for wanting to look out for those who seem to be looking out for them, now can you? Not when the government seems content to forget them and their problems. Unless they start causing them trouble."

"I suppose not. And I empathize, I do," I assured him, feeling that uncomfortable knowledge about the nature of privilege stir inside me again. "But that doesn't mean that the men who shot and killed Gregory Reed and severely injured my father-in-law should go unpunished. If we allow such clear instances of wrong to go unchecked, then what does that say about us or our society?"

"Yes, of course," he agreed. "There must be justice and balance."

I turned to peer out the window, weary in every bone of my body. It had been a tiring week and a half, and the lengthy days ahead would be no easier.

Long shadows reached across the gravel drive toward the house, and through the panes of glass I could hear the distinctive churring call of a nightjar in the brush nearby. The afternoon had grown later than I'd realized, shifting into evening, and sunset would not be far off. A pulse of anxiety thrummed along my nerves. One that Mr. Butler seemed to share.

"Mr. Gage should be completing his tour. Let's go out to meet him."

I agreed, accepting his proffered arm. By the time we reached the front drive, I could see Gage striding toward us around the corner of the building. His scrutiny was fixed on the western sky above the tree line, and the golden light reflected back from the thickening clouds.

Mr. Butler's attention also seemed set upon this point. "I trust you found everything in order?" he asked as Gage drew close enough to hear him without shouting.

"I did," Gage acknowledged civilly, though I could tell there was more he was not saying.

"Then, I hate to be rude, but you really should be on your way before the hour grows later. And please, allow me to send a pair of outriders with you. It will ease my mind," he added when it appeared Gage might argue.

He considered our host for a moment longer before nodding. "Yes, thank you. I should have recognized sooner how late the hour was growing."

This acknowledgment from both men that we were at some risk traveling at this hour made my heart beat faster. The sun had not even set. We should return to the Barkers' cottage under twilight, before full darkness had fallen. Yet they were both intent on these precautions.

"Give me a moment to summon two of my best men," Butler proclaimed before striding off in the direction Gage had come from. We had seen only one member of his staff, but that didn't mean they weren't lurking about elsewhere. In fact, I now wondered if this impression of the manor being short of staff had been done to some purpose, creating the illusion that the estate was all but vacant when the opposite was true.

But I had little time for such contemplations. "Are we truly in danger?" I asked my husband once we were alone.

I could tell before he spoke that he was about to lie. "Probably not, but it's best to be cautious."

I might have argued with him, but I decided doing so would be pointless. After all, I had my answer. Belaboring the point would only distract him when his focus was needed elsewhere.

Our carriage rounded the drive and drew to a halt, evidently having already been summoned by Gage. He approached to speak with Joe, our coachman, and then clambered partially inside to dig in the compartment beneath one of the seats. I knew he was removing a pair of pistols he kept stored there. Between those, the gun Gage often carried on his person during the course of our investigations, my percussion pistol, and the rifle I watched Joe check before storing it securely back into the slot on the box next to him, we were well armed. However, the outriders would be far more mobile and serve as a much greater deterrent to any highwaymen we encountered.

I should have realized sooner what a target we'd made ourselves—asking questions, poking around where the culprits who'd attacked Lord Gage's carriage would not want us to. If they were still in the area, it made sense they would be monitoring us and our movements as best they could. And whether they were the same gang playing Robin Hood or not, they had nearly an entire village to help them do so.

Fighting a growing fear and a near desperate desire to hold Emma and ensure she was safe, I almost climbed into the carriage without waiting to politely take my leave of Butler when he returned with the pair of outriders he'd promised us. Even so, he sensed my impatience to be away.

"Dawkins and Sharp are stout men. They'll see you back to Wentbridge safely," he assured me.

A swift scrutiny of the men in question showed me they certainly looked strong and capable. Both displayed a brace of horse pistols and may have been armed with other weapons underneath their dark greatcoats.

"It's been a pleasure," he ended with, bowing at the waist again before helping me up into the carriage.

He and Gage conferred in low voices as they shook hands, and then Gage climbed in beside me. The step was thrown up, and we were on our way. I eyed the pistols laid across the seat opposite us while Gage leaned forward to lower the windows.

"It may grow cold in here," he warned me, passing me a blanket.

He didn't elaborate, but I heard the words as surely as if he did. If we were ambushed, he couldn't waste precious seconds letting down the windows.

A chill swept through me that had nothing to do with the wind.

I draped the blanket around my shoulders rather than over my lap—so that I could toss it off if needed—and tried to focus on the passing scenery rather than the hammering of my heart. My ears strained for any sign of trouble, but the carriage wheels and the pounding of the horses' hooves drowned out anything else. It was pointless to try to converse. We would have to raise our voices, and Gage's attention was fixed on the roadside. It seemed best not to create any distraction, despite my desire for just that.

We returned to the Great North Road without incident and turned north toward Wentbridge. I'd heard enough of Gage and Butler's brief conference to understand they'd been debating the merits of which route we should take. The consensus had been we should take the quicker, more direct road. It was the route the highwaymen were expected to patrol, but it was also well traveled, even at dusk. The minor roads which zigzagged northward might be less monitored, but they were also infinitely slower and less populated. Should the highwaymen have gambled on our taking that route, they would have a far easier time waylaying us.

The land between Skelbrooke and Wentbridge was nothing but fields and forest, and the road was particularly exposed, perched high on the hilltops across this lonely expanse of country. It was not a stretch of road you would want to be caught on during a storm, and fortunately, the clouds amassing in the west did not appear to be bringing rain. Or perhaps unfortunately.

An approaching storm might have driven any waiting highwaymen out of the tall grasses and woodlands and inside to crouch before a roaring fire.

On and on we drove through the medieval vale of Barnsdale, the sun setting and the sky deepening to twilight. The road had just begun its descent into the gorge through which the River Went flowed, and I had started to ease my terrified vigil, when the crack of a gunshot made me sit rigidly upright. Gage reached for one of the pistols and eased his head and arm outside the window while I peered in terror out the opposite side.

Recognizing I was doing none of us a bit of good sitting there stiff with fright, I removed my percussion pistol from my reticule and cocked the hammer. I could hear shouting and then another gun fired. Our carriage wove right and then left before straightening, jostling me about and forcing Gage to grasp tight to the carriage frame as we continued to gather speed. I feared Joe had been shot, and I shifted to the opposite seat, thinking to open the door in the wall above the squabs to check on him.

Until a rider suddenly came thundering past. I hadn't been able to tell if it was one of Butler's men or a highwayman, but I soon got another chance. Having noticed the window of the carriage was open, he'd dropped back to gallop alongside us. A cloth was wrapped around the lower half of his face, and a hat was pulled low over his eyes. In the gathering dark, I couldn't make out any of his features, though I might have been able to if the carriage lamps had been illuminated, but we'd left them unlit so as not to draw attention or give the highwaymen greater forewarning of our approach. I opened my mouth to yell to my husband, but then the highwayman lifted his pistol, aiming it inside the carriage straight toward Gage.

CHAPTER 13

I reacted by instinct, lifting my own weapon before he could steady his shot, and fired. The buck of the pistol rocked me back against the squabs, but it did far worse to the rider. I saw his body react to the shot almost as if time had slowed, and then he disappeared from sight as his horse veered away.

Gage glanced at me with wide eyes before turning back to his window to confront whatever was happening there. How much time passed then, I didn't know, for my ears and my mind still seemed to be ricocheting from the gunshot, but the next thing I knew he was seated across from me, clasping my upper arms. At first, I couldn't seem to hear what he was saying, but he shook me, jarring me out of the daze I'd fallen into.

"Kiera," he repeated, inches from my face. "Have you been injured?"

It took me a moment to convince my muscles to respond so I could shake my head.

He pulled me into his arms, lifting me from the rear-facing

seat and onto the forward-facing seat beside him. I was awkwardly sprawled across him, but I didn't care. Not when I needed the comfort of his embrace.

"I thought that gunshot was for you," he said in a broken voice next to my ear.

"No," I managed to croak, though I wasn't sure he could hear me. "I was the one. I shot . . ." My throat closed around the words, and I couldn't finish the sentence.

He lifted his head, holding me away from his body so that he could see my face. "You've never shot anyone before."

I shook my head.

I'd threatened to shoot people. I'd pointed my pistol at others a number of times. I'd even pulled the trigger as a distraction. But I'd never actually fired a bullet into another human being. And knowing that I now had made me physically ill. For a moment, I thought I might cast up my accounts all over the carriage floor.

Gage turned me toward the window so that I could take deep, gulping breaths of the cool air rushing past. "Slowly. Or you'll make yourself light-headed."

I already felt light-headed, but I obeyed, forcing myself to count between inhales and exhales. By the time the carriage slowed to cross the bridge over the River Went, I had myself more in hand.

"The first time is the most difficult," Gage told me. "Though, the truth is, it's never easy. It's not supposed to be."

I looked up into his shadowed eyes, haunted by memories of men he'd shot and even killed as a gentleman inquiry agent and in his time fighting during the Greek War of Independence.

"He . . . he had his gun raised. He was going to shoot you," I choked through the tears I realized were now streaming down my face.

It was clear he didn't know how to respond to that, so he

pulled me into his arms again. He held me so tightly it hurt, but I didn't protest the pain. I needed to be this close to him, just as he seemed to need me close to him.

When the carriage slowed to a crawl and then stopped, he released me, and I felt better able to face whatever came next. Gage clambered out before the step was even lowered and paused to help me down before approaching the outriders Mr. Butler had sent to accompany us. I turned to speak to Joe, having forgotten until that very moment that I'd been concerned for his safety when I switched sides of the carriage.

"No' to worry, m'lady," he assured me. "I'm no' harmed."

I pressed a hand to my chest in relief. "How many were there?"

He rubbed a hand down over his thick auburn beard threaded with gray. "Mmm . . . I counted three, but there may've been four."

"Four," one of Butler's outriders confirmed. He shrugged his shoulder toward his compatriot. "Sharp shot one o' 'em." His gaze dipped to me, bright with interest. "And it seems her ladyship clipped the other."

My stomach dipped at the reminder.

"Then at least two of them are injured, which could help us identify them," Gage interjected before turning back to Sharp and Dawkins. "I'm sure we could procure you a bed for the night," he offered.

"Nay, we'll be headed back," Dawkins replied, speaking again for them both. "Mr. Butler will want to know you've made it safe."

"But the highwaymen?" I protested.

"They're no' likely to be botherin' anyone else tonight." His face split into a vindictive grin. "Or any time soon. In any case, we ken the back trails from here to there. They'll no' catch us."

I nodded uncertainly.

We watched as the outriders rode off into the night, the sound of their horses' hooves reaching us long after they'd already disappeared from sight. When we turned to enter the house, we found Anderley and Henry standing on the doorstep, ignoring the glare of the Barkers' butler.

"What's happened?" Henry asked first.

Gage's jaw hardened. "We were ambushed by highwaymen."

Henry and Anderley both stared in the direction the riders had gone.

"No. Those two were members of Butler's staff." His brow furrowed, as if he'd forgotten something, and then cleared. "And we were fortunate he sent them to accompany us, or else the results of our encounter might not have been so lucky."

We strode past them into the entry hall while Joe pulled the coach around to the stables.

"Then you don't believe Butler is behind the attack?" Henry queried, following us.

Gage passed his hat to the butler and scraped a hand back through his hair, making tufts of it stand on end. Though he'd maintained his composure for most of the drive and throughout the encounter, expressing emotion only after the attack was over, thick agitation now rolled off him in waves. As if by suppressing it he'd only compressed it into something darker and sharper . . . and now it was demanding release. He glanced at me before turning to pace in the opposite direction. "No," he huffed. "No, it wasn't Butler."

We'd not yet had a chance to confer, so I was somewhat surprised by this admission, having expected him to insist that Butler remain a suspect. But perhaps this evening's incident had convinced him of the unlikelihood.

"But *someone* with a strong motive was behind it." His voice hardened. "Someone who doesn't like us asking questions. Someone who has much to lose and isn't going to just slink away quietly." He looked up toward the head of the staircase, where Dr. Barker appeared. "Is my father awake?"

"His valet is helping him to bathe," he replied as he descended, searching first Gage's face and then mine. "Something has happened."

"Yes, something has happened." His eyes glittered in the light of the wall sconces. "Something that I wager could have been prevented had my father told us everything he knows instead of selectively choosing what he *wants* to share."

He wasn't wrong. Lord Gage had done so in previous inquiries we'd undertaken on his behalf. He'd professed to want the truth and then withheld information critical to uncovering it simply because it was something he or his client had wished to conceal. Why should we imagine this time was any different?

Gage pivoted to resume his pacing, though the space was too tight for it, making him resemble nothing so much as a caged tiger I'd once seen in a menagerie. "Something that he's hidden and *we've* now been *attacked* because of. My wife . . ." He broke off with a smothered curse, not finishing whatever he'd been about to say, though I could easily guess it was something to do with the threat to my safety or the fact I'd been forced to use my pistol to defend us. The others turned to look at me, but I had no intention of elaborating either.

"Darling, come into the drawing room," I coaxed, hoping to calm him. The anger rippling through his frame was making my muscles tense.

The others obeyed my urging, more or less forcing Gage to do so, though that did not stop his pacing. He just had a larger chamber to do it in. I was debating what to do—whether I should attempt to soothe him or leave him to rant to the men while I hurried off to feed Emma—when Mrs. Barker swept into the room. "I requested that dinner be delayed an hour . . ." She broke off at the sight before her. "Oh, my! What has happened?"

"We were ambushed," I explained.

Her eyes widened to saucers. "On the road?" She inspected me and then my husband. "Was anyone hurt?"

"*We* weren't," Gage muttered. "Though it was a near thing."

"But the highwaymen were?" Anderley queried, catching the implication.

"Two of them were shot," I forced myself to say.

Mrs. Barker made a shocked sound at the back of her throat, and I turned to see she'd pressed a hand over her mouth. "Oh, my! How terrible." She appeared distraught. "*Why* are these men doing such foolish, wicked things?!"

"That is something you'll have to ask my father, ma'am," Gage bit off crisply as he pivoted to stride back in her direction. "He *must* have some inkling." He scoffed. "But being my father, he can't simply give us a straight answer."

Dr. Barker, who had crossed to his wife, wrapping an arm around her shoulders in comfort, looked up at this pronouncement. "But why would he *lie*? Or . . . if not lie . . . why would he not tell you the complete truth?"

"Because he is Stephen Henry Gage, Baron Gage." He pantomimed his father's vainglorious posture, deepening his voice. "And he is *above* the truth."

I frowned at Gage's mockery of his father. Deserved or not, my husband didn't normally stoop to such antics. And from Henry's taut expression, it appeared I wasn't the only one taken aback by it. But there was *one* benefit to this twist in his behavior. His rage was now more irritating than alarming.

"Perhaps so, but confronting him while you're in the pet you are now will not do a bit of good," I told him as I untied my bonnet. "You need to be in a calmer frame of mind before you try to speak with him."

He turned his scowl on me, but I ignored him.

"I need to see to Emma," I declared, moving toward the door as I directed a pointed glare at both Henry and Anderley in turn, telling them I was relying on them to keep Gage away from his father until his temper had cooled.

But twenty minutes later, I discovered they'd failed to do so rather spectacularly.

Mrs. Mackay had returned to my chamber to collect a now slumbering Emma. Her face was sweet with repose, her tiny fingers gently curled around the edges of the fabric of my bodice, and after the fright of the evening I was reluctant to give her up. As such, I was delaying doing so while Mrs. Mackay and I exchanged a few words about the evening when the sound of raised voices made both of our heads whip around.

"Good heavens!" Mrs. Mackay gasped, pressing a hand to her chest. "Noo, that's a right stramash. What on earth do ye suppose they're arguin' so loudly aboot?"

I closed my eyes, inhaling a long-suffering breath. For I already knew. There was no supposing.

"Take Emma, please," I directed Mrs. Mackay as I transferred her into her arms, an abrupt end to my peaceful moment. "And I'll put this stramash . . ." borrowing her Scottish word ". . . to an end before they wake her."

Mrs. Mackay nodded in approval but said no more. Perhaps because she recognized the icy ferocity I was restraining and didn't want the cold wind blowing in her direction.

I strode around the corner and down the corridor toward Lord Gage's assigned chamber to discover the perfect idiots had left the door open for all the house to hear. Anderley hovered closest to the entry and had the good sense after catching sight of my frosty glare to beat a retreat toward the servants' stairway. Next nearest stood Henry, his face a contorted swirl of emotions, none of which were pleasant, as he watched his natural father and half brother argue vociferously. Gage leaned over his father, his complexion bright red with rage, while Lord Gage scowled up at him contemptuously, as if he were naught but a foolish boy.

I hesitated a moment before crossing the threshold, my shoulders inching up toward my ears and my stomach dipping. Displays of anger always brought forth some of my worst memories, often unconsciously. In my sweating palms, my pounding heart, my trembling knees. They never forgot that anger often prefaced pain. Perhaps the most unpleasant consequence of my marriage to Sir Anthony Darby. And given the number of unpleasant consequences I had to choose from, that was saying something.

However, I was determined not to let it master me anymore. I'd learned that the trick was to acknowledge it, and then push forward. That I could not erase the memories my body held, or prevent my reaction to them, but I *could* choose not to let them hinder me.

I lifted my foot, and I crossed the threshold. And then I lifted my foot again before turning to firmly shut the door—loud enough that it would draw their attention while not rattling the frame or waking Emma on the opposite side of the house. When I swiveled back to face them, Henry's gaze was the first I met, and *he* at least had the grace to flush. My husband and father-in-law, not so much.

"Gentlemen," I proclaimed severely in a voice they would have to strain to hear. "This is quite unbecoming and thoroughly inappropriate."

Lord Gage pointed his finger at Gage. "My son thinks to come in here and . . ."

I cut him off, raising the volume of my voice for only the first four words. "There is a *sleeping* infant upstairs. Should either of you wake her, I will *not* be held accountable for the consequences. But I can promise you that you'll *wish* I'd merely set the highwaymen after you again." I turned my glare on my husband to make certain he understood he wasn't excluded from my wrath. "Why are you here?"

He flung his hand out toward the bed. "Father . . ."

"Is a liar, a philanderer, and content to play fast and loose with our lives. Yes, we've established that."

Lord Gage straightened in outrage. "Now, see here . . . !"

"No," I interrupted again. "That's the trouble. We *don't* see, because *you* won't tell us!" I gestured broadly with my hand. "You tell us what you wish, when you wish, with no respect for our intelligence or concern for our safety."

"I respect your intelligence and have concern for your safety," he countered mutinously.

"Really? Then you have an unusual way of showing it." My temper spiked. "If you know something and you haven't shared it with us . . . If you sent us into danger . . ." I broke off, turning away to force a calming breath deep into my lungs. Tears were beginning to threaten, and the last thing I wanted to do was cry in front of my father-in-law.

It was a testament to the force of my own fury that none of them spoke as I gathered myself. "We will speak tomorrow," I informed Lord Gage before eyeing my husband sideways. "But if Sebastian did not make it clear in all of his yelling, it is highly unlikely that Mr. Butler is in any way responsible. But someone is. Someone who has a personal vendetta against you. So I suggest you think long and hard about who that might be."

Much of the anger had drained from his features, leaving Lord Gage's face very pale. Dr. Barker had warned us he must not be overexcited, and tonight's argument had undoubtedly done that. Dark circles ringed his eyes, and a tight furrow had formed between his brows.

Even so, he wasn't done protesting his innocence. "I have not lied." He arched his chin. "You have no right to make such accusations against me."

I threaded my arm through Gage's, urging him toward the door. "Just because you deny it," I answered softly, "doesn't make it untrue."

He winced, but whether that was because of the pain of his wounds or the truth of my statement, I didn't know. Perhaps both.

Henry followed us from the room, closing the door behind us.

"Kiera," Gage exclaimed after we'd ventured several steps down the corridor. "You were magnificent!"

"Stubble it," I snapped, rounding on him. "You knew better than to go in there. You knew it would only devolve into a sense-less quarrel."

Henry drew up beside me, crossing his arms over his chest as I had done. Together we formed a united front, though that didn't stop me from feeling a tick of annoyance that he'd not prevented Gage from going there in the first place.

Gage turned his head to the side, clearly not wanting to face our scowls.

"So why did you?" I pressed.

He didn't answer immediately, struggling with himself. "I'm *tired* of him worming his way out of taking responsibility for his actions."

"He's not wormed his way out of anything. Not this time. Not while he's still injured." I tilted my head, assessing the frus-tration stamped across his features. "He's not going anywhere for the time being. And in any case, he was actually coming to see you. To see Emma," I amended. "When this all happened. I don't believe he intends to slink away once he's recovered enough to do so."

"But his stubborn refusal to tell us all he knows is hindering our inquiry and may have put us in danger tonight. He must answer for that."

His voice was rising again, and I reached out a hand to touch his arm, seeking to soothe him. "I agree. But tomorrow is soon enough."

He grunted, but I couldn't tell if it was in agreement or denial.

"You know how he is," I pressed. "Approaching him while you were in such a fury only had hope of being met with the same furiosity. Accusation for accusation. Tit for tat."

"I warned you of that exact thing, but you charged past me like a raging bull anyway," Henry grumbled.

Gage frowned at him. "How can you be so calm about this? The man brushed you aside and then blackmailed you and your mother to keep your relationship to me hidden." His arms gestured broadly. "He's treated you in a deplorable fashion. How are you not angry?"

"I *am* angry!" Henry's gray eyes flashed with quicksilver as he leaned into his half brother. "But lashing out at him does no good. It only makes the problem worse. *You* are only making the problem worse."

Gage appeared taken aback by this remark.

"Yes," Henry stated, letting him know his last remark was not a mistake or a slip of the tongue. "Anger and accusations are not going to solve this. If it can even be solved at all," he added under his breath before turning on his heel and striding away.

Gage stood staring after him.

I waited a moment, allowing time for Henry's words to sink in, for he hadn't been wrong. Gage's clashes with his father weren't helping. Then I pressed a hand to his lower back, urging him forward. "Come. We need to dress for dinner."

CHAPTER 14

Dinner was a somewhat stilted affair, each of us feeling self-conscious about the events that had unfolded earlier. That is, until Dr. Barker began to tell us stories of his years spent as a military surgeon with the army. He soon had us alternately gasping in shock and awe or clutching our sides with laughter over some of the soldiers' antics.

"You have led a far more adventurous life than it would at first seem," Gage remarked after hearing about the successful cesarean section he had performed on a mother and child in Cape Town, South Africa. Such a procedure was tremendously risky, particularly to the mother, and was usually performed only as a last resort when the mother was dying anyway.

He sat back, clasping his hands over his trim waist. "Yes, well, 'tis all a mixture of thorough preparation, good fortune . . ." His eyes twinkled. "And the king's soldiers' remarkable capacity to injure themselves—even when *not* in the heat of battle—in the most extraordinary ways." He chuckled. "In fact, I daresay they were *more* creative about it when at leisure."

"I suspect my father has told you tales," Gage surprised me by saying. Though casually spoken, I could tell there was much more to the statement than passing interest.

"Oh, aye, we swapped a few stories. His ship having manned the blockade for much of the war with France, he contended with more than his fair share of antics." Dr. Barker nodded his head in emphasis. "And he'll tell ye the same as me—boredom can breed as much trouble as battle. Idle men weave intrigues."

Gage's gaze shifted to meet mine, and I wondered if he was thinking the same thing I was.

I soon had the chance to find out when Dr. Barker and his wife retired early, allowing Gage and me to gather with Henry, Anderley, and Bree in Gage's chamber again. We each gravitated toward the same seats we'd occupied before after Anderley shut and locked the door.

"It seems to me we're looking for a group of retired soldiers, possibly cavalrymen," my husband declared.

I leaned forward, grasping the train of his thought. "It would explain their precision and prowess in ambushing Lord Gage's carriage. Especially if they're not the same men as the gang who's been at work in this area, acting as Robin Hood and his merry men."

I told them what Mr. Butler and I had discussed. How the success of the first gang might have actually made the existence of the second gang more likely. How emulating the first gang's methods would not only improve the second gang's chances of success, but also serve to cast the blame elsewhere so that they could evade capture.

They each appeared to give this suggestion due consideration.

"That's a possibility," Gage replied, rubbing his chin.

"What of Butler's stables?" I asked him. "Did you find nothing of interest?"

"No horses matching those described by my father and Melton, or any of those mentioned by Mr. Robinson. Nothing of suspicion, really." His mouth pursed before he added, "Though I also couldn't help but note how vast the Skelbrooke property seems. There could be another stable concealed somewhere on the estate."

So he hadn't given up on the idea of Butler remaining a suspect, even if he had to grasp at straws to do so.

"What of you, Anderley?" Henry remarked. "Did you learn anything at the Blue Bell?"

Rather than sitting in strict politeness, the valet had chosen to straddle the ladder-back chair, propping his arms along the back and resting his chin on his forearms. He looked tired.

This shouldn't have been surprising to me. After all, he'd ridden as long and hard as the rest of us. More so, as he'd been responsible for overseeing all our baggage and coordinating accommodations and meals. He'd also doubled as Henry's valet when required, since Henry's valet was old and near pensioning, and thus unable to travel by horse. As such, he'd been left behind at Barbreck, assigned the task of seeing to the trunks and crates we'd left there in our haste to be on the road to Yorkshire. Even since arriving in Wentbridge, Anderley had been dashing to and fro, aiding us in the investigation. It was no wonder his normally dynamic personality was somewhat muted. The poor man must be exhausted.

He lifted his head to shake it. "Not in particular. But you're right." His eyes narrowed. "There is something havey-cavey going on. Something they'd been warned not to speak to me about. There was someone always watching." His eyes flickered toward Bree. "Particularly when I spoke to the maids."

"They didna want ye to have a chance to charm 'em," she said, stating aloud the same thing I was thinking.

He nodded.

"Which they wouldn't have done if there wasn't something to conceal," Gage further extrapolated. "Did you get a sense what it might be?"

"No. Though . . ." He frowned, his thumb drumming against the top of the chair. "I got a sense they didn't want me near a particular room. Their eyes kept darting to it, almost not of their own volition. And they hustled me outside whenever they could."

Bree had stiffened beside me, and I could sense the direction of her thoughts. Though I still didn't believe the innkeeper was concealing a pit of bones or any other such nonsense.

"Which room?" Gage pressed.

"It's located off the main taproom," Anderley replied. "Not far from the entrance."

The same room from which someone had entered during our interview with the innkeeper before they'd disappeared back inside at the signal of his headshake? Mr. Fryston had been intent on concealing someone or something from us then as well. Were they connected?

Gage turned to Bree. "Have any of the servants mentioned anything about the Blue Bell? Any goings-on there?"

She shook her head. "And I did try. But none o' 'em wanted to discuss it. And that maid I spoke to before is still avoidin' me." She spread her hands down over her skirts. "I'll try to talk to her again tomorrow. But for noo, she's stayin' button-lipped."

The room fell silent, each of us lost in our own contemplation, though I suspected we were all contemplating the same thing.

Gage had turned his head toward the windows across which the long goldenrod damask drapes had been drawn against the night. "Then it seems to me, we need to figure out what they're so determined to hide from us."

"That does seem the next logical step," I admitted. "But how do you propose we do so?" I gestured toward his valet. "They're already aware of who we are. If we were to show up and start poking around, they would immediately be on their guard."

"Yes, but they've not met *all* of us."

At this remark, he turned cautiously toward Henry, perhaps wary of offending him after his harsh words earlier.

Henry looked back at him steadily. "Is that the actual reason you didn't wish me to accompany Anderley earlier today?" he queried lightly, though there was an ironic lift to his eyebrows.

"I admit the thought did cross my mind that it might be to our benefit to have at least one member of our party unknown to the proprietors at the Blue Bell. One of our party of men, that is," he amended with a glance at Bree. "But I was also sincere earlier when I told you I didn't want my daughter and father left here without protection." His expression turned deathly serious. "And that holds true from here on out. I want one of either myself, Henry, or Anderley here at all times. If tonight's ambush of our carriage proved anything, it's that the men who attacked my father are still about, and they're not going to sit idly by while we investigate. We may have injured two of them." Our eyes met. "But that does not make them any less dangerous. In fact, it might make them more so if they grow desperate. They could make another attempt on Lord Gage's life or try some other dastardly trick."

A chill ran down my spine at this suggestion, particularly since he'd specifically mentioned watching over our infant daughter.

"Until they're apprehended, we must remain vigilant," he finished.

"Then, beg your pardon," Bree began, her concern directed

at me. "But maybe we should be askin' the question whether we *should* be investigatin'. I mean, is it worth the risk?"

Clearly, I'd not done a good job of concealing my alarm.

For a moment, no one spoke. Not until Henry tentatively voiced, "It *is* worth considering. After all, we are rather isolated here. And obviously these men are willing to do violence if that rider was aiming his pistol through the window of the carriage at you."

Gage's mouth opened as if to argue, but then fell shut, and I could tell from his furrowed brow that he was mulling the matter over. Henry was right. We were isolated. But we'd been in such situations before, and we'd faced direct threats, albeit not with our infant daughter in tow.

"You said the parish constable seemed earnest in his duties," Henry continued. "And Dr. and Mrs. Barker have proven their willingness to help. But can their staff truly be trusted? How would they react if we were threatened? Would they lift a finger to defend or assist us?"

The chamber we occupied suddenly seemed far less cozy than it had before. My eyes darted to the door. Was someone even now standing with their ear pressed to it, attempting to hear what we said? Then I looked upward at the ceiling, wondering if I should check on Emma in the nursery above.

I inhaled a deep breath, attempting to calm my racing heart and quell my unfounded fears. I needed to think logically. Emma was sleeping. If there was a problem, Mrs. Mackay would send for us or come to us herself. She was more than capable. That was one of the reasons why we'd hired her. In any event, the dark suppositions that had begun to form in my mind were irrational.

"I take your point, but I also struggle to believe that any of them would stand by while these highwaymen stole into the

Barkers' home to harm an innocent child. I suspect most of the villagers would balk at that as well," I argued. "The villagers may not wish us well in our investigation and desire us gone, but I don't believe that means they wish any of us ill."

"But my father may be another matter," Gage said, and I had to concede he was right. Though if the highwaymen's intention all along had been to kill him, then why did they make such a hash of it the first time? Why had they lowered the pistol and shot him in the leg when they could have shot him in the chest? It would have been far more deadly, and more in accordance with what they'd said about "taking his black heart."

Gage grasped the arms of his chair. "Until he can be moved, he will be at risk."

"And we can't forget, he's not the only victim," Anderley asserted, his eyes fixed on the twine-patterned rug before him. From the hard set to his jaw, I could tell he was suppressing some strong emotion, and I thought I knew what it was.

"Anderley's right," I murmured. "Doesn't Gregory Reed deserve justice as much as any other man?" I posited, knowing that as a fellow male servant, my husband's valet must identify with the footman. "Is that not what we've come to understand over the course of the past year? That the pursuit of justice is often biased, and yet if we wish it to change, then it must start with us."

"You're right." Gage scowled in determination. "We must continue. For Gregory, if for no one else." He added this last out of residual anger toward his father, but I knew the harsh edge of his voice was indicative of love, not hate. He could bluster all he wanted, but the truth was, he was afraid for his father, and anxious that his attackers be caught. The slight tremble in his voice as he inhaled before speaking again only proved it. "At any rate, it may already be too late to stop. The culprits may have their minds set. Our ceasing the investigation at this point might make no difference, other than to give them time to strike again."

Anderley straightened. "Which means we need to catch them before they do."

Henry had sat with one arm across his chest and the other bracing his chin through these pronouncements, but now he brought us back to the topic we'd been discussing before. "Then if my paying a visit to the Blue Bell to uncover what they're hiding will help, I'll go."

Gage leaned toward his half brother. "You will?"

He peered at us earnestly. "You and Kiera, you are my family. And if there's something you need that is within my ability to give, I will do it. Besides, Lord Gage is family, too." His brow quirked wryly. "Whether he wishes to be or not. I would see justice done for him and for Gregory."

My husband cleared his throat, his eyes bright with emotion. "Then the trick will be getting you there without arousing suspicions. After all, you can't simply stride up the road."

"And both coachmen have been seen there," Anderley contributed, speaking of our Joe and Lord Gage's Melton.

"If ye want to draw the least amount o' attention, ye should arrive like any other traveler," Bree suggested.

"On the stagecoach or mail coach," Gage supplied, following her line of thought. "Though they move on rather rapidly, so you'll have to claim an indisposition and take a room for the night before procuring a seat on another stage the next morning."

Henry's expression had turned bemused. "Then you want me to travel to . . . What's south of here?"

"Doncaster should be far enough for Joe to take him without anyone uncovering our ploy," Anderley said.

"To Doncaster," Henry repeated uncertainly. "To catch a stagecoach north. Then I'll disembark at the Blue Bell . . ." His eyebrows arched and his voice lowered in displeasure. "Claiming an indisposition. And take a room for the night. Then somehow I'll uncover the answers to all our questions . . ."

"Wi' oot bein' seen," Bree cautioned.

"Of course. And secure a seat on another stage headed north, where I'll disembark at . . . ?"

"Ferrybridge." Gage looked to Anderley, who nodded in agreement. "Joe can meet you there the next day."

"Ferrybridge," Henry finished, perhaps wishing he'd not agreed to this scheme.

"It's the only way to be certain your connection to us remains unknown."

"Yes, I realize. And I can think of no better plan, unless I arrived on my horse. But even that may be suspect. After all, Janus is a prime bit of horseflesh, and certain to draw speculations as to exactly who I am." He sighed. "Yes, I suppose this is the way I must go."

"Though, I don't like the idea of Henry staying there alone overnight," I muttered, pleating the amaranth silk of my skirt. "What if he encounters trouble? There will be no one there to help him." Mr. Fryston had not seemed like the most forgiving sort of man. What would he do if he found someone spying on him and whatever he had been so intent on keeping from us?

But there was no one from Lord Gage's or our staff we could send. No male anyway. They were all known. And sending Bree would be the height of ridiculousness and draw the sort of attention we didn't want.

"He'll simply have to take care he's not caught," Gage said, sounding as if he was trying to reassure himself as much as me.

Henry's eyes crinkled with warmth and affection. "Don't fret, Kiera. I may not be as experienced in these matters as some, but I know how to handle myself."

"Even so, maybe I should stroll over for a drink late tomorrow evening," Anderley ruminated, one corner of his lips curling into a sly smile. "Just to be sure all is well."

"Except that may only put them on guard," Gage argued. "We want them to relax."

Henry nodded. "Sebastian is right. We want them to think no one is watching so they'll carry on as they normally would." He glanced at Gage and me again. "Don't worry. I'll be fine."

I still wasn't convinced, but I allowed the matter to drop.

"In the meantime, I'd like to speak with Sir Reginald Oxley, the local magistrate." Gage rolled his shoulders before settling deeper in his chair. "I'd like to make myself known to him and hear his thoughts on these highwaymen and the attack on my father." That he would have a few choice words for him if he didn't like what he heard was plain.

"And I'd like to speak to the proprietor at the Bay Horse again," Anderley said. "When I spoke with him today, he seemed to have more to say about the Blue Bell, but two coaches had just arrived, and he needed to be sure his staff was seeing to them." He shrugged one shoulder. "Perhaps the words I sensed he was withholding were merely a rival's jealousy, but it could be worth finding out."

"Go in the morning," Gage told him before nodding at me. "We'll need to wait to pay Sir Reginald a visit until Joe returns with the carriage from taking Henry to Doncaster."

"Then it sounds like we have our plan," I declared, rising from the sofa. "It's growing late, and we're all undoubtedly tired." I couldn't help glancing in Anderley's direction as I made this remark, noticing how sluggishly he pushed to his feet. I wanted to order him not to visit the Bay Horse too early, hoping he might slumber later, but I knew he would not appreciate my interference. Indeed, it might embarrass him.

However, I felt no qualms about approaching Henry and clasping his upper arms. "Do be careful," I murmured.

His face softened under my anxious regard. "I will. I promise."

I nodded, forcing a smile to my lips. "Good. Because if something should happen to you, I daresay the duchess and duke, and all your brothers and even your sister, would be out for our heads." Of course, this was meant in jest, but I also hoped by reminding him of all the people who cared for him that it would not only persuade him to be more cautious, but also soothe some of the hurt Lord Gage's continued rejection had caused him.

His eyes glinted with the mirth I'd hoped. "Duly noted."

Arching up on my toes, I pressed a kiss to his cheek before giving his arms one last squeeze and turning toward the dressing room which would lead to my own bedchamber. Bree followed somewhat reluctantly. The way her eyes kept turning to Anderley told me there was something she wanted to say to him, though it was neither the time nor the place.

In any case, I pretended not to see it, as did Gage and Henry, if they even noticed. Men often didn't. But I did hasten through my preparations for bed so that Bree could retire. Once she'd gone, a peek at the clock on the mantel told me Emma wouldn't wake for at least another hour or two. She had begun to sleep longer between feedings in the middle of the night—a blessed development, but also unpredictable. I might fall asleep only to be woken up in an hour. Or if I remained up, waiting to nurse her before resting, she might decide instead to sleep for four more hours.

I was seated on the bench before the dressing table, my braid draped over my shoulder and running the end of it across my palm like a paintbrush, when Gage entered from the dressing room. His mouth was compressed into a tight line and his eyes stared unfocused at the floor. Such was his distraction that he didn't notice me watching him until after he'd taken half a dozen steps toward the bed. His footsteps halted, and I arched my eyebrows in question, curious what had so absorbed his attention.

"Thinking about Henry?" I guessed.

"Partly," he admitted, advancing toward me.

"Your father?"

He sighed. "Partly." He reached for my hands, pulling me to my feet.

A devilish urge rose inside me to tweak his nose. "Mr. Butler?"

His face screwed up into a disagreeable scowl.

I couldn't help but laugh. "Why have you taken such a disliking to him?"

"He's slippery. A shuffling fellow."

I slanted a look of mild reproach at him while still maintaining my good humor.

"He was hiding something," he emphasized.

"Oh, unquestionably. Just like everyone else we've met," I reminded him with no small sense of irony. "But while he was shrewd and gumptious, I wouldn't have dubbed him deceitful. Not any more than everyone else. Including the Barkers."

"Yes, well, the Barkers appear to live perfectly ordinary lives to me. While Butler . . ." He shook his head in some sort of combination of irritation and puzzlement. "He's a rum duke."

"Maybe so." I lifted my hands to smooth the lapels of his claret silk dressing gown. "But eccentricity doesn't make one untrustworthy. Lest you forget, I'm also considered eccentric. And you married me."

His eyes snapped in accusation. "I see he's managed to charm you."

I arched a single eyebrow, not appreciating his implication.

"I saw the way you reacted to him."

I felt a mild stirring of discomfort but squashed it. "Now you're simply being foul," I told him. "Yes, I noticed he was attractive. Just as women notice how attractive *you* are. *Frequently.* That has no bearing on any of my impressions of what followed other than to analyze how that factor plays into his own perception of himself and others' interactions with him." I tilted my head. "Is that why you turned so confrontational with him? Because I noticed he was handsome."

He scowled. "Of course not. The man was being obstructive and . . ."

"He was being entirely reasonable," I countered. "Until you insulted his honor."

At least he had the grace to flush.

"From a man whose honorability is one of his most admirable traits, it was a startling and uncharacteristic act." I waited for him to explain, but when he failed to do so, instead continuing to glare back at me, I elected to turn the screw tighter. "Particularly when that act forced me into a somewhat undesirable situation."

At this, some of his ire faded, leaving behind a look of misgiving. He turned his head to the side, exhaling a long breath. "Yes, I misjudged that rather badly, didn't I?"

But I wasn't about to leave it at that. "I *believe* the words you're looking for are *I apologize.*"

His lips quirked and then flattened again at my deadly earnest expression. "Yes, of course. I apologize. I really put my foot in it, didn't I?" He scraped a hand back through his hair, rumpling it attractively. "I don't know what I was thinking."

"I suspect the problem was that you weren't. Thinking, that is," I clarified, even as my eyes dipped to the chest muscles revealed by the gap that had formed between the two sides of his dressing gown. "You let your anger and frustration do the talking." I lifted my eyebrows. "Just as you did this evening with your father."

He gritted his teeth, grumbling under his breath in agreement and now directing that frustration at himself, which had not been my intent.

I reached up to cup his warm jaw, forcing his gaze back to mine. "Henry was right. Anger and accusations aren't going to solve any of this. *Including* accusations at yourself."

His pale blue eyes shimmered with misgivings.

I shrugged one shoulder. "So you lost your temper. It was bound to happen. Especially with your father involved." When my attempt at a jest didn't elicit even a flicker of amusement, I grimaced in apology. "The trouble is, darling, you're too close to this one. There is too much at stake for you, and so you're naturally at risk of losing your objectivity." I tilted his face closer to mine. "*Which means*, you need to rely on the rest of us to help you. So the next time I tell you not to go poking and prodding the ogre . . ."

This quip did garner a tiny glimmer of good humor.

"Please listen."

He nodded. "I will try."

I searched his beloved features, eager to soothe the insecurities I sensed were never far below his mask of self-possession these days. "That's all I ask. Now." I lifted my arms to drape them around his neck, offering him a melting smile. "I do believe, before our arrival at Skelbrooke, we were discussing what a well-matched pair we are."

His hands lifted to my waist, pulling me flush against his lean, hard body. "Oh, yes? I do seem to remember that." His voice deepened, stroking along my nerves like a finely plucked viola string.

I drew the musk of his sweat and skin, and the spicy scent of his cologne deep into my lungs as I lowered my mouth to his neck, leaving a trail of kisses upward toward his ear. My fatigue from minutes earlier all but gone. "What do you say we put that to the test?" I purred, capturing his earlobe between my teeth. The swift inhalation he took made me grin like the cat that got the cream.

He turned his head, forcing me to let go of his ear. His eyes burned with intent. "I thought you'd never ask."

CHAPTER 15

When I woke the next morning, or rather was summoned by Emma, I discovered an unpromising sky of leaden gray and mist clinging to the ground, obscuring much of the landscape. Gage still being asleep, and in need of restful slumber after weeks of anxiety and uncertainty, not to mention his vigorous efforts the previous evening, I elected to tend to her in the connecting bedchamber rather than risk waking him. When he remained asleep even after Emma had finished, I had Bree dress me in a simple morning dress of cerulean blue there as well.

My daughter was particularly alert and playful that morning, and no wonder. She'd slept for six hours at one stretch! I could almost imagine enjoying a full night's rest again. But I'd been warned by my sister and female cousins not to expect this to last, or else the child would somehow unerringly sense it and revert to the feeding habits she'd exhibited during the first weeks after birth, demanding to be fed every two hours. It was better to be pleasantly surprised by their long slumbers than crushed by disappointment and driven to exhausted tears when they failed to repeat them.

Watching her happily kick, coo, and roll across the counterpane, I began to ponder whether a bit of that deviousness Gage had accused Mr. Butler of the night before might be in order.

"Do you know if Lord Gage is awake yet?" I asked Bree as she was emerging from the dressing room, where she'd stowed my nightdress and other accoutrements until my husband woke.

She seemed a bit taken aback by the question. Or else her thoughts had been absorbed by a far more interesting topic. Judging from the private little smile that had played across her lips, I suspected the latter.

"I think so," she said. "Least, I saw Lembus collect his lordship's breakfast tray."

I reached down to swing Emma up into my arms, making her giggle. "Then I believe we'll pay him a visit." I cast an impish smile over my shoulder. "If Mr. Gage should ask, don't tell him where we are."

"Aye, m'lady," she replied without any questions, though I knew she must have them.

I chattered softly to Emma while we strolled, and occasionally she babbled back. The gap-toothed maid dipped a brief curtsy as she passed us, avoiding my eyes, though I could see a smile lurking on her lips. I laughed to myself as I continued on. I was becoming as bad as Mrs. Mackay. But then, I now knew there was a purpose to her incessant prattle to our daughter. During the long carriage ride from Barbreck, her chatter to the waking infant had at first threatened to drive me batty. However, when I'd asked her about it, she'd explained that was how the wee ones learned to talk. The more you gibbered at them, even engaging them as if you were having a conversation and could understand what they were cooing back to you, the faster they grasped the language. She'd then proclaimed with pride that all her past charges had spoken in full sentences by the age of eighteen months.

I supposed this meant there was a good chance Emma would begin life speaking with a rolling Scottish accent like her nanny. At least until a governess taught her the correct elocution the members of the Quality were all required to speak in order to be taken seriously. But I didn't mind that possibility in the least. After all, I was half-Scottish. Though I now had to wonder what Lord Gage would think of his wee granddaughter speaking with a brogue. Not that I cared what his opinion on the matter was.

As we reached Lord Gage's chamber, Dr. Barker emerged, closing the door behind him. His thick cinnamon brown hair continued to defy restraint, bristling about his head like a hedgehog's quills. He smiled at the sight of us. "Ah, Mrs. Gage, a pleasant morning to you. And to you, little lady," he leaned forward to say as he gently squeezed Emma's foot, earning himself a slobbery grin in return. "His lordship will be happy to see you," he added before glancing significantly over my shoulder. "And I take it this morning's visit will be calmer than the one yesterday evening."

"I've had a chat with Mr. Gage," I explained, catching his meaning. "He recognizes that last night's row cannot be repeated."

"Good." He looked troubled. "Because I should hate to have to forbid his visits altogether. But I will, should it become necessary. For the good of his lordship."

"I understand."

Dr. Barker's responsibility had to be first and foremost to his patient and his recovery. I even appreciated his taking such a stance. Gage's outburst had placed him in an awkward position, especially as he was also our host. So he was relying on me to keep the peace.

"Good," he repeated, seeming relieved that I'd not disputed

the matter with him. He nodded his head and hefted his black medical bag as if to move on.

I hastened to speak before he could. "Dr. Barker, may I ask a question?"

"Of course," he replied, with every indication that he was pleased to answer anything I might ask. Only the flutter of anxiety that rippled across his features like a rock thrown into a still pond told me otherwise. Even then I might I have believed I'd imagined it if I'd not looked downward to see the white knuckles with which he gripped his bag. It distracted me from what I was saying for long enough that he caught the direction of my gaze and loosened his grasp, opening and closing each of his fingers in quick succession.

He cleared his throat. "What did you wish to know?"

"The garden. Might Lord Gage be well enough to venture out to it from time to time, with the aid of his valet or a footman or even his son?" I glanced toward the window at the end of the corridor. "Obviously not on a day like today, but tomorrow maybe." I smiled as if we were sharing an inside jest. "I wondered if perhaps the sunshine and flowers might improve his mood and speed his healing."

His shoulders relaxed, and a grin tickled the corners of his lips. "As you may have noticed, I am not the type of surgeon who believes in smothering their patients. Fresh air and light can work wonders of their own. I will see what can be done."

"Thank you," I replied sincerely.

He nodded once more and then turned to go.

I watched him for a moment, noting his short quick steps, and pondering what he had been so apprehensive of me asking. I supposed it could be a simple matter of class. After all, the aristocracy were accustomed to demanding things of people, specifically those of a lower social status. How many times had I heard Sir Anthony complain about the nonsensical demands of one nobleman or another, and he himself had been a baronet? I could only imagine how a surgeon of no rank might be treated by those same people. Of course, Sir Anthony had taken umbrage at anyone questioning his professional opinions or even asking for greater clarification, so perhaps that wasn't a just comparison.

Regardless, I was certain Dr. Barker faced his own pressures and high-handed behavior from his genteel clients. Had not Mrs. Barker mentioned one such patient at dinner some nights past? So perhaps that could explain his uneasiness. Nevertheless, I felt it was something worth storing at the back of my brain.

I adjusted Emma in my arms and then rapped on Lord Gage's door. A few moments later, Lembus opened it. He favored us for one moment with his dyspeptic scowl before turning to report our presence to his employer.

"Yes, let them in, and then leave us," Lord Gage replied peevishly.

Oblivious to Lembus's disfavor toward us, Emma cooed at him as he stepped back to allow us to pass, but not even her charm seemed to soften him.

"I've heard mint can help with that," I couldn't resist telling him.

His eyes narrowed, not appreciating my jest nor seeing it as a genuine attempt to help. How was I to know whether he genuinely suffered from indigestion, or he simply insisted on being disagreeable?

He exited, closing the door more sharply than necessary, and I turned to find Lord Gage sitting upright in bed, recently groomed. A glint of amusement flashed in his eyes.

"Did you just suggest he try using mint?" he asked.

"Yes."

He tipped his head back, emitting a bark of gleeful laughter. An act I'd never expected to witness from my father-in-law, and one in which I could see my husband's resemblance to him. The smile, the laugh, the crinkles at the corners of their eyes—they were all the same.

He wagged his index finger at me. "I'd not realized what a sly sense of humor you possessed, but I suppose it's to be expected, having endured everything you have."

I didn't know whether to be more astonished that he'd laughed or that he was referring to my macabre and scandalous past with a modicum of compassion rather than derision.

His brow quirked in irritation. "And yes, I can appreciate a cunning jest as well as the next man. You've simply never given me any reason to," he quipped, digging in the dagger.

Now, that was the man I knew.

"Stop gawping and bring my granddaughter closer."

I complied, only because his eyes lit with such eager delight that I couldn't deny his demand. In any case, it was why I was here. With Emma present, he would be forced to remain civil, and perhaps I might be able to get some useful answers out of him.

I perched on the side of the bed, turning Emma so that they could see each other. He reached for her hand, telling her good morning and what a darling girl she was.

"Sebastian has your laugh."

Lord Gage looked up at me, perhaps arrested by the tone of my voice. "Yes, well, he is my son," he replied, returning to his granddaughter. "There's no contesting that."

I wanted to say something about Henry's obvious resemblance to him as well, but sensed this was not the time to press it. Not when I hadn't yet gotten the other information I'd come for. Instead, I tried a different tack.

"Just as it's evident Emma is your granddaughter," I murmured, grinning down at her.

His eyes lifted to me again, sensing there was more to this remark than idle observation. "Let me hold her."

I passed her and the blanket I'd used to protect my gown from any spittle into his arms, avoiding his injured leg. Her favorite ragdoll—whom we'd taken to calling Rosie on account of the rose-printed dress Bree had stitched for it—slipped from her grip, and I retrieved it for her, wiggling it in front of her face so that she could practice reaching for it.

"I just find it baffling how kind and affectionate you are with her," I said, careful to keep my voice even and my eyes on my daughter. "And yet you are rarely more than cold and provoking toward your son."

He didn't answer at first, content to join me in this fiction that we weren't discussing anything important as we played with Emma. He marched his fingers up one leg and over her belly to her neck, making her giggle. "I suppose it's because my granddaughter hasn't yet disappointed me."

A cold lump of fury settled in my gut, and I knew with quiet certainty that he was goading me. That alone helped me swallow the bubble of anger pressing against my lips rather than vent it. I was not going to be incited into lashing out at him, no matter what hateful thing he said. However, I was also not going to let that pass without calling him on his nonsense.

"That's balderdash," I stated coolly, lifting my eyes to his long enough to allow him to see my firmness of mind. "And you know it. When has Sebastian ever disappointed you?"

"When he did not join the Royal Navy as a young gentleman, as I wished."

"But that was his mother's doing, was it not?" I countered before he could continue in what I could tell would be a list of his son's perceived faults. "She was the one who begged you not to take him from her while she was ailing."

He exhaled in displeasure before continuing. "When he went to Greece on that ridiculous crusade rather than return from his Grand Tour as I ordered."

I knew Gage had joined the Greek War of Independence for very specific ideological reasons. That he'd felt a very strong moral obligation to be there. At least at first. Though everything he'd witnessed had resulted in his becoming the rather listless and cynical person he'd been when he returned. He had begun to emerge from that period of his life before I ever met him, but it pained me to think of him as such, even though his father seemed to prefer it.

"When he went haring off to Scotland just as I'd arranged a brilliant marriage for him."

I arched my eyebrows mockingly. "I suggest you think very carefully before you list his marriage to me." I tipped my head sideways toward the child in his lap. "For otherwise your granddaughter would not be here."

He did not speak the words, but I could tell from his clamped lips he was thinking it. I supposed he believed Lady Felicity would have birthed the same sweet child. One that was perhaps more biddable.

"When he departed London last December rather than remain as I asked."

My gaze was arrested by his silvery one, for I hadn't known that he'd asked Gage to remain. Albeit, *asked* was probably the wrong word. He'd more likely *ordered* it. But Gage had still not told me. Of course, we'd already decided to spend Christmas and Hogmanay at Blakelaw House with my family before continuing on to Sunlaws Castle for the Duke and Duchess of Bowmont's Twelfth Night Party. Then we were bound for Edinburgh, where I'd made it clear I wanted to give birth to our child, utilizing the same physician accoucheur who had delivered my sister's fourth child. Given those factors, matters would not have changed even had he informed me, but I found it curious that Lord Gage had even asked . . . *ordered* it of him.

"Well, when do children always do as their parents wish?" I replied, trying to make light of the matter. "I'm sure you caused your parents their fair share of worry and aggravation. That doesn't mean you disappointed them."

A flicker of acute pain flashed in his eyes before he dropped them, stilling my heart. Plainly something I'd said had caused it. Or had aroused a memory that caused it.

Had he been a disappointment to his parents? Or been made to feel he was?

Gage had told me very little about his paternal grandparents or *any* of his paternal relatives. I knew his grandfather had been Sir Henry Gage, a minor baronet from Cornwall, and his grandmother had been born to the Roscarrocks, who Lord Gage had once let slip were naught but smugglers and rogues. Apparently, their roots ran deep in Cornwall. Or at least that's what the number of Cornish ancestor names Gage had teasingly proposed for our as yet unborn child had led me to believe.

I suddenly found myself very curious about these relatives—Emma's great-grandparents—and about their relationship with their son. How much had they shaped the man before us into who he'd become? After all, the person Gage had become was at least partially a result of his childhood and the connections, or lack thereof, he'd had with his parents. The same could be said of me. Of any of us. So what pieces had molded my father-in-law into the stubborn, critical, ruthless, sometimes cruel man he was? And why, despite ample evidence he was capable of warmth and affection, did he withhold those from his son? From *both* his sons.

Before I could think of any way to prod at these truths, Lord Gage turned the subject.

"I know why you're here," he declared almost belligerently, punishing me for having witnessed his moment of weakness.

"Sebastian couldn't bludgeon it out of me, so he sent you . . ." His regard dipped to Emma. "Or rather Emma, to charm it out of me."

"Actually, he doesn't even know we're here," I said as I lifted Emma's blanket to dab a bit of slobber from the corner of her mouth, refusing to be provoked.

This remark seemed to interest him, though I didn't give him time to press me on it.

"Though I'm not sure I understand why we should need to bludgeon or charm anything out of you. Not when it pertains to the investigation into your own attack and the murder of Gregory."

He aimed his scowl at me, but Emma still sensed his anger. Her eyes widened and her bottom lip began to tremble as she emitted her first tremulous whine. Rather than interfere, I waited for him to adjust his expression and soften his voice to soothe her.

I noted that the pallor of his wind-roughened skin was healthier today, but it could still have used some improvement. I suspected some time outdoors would bring a bit more color back into his cheeks. So long as he didn't overtax himself. I hoped it also improved his appetite, for his cheekbones were sharper than usual, and the skin around his strong jawline seemed to sag in a manner it hadn't eight months ago.

Once Emma was cajoled back into a good humor by his animated prattle and happily gnawing on Rosie, I ventured to speak, but once again Lord Gage was quicker.

"I never expected harm to come to you or Sebastian." He lifted his eyes to show me he was in earnest. "I certainly never expected those highwaymen would dare attack you. To be honest, I thought they would have enough sense to quit the vicinity for the time being." He frowned. "But perhaps they are not afraid of the repercussions of attacking my carriage. Maybe my reputation is not as fearsome as I imagined it," he quipped sarcastically.

"It seems to me that either they don't have the means to quit the vicinity, either because of poverty or current obligations, or they believe they'll be protected from either discovery or the consequences."

He scoffed. "If they were suffering from poverty, why didn't they take my purse when I offered it?"

"Poverty doesn't make one a thief, sir. And whatever their motives were for waylaying your carriage, it was not robbery."

"I still think it more likely they've remained because they feel protected. You said the villagers have been uncooperative."

"Yes. Though their protection may derive less from the people involved and more from their ploy." I explained what Mr. Butler had pointed out about how the gang of highwaymen who had attacked Lord Gage's carriage might be a separate group from the Robin Hood gang. That they might have masqueraded as them in order to conceal their activities.

He appeared to be listening with interest to this theory, but when I finished, I discovered he'd latched on to another aspect entirely.

"It sounds as if you found Butler to be credible, then, if you were discussing theories with him." There was a sharp glint in his eyes I did not appreciate.

"If you're asking whether I believe he was responsible for your attack at the urging of his brother, Lord Portis, then, no, I do not." I narrowed my eyes. "And neither do I believe did you. Not truly. It's flimsy reasoning at best."

We stared at each other a moment longer before he surprised me by being the first to relent. "Maybe so."

He gritted his teeth as Emma lashed out with a swift kick. Having slid lower in his arms, her lower limbs were now able to reach his injured right leg. I reached out to take her, but he shook his head, lifting her to sit upright across his left thigh. In this position he could no longer see her face, but her back was cradled against his chest, and more importantly, her kicks couldn't strike his injury.

"Then why did you suggest him?" I asked, picking up the threads of our conversation.

He sighed, lifting his mouth from where he'd pressed it to Emma's sweet-smelling golden curls. "Because at the time I couldn't think of anyone better."

"But you *have* thought of someone since then?" I hastened to say, latching on to his use of the phrase *at the time*.

A pucker of irritation formed in his brow. "No. At least . . ." He broke off in consideration, but then shook his head. "No."

I struggled to stifle my vexation. "You need to share everything with us. Even those things that may only seem vaguely pertinent. You know as well as we do that sometimes they can be the key to the entire matter."

But I could tell from his jaded expression that this speech had little effect on him. "Lembus said you're taking a closer look at the Blue Bell, and I concur that's a good idea."

Except I had a strong intuition that was not what he'd stopped himself from telling me. "Have you remembered something from your time there?"

Emma lurched forward, reaching for her dropped doll, and he retrieved it for her, readjusting her in his arms. "No, but I've been recalling some whispers I heard last summer at the White Swan." The inn he preferred in Ferrybridge—the one he'd been aiming to reach on the night he was attacked. "Apparently, the White Swan had been losing some of its regular custom to the Blue Bell, and the proprietor was convinced it was because the Blue Bell was serving unlicensed spirits."

"Then . . . you believe you may have been attacked because of smuggled whisky?" I struggled to keep my skepticism from coloring my voice. "That they recognized you and were afraid you were there to investigate, or that you would notice something?"

His jaw hardened. "Smugglers are a ruthless breed, daughter mine. Do not underestimate their capacity for callousness and violence when they are crossed."

I recognized that these were the men he was accusing of shooting and beating him, and leaving him for dead, but even so, the intensity of his voice when he spoke of smugglers in general suggested his feelings were far more personal. This must not be his first encounter with them. But of course, he'd undoubtedly had at least a few clashes with them during his time serving with the Royal Navy, particularly when he was manning the blockade. There had been a number of enterprising fisherman and merchant seaman who had been willing to overlook the fact that we were at war with France in order to smuggle brandy, genever, lace, silk, and other contraband into the country for a sizable profit.

Lord Gage was also from Cornwall—the county perhaps most notoriously synonymous with smuggling, given its isolated location far from the authorities in London; its long, winding coastline; and its many hidden inlets and coves. Hadn't I just recalled how he'd described his mother's family as smugglers and rogues? Perhaps that description was quite literal.

"Well, regardless, we should know more on that front tomorrow," I replied.

He squinted at my curiously. "Why?"

I remembered then that he had not been partial to our ploy to send Henry there to uncover more information. I hesitated to speak, but then decided it could do no harm to tell him. In fact, it might do some good. Perhaps hearing how the natural son he'd insisted on keeping at arm's length had placed himself at potential risk in order to find out the truth about the ambush of his carriage might evoke some sort of emotional response.

"Henry is traveling south to Doncaster to board a stagecoach north in order to contrive a way of begging a room for the night at the Blue Bell without rousing suspicion."

His pupils dilated, and he remained mute for a few seconds before forming a response. "If he's dam—" He glanced down, recalling Emma's innocent ears. "Dashed fool enough to place himself in harm, that's his own affair."

"I think it's rather noble. After all, Gregory Reed deserves justice."

Lord Gage grumbled under his breath in a voice too muffled for me to make out the words, but I knew from experience they wouldn't be complimentary. Even so, I hid a smile, for this was at least proof that he was far from indifferent about his second son.

And I wasn't the only one who found his grousing amusing. Emma tipped her head back to look up at him, offering him a lopsided grin as she reached up to try to grasp his chin. Faced with such a sight, only the most coldhearted of individuals would have been able to continue, and it appeared my father-in-law was not one of those after all.

"If the weather clears, Dr. Barker has agreed to allow you to join me and Emma in the garden for a short while tomorrow," I said.

He seemed astonished by this pronouncement. "Truly?"

"Yes."

I puzzled over his reaction. Gage had said he'd found his father seated in a chair when he'd been called to his room the previous afternoon. That Lord Gage had made several laps around the room. So I didn't think it was the fact of being allowed to leave his chamber that so surprised him, but rather my having desired and arranged it.

Seeing the genuine joy lurking at the corners of his mouth as he pretended to gobble Emma's tiny fingers, I vowed to be kinder and to try to include him more. Perhaps he was so harsh and critical because he didn't know *how* to behave any differently toward his family. After all, his wife's family had not exactly been welcoming, and I was beginning to suspect his own family had not been as loving and accepting as they might have been.

I had so many questions I suddenly wanted to ask him. Why had he joined the Royal Navy at age eleven? Had it been by choice, or had his family forced him to do so? I wasn't aware of any other naval men in his family, so it didn't appear to be a family trade, so to speak. And why was he so averse to smugglers and tight-lipped about his past?

But I could see that he was tiring, and when Emma cracked a yawn, I knew it was time to withdraw. Such discussions were best left to the well rested and even-tempered, and even if Lord Gage might be convinced to share some of what I wanted to know, Emma would begin fussing soon, needing to lie down for her morning nap.

So I gathered her up with the renewed promise we would visit him again the next morning, if not sooner, and hopefully in the garden, and then took my leave. Closing his door, I was struck by the fact that it might have been the first time I'd been given a smile rather than a scowl or a glare as I departed his presence. I couldn't help but feel it was a welcome change.

CHAPTER 16

I encountered Gage striding down the corridor toward his father's bedchamber as I was leaving it. He slowed his steps, waiting for us to approach. His hair was still damp at his temples, and I could smell the bay rum from his aftershave, telling me he'd just finished his grooming, presumably sans Anderley, who had departed for the Bay Horse earlier. Emma cooed at the sight of her father, reaching her arms up to him.

His face lit up as he took her from me. "Good morning, sweet girl," he told her as he pressed kisses to both her cheeks and then mine before glancing significantly in the direction we'd come. "Is he resting?" It was obvious whom he was speaking of.

"If not already, then soon," I replied, falling in step with him as he pivoted to return toward our chamber.

"How long have you been awake?"

"A while," I answered vaguely, not wishing him to feel guilty.

"You could have woken me."

I reached up to grasp his arm above the elbow. "You needed your rest, darling. I've watched you toss and turn. It's been an exhausting few weeks."

"*And* I imagine you decided this morning's interview would be a bit tamer without me present."

"I admit that I wondered if I might get more information from him without you."

He arched his eyebrows knowingly. "You wanted to test the theory that honey catches more flies than vinegar."

"Did you just equate our daughter with honey?" I replied, attempting to divert his focus.

"I did."

"Which would then make you the vinegar in this scenario. And your father a *fly*." I tilted my head. "I would have deemed him more of a wasp."

The good-humored look in his eyes told me he knew what I was doing. "The point still stands."

I sighed, admitting to being caught out. "I decided that, given your father's history of playing fast and loose with the information we need in an investigation, the use of a little persuasion would not be out of order."

"I see. So now our daughter is the 'persuasion.'"

I looked up at this rebuke to find him grinning.

"Actually, I woke with a similar thought," he admitted. "You simply got there quicker." He shifted his head to the side to look down at Emma, who had snuggled into his shoulder before glancing at me in question.

"Nap time," I confirmed.

He nodded, turning to climb the stairs toward the nursery while I continued to my chamber. A few moments later he joined me, finding me standing at the window, staring out at the rain-soaked drive. A steady drizzle fell from the sky, casting a misty curtain over the trees in the distance. I'd taken a shawl from the clothespress and now hugged it around me against the chill of the day.

"What did my father have to say?" Gage asked, clasping his hands behind his back as we stood side by side. "Anything pertinent?"

"Not much, unfortunately. He admitted to hearing whispers over a year ago that the Blue Bell might be selling unlicensed spirits."

"Whisky?"

From one or more of the dozens, if not hundreds, of Highland distilleries that had not been granted a license by the Crown in the government's changes to the law in order to impose a greater tax on the commodity.

"He didn't give specifics, but that would be my best guess." I frowned. "Though he didn't share this until *after* I mentioned the Blue Bell. And I'm almost certain there's something else he's not saying. He nearly spoke of it, but then stopped himself. I don't know why."

Gage scoffed. "Because he's my father. He doesn't need a reason, other than to plague us."

But that wasn't true. During the other times Lord Gage had failed to share pertinent details with us, there had always been an underlying reason, even if it was purely to protect someone's reputation, including his own.

"Well, I'm hopeful, in time, I can wheedle it out of him," I said.

"Just so long as his hesitance doesn't cause us complications in the meantime. *Dangerous* complications."

"It would help if we knew the right questions to ask. Perhaps Sir Reginald Oxley can help us with that," I ruminated, though it seemed doubtful that a magistrate in rural Yorkshire would be aware of a connection between Lord Gage and his constituents. At least, nothing stronger than the broadest of contexts.

Gage didn't respond, telling me he hadn't any greater hope than I did that Sir Reginald would be able to help us. Nevertheless, the call still needed to be made, if for nothing but to remind him the victims and their families were real people, and that some of us possessed rank and pull. Unfair as it might be, neither of us was above exerting our influence to obtain information when necessary. Gregory Reed's family might not possess the wealth or power to do so, but we could apply pressure on their, as well as Lord Gage's, behalf.

I only wished it weren't raining. Then at least the sojourn might be made more enjoyable on horseback. But in this weather, we would have to take the carriage.

Gage tipped his head back, looking up toward the dripping eaves overhanging the window. "I suppose we should be grateful the rain will provide Henry an even greater excuse for begging a room at the Blue Bell. But I hope he isn't forced to take a seat on the outside of a mail coach to reach Wentbridge."

I hadn't thought of that. The seats on the top of any conveyance were the cheapest and least coveted, for obvious reasons. Though the interior could be made just as unpleasant depending on the travelers you were forced to share the space with. On her journey home to visit her family in late December, Bree had told me she'd dosed her scarf with some of the precious lavender oil she'd purchased her mother as a Hogmanay gift just to be able to survive the journey seated beside a woman who had packed onions to eat like apples and a farmer who'd clearly never cleaned his boots. Of course, to hear her tell it was far funnier. And the lecher who'd sat next to her during one leg of the journey had gotten his just deserts when she'd pretended to stumble as she rose to exit the coach, slamming the edge of the book she clutched in her hands down into a rather sensitive place in order to catch her balance.

Depending on the circumstances, Henry's journey might be uncomfortable, indeed. As might be whatever accommodation was left to him at the Blue Bell. Masquerading as he was as a more common man, he also wouldn't be given the best room. I hoped he didn't catch ill from the experience. Or find himself covered in lice.

I squirmed at the notion and forbade myself to think of the cholera morbus still raging in pockets about the country.

"You're worried about him, aren't you?" I asked, seeing the tight furrow between Gage's eyes.

"I'm wondering if I made a grave mistake suggesting the idea," he admitted. "But what's done is done. He's probably in Doncaster by now, if not already boarded on a coach headed back toward us." He closed his eyes, the muscles on either side of his neck tensing. "If something should happen to him . . ."

"It won't," I interrupted gently, turning to press a hand to his back.

He nodded in agreement, but I knew he hadn't released his anxiety. I could feel it in his taut muscles. Stepping closer, I wrapped my arms around his torso, offering him what comfort I could. He unclasped his hands, draping his arms around me in turn. In time, I felt his rigid posture soften.

Outside the windowpane, a ginger cat emerged from the hedges, picking its way across the yard despite the rain, and then disappeared from sight.

With my hand resting against his abdomen, I could feel his breath moving in and out of him, deep and even, and I almost hated to broach the next topic. But my curiosity would not be assuaged. It pecked at my brain like an angry crow.

"What do you know about your grandparents? The Gages," I clarified. "You've never told me much beyond the barest facts."

"Well . . ." He paused, as if gathering his thoughts. "I didn't know them very well. I only remember meeting them once. And I was too young at the time to recall much of that, but . . . they seemed rather austere people." He frowned. "I don't believe I ever felt much affection for them. When my mother told me they'd passed, I was old enough to know I should feel something, but I didn't."

I felt a pulse of sadness for him. I had known and loved both of my sets of grandparents. Both of my grandfathers had passed when I was very young, but I still had vague memories of kindly smiles and soft laps. Apparently as a child, I'd believed that grandfather laps were the best place to curl up and take a nap. Or so I'd been told by my brother and sister, who liked to tease me about my propensity for doing just that. I was the youngest, and I strongly suspected they'd done the same when they were still toddling about.

"What about your father? Has he not told you about them?"

"No. He's never liked to talk about them. I always gathered he was rather ashamed of them. That their origins were too humble for his liking."

Hearing the bitter note in his voice, I tread carefully. "Are you sure that's it? Has he ever actually said that?"

He didn't speak for a moment, and I waited, allowing him to ruminate on the question. "I suppose that's just a presumption on my part given how pretentious he can be. Perhaps he had other reasons for not mentioning them." His left hand lifted to swipe away something from the window glass. "My mother told me once when I was complaining about the type of punishment her father had given me after I'd gotten into some sort of mischief that I was lucky it wasn't my Grandfather Gage reprimanding me." He hummed in surprise. "I'd forgotten that. The inference being that Sir Henry Gage must have been a rather harsh disciplinarian."

His words turned pensive. "I don't think he was able to attend their funerals, since it was during the war. But I know he went to his brother's some years back. I was cross with him about it because he didn't even tell me my uncle had died—not that I was all that close to the man—until after he'd returned to London. He claimed he only made the trip to Cornwall so that he could evaluate the land steward his brother had employed and survey how poor the condition of the house was before closing it up."

My eyes widened at the cruelty of his claim. Such an action certainly fit the cold and callous man my father-in-law had always seemed to be. But I couldn't help but think there was something more to it. Perhaps that was wishful thinking on my part. Perhaps Lord Gage was as heartless as he seemed. But then he'd already proven that not to be true by his behavior toward his granddaughter. By the compassion and sensitivity he'd shown me once upon a time in a carriage in London when I was too vulnerable to protect myself from his slings and arrows.

"Then your father inherited all of his father's property and titles?" I clarified, lifting my head to look up at him.

"After Uncle Arthur died, yes. Though the king elevated him to a baron less than a month later, granting him property along with it. So the matter was almost null and void." He squinted out into the rain. "He's not been back to Cornwall since. At least, not that I'm aware of."

I turned to see what he was looking at and spied a rider entering the yard, water sluicing from his hat and greatcoat. He slowed his horse's canter but, rather than stop at the front door, continued on around the side of the house toward the stable yard.

"That'll be Anderley," Gage declared, disengaging from me in his eagerness to hear what his valet had to report, even though it would take him several minutes to remove his wet outer garments and make his way up to us from the servants' quarters belowstairs. I took this to mean our discussion about his father was at an end, though I now had even more questions than answers.

He paused to look back at me, and I could tell I was an afterthought. "Was there . . . something else?"

"No, go on," I told him, shooing him toward the dressing room door. "Let me know what he says. I have some letters to write before Joe returns with our carriage." And some deep thinking to do in the meantime.

O xley Manor stood a quarter of an hour's drive from Wentbridge, near the village of Badsworth, and not far from the old Roman road which ran parallel to the Great North Road to the east. It was a handsome house of warm yellow stone punctuated periodically by protrusions of long, narrow windows. Inside, dark wooden panels covered the walls and ceilings, and ornate parquet flooring was showcased below. Everything gleamed with spit and polish, including the ancient suit of armor displayed in one corner of the drawing room.

Sir Reginald was a man of no fewer than threescore years. He possessed a head of snow white hair and a trim mustache which swept his upper lip. Our having already been shown into the room, he joined us not two minutes later, striding forward to bow before each of us in turn. "I'd heard you'd come to your father's aid." He glanced toward the windows, outside of which the rain continued to fall, as he lifted aside his coattails to sink into a deep leather chair. "I intended to call on you myself this morning, but another matter demanded my attention, and the damp affects my rheumatism, so I avoid going out in it when I can. But here you are, come to me." He propped his elbows on the arms of his chair, clasping his hands before him. "What can I do for you? What can I tell you?"

I was certain Gage was as grateful as I was for the direct opening.

"I've already spoken to Mr. Robinson," Gage informed him, settling deeper into the matching chair he occupied. "In fact, he paid me another call this morning before we set out to see you. He'd heard our carriage was attacked yesterday evening."

"Yes, I received a message informing me of that not long ago." He scrutinized us in what appeared to be genuine concern. "I'm relieved to see that you're unharmed, but what of your staff?"

"They also escaped without injury, but I cannot say the same for our attackers." Gage frowned. "We were forced to defend ourselves."

"Of course," he agreed without hesitation, but then seemed undecided how to voice his next question. "Then you believe your assailants were wounded?"

"We believe two of the four were shot, though we don't know how seriously." My husband's gaze shifted to meet mine briefly, perhaps aware of how unsettled I still felt that I'd fired one of those bullets. "It was dark, and they fled after the second man was hit."

Sir Reginald nodded. "Then perhaps this will finally put an end to these benighted highwaymen and their raids. They've been a plague and a nuisance to this stretch of the Great North Road for long enough. I'm only sorry your father and yourselves have been caught up in it." He pounded his fist down onto the arm of his chair. "By all rights, the dastards should have been stopped ages ago. But as I'm sure Robinson told you, the people in these parts only wish to see the good in them, and so they've foiled our efforts at every turn. Robin Hood and his merry men, bah!"

"We understand from Mr. Robinson that these highwaymen had committed no violence beyond a bit of shoving until the incident with my father."

"That's true."

"Which forces us to consider whether they're the same group of men who perpetuated the other robberies."

He frowned. "What do you mean?"

Gage explained our theories and suppositions while Sir Reginald listened with his chin propped on his fist.

"I admit," he replied once Gage had finished, "there is some merit to the argument, and Butler is a good man. Though the same cannot be said for all the ancestors that shared his name. One Robert Butler from the thirteenth century was pressed to death rather than admit to theft and murder."

I blinked in surprise at his sharing this seemingly incongruous bit of information.

"But not this Robert Butler. He's done a great deal of good for the parish since he took up residence here some seven or eight years ago. I've tried to get him appointed to public office several times, but he prefers to do his civic duty quietly. However, in regards to the highwaymen, I'm not so certain matters need be so complicated." He leaned forward, lacing his fingers over his abdomen. "Seems to me we have a simple case of arrogance. These men have carried on with their crimes for so long without suffering repercussion that they begin to believe themselves invincible. Intensification then becomes inevitable. So when Lord Gage and his staff challenged them, they reacted with greater violence."

"Except from our understanding, Lord Gage and his staff didn't challenge them," I argued. "His lordship even offered them his purse, and they rejected it."

Sir Reginald's brow furrowed as he considered this. "Then perhaps having recognized him, they expected a challenge, and when instead they were met with compliance, they attempted to stimulate a challenge."

"Are you suggesting they were bored?" Gage's voice rang with doubt.

"Part of the appeal in committing these crimes lies in the boldness and excitement these men derive from the exploit. But if they begin to believe they'll be allowed to operate unchecked, it deprives the act of the bravery and audacity required."

My husband nodded, rubbing his hand over his clefted chin. "Much like a cavalry charge. If a squadron believes they won't confront much resistance, it robs the maneuver of much of its peril and therefore requires less courage to complete it, which therefore deprives them of much of the exhilaration of victory, not to mention the glory."

"Precisely," Sir Reginald said.

"But if their motive for waylaying carriages is to rob from the rich to give to the poor, it seems foolish that they would risk everything merely for a bit of a thrill," I argued.

He sank back in his seat. "Ah, but you are making the same mistake as the villagers by ascribing noble motives to these brigands."

I scowled, disliking the implication he made about me with this statement.

"*I* do not believe they are so honorable."

Gage could clearly sense my irritation, and so picked up the threads of the conversation before I could speak again. "I don't believe my wife intended to suggest that they are. Nor do I think that their sole motive for attacking my father was to stimulate a challenge. The words they spoke to him were much too personal." He crossed one leg over the opposite knee. "Which makes me suspect they had a very specific reason for doing so. A past connection of some kind. Something they blame him for." Gage's eyes narrowed, scrutinizing the other man. "Are you aware of any reason someone from this district might hold a grudge against my father?"

Sir Reginald glowered in thought, his lower lip nearly disappearing beneath his mustache.

"It may have happened many years ago," I prompted. "Perhaps involving someone who was shot in a lower limb." Which might explain why Lord Gage's attacker had lowered his weapon to wound him in the leg after threatening to take his black heart.

He shook his head. "Nothing springs to mind."

"Maybe it's the date," Gage pressed. "Or the timing, or the location."

The last appeared to jog something in Sir Reginald's memory, for his head lifted. "There was one incident. A shooting that took place near that same spot some, oh . . . it must be fifty years ago now. And it involved a highwayman. Or someone mistaken for one. A poor tapster up at the White Swan in Ferrybridge was killed when he rode after a gentleman—an officer with the Guards, if I remember rightly—who had left his purse behind. Yes, yes," he declared, warming to his story. "I believe Vanburgh was his name. He and his new wife were just returning from making a 'matrimonial excursion' to Scotland, if you understand my meaning."

I nodded. Having grown up in a Borders town, I was well aware of the laxer matrimonial laws in Scotland which sent many eager couples whose families didn't approve for various reasons, or who didn't wish to wait the three weeks for the banns to be read in their local parishes, scurrying over the northern border to be married over the anvil, as they said, because of the idea that blacksmiths often performed these marriages by declaration. In truth, anyone could do it, be they weaver, fisherman, horse saddler, or mole catcher. But the idea of the blacksmith soldering the couples' eternal bonds sounded more romantic.

"When the tapster caught up with their carriage—somewhere about the place Lord Gage was accosted—he made the mistake of not making his intention clear. Instead, he drew up alongside the carriage and shouted, 'Your purse, your purse, sir!'"

My eyes widened. "And they thought he was a highwayman demanding their valuables."

"You've the right of it." He shook his head sadly. "'Twas an understandable mistake. They say it was pitch-black that night, and highwaymen were known to operate in the area. In his fright, not only for himself but for his new bride, Vanburgh shot the tapster in what he believed was self-defense. 'Twas only later that he realized his mistake."

"I assume he was acquitted," Gage said. The shooter being a gentleman, this was a foregone conclusion.

"The coroner's jury ruled it an unfortunate accident. Though the gentleman was suitably remorseful and tried to do his best by the tapster's widow and three young children by sending them money. He even settled a ten-pound yearly annuity on the young-est child, who was just three months old when her father was killed."

I supposed those were small amends, but rather a cold comfort to his family, particularly the infant who would never remember her father. However, I couldn't say that prosecuting Vanburgh for his mistake would have made anything better.

"What was the tapster's name?" Gage asked, for Sir Reginald hadn't even mentioned it. He'd swiftly recalled the gentleman's name, but not his victim.

The magistrate tapped his fingers against the arm of his chair. "Let me see. Was it Thomas? Tompkin? Thomson? No . . . Thomp-son! That's it. Gervase Thompson." He heaved a sigh. "'Tis a sad tale. Though I don't know how it could possibly relate to his lordship's attack."

"And Gregory Reed's murder."

Sir Reginald's brow wrinkled in confusion.

Gage's jaw tightened in irritation. "His footman."

"Yes. Yes, that's right." He tilted his head. "Was the lad from Yorkshire, then?"

"No. London."

Sir Reginald nodded, misunderstanding my husband's rea-son for mentioning Gregory. "Well, I will think on the matter further and speak to some of my colleagues and predecessors. Perhaps they are aware of an incident I am not." It was obvious he didn't believe this was likely. "In the meantime," he declared, pushing to his feet, "please express my good wishes to his lordship that he continues to recover. And . . . a bit of friendly advice."

I could already tell we weren't going to like whatever he had to say.

"Leave the investigating to Mr. Robinson. He's a bit plodding, but a sturdy man, nonetheless. And he follows direction well." He patted Gage on the shoulder. "Send him to gather whatever you wish to know, and keep yourselves out of the line of fire, so to speak."

CHAPTER 17

Iknew better than to speak until we'd passed between the two gateposts topped with lion statues and turned northeast toward Wentbridge. I could tell Gage had been holding back some choice words from and about Sir Reginald. Choice words I might have echoed. But once we were ensconced in our carriage and had driven off his property, we no longer needed to worry about our giving offense when we might need the magistrate's assistance in the future.

"*Clearly* we're going to ignore him," I said, staring out at the lush green countryside. It was no wonder this landscape could boast of so many battles throughout English history, from white versus red rose to king versus Parliament. The sky from horizon to horizon in places was broken only by hedgerows, the occasional tree, or the tall spire of a distant church. Even with rain falling from heavy gray clouds, ones could see for what seemed to be miles. And yet, forests still dotted the countryside here and there, a welcome haven for woodland creatures and outlaws.

Gage made a very rude noise at the back of his throat. "Does he not know who we are?" He tossed his walking stick, which doubled as a cudgel when necessary, into the seat opposite, grumbling under his breath. "A bit of friendly advice, indeed."

"What did you think of his tale about Gervase Thompson?"

"I think it was a great deal of nonsense."

I turned to him in surprise.

"An anecdote he likes to trot out for guests."

"He did seem to recall a surprising amount of details about an event that happened fifty years ago, long before his time as a magistrate," I conceded. "Even if he *pretended* he had to struggle to remember."

Gage arched his eyebrows as if to emphasize his point. "But I don't think it has *anything* to do with my father. I don't see how it can! He would have been approximately eight years old and living in Cornwall." He shook his head in frustration. "I've never heard of Vanburgh *or* Thompson."

But the question remained, had his father? He would have to be asked.

Gage muttered a sharp curse and then apologized. "I forgot to ask him about the Blue Bell."

"Do you want to turn back?"

He exhaled in aggravation. "No, I think I already know what he'll say."

Leave matters with Mr. Robinson.

Anderley had returned from the Bay Horse that morning to tell us that its proprietor could make no concrete complaints about his rivals' business practices, but that in recent years a number of coachmen and their routes had changed their place of call to the Blue Bell without any apparent reason. An opinion which was, of course, subjective. There were any number of reasons why those coachmen might have switched their custom to a different inn—softer beds, better food, friendlier staff, a coach yard that was easier to navigate. The cause need not be nefarious.

However, the strange deliveries the Bay Horse's owner had reported seeing made to the Blue Bell at odd hours of the night did raise our suspicions slightly. Perhaps Lord Gage's claims about smuggling were not as outré as they'd first seemed.

Which sent a stab of concern through me, knowing Henry was there now and ignorant of this new information.

"Maybe we *should* pay a call on Mr. Robinson," I suggested, avoiding my husband's eye. "He could drop in for a pint and make sure everything is well in order."

His hand stole into mine where it rested against the seat, coaxing me to look at him. "How is that any different than Anderley doing so?"

"But we know more now," I replied anxiously.

"Yes, but that doesn't change the fact we need to trust Henry to conduct this stage of the inquiry in his own way."

I offered him a shamefaced smile. "You're right. I just hate that he's on his own." In this, and so many things.

Gage's pale blue eyes softened as if he'd heard the unspoken sentiment. "Whether surrounded by loved ones or not, there are some things we all still must face alone. You know that as well as I."

I sighed, leaning my head against his shoulder and nodding. Indeed, despite all the support of Gage and my family, I'd still had to be the one to wrangle with the shadows of my past. No one could have done it for me. *I* had to be the one to confront it, and to ultimately overcome it. And so would Henry.

Gage wrapped his arm around me, pulling me closer. "But my brother knows he's not actually alone. If he needs help, he will reach out." Then lest I failed to understand, he specified. "And find a way to contact us, even if it means destroying the fiction that he is a lone, ailing traveler."

"Then I suppose we should return to Bowcliffe House so that we're close at hand should that occur."

So return we did. But my mind would not lay quiet all afternoon and evening and into the night. Not when it felt like we were waiting for something to happen. For Henry to return. For Lord Gage to share everything he knew. For evidence to drop into our laps. I knew it was the nature of investigations—to feel as if you were stumbling about blindly until you finally hit upon the correct trail. And more often than not you would venture partway down the wrong path at least once before turning back to search again for the right one. It was infuriating and disquieting, and rather like the maze at my brother-in-law's Highland estate. It was only after you'd reached the heart of the matter that you could look back and feel that you should have known which way to turn, which snapped twig to avoid, what path had been worn before.

I just wished Henry wasn't off on a trail by himself, with no way to know whether he'd hit a blind corner, or worse, some sort of trap. I'd heard tell of mischievous gardeners who'd laid puddles or low-hanging swags of greenery for unsuspecting walkers. Though, in this case, the traps awaiting Henry could cause much greater harm than a wet shoe.

After tending to Emma in the wee hours of the night, I found myself unable to settle. Wandering over to the window, I peered out between the curtains to see if the weather had cleared. Water dripped from the eaves, but a milky moon peeked through the clouds showing that, at least for the moment, the rain had moved on. All was still and quiet. Even the animals of the night remained tucked up safe in their nests and burrows. It seemed I was the lone being in the world awake.

And then a movement to the east near the tree line caught my eye. If not for the clouds drifting away from the moon to briefly reveal its glow, I'm not sure I would have seen anything. Even with such illumination, the figures were naught but hazy shadows in the distance. One approached the other across the expanse of the lawn, and then they turned together, fading away as the clouds once again blanketed the moon.

I strained to catch another glimpse of them, but the night was too dark, and by the time the clouds shifted again to allow the moon to wink through, they were gone. They must have disappeared into the woods bordering the property. But who were they? The highwaymen? Were they watching us?

I turned toward Gage to tell him what I'd seen, but then I hesitated. He was resting so peacefully, one arm curled up under his pillow and his handsome face relaxed. If I woke him, it would only disturb his slumber, for there was nothing he could feasibly do at this hour. Not unless he took it into his head to go traipsing off into the woods to search for the figures I'd seen. I could just imagine him stubbornly insisting on such a course of action, and doing so alone so that Anderley could remain here to guard the rest of us. No, it would be better not to say anything until morning.

If the highwaymen had been here scouting, then it appeared they were gone now. Though I was tempted to steal along the corridor to look in on Lord Gage and his valet, Lembus, who was sleeping in his employer's chamber on a cot, lest he need assistance in the middle of the night.

It was then that I realized the highwaymen might have come to Bowcliffe House for a different reason. After all, we believed that two of them had been shot. If so, depending on the wound, they might not have been able to tend to it themselves. They might be in desperate need of a surgeon.

My hands tensed with the urge to do something, but I wasn't certain what. In the time it had taken those figures to make their way across the lawn, any evidence of Dr. Barker having tended them would almost certainly have been cleared away. Which meant that my going in search of it might only alert them to the fact I'd witnessed something, which in turn might place all of us in greater danger. One hoped that Dr. Barker would tell us if he'd been called upon to assist the men either by force or his own adherence to the Hippocratic oath. That he would even send for the parish constable as soon as he was able to do so. But despite the Barkers' hospitality and their care for Lord Gage, we didn't know them well enough to judge how they would respond or where their sympathies truly lay.

With each minute I stood there, undecided, the less chance I had of uncovering anything pertinent. Then I heard the faint sound of a door opening somewhere along the corridor. Before I had time to reconsider, I checked the buttons on my indigo dressing gown and padded softly toward the door. I opened it and stepped out, deciding to pretend I was on the way to the nursery to tend to Emma if asked. It turned out there were some advantages as an investigator to being a new mother—I had an excuse to be wandering the upper corridors at night.

When I looked up to see Dr. Barker standing just outside his door farther along the corridor and across the way, I feigned surprise. A surprise he also seemed to feel. He reached up to clasp his green and gold banyan closed at the neck. A motion that seemed out of place. His thick hair was tousled and matted on one side, and while it was too dark to see his face, his voice when he spoke sounded bleary, as if he'd just woken from sleep. But perhaps he was also dissembling.

"Dr. Barker," I murmured after closing my door and moving several steps toward him. "Is something the matter?"

"No, I . . . I thought I heard a noise." He shuffled his feet, still awkwardly clutching his banyan closed at the throat.

"I didn't hear anything. What did it sound like?"

He glanced about him uncertainly, closing his own bedchamber door. "I'm not sure . . . but something woke me." He cleared his throat, lowering his tone as he next spoke. "I thought I might check on my patient."

I nodded, watching as he hastened down the corridor and turned the corner. To complete my charade, I should go upstairs to check on Emma. But then I might be trapped up there for some time, lest I return downstairs too soon to encounter Dr. Barker again and ruin the pretense. And Mrs. Mackay slept lightly, so if I woke her, I would have to explain. Instead, I opted to tiptoe quickly back to my chamber and dart inside before he could return to catch me. Each click of the door handle turning made me grit my teeth lest anyone hear.

Swiveling about, I pressed my back against the door, listening. For several minutes there was only the sound of my breathing and the clock ticking away on the mantel. I was about to abandon my vigil when I heard a door open and then shut—presumably Dr. Barker returning to his chamber.

Crossing the room, I removed my dressing gown and slid between the covers, nestling closer to Gage's warmth. I felt my muscles relax as it seeped into my bones, but my mind was still alert with questions.

What had Dr. Barker been doing awake at this hour? Had he been entering or leaving his chamber? Ostensibly, from his sleepy appearance and the manner in which he'd been standing just outside his doorway when I'd exited mine, he'd appeared to be leaving. Or at least, considering leaving. Perhaps he truly had heard a noise. Much like nannies and mothers, I suspected doctors were highly attuned to sounds that others might not hear. Especially those who had once worked in a military hospital.

But maybe all of that had been a pretense. Maybe he had paused in his doorway as if trying to remember if he'd dampened the fire in the room where he'd hypothetically operated on that figure I'd seen moving toward the woods, perhaps removing a bullet. Or maybe his conscience had been troubled, and he'd been torn about whether to alert us or Constable Robinson to what had happened. If it had been the latter, evidently he'd opted to remain silent. At least for the moment.

And why had he kept his banyan clasped shut so tightly around his neck? It was the type of gesture a woman might make to preserve her modesty. I supposed it was possible he'd been bare beneath his dressing gown. After all, Gage slept without a nightshirt most nights. Though I'd never seen him go to the trouble to conceal any skin that might appear at the top of his dressing gown from others' eyes. Of course, my husband was also an attractive young man, comfortable with his own physique. Dr. Barker might not be so confident or unselfconscious. Or perhaps he meant to spare me any embarrassment.

Of course, there was also another possibility. He could have been concealing something beneath. If he'd been operating, his clothing could have become soiled and splattered with blood. Perhaps he'd feared I would notice it.

I sighed aloud. Of course, all of this was conjecture. I had no proof of any of it. No proof even that the figures I'd seen near the woods were the highwaymen who had attacked us and Lord Gage. Regardless, I vowed to keep a closer eye on Dr. Barker. I would also ask Bree to be mindful of the laundry that appeared belowstairs, and whether any items were bloodstained, be they garments or linens.

Gage hummed in his sleep and rolled over, draping his arm about my abdomen. Turning to my side, I snuggled into the slight curve formed by his body, attempting to release my worries for the next few hours. But it was still a long time before sleep found me.

I told you I could do it myself," Lord Gage gasped defiantly as he collapsed into the carved armchair which had been carried out into the garden for him near the terrace. Though I noticed he didn't protest when Lembus shifted the matching footstool closer and helped him to prop his injured leg atop it. He might have made the journey down the stairs and out to the garden, but it had not been completed without taking a toll. His face was red from exertion and his breathing labored, sawing audibly in and out of his chest which rapidly rose and fell beneath his silver waistcoat and cornflower blue and yellow striped banyan.

The sight of the garment caused my gaze to lift to Dr. Barker where he hovered near the doors to the house, observing his patient's progress. I'd exchanged a brief greeting with him earlier that morning as I was entering the breakfast room and he was leaving, but we hadn't spoken otherwise. In truth, I couldn't tell if he was avoiding me or simply busy with his normal duties, but I felt quite certain—as his eyes met mine and then skittered away—that he was not eager to be drawn into a lengthy conversation with me. Seemingly content to see his patient settled, he retreated into the house along with Lembus, leaving me, Emma, and a scowling Gage to Lord Gage's company.

From the sounds of grumbling and haranguing I'd heard since they'd reached the terrace, I gathered that escorting my father-in-law downstairs had been a rather thankless endeavor. He must be embarrassed by the idea of needing assistance to complete such a previously mundane task, and so to hide that and any pain he felt in the process, he'd vented his displeasure on his son and valet instead. It almost made me wish I could retract the suggestion I'd made the day before that had set this in motion. But it was a lovely day. The skies overhead were a brilliant blue dotted with puffy clouds like sheep strewn across a meadow. The windows throughout the house, including those for the chambers above the terrace, had been thrown open to allow the fresh air to circulate. And I had high hopes it might bolster my father-in-law's recovery and improve his mood and cooperation. If he let it.

The entire household appeared to have gotten a late start to the day, so the morning was already more than half-gone, allowing ample time for the puddles from yesterday's rain to dry. I had found a sunny spot to spread a thick blanket, and I sat with my legs folded beside me, watching my daughter lie on her back and chew on one of her feet.

I offered my husband a smile of commiseration, knowing he was probably still wishing his father to perdition. Perhaps recognizing he wasn't doing a very good job of concealing his vexation, he turned to stare across the sea of alstroemerias and zinnias, his shoulders rising and falling before he dragged a second chair closer. Meanwhile, his father had leaned over to stare down at his granddaughter. His color already much improved, he chuckled at the sight of her engrossed in exploring her own toes. "Yes, they are terribly cute," he told her.

She looked up at the sound of his voice, but soon returned her attention to what was apparently a more important matter.

Leaving her to her exploration, he sank back into his chair, lacing his hands over his stomach and gazing out at the riot of colors before him. He inhaled a deep breath of the sweetly scented air, his nostrils flaring. "Now, this is lovely." A soft smile curled his lips. "Your mother had a garden much like this at our cottage outside Plymouth," he told Gage. "Not this large, but just as colorful."

From the look on my husband's face, I suspected this was the first he'd heard of it. Or at least, the first he'd heard his father refer to it.

Lord Gage waved his hand. "She adored those purply pink bushy ones."

"Dahlias?" I supplied.

"Yes, those are the ones!"

"She planted them at Windy Cross as well," Gage murmured, referring to the cottage on his maternal grandfather's estate at the edge of Dartmoor where he had moved with his mother at about the age of three, when she had fallen ill and his father had been away fifty weeks out of the year, serving with the Royal Navy in the war against France. There was a hint of wistfulness in his voice. One that his father also seemed to note.

"In her weekly letters she used to tell me how you would toddle about, trying to help her weed, and how nine times out of ten you would pull up a fistful of flowers at some point." His eyes lit with amusement as he shook his head. "But she didn't have the heart to chide you or make you stop because you looked so proud." A laugh rumbled up from his chest. "Whenever I would come home for leave there would be a vase of assorted blooms on the table. Your contributions to the weeding effort."

A grin split Gage's face. One that took on an impish twist. "When I was a bit older, I used to pull flowers from Langstone Manor's garden and bring them home to her, saying I'd found them on the moor."

His father laughed outright.

"Of course, she knew better, but she never scolded me. Perhaps because she knew Aunt Vanessa did more than enough for two people. And the gardeners seemed to overlook it with benign indifference."

Benign indifference it might have seemed, but I wondered if those gardeners had been more aware of what was going on than he realized. After all, servants heard most everything, and shared it with one another. It seemed likely to me that they'd known his taking the flowers was both an act of defiance against his aunt, who didn't want him there, and his grandfather, who had not been the easiest man to live with, as well as a token of love to his mother, who—while allowed to come home—had not been entirely welcomed back into the fold because of her defiance in marrying Stephen Gage against her family's wishes. They'd known, and they'd chosen to overlook it out of compassion for an angry, anxious boy.

Both Gage men fell silent, lost in their own ruminations. Until Emma caught sight of her ragdoll a short distance away and rolled over to try to reach it. This seemed to prod Gage into speech.

"Mother's letters. Did you keep them?"

He turned to look at his father, who slowly lifted his gaze to meet his, seeming to sense the importance of this question to his son. "Yes. Every last one."

Gage nodded, a slight furrow forming between his brows, and turned away. I knew what that furrow was about. That he wanted to know how the man who'd kept every one of his wife's letters—especially when personal space on a ship was limited—could then be unfaithful to her. But he didn't ask it.

Instead, he shifted his thoughts to the investigation. "Are you familiar with a Gervase Thompson or an officer from the Guards by the name of Vanburgh?"

Lord Gage frowned. "No. Should I be?"

Gage leaned back deeper in his chair and shifted slightly to the side so that he could drape one elbow over the back of it. "Sir Reginald mentioned an incident involving them which happened fifty years ago in the same spot where your ambush took place." He reached up with the opposite hand to brush back a twist of golden curls that had fallen over his brow. "It seemed to me to be unrelated."

His father's mouth hardened. "Sir Reginald Oxley is a fool." He harrumphed. "And he knows that's what I think of him. That's why he hasn't come to call on me."

My husband and I shared a speaking look.

"I was under the impression you weren't acquainted," Gage said. Or at least, that was what Sir Reginald wanted us to believe.

"We're not," Lord Gage replied flatly. "But his reputation precedes him."

My eyebrows arched in surprise—a motion he caught sight of.

"Yes. That bad," he emphasized. "Sidmouth deemed him worthless."

"Viscount Sidmouth?" Gage asked, evidencing the same confusion I felt.

As a statesman, Lord Sidmouth had served in various cabinet positions, including prime minister around the turn of the century and more recently as home secretary for about a decade between 1812 and 1822, remaining active as a Tory in the House of Lords since then.

Lord Gage's lips clamped together, and he looked as if he wished he could retract his words, but his son continued to press him.

"What dealings has he had with a provincial magistrate in rural Yorkshire?" The seat of Sidmouth's viscountcy lay in Devon in southwest England, far from Yorkshire in the north. I supposed he'd possibly had dealings with Sir Reginald in his role as home secretary, but that had been a decade ago. Had Sidmouth made a passing remark about Sir Reginald to Lord Gage then, it was doubtful either of them would remember it now. And why else would Sidmouth have discussed the magistrate with Gage's father?

But before either Gage or I could extract more information, a familiar figure emerged from the house.

"Henry!" I gasped.

CHAPTER 18

I jumped to my feet and hurried up the three steps leading to the terrace to throw my arms around Henry in relief. If he was embarrassed by my display of affection, he didn't show it, embracing me in return. I pulled back, grasping hold of his upper arms so that I could survey his appearance. Besides the dark circles under his eyes and a rumpled coat and neckcloth, he looked none the worse for wear.

"Thank heavens you've returned in one piece," I declared, attempting to make light of my worry.

His gray eyes crinkled at the corners fondly. "Yes, whenever I was tempted to take a greater risk than might be necessary, I reminded myself that my sister-in-law would maul my carcass if I came to a bad end."

I smacked him on the shoulder, and his teeth flashed in a wide grin.

"I am well," he confirmed more gently, cupping my elbows when I would have turned away.

I nodded, exhaling the breath I hadn't realized I'd been holding.

He released me to accept Gage's proffered hand, and I became aware of Emma whimpering. Evidently, she wanted to know what the fuss was all about, and why she hadn't been included. I returned to the blanket, finding Lord Gage leaning over as far as he could in his chair, attempting to soothe her while trying to seem like he wasn't interested in what was happening above him on the terrace.

I pressed a reassuring hand to my father-in-law's shoulder as I passed, and then sank back down onto the blanket to lift Emma up onto my lap. "Now, what's this stramash?" I crooned, borrowing one of Mrs. Mackay's Scottish words. "Did I scare you when I leapt up?" She blinked up at me, tears still clinging to her lashes. I dabbed them away with the hem of her gown. "Or did you just lose Rosie?" I plucked her ragdoll from where it had fallen and handed it to her, earning myself a toothless smile. Chuckling to myself, I kissed each of her soft, chubby cheeks before turning her so she could see the others.

Lord Gage sat watching us with interest, his gaze resolutely turned away from his two sons. But in spite of, or maybe *because* of, how indifferent he wished to appear, I could tell he was far from apathetic about either of them. His eyes narrowed at me, perhaps realizing I saw more than he wished, and I couldn't help but grin at him. A move he had not expected from the shock that registered across his features.

Did he not realize how silly it was to pretend he did not feel these tender emotions, particularly when far from belittling them, his sons would *welcome* them? Why was he so intent on concealing what he felt? What had made him so stubbornly taciturn when he had no need to be?

Recognizing he would find the pending conversation easier

if he was distracted, and that he would also be less likely to provoke Gage and Henry, I pushed up onto my knees. "Would you like to hold her?"

"Of course. If it will be a help to you," he replied, his voice a trifle rougher than before.

I gave him a look only he could see as I passed Emma into his care, letting him know I wasn't going to pretend he wasn't perfectly eager to hold her. Rather than responding with the frown I'd anticipated, he seized the opportunity to surprise me by relenting with a soft smile. Then, realizing he'd bested my expectations, his silver eyes gleamed triumphantly. Recognizing when it was best to concede gracefully, it was all I could do not to laugh out loud and destroy the moment by drawing the others' attention. As it was, I was forced to spend a few moments feigning great interest in settling my skirts to my satisfaction while Gage offered Henry his chair before sinking down onto the blanket next to me.

"Now, tell us what you've learned," he urged without preamble, drawing one knee up and resting his elbow against it.

Henry glanced at Lord Gage uncertainly, perhaps wondering if we should be speaking in front of him. Or maybe his hesitancy stemmed from the fact his natural father wasn't insisting he leave his presence—a marked improvement over his behavior toward him three days prior. Whatever the case, he cleared his throat and turned to focus on his half brother.

"Your instincts were correct. There are undeniably some strange goings-on at the Blue Bell."

"Did you encounter any trouble?" I asked.

"No. Your ploy worked," he told Gage. "I was largely ignored." His eyebrows arched tellingly as he leaned forward. "Except when I tried to inch closer to the door of a private parlor where some sort of meeting took place yesterday evening. A contentious one from the sound of their raised voices and arguing. I might have tried to enter, but there was a man at the door verifying identities, and it appeared newcomers had to be vouched for by an existing member."

"Then you did right. Being turned away at the door would have drawn attention to yourself and raised suspicions." Gage brushed aside a bee as it buzzed about his head. "Could you hear anything they were saying?"

"Not as much I would have liked. But it seemed to be political. I heard someone yelling about the Reform Act once when the door was opened and closed."

I frowned, wondering why the recently passed Reform Act was being discussed in such vociferous terms in rural Yorkshire. I would have thought most men of the classes in this area who frequented the inn would have supported it. After all, it would amend the current electoral system, restructuring the districts to be more representative of the actual population and abolishing the so-called rotten boroughs containing a small number of voters dominated by a wealthy patron, usually from the House of Lords. It also expanded the franchise to more men.

Out of the corner of my eye, I could see the displeasure stamped across Lord Gage's features. For he had been in alignment with the Tories in opposing the Reform Act. In fact, they had managed to stymie two previous attempts at passing such a bill. Only the Whigs' stealthy maneuvering and the threat of continued rioting and possible outright rebellion by the populace had forced the measure through. However, my father-in-law was still bitter about it, especially knowing his son had supported the measure.

"Anderley was just telling me something he'd overheard about that the other day," Gage ruminated as he pushed to his feet. "One moment while I send for him."

We waited as he hurried up the steps and ducked part of his

body inside, presumably speaking to a passing servant or a footman positioned somewhere nearby. Henry shifted in his chair, appearing uncomfortable as he eyed a surly-looking Lord Gage out of the corner of his eye. Anxious for the conversation not to turn contentious, I scrambled for something to say that Gage wouldn't need to hear, but Emma came to the rescue instead. She gave one of her little squawks and began kicking her legs excitedly.

Fortunately, Lord Gage had a good grip on her. "We want to stand, do we?" he asked her, his face softening.

Her legs weren't strong enough to hold her up yet, so when he lifted her so that her feet rested against his left thigh she merely bobbed up and down, but she appeared to like it. So much so that I feared he might tire before *she* did. I leaned forward to tell him so, but then stopped myself. He wouldn't thank me for pointing out his weakness and would likely revert to his grumbling demeanor. I elected to hold my tongue.

The sun passed behind some clouds, casting us in shade. It was turning into a warmer day than I'd anticipated.

"Did you recognize any of the men either coming or going to the meeting?" Gage asked when he returned, lounging once again on the blanket.

Henry leaned back. "There was Fryston, the proprietor of the Blue Bell. I know you met him."

Gage nodded in confirmation.

He glanced toward the house, lowering his voice. "And maybe one of the stable hands from here."

That was a tad alarming, though it didn't necessarily mean anything. Most of the men at that meeting were probably there to listen.

"I didn't get a good look at him," Henry hedged. "But I also thought I saw a man with two different-colored eyes."

"Like Melton noted about one of the attackers?" Gage confirmed.

His brother nodded. "And he was promptly sent away."

Gage's eyes shifted to first me and then his father. "So he wouldn't be recognized." After all, the constable had been asking around about a man with such a feature, so the highwaymen knew that had been noted.

"What about a man of about thirty with an unlined face, but his beard is already grizzled?" I asked on a sudden inspiration. "He would have been dressed as a laborer."

Henry straightened. "Yes, I believe I know the man you're talking about."

My and Gage's eyes met and held.

"When the meeting broke up, he stood near the corner, watching everyone coming and going." Henry laughed without humor, scraping his hand back through his auburn hair. "I had to make myself scarce because I was afraid at one point he recognized me. He didn't talk much, but when he did, they all seemed to listen."

"Who is he?" Lord Gage asked, lowering Emma to his lap. She immediately protested, and he lifted her again, though I could tell it was exhausting him to do so.

"Tom Hutchinson," Gage supplied, his eyes on his father and daughter. Clearly, he'd seen the signs of his tiring as well.

"We met him outside Constable Robinson's home," I explained. "And then saw him again inside the Blue Bell. He was staring daggers at us. And recall, Mr. Robinson told us he'd been in trouble with the law before down in Barnsley," I said to Gage. "That he'd been arrested for taking part in the Grange Moor Rising."

Suddenly, Lord Gage's arms seemed to give out, and Emma flopped down on his lap and nearly rolled out of his arms. Gage and I both sprang into action, reaching out to stop her from tumbling. My heart was in my throat when I realized my father-in-law still had a grip on her—tenuous though it was.

"I've got her. I've got her," he protested.

"I see that, Father," Gage told him calmly as he took her from his arms. "She gets awfully fidgety when it's time for her nap. Like a suspect who knows we're aware of them."

"Our daughter isn't a criminal, Sebastian," I chided faintly, still trying to steady my frantic pulse.

He smiled, bouncing her lightly as he paced beside the blanket. "She's a fugitive from sleep."

I shook my head at his terrible joke but couldn't stop my lips from curling of their own volition nonetheless—more from relief than amusement. I turned to my father-in-law, taking hold of his hand. He appeared paler than I would have wished, but that might have been from the shock. "Would you like a glass of water?"

"Yes, please," he answered meekly, telling me he was feeling poorly. I considered whether we should insist he return to bed, but then realized we needed to give him the autonomy to make that decision. If he was unwell enough that he needed to go back to his chamber, we needed to trust he would tell us.

Anderley appeared on the terrace then, and before Gage could begin questioning him, I sent him to fetch a glass of water. When he returned, I knelt beside Lord Gage as he drank deeply, first with trembling hands and then limbs that were steadier. Once he was settled, Gage addressed his valet, who stood more or less at attention just behind Lord Gage's and Henry's chairs.

"You were telling me about some rumblings you heard the other day regarding the Reform Act?"

"Yes, sir," Anderley replied formally, given Lord Gage's presence. "At the various inns you asked me to visit and gather information. It appears a number of the local men don't believe the Reform Act went far enough. There seems to be a great desire that the franchise should have been extended to all men."

For all that the Reform Act had done to address long-standing problems in the electoral system and expand the franchise, it still had its limitations. Eligible men still had to hold land or pay rent worth at least ten pounds annually, along with other stipulations. While it would undoubtedly expand the size of the electorate, this left many poorer men still without the right to vote. Men like Tom Hutchinson.

"What rubbish!" Lord Gage shook his finger at his son. "Now, you see what the Whigs have started. Give these men an inch . . ." He scoffed. "Soon it'll be France all over again. Or God forbid, the colonies." He shuddered.

Gage ignored him. "But that must not have been the sole objective they discussed. Not unless Fryston was there simply to lend his support to his local patrons." For surely, the innkeeper met the qualifications for franchise.

Henry dipped his head, conceding his point. "And he wasn't the only one." His expression turned grim. "I believe your Mr. Butler may have been there."

Gage's gaze dipped to mine, a glint of almost triumph in his eyes. "Handsome-looking devil with shaggy brown hair and a bronzed complexion?"

"That's him."

I might have rolled my eyes at him, but I had to give him his due. Butler's presence there was suspicious. "I wonder why *he* attended the meeting?"

"Or why he didn't inform *us* of it, or his knowledge of a man with two different-colored eyes?" Gage charged, the sharp edge of his voice making Emma roll her head fitfully against his shoulder. He pressed his hand to her back, rubbing it in circles.

Both were legitimate questions.

"Then perhaps we should ask him," I answered evenly, before looking at Henry and then the others in turn. "Maybe he can tell us more about what this meeting was all about rather than us guessing based on the limited information we *do* have."

"If we believe he'll tell us the truth."

I cast a quelling glare at my husband. "Which is why we're also going to pay a call on Mr. Robinson. Surely he must be aware of these political meetings and monitoring them."

"He should be arresting the lot," Lord Gage groused. "Sounds like agitation to me."

"The Seditious Meetings Act is no longer enforceable, Father," Gage scorned. "Nor many of the other Six Acts."

The Six Acts were a contentious series of laws that had been promoted by then home secretary Lord Sidmouth and passed through the Tory-controlled Parliament in late 1819 in reaction to the wave of reform-minded protest meetings that had swept through a large portion of the country following the Peterloo Massacre. In August of 1919 in St. Peter's Fields in Manchester, more than a dozen people had been killed and hundreds injured when a body of yeomanry cavalry charged into a massive crowd of more than fifty thousand people gathered to rally for parliamentary reform, among other things. The Seditious Meetings Act essentially made it illegal to hold a meeting of more than fifty people that discussed anything to do with the church or state.

"Then maybe Melbourne . . ." the current home secretary ". . . needs to bring it back," Lord Gage retorted.

Gage didn't dignify that with a response, given the fact that the Whigs were now in power, and they had been opposed to the Six Acts when the bill were passed in 1819 and fought to mitigate them.

"The meeting wasn't the only thing of note at the Blue Bell," Henry remarked, helpfully redirecting the conversation.

However, Gage's attention had been snagged by something behind his brother on the terrace. Mrs. Mackay peered out the door, apparently having recognized Emma must be ready for her nap. "Go on," he told Henry as he crossed to pass Emma into her nurse's care.

"My room happened to be positioned so that I could see the back of the inn, and they received a rather late delivery." He arched his eyebrows. "One they didn't wish to draw attention to, because they didn't light any lanterns and spoke in low voices. I suspect the only reason I caught them at it was because I'd decided not to risk sleeping."

This last comment made my skin flush in alarm. "What made you decide that?"

His expression turned sheepish, and I could tell he wished he hadn't mentioned the last. "Perhaps it was merely my own anxiety, but I couldn't shake the suspicion that I was being watched somehow."

No wonder he looked so tired.

"You mean, while you were alone in your room?" Gage clarified, remaining standing with his arms crossed over his chest.

Henry nodded. "Ridiculous, I know."

"Maybe not," I ruminated.

The men turned to me.

"I'm sure you've all heard of a laird's lug. There's a rather famous one in Edinburgh Castle near the fireplace in the Great Hall, where the king could eavesdrop and even watch his guests gathered there. A number of Scottish castles have them. As well as English ones, I'd wager," I added, lest Lord Gage make some snide comment. "So why couldn't an inn have something similar? A type of peephole, if you will."

I thought of Bree and the lurid tales she'd read about disappearing travelers and bone pits. One of the stories she'd told me about—which had seemed slightly more believable than the rest—had featured a woman who had been certain that the set of eyes in a particular painting was watching her. Readers had later discovered she'd been, in fact, correct, and because of the woman's vigilance and her faithful coachman's skill she'd escaped a terrible fate.

Perhaps Henry had encountered a similar contrivance, though perhaps not something as trite as removing the eyes of a portrait.

"They could have peepholes positioned in multiple rooms throughout the inn." Gage's scrutiny landed on his father. "Including the parlor where you took your ease the evening of your attack while a team of fresh horses was added to your carriage."

I rose up on my knees. "That might explain how they knew you carried two pistols rather than just one."

"Did you remove them from your person while you thought you were alone?" Gage asked him.

Lord Gage scrubbed his face. "Maybe." He frowned. "Yes, it's likely."

Gage began to pace again. "Perhaps that's how these highwaymen are choosing their victims. They're spying on them from these peepholes to find out which travelers have flush purses."

"When you believe you're alone, it can be tempting to check to be certain your coins are secure," Anderley supplied.

Gage swiveled to point his finger at him. "Precisely. Which means these highwaymen are working with the Blue Bell. The inn is the connecting factor."

"Let's not be hasty," I argued. "I agree this theory is worth looking into. At least for the band of men who attacked his lordship and killed his footman. But don't you think Mr. Robinson would already have noticed if all the carriages who'd been robbed by highwaymen had made stops at the Blue Bell beforehand?"

"We'll have to ask him."

I nodded, still feeling like we were missing something.

"What was in the delivery?" Lord Gage asked Henry, who turned to blink at him. "Could you tell?"

I realized then that this might have been the first comment Lord Gage had made directly *to* him since our arrival in Wentbridge. Everything else had been directed at us or to the room in general. Given that, it was no wonder that Henry seemed a bit stunned.

"I . . . I couldn't tell," he finally managed to say. "Not for certain." His voice turned wry. "But they did seem to have a rather extensive selection of whisky."

Lord Gage tipped his head back. "I told you there was some sort of smuggling going on."

I frowned, unwilling to hide my impatience that not only had my father-in-law failed to recognize the momentousness of his addressing Henry without rancor—or perhaps sought to deliberately ignore it—but also that he saw this discovery as in any way *his* success. I'd had to badger that small suggestion out of him, and he'd shared it only in order to withhold something else. Though I was beginning to suspect what that something else might be.

"We also need to find out more about this Grange Moor Rising," I remarked, eyeing Lord Gage closely. It had not escaped my notice that the moment he'd almost dropped Emma had also been after I'd mentioned that unrest. "It may have happened a dozen years ago, but given the fact some of the same men from that uprising attended the meeting last night, and they both seem centered around reform, I can't help but think in some way it has a part to play."

I knew better than to expect an overt reaction from my father-in-law. He was much too sly for that. But the deep furrows that creased his brow and the very stillness of his muscles were answer enough. However, most telling of all was his willingness to ask for the one thing I'd thought he would rather collapse than accept, let alone *request*.

"That's a good point," Gage replied. "Father, you surely would have been in connection with Lord Sidmouth by then. Do you remember . . ."

"I apologize, Sebastian," Lord Gage interrupted in a brittle voice. "But I . . . I'm not feeling well."

Gage hurried to his side, concern stamped across his features as he knelt beside his chair. Even I had to admit to a pulse of worry, for Lord Gage did appear rather ghastly. The sun had reemerged from behind the clouds, and he was holding one arm up to shield his eyes where his head had fallen listlessly back against the chair. But the steadiness of his movements and the watchfulness of his gaze shadowed by that arm told me my suspicions might still be correct.

"I think . . . I'd best return to my chamber," he murmured so softly it was almost a whisper. "Would you assist me?"

"Of course." Gage rose to his feet. "Give me your arm. You can lean on me."

"No. I think you'd better carry me."

Hearing this, and suspecting he was feigning the extent of his weakness for his own benefit and ignoring its effect on his son, twisted something dark and cynical inside me. I could not find the humor in this desperate ploy, nor could I feel any grace for his foibles. It simply made me bitterly angry on my husband's behalf.

Gage, being the good man and loving, dutiful son he was, stooped to lift his father into his arms, urging Anderley to walk ahead of them to open doors.

I sat very still, lest I mutter a foul curse.

After they'd gone, I could feel Henry observing me. Even so, I forced myself to take a deep, even breath before looking at him. His eyes were stamped with the same stark contempt I felt.

"Go ahead. Say it," he urged me. "I won't tell." One corner of his lips quirked upward. "If you don't say it, I will."

I exhaled, allowing my spine to release its rigid posture. "No, I won't give him the satisfaction," I said as I rose to sit in the chair Lord Gage had vacated. When I'd settled my deep red and straw yellow skirts and turned back to Henry, I was startled to discover his wry amusement had vanished.

"When you hear what I have to say next, you'll wish you had."

CHAPTER 19

Unfortunately, Henry would say no more until Gage returned, though I tried to pry it out of him, wanting to be inured so I could lend my support to my husband. Given the alarm Gage had plainly been feeling when he departed carrying his father, and the lines of deep concern that still grooved his face when he returned, I dreaded whatever news Henry had to share and what it might do to him. However, I also understood Henry's loyalty. Whatever it was, if it touched on their father, then Gage should be the first to know.

"Is he settled?" I asked, lifting my hand to grasp his when he offered it to me.

"Yes. Lembus is with him," he replied dimly.

I squeezed his fingers, urging him to sit down on the footstool adjacent to my chair. "He'll recover. He just needs some rest." I'd intended to share my suspicions about why he'd suddenly been so anxious to retire, but I was wary of what Henry had to tell us, so I held my peace. And was soon glad I had.

"He was light as a feather, Kiera." He blinked at me, clearly stunned. "He's lost so much weight." His eyes pleaded with me for reassurance.

I clasped his hand more tightly between my own, unable to dispute such evidence. Lord Gage's loss of weight *was* concerning. "It's not unexpected," I reminded him gently. "Considering his injuries and the fact he was ravished by a fever from an infection. It will take time for him to regain his strength and the weight he's lost. But he *is* making progress."

He nodded, attempting to gather himself. "Yes, of course. You're right." He frowned. "And I daresay he was exaggerating his infirmity a bit to avoid answering our questions."

I should have known better than to think this possibility had slipped my husband's notice. Nonetheless, he seemed to find the idea of his father's ploy more comforting than upsetting—preferring it to the alternative—so I continued to keep my antipathy to myself.

He turned to Henry. "I'm glad you've returned safely, and I'm grateful to you for taking such a risk. I'm not certain how we would have uncovered everything you have otherwise."

"Of course." Henry crossed and recrossed his legs, appearing uncomfortable with his brother's warm regard. Perhaps because of what he had to say next. He cleared his throat. "There is one more thing."

Gage's shoulders had slumped, his attention drifting toward a patch of orange tithonias nodding in the sun, but at these words, he straightened again, alerted to the tension in Henry's tone.

Henry appeared reluctant to continue. "This was waiting for me when I returned," he said, reaching into the inner pocket of his hazelnut-colored frock coat to extract a letter. "It's from my mother. I took the liberty of writing to her once we'd arrived to update her on our circumstances."

"Is the duchess well? What of the rest of your family?" I asked politely, already knowing that whatever the letter contained that had so unsettled him had nothing to do with his acknowledged family.

"They are all well, as far as I know. Most of them are gathered at Sunlaws." The Duke of Bowmont's country seat in the Lowlands of Scotland. "As I'm sure you must have surmised."

Most of the ton departed London in late June or early July, once the season had ended and the latest session of Parliament had closed, but before the heat of summer turned the city into a stinking cesspit. They all fled for cooler climes and fresh air.

I wondered if Henry was wishing he was at Sunlaws rather than here, embroiled in this mess. After all, the duke and duchess—his father and mother—and his four older brothers and one sister, as well as their assorted families, all loved and adored him. Of course, they had their disagreements just like any family, but they accepted one another, for better or for worse. I struggled to see how we could even begin to compare, especially when his natural father would barely speak to him.

"What does she have to say?" Gage prodded woodenly, perhaps anticipating, as I was, that his father had done something to follow through on his threats to reveal certain secrets about the duchess should she or Henry reveal Henry's true parentage to Gage.

He stared down at the folded missive. "She asked me to offer you both her sympathies. That she hopes, for our sakes, that his lordship makes a full recovery."

Though, not for his sake? I supposed it was understandable that the duchess might not harbor goodwill toward Lord Gage given his behavior. But this was still not the reason for his sudden reticence.

He lifted his gaze to his brother with his head still bowed. "And she divulged something that she suspected Lord Gage would be disinclined to disclose."

Gage's fingers tightened around mine.

Henry took a deep breath, as if preparing to dive into the deep end of the loch, and then laid it out before us. "She said that a few years ago he indulged in an affair with one Georgiana Lane-Fox, and that upon finding out about it, her husband, George Lane-Fox, had rather publicly vowed revenge." Henry paused, perhaps waiting for his brother to react, and when he didn't, carried on. "Lane-Fox resides at Bramham Park, about twenty miles to the north."

I turned to Gage, curious what he thought of this revelation.

"I knew about his affair with Georgiana Lane-Fox," he answered stoically. "It happened just four or five years ago, and I was living in London at the time." His stony countenance began to crack as a scowl settled over his features. "And given how indiscreet she was, I would have had to be a complete imbecile not to realize what was going on. That and Lane-Fox made a top-heavy spectacle of himself in Brooks's, promising bloody retribution. That's when Father dismissed her. He can't abide such drama." He spoke the last as if talking about someone he'd read about in the gossip columns, not his own parent. "But I'd forgotten the incident. So I'd not considered how close Bramham Park lay to Wentbridge."

It was apparent to me that Gage didn't know how to react. He may have known his father was indulging in affaires de coeur after his mother had died—known it and accepted it. But that didn't mean they didn't cause a conflict within him, particularly since learning his father had indulged in at least one of those liaisons before the mother he'd adored had passed, and that liaison had resulted in a brother his father had kept hidden from him for almost three decades. However, now was not the time to delve into those complicated aspects or the emotions they evoked. Now was the time for cold, hard facts.

"I'm not sure I'm familiar with George Lane-Fox," I told them, maintaining my grip on Gage's hand. As long as he wished to sustain contact, I would keep my fingers intertwined with his larger ones. "Who is he?"

"He was a member of Parliament for a number of years about a decade ago," Gage supplied. "A supporter of the Liverpool ministry." In other words, a Tory. "Though I don't know how obsequiously. But the most noteworthy thing about him seems to be his notes of hand."

My eyes widened at this dry jest. "He frequently owed others money, then?"

"Supposedly gambled away half his fortune at the horse races. His father had been a particular friend of George IV in his younger days as the Prince of Wales," he concluded, as if this might explain some of Lane-Fox's character, and perhaps it did. After all, Prinny and his cronies had not exactly been known for their fiscal responsibility. One need only look to the refurbishment of Carlton House and the construction of the Royal Pavilion in Brighton as an example of George IV's spendthrift ways.

Gage turned to look at Henry to see if he had anything to add.

"Mother said to warn you that the mansion at Bramham Park is in ruins. That it was destroyed by fire several years ago. Though, I guess Lane-Fox had been living at a smaller adjoining house even before that, being unable to afford the larger mansion's upkeep."

This bit of news went a long way to confirming the family's profligate practices.

"I suppose we should pay him a visit to at least explore the possibility he's our culprit," I acceded before allowing my doubt to tint my voice. "But do we truly think it's possible he *hired* a crew of ruffians to waylay your father because he cuckolded him several *years* ago? That seems like a rather long time to wait to enact his revenge, and a waste of his already depleted funds."

Gage scrubbed a hand through his hair. "I admit it seems unlikely, particularly given the other things we've discovered today, but I learned long ago never to leave any stone unturned, no matter how tedious or unpleasant the task might seem. A snake or spider might lie in wait underneath, unheeded and unseen, waiting to strike."

I refrained from pointing out that the vermin might also have nothing to do with the matter at hand and be entirely content to leave one alone, until you *kicked over their home*. But I recognized the wisdom in what he was trying to say. Sometimes you didn't know where the crucial piece of information that would solve an inquiry would come from. All you could do was listen and sift and gather until all the pieces fell into place.

"Then you will have to take Henry," I told him. "For that is too far for me to venture away from Emma. But tomorrow is soon enough." If they tried to venture to Bramham today, I feared Henry would fall asleep in his saddle. "Get a fresh start in the morning."

Both men indicated their agreement, and watching them as they conferred over the details, I felt hopeful that their trip might actually prove fruitful. If not in finding answers to who had attacked Lord Gage, then in the depth of their bond as brothers, and their reconciliation with the man their father was.

After the midday meal, Gage and I set off to visit Mr. Butler again, eager to attain some answers to the questions raised by Henry's discoveries at the Blue Bell. Unfortunately, Butler wasn't at home, and this time, the man who answered his door—I was hesitant to call him his butler, for he didn't look like one—seemed anxious to see us off his property.

I sat puzzling over the differences in our reception during the drive back to Wentbridge, wondering what it meant. Had I been wrong about Butler? If so, Gage was gracious enough not to say so, and wise enough not to let me see any satisfaction he might take in it.

In any event, I wasn't ready to deem him a villain just yet. After all, butlers and majordomos—or whatever the title of that man's position was—were notorious for being pretentious and rather high in the instep. More so than even their lordly employers. His haste to close the door in our faces might easily have been attributed to that.

Nevertheless, it made me suspicious and impatient to uncover the truth, no matter what that meant for Butler or my own intuition.

Our next stop was Mr. Robinson's cottage, where we were directed to a sheep farm not far from Bowcliffe House. The pretty stone farmhouse stood at the edge of a valley the constable soon told us was called Brockadale. He met us at the end of the lane and, upon discovering we had a number of questions for him, suggested we take our ease beneath a tall beech tree.

The late afternoon was a fine one, and I soon found myself glad of his suggestion. The slope stretching downward before us was carpeted in varying shades of purple with clustered bellflowers, knapweed, and field scabious. Butterflies fluttered from bloom to bloom, much as they'd done in the wilder area of Mrs. Barker's garden. Emma would have been enraptured by the sight, and I resolved to bring her here one day before we departed Wentbridge or the flowers wilted.

Spreading out my deep red and straw yellow skirts, I found a comfortable spot beneath the boughs of the tree and loosened the red ribbons of my bonnet tied beneath my chin. The breeze being light, I knew there was little risk of it becoming dislodged. The air was flush with the scent of living things, and I felt a twinge of regret that rather than simply enjoying it, we would have to turn our thoughts to less cheery topics.

"Now, how can I help thee?" Robinson asked after he'd lowered his brawny frame to the ground a few feet away, leaning his back against the broad twisted trunk of the tree. So broad, in fact, that Gage could also settle against it and still leave more than a foot of space between them.

Beyond them, Joe, our coachman, had pulled the carriage to the verge of the road so that the horses could graze on the tall grasses growing there alongside Robinson's steed. Meanwhile, Joe crossed his arms with the reins still looped in his grasp and slouched backward in the driver's seat, tipping his hat forward to shade his eyes from the sun. Seeing how content he looked on his perch, I suspected this was a stance he often took while waiting us out whenever he delivered us to various locales.

"It's come to our attention that a rather . . . spirited political meeting occurred at the Blue Bell last night," Gage declared, stretching his long legs encased in Hessian boots polished to a high shine out before him. "And that some of our suspects may have attended."

"Aye, like the man with two-colored eyes?" He nodded at our interested looks. "We've been monitorin' the gatherings at the Blue Bell for some time. Though, they would take issue with thee callin' 'em 'political meetings.' They're 'union societies,' is what they'd call 'em, though they're political all the same."

This was clearly a holdover from the time of the Six Acts and possibly even before, when there were laws against such things, and so they'd taken to naming it something else in hopes of masking their activities.

"And the man with the two different-colored eyes?" Gage pressed. "It sounds like you know him."

"I've had a suspicion who his lordship's coachman saw, but last night was the first he's poked his head out from wherever he's been hidin'."

"Why didn't you tell us?" he demanded, straightening.

"Because it wouldn't o' made heads nor tails to thee," the constable retorted, his own temper sparking. "No one would've told thee where he was. And thou askin' around about him would only o' made 'em guard their tongues around me, for who else woulda told thee his name."

He made a sound point.

"Then you've been trying to catch him out?" I clarified.

His voice gentled as he addressed me. "Aye. And sniff out who he might be workin' with. Haigh . . ." He turned to Gage, his tone hardening again. "That's his name. He's certainly not the brains behind their operation, but he served in the army. And he knows his way around a horse."

"What about Tom Hutchinson?" I asked.

Robinson studied me more closely. "Heard he was there last night as well." He lifted his chin. "Aye, he's got the brains." He glanced between us. "And my man noted he seemed to be favoring one arm."

Gage and I shared a speaking look. Henry hadn't observed this, but then he'd also been trying not to be noticed himself. Did this mean Hutchinson was one of the men we'd shot?

Robinson turned to stare at the field of flowers, his eyes narrowing against the glare of the bright sun. "Though I haven't been able to figure out why he would plan such a thing." He sounded genuinely baffled.

Gage plucked a piece of grass, running it between his fingers. "Then you don't think they're part of this Robin Hood gang of highwaymen?"

The constable gave a humorless huff of laughter. "Oh, I know they're not. They would never have continued for this long undetected. And more to the point, I'd had Haigh detained for drunken disorderliness during one of the robberies, and Hutchinson was in my company for another."

It would be difficult to argue with that. Not to mention the fact that Robinson knew these men far better than we did. If he felt certain they weren't the Robin Hood gang, then that was good enough for me. All our other evidence seemed to be leading us to that conclusion anyway.

"What of the Blue Bell and its connection to all of this?" Gage ruminated. "We've begun to suspect the inn is fitted with a few distinctive features."

"Peepholes and the like? Aye, I've wondered the same. Though I've never been able to prove it." He swatted at the sole of his boot idly with his riding crop. "But to answer thy question, I've no' been able to work out a direct connection. Sometimes the highwaymen strike after they've stopped to change horses at the Blue Bell and sometimes not. Sometimes the carriage is waylaid before they even reach Wentbridge. The inn *is* at the center of the area in which the robberies occur, and I've a feeling at least some of the men have enjoyed a glass of ale beneath her roof, but that's not proof of owt."

"And their smuggled whisky?" Gage pronounced leadingly.

A cynical smile twisted his lips. "Aye, I'm aware of it. But every time I call the excise officers in on 'em, they can't find anything. And I'm left looking like a bottle-head."

Whether this meant the Blue Bell had an ingenious hiding place for its contraband or that the excise officers were being bribed, I didn't know. Perhaps Robinson didn't either. Hence his cynicism.

I looked up into the branches of the tree, searching for the chiffchaff rather insistently making its distinctive call. "Maybe the political meetings are the connection."

Robinson appeared troubled by this. "Aye. 'Twouldn't be the first time such things have instigated trouble."

"You're speaking of Grange Moor," Gage said.

"Aye. And the like."

He bent one knee, raising it toward his chest to drape his arm over. "What do you know about the risings that occurred a decade ago?"

"You think they're connected?" Robinson tilted his head, and I noted he'd had his hair cut since last we'd met. "Aye," he said on a sigh. "Could be. Most o' the troubles happened south o' here. In Huddersfield and Barnsley and Sheffield. Thee might be too young to remember or . . . too removed from the problem . . ." Which I took as his diplomatic way of saying that most people from polite society had been little affected and so had been content to ignore the situation. "But the years followin' Waterloo were difficult for many. People had been expectin' prosperity, and instead were met with hardship."

Several hundred thousand soldiers had returned from war, he reminded us, and there hadn't been enough employment for all of them. Agricultural prices fell, and to curb their own losses, Parliament had passed the Corn Laws, imposing tariffs and restrictions on imported foodstuffs, which raised the price of grain to crippling levels for many. Concurrently, the wages in several trades plummeted. So those working in the industries of hand-loom weaving and linen weaving—both large industries in the West Riding of Yorkshire—were some of the hardest hit.

In response, these men had formed "union societies" to band together to discuss reform. At first, they'd been largely peaceful, petitioning the government and planning nonviolent marches and demonstrations. However, their pleas were met by deaf ears in Parliament. So in anger, they'd grown increasingly more determined and willing to consider the use of violence, though most continued to remain peaceful.

Then the Peterloo Massacre had occurred, spurring more protests in response. But rather than address the public's grievances, the government had instead responded with repression—passing the Six Acts, which restricted public meetings and demonstrations, outlawed drilling with weaponry except if conducted by municipal bodies, curtailed the radical press, and allowed magistrates to search houses without warrants. And so these union societies began to embrace more extreme positions, prepared to call the government to account.

This all came to a head in the spring of 1820, when a joint uprising was planned. However, it turned into a botched affair. A couple thousand men gathered to march on the lightly defended town of Huddersfield, but then it was called off with little incident. Two weeks later, rumor of a second attempt to take Huddersfield spurred the men from Barnsley to gather on Grange Moor, but on finding no contingents from other societies, they also disbanded and fled. A similar outburst also took place the same night in Sheffield, and on successive nights in a few other places.

"There was a general strike in western Scotland at about the same time," I interjected. Though we'd still been removed from it, living in the Borders region, I recalled my father discussing it with other local landowners. Many industries surrounding Glasgow had ground to a halt for several days.

"Aye. It makes one wonder if they were supposed to be coordinated attacks." Robinson frowned. "Whatever the case, they all failed."

"You said Tom Hutchinson was arrested for his involvement in the Grange Moor Rising and then let go," Gage prodded.

"Aye. 'Tis a better fate than some of the fifty or so rebels who were arrested faced. Those who weren't released were detained in the hulks . . ." decommissioned ships on the Thames that had been transformed into floating prisons ". . . or transported to Van Diemen's Land."

"So he's no stranger to political intrigue."

"The brother he lost to violence," I murmured, recalling something else Robinson had said. "Do you know how or when it happened? Could it have had anything to do with Grange Moor?"

He paused, seeming to give this consideration as he flicked away a bug crawling over his boot with his crop. "I don't know. But if it did . . ." His voice trailed away, leaving the thought unfinished. He frowned. "What does the attack on his lordship have to do with any o' that? Surely, *he* wasn't at Grange Moor."

"Not that we know of," I replied, turning to look at Gage, whose pale eyes reflected the same uncertainty I felt.

"Then how does Huddleston bein' at Grange Moor connect to his attackin' his lordship?"

"It might not. It's merely a notion."

It was more than that. It was a feeling in my bones. But I was leery of admitting such a thing in front of a man like Robinson, lest he scoff at the idea. Even so, it was obvious he suspected I wasn't telling him everything.

"Did Hutchinson serve in the army?" Gage asked, distracting him.

"Nay. Though the Barnsley society he was part of had a number of former military men. Reports were they were well organized, marchin' in lines to the beat of a drum, and carryin' pikes and guns. Even had scouts who surveyed ahead to determine which houses had weapons they could confiscate, and they issued receipts to those they took items from. So Hutchinson's no stranger to army tactics."

They must have seemed a formidable sight marching toward Grange Moor. One that any militia sent to confront them would have taken seriously. But Lord Gage had never served with the militia or the yeomanry or any ground troops at all. He'd been a Royal Navy officer. What possible connection could he have had with the uprising at Grange Moor?

I could understand Robinson's skepticism, for ostensibly it

made no sense. Yet I'd seen the way Lord Gage had reacted to the mention of Grange Moor. Gage had noticed it, too. And my instincts were clamoring at me that this was important. I just didn't understand why.

A butterfly fluttered past, charting a swerving flight toward the slope of bellflowers before it reached the blossoms. Perhaps it was time to stop weaving around the problem and go straight to the source. Of course, if we confronted Lord Gage, he could always continue to fob us off as he'd done before, but then his reaction might at least tell us if we were on the right path. If we were circling the bloom or hovering over the wrong field entirely.

CHAPTER 20

By the time we returned to the Barkers' home, the sun was already beginning its descent, casting long shadows across the floor of Lord Gage's chamber. He appeared to have recovered from his fatigue that morning and was even perched in a chair near the window, with his leg elevated on a footstool, rather than reclining in bed. Though the food on his dinner tray appeared as if it had been barely touched. This could have been a result of his taking laudanum. It was a fine balance prescribing the right dose to stave off the pain while not causing the rest of the patient's health to suffer. I would have to remember to ask Dr. Barker about it.

Upon our arrival, the first thing Lord Gage did was look for Emma. "Is she napping?"

"I'm afraid so," I lied, knowing it was doubtful she was resting yet. Not when I'd just fed her and passed her back to Mrs. Mackay wide awake. But I didn't wish to explain why I'd opted not to bring her with us. Not when the conversation was likely to be fraught enough without my giving him advanced notice of such.

Even so, he must have sensed something—or he'd realized his act earlier had not fooled us—for he searched our faces. "You've uncovered new information?"

Gage allowed me to take the chair adjacent to his father's while he perched on the side of the bed. "You could say that," he replied, keeping his emotions carefully controlled.

We'd both freshened our appearance so that we would be ready to go down to dinner following our conversation with his father. Gage looked handsome, as always, in his black evening clothes with his golden hair arranged in its artless tousle, but the sparkle that normally lit his pale blue eyes had dimmed, and his charming smile had been replaced by a more brooding countenance. The charismatic mask he normally wore for the world had been discarded. Perhaps he'd realized he could not fool his father, or he'd decided genuineness was the only way to reach him. Perhaps he hadn't the will to maintain the façade. Either way, it made my heart twist to see his vulnerability on display, laid open for the man who had already hurt him so terribly.

"We've spoken to Constable Robinson," Gage informed him. "He has a strong suspicion who two of the men who attacked your carriage are." He arched a single eyebrow. "And one of them has a rather interesting connection to the Grange Moor Rising."

"Yes, you said that before," Lord Gage replied impatiently. "Does he intend to apprehend them?"

But Gage was not going to be diverted this time. "Yes, we said it, and *you* seemed rather determined not to discuss it."

His father scowled, his voice rising in agitation. "I couldn't have been determined because there *is* nothing to discuss." He narrowed his eyes. "Or are you speaking of my moment of weakness." He scoffed. "I should have known you would attempt to use that against me."

Guilt pierced me. Had we misread the situation? Had he truly been overcome?

But then I squashed it. No. This was exactly what Lord Gage *wanted* us to feel. He was chronically averse to any display of weakness. He would do all in his power to avoid it, including using the very word. Even in the days since our arrival, when his physical weakness had been apparent, he had tried to arrange every matter, every encounter, to his advantage. For him to invoke the notion now in order to manipulate our emotions told me just how desperate he was not to discuss it.

What thoughts Gage was entertaining about this I couldn't tell, but he did not lose his nerve. "Stop evading the question, sir," he told him in a slightly sharper voice. "What do you know about the Grange Moor Rising?"

His father scoffed again, muttering uncomplimentary things under his breath.

"Were you there?"

A twist of curls dislodged to fall over his forehead, much like what happened to Gage and even Henry when they were agitated or excited. "Do I seem like the sort of man who would take part in a rebellion against my government?" he snarled.

But that wasn't actually an answer, so Gage pressed again. "Were you there?"

"No, of course not!"

However, there was no "of course" about it, and my father-in-law was acting distinctly like he'd been backed into a corner. Because of that, I was nearly certain he was lying.

He gestured broadly with his hand. "And I don't know any more about Grange Moor than you do."

This was definitely a lie. Particularly as he had already admitted to a strong acquaintance if not a friendship with Lord Sidmouth, the home secretary at the time of the uprising. As such, he likely knew *far* more than we did, whether he was directly involved or not.

I looked at Gage, curious how he would proceed. We didn't know enough to press him on any particular points, and it was doubtful asking the same question over and over again would yield different results. Given his silence, I suspected he'd already realized this. In truth, his expression of offended disappointment was likely to have a greater effect on any normal feeling person than words, but no one had ever described Lord Gage as such in my hearing.

"What of the smuggling?" Lord Gage charged, brushing back the wayward gray curl. "Was he aware of *that*?"

Gage's brow tightened. "Yes. Though it appears the local excise officers are being bribed to look the other way."

"Well, we'll just see about that," his father spat. "I'll be sending Lord Althorp a letter on the matter." Who was presumably the man who oversaw the Excise Office.

If that had been the fate the attackers had wished to avoid, then they'd just failed. But I still didn't believe that was their motivation. For one, Lord Gage had spent very little time at the Blue Bell—perhaps a quarter of an hour. If they'd feared he was there intending to investigate, wouldn't his swift departure have been the result they most wished for? Attacking him would only draw greater attention.

"What about a man named Tom Hutchinson?" Gage said, still harking back to the Grange Moor incident. "Do you know him?"

"The man you said had been at Grange Moor?" his father retorted snidely, recalling our earlier conversation. "One of the men you suspect of attacking me? No! I don't know him."

"What of his brother?"

Lord Gage suddenly took great interest in straightening the lapels of his cornflower blue and goldenrod striped banyan.

Gage's scrutiny grew more intense. "We understand he was killed by the authorities."

"When? At Grange Moor?" He looked up, his face a study in affected boredom. "I already told you I wasn't there."

My husband's gaze shifted to meet mine, and I could tell he was harboring the same suspicion I was. And that his patience was near snapping. Yet we still had an even more fraught subject to broach. I offered him what consolation I could with a simple look, hoping it would be enough to see him through.

"As you're insistent this has nothing to do with Grange Moor, and I can't see the logic in smuggling being the reason for the attack on you and the murder of Gregory, we're forced to turn our attention to another suspect that has emerged." His words were clipped but even, and I knew he paused before saying the name as much for dramatic effect as it was because it was difficult for him to raise this specter. "George Lane-Fox."

"Lane-Fox?" his father repeated in what appeared to be genuine bafflement. "Why would he . . . ?" He broke off, his silver eyes hardening to chips of ice. "Because of his wife?" His voice rose at the end, incredulously.

"Yes. Or do you often have men threaten to unman you because of your dalliances with their wives?" Gage drawled coolly, proving he wasn't yet so furious he was incapable of sarcasm.

Lord Gage appeared to be grinding his teeth together. "Lane-Fox is an imbecile," he finally answered. "And his wife's virtue was dubious long before I took up with her. Just as it has remained dubious since. If Lane-Fox were to suddenly decide to defend her, *and his*, honor, there would be a long line of targets."

"Georgiana Lane-Fox is younger than *I* am," Gage snapped.

His expression turned disdainful. "Don't be a saint, Sebastian.

She was perfectly willing." He flicked a speck of dust from his sleeve. "Though I concede our relationship was a mistake. Beautiful she might be, but she can't keep her tongue between her teeth."

His son's face was flushed, and his eyes glittered with repressed fury, but Lord Gage continued speaking, either unaware or uncaring.

"Who told you about Georgiana? Oh, wait." His sharp gaze flicked toward the door. "It was Selina, wasn't it? She wrote to her son. Couldn't keep her nose out of it."

"His name is Henry," Gage informed him. "And the duchess was merely trying to help. She knew you would never tell us."

"Because there's nothing to tell. So Lane-Fox threatened me years ago? So he lives, what, fifteen, twenty miles distant from here? The man would never expend the effort to hire ruffians to attack me, if he could even scrounge up the blunt to do so." He turned toward the window through which the crisper scents of the garden in evening filtered. "Selina is simply making trouble. You would *think* she'd learned her lesson, but then I was the dolt who didn't follow through on my threats when I should have."

"If you do, then as I told you, I shall be forced to reveal some of your past questionable actions as well," Gage warned.

His father's head whipped around so that he could glower at him. "Don't be a fool, Sebastian. You don't even know what secrets I hold over the duchess. If you did, you might not hold her or her son in such high regard."

My eyes widened, for he'd said something similar a few days ago, and they didn't seem like idle remarks.

"Whatever the duchess has done, that is not a reflection on Henry." Gage pushed to his feet. "And I had a *right* to know I had a brother. You should have *told* me."

"Why? So he could swindle and bamboozle you?"

"Do not try to make this about Henry. You know nothing about him. This is about you!" He loomed over his father, and I rose to my feet, anxious to calm him.

"Sebastian," I murmured.

"This is about the fact you didn't want me to know what a faithless, deceitful philanderer you are."

"Sebastian."

He turned and paced several steps away, scrubbing his hands back through his hair. "Do you know how much she loved you?" He pivoted sharply. "She counted the days until you would return to us. Literally counted the days. She would read your letters over and over until they fell apart. She would beg acquaintances for news of you, any news at all. And she . . . she refused to travel farther than an hour or two from Langstone and then Cambridge out of fear you would return for leave and she wouldn't be there."

I cupped my hands over my mouth, overcome by the anguish laid bare in his face. It was all I could do not to openly sob.

He stabbed his finger at his father in accusation. "She *loved* you!" His voice fell away to barely a murmur. "Did you love her?"

Lord Gage had listened to this stiffly, his face a pale mask. "Of course I did. But these things were between *us*—husband and wife." He arched his chin. "She knew who I was. Knew it and accepted it."

I couldn't tell if he was simply being defensive, or if he was saying she'd known about his infidelity. Had known about it and understood it. Whatever the truth, Gage was not willing to believe it. He shook his head and kept shaking it, his jaw clamped shut around words he either couldn't or knew he shouldn't say.

Recognizing it was time to retreat—for Gage's sake, not his father's—I pressed my hand to his back and urged him from the room. Only when we'd passed through the doorway did I look back to find Lord Gage watching us with a look of such bleakness that it nearly stopped me in my tracks.

But if he felt that way, why didn't he *say* something?! Why did he instead do everything in his power to deflect and belittle his son's concerns, to push him away? Even in my brief glimpse of him before the door shut behind us, he closed his eyes and turned resolutely to the side, breaking all connection instead of reaching out.

It left me with an aching hollow of bewilderment, frustration, and grief. Things did not have to be this way. So why didn't he do something about it?

Gage's muscles quivered beneath my hand—his rage and sorrow still bottled up inside him. He could not join the others for dinner like this, and so, anxious to protect him from prying eyes, I rapped in warning on the next door before opening it to usher him inside. Fortunately, no one was on the other side.

It appeared to be a sitting room of some sort—one decorated with delicate feminine flourishes. The windows were open to the evening air, their eyelet curtains fluttering in the breeze, which also riffled a stack of papers held down by a pretty porcelain figure on the writing desk nearby. An embroidery hoop lay discarded on the sofa, its design partially finished—and a companion to several patterns that adorned the other pillows. These things convinced me this was Mrs. Barker's private parlor. I hoped she wouldn't mind our using it.

Gage strode several feet into the room and then stopped, his hands coming to rest on the back of the sofa. They clenched the warm oak and pale blue upholstery, his knuckles turning white. I circled around him, giving him ample space as he wrestled with himself—both for his own peace of mind as well as my own.

I paused next to the windows, gazing down at the garden in

the velvety evening light. From this vantage, I could see the entire garden from the edge of the terrace out to the wildflowers planted in the back corner and beyond. This way, Mrs. Barker need never be far from her beloved blooms.

My gaze fell to the spot where we'd sat earlier that day with Lord Gage and Henry, discussing all we'd learned. I wondered if our voices had carried to her here. It was an unhappy thought. Not because I suspected Mrs. Barker of anything nefarious. But because we should have taken greater care not to be overheard. Anyone might have eavesdropped on us from these rooms above, particularly with the windows opened to the fine day.

Gage emitted a growl of frustration, pushing away from the sofa he gripped. "Why does he have to be so . . . so . . . self-righteous?" he demanded to know, gesturing broadly toward Lord Gage's room next door as he paced back and forth. "He enumerates the Lane-Foxes' and the duchess's faults when he should be the *last* person casting aspersions. He . . . he pontificates about everyone else, but when it comes to his own sins, they suddenly become a private matter or a trifle thing." His hand scraped back through his hair, destroying its artless arrangement. "For God's sake, he won't even say Henry's name, let alone acknowledge him, or admit that I had a right to know him! And then he tries to say that my mother . . ."

He broke off, his words growing too tangled around his tongue.

I moved several steps closer to him before answering in a calm voice, trying to speak to the heart of his pain. "Could she have known?"

His head whipped around. "What? No! How?"

"If there were no rumors . . ." I left the rest of that unsaid, knowing he would grasp the implications. That if there had been, and if they'd made it into the gossip sheets or private letters, how his Aunt Vanessa would have been only too pleased to inform her sister-in-law of them. But I didn't need to open that old wound any more deeply than a glancing scratch. "Maybe he told her himself."

He laughed mirthlessly. "Can you honestly imagine my father doing that?"

"Or she guessed."

He had no response to this, though he continued to pace five steps one way and then five steps back. I took that to mean it was possible.

"How do you think she would have reacted had she known?"

"She . . . I . . ." He fell silent after these few vehement false starts, coming to a stop just behind a chair. I could tell he was giving the matter some deep thought and did not like the answers that were coming to him. "She likely forgave him. If she said anything about it to him at all." His eyes lifted to meet mine, simmering with anger and pain. "She loved him. And what other choice did she have? She'd already almost been estranged from her family for marrying him. Her continued illness kept her beholden to nearly everyone. She couldn't exactly cast him aside or admit to her family how faithless he was."

He was right. She'd had no choice.

"But what about privately—in her heart of hearts?" I pressed, even knowing he didn't want to contemplate this. "Do you think she *actually* forgave him, or was she merely pretending?"

When once again he didn't speak, I took that for another answer.

"But you don't think she should have."

His temper flared, his skin flushing. "Not if he didn't apologize. Not if he didn't express remorse and promise to never do it again."

I nodded, for of course that would have been ideal. "But

given her circumstances which you've already enumerated, who would her refusal hurt most? Not your father. He saw her two weeks out of the year, and his failure to express regret would seem to indicate it didn't bother him overmuch. Not her family or you, whom she kept the matter from."

He turned to the side, still not wanting to face this.

"I'm not excusing what your father did," I told him, taking a few steps closer. "But given the life your mother was forced to lead, I understand why *she* might have. For her own self-preservation. You shouldn't be angry at her for that."

"I could never . . ." He broke off, closing his eyes as he winced. After a few moments, he hiccupped as he forcefully inhaled and then exhaled before bowing his head to me in acceptance of this. His eyes suddenly narrowed. "But that doesn't mean *I* have to forgive him."

"No," I conceded, lifting my hand to smooth his rumpled lapel. "But whom does that hurt?"

"Him," he challenged belligerently.

I tipped my head in gentle rebuke, telling him I wasn't going to let him hide from the truth. "Probably. But whom does it also hurt?"

His lips remained clamped shut, and I lifted my hands to cup his freshly shaven jaw.

"Darling, you are holding so much anger and hurt and resentment toward your father. And I'm not saying it's not justified. Heaven knows, I have my own reasons for disliking him. But allowing it to churn away like a storm only wreaks havoc inside you. Except when you, intentionally or not, vent some of that fury on others."

He made a sound under his breath I took as assent.

"Whether or not he admits guilt or expresses remorse, you need to find a way to forgive him." I clasped his jaw more firmly when he would have pulled away. "And *then* you need to decide what kind of relationship you want with him, if you want one at all."

He blinked down at me as if surprised by what I'd said.

"Just because you're willing to forgive someone doesn't mean you also have to give them leave to continue hurting you," I explained as I released his face. "Would I like to have a better relationship with my father-in-law? Of course, I would. Just as I know you wish your father would respect the man you've become instead of constantly trying to bend you to his will. Just as I know we both want our daughter to be fond of her grandfather." My voice turned icy. "But not at the risk of his berating or belittling her in the future."

His gaze drifted toward the window. "If my father said to Emma some of the things he said to me when I was yet a boy . . ." His jaw hardened, allowing me to imagine how fierce he would become to defend our daughter.

The soft rumble of voices drew my eyes to the wall which separated Mrs. Barker's parlor from Lord Gage's bedchamber. The walls were thin here as well, then. I couldn't make out any of the words my father-in-law or the other man—likely Lembus—were saying, but if they'd spoken loud enough, I might have been able to. Too bad. It would have been nice to know what Lord Gage was thinking in his more private moments. Though, it was true, he was unlikely to share them with his valet.

I recalled again the look that had flashed across his face as we were leaving, when he'd thought no one would see. And the expressions I'd seen at other times, like when Gage had gone to greet Henry after his return that morning. I was certain he felt much more than tolerance and indifference for his sons. There was a well of deeper emotions he never gave sway, and a reason why. The trouble was convincing him to admit to it.

It was a challenge I wasn't sure we were equal to. But we had to try.

"Do you want my advice?" I asked my husband softly, lest we be overheard.

A dry smile quirked his lips. "Won't you give it to me anyway?"

I crossed my arms over my chest in mock affront. "Only if you wish to hear it."

The cynical light in his eyes dimmed, and his hands lifted to grip my shoulders. "I do want to hear it. It can't be any worse than the hashed approach I keep taking."

"Tell him how he's hurt you."

His brow furrowed.

"Don't accuse him. Just . . . tell him how each of the actions he's taken and the words he's spoken has made you feel."

"Why? You know he'll mock me."

"Maybe," I conceded. "But . . . maybe not." I pressed my hands flat to his chest. "Tell him, and then explain to him exactly what you want from him, exactly what you hope for. Make clear the bare minimum of what you expect from him, as well as those things you *refuse* to accept. Lay it all out before him in clear lines. Leave no room for uncertainty. And then tell him the choice is his." I spread my hands wide, raising the right up and then the left. "He can accede to your wishes, and we will stumble forward, finding our feet together. Or he can refuse, and after he is safely returned to his home, we will resume our chilly distance from each other."

Gage's pale blue eyes flickered over my features, appearing to try to take them all in at once. "It's the only choice I have, isn't it?" he asked in a weary voice.

My heart ached for the pain and disenchantment evident behind those words. "If you wish to make him understand. If you want things to be different."

His head sank forward and then he nodded.

I knew this wouldn't be easy for him, exposing so much to his critical father, but it was the only way I could see to break through to Lord Gage. I just hoped I wasn't wrong about my father-in-law. That the heart I believed still beat inside his chest wasn't a figment of my own wishful thinking.

CHAPTER 21

We were late for dinner. Although everyone was too polite to say anything when we appeared. We sat down to a table graced with haricots verts, stewed artichokes and cardoons, pigeons in port wine sauce, sliced pork, and parkin—a gingerbread cake made with oatmeal and treacle. Fortunately, none of it had gone cold, though I was certain the cook and her staff had been cursing us belowstairs as they'd tried to keep the dishes warm but not overcooked.

We began the meal with little more than sporadic small talk about the food and the weather. For my part, I was struggling to find a way to introduce weightier subjects without ruining the meal or insulting our hosts, while Gage and Henry both appeared distracted. Dr. and Mrs. Barker each eyed us with more misgiving than they had previously. Perhaps they were merely tired of the inconvenience of our presence, and the potential danger we'd brought to their door, but I also couldn't help but think of Dr. Barker's appearance in the corridor in the middle of the night. Gage and I had not yet had a chance to speak with him, because he'd been called away to see to a feverish child and then stitch up a local lad's leg. Or so his wife had claimed.

"I hope the patients you tended this afternoon weren't seriously injured," I told Dr. Barker as I sliced into the pigeon on my plate.

He swallowed the drink of ginger beer he'd taken before answering. "Just a touch of catarrh and a farming accident. Nothing to be concerned about," he assured me, perhaps thinking I was worried about the cholera morbus and other diseases which seemed to spread quickly in the August heat.

"I can't imagine there are a great number of surgeons in this area," I remarked offhandedly. "You must get called away to some distance at times."

He nodded. "I do. Or they come to me. That's why I keep a room set aside belowstairs for anything that cannot politely be handled in the drawing room."

I understood what he was saying. Anything that involved blood or other bodily fluids would be treated belowstairs. Things like extracting bullets and suturing wounds.

I turned my head to catch my husband's eye across the table, and I could tell that he'd emerged enough from his preoccupation to recognize this for the opportunity it was.

"Then if someone was sliced with something sharp, or fell and broke a bone, or was struck by a bullet . . ." Everyone fell silent at Gage's mention of the last scenario. Even our cutlery stood still. "They might come here to be treated."

Dr. Barker's gaze held his steadily. "Yes. As a medical man I have an obligation to help all those who are sick and injured, regardless of who they are . . . or what they've done."

Gage tipped his head in acceptance of this. "I respect that. But your treating them doesn't also preclude you from informing the authorities of something suspicious, does it?"

They might be speaking in abstract terms, but it was clear we all knew to what they were referring.

Dr. Barker's chin raised an inch and then lowered as he spoke very precisely. "If a wounded individual came to me for help, I would give it to them. No questions asked. *But* . . . if their story—and there's always a story—as to how they received the injury was not credible . . ." His voice turned dry. "And there is rarely a credible reason for a gunshot wound. Then I would report it to the authorities and allow them to deal with the matter as they saw fit." Dr. Barker picked up his fork, indicating the matter was closed.

But Gage wasn't finished. "Have you recently reported any incidents to the authorities?"

Genuine anger furrowed the surgeon's brow as he looked up at him—the first of that emotion I'd witnessed from him. "Not since your father."

"You understand why we're asking," I murmured.

His sharp eyes turned to me, cutting off anything else I might have said. "I do."

We all sat stiffly staring at our plates, slow to resume eating after the confrontation.

Mrs. Barker's hands fluttered nervously before her. "Dr. Barker takes his duties very seriously. Thou can be assured . . ."

"Let them ask their questions, Prudence," he interrupted her in a gentler voice. He lowered his hands to the sides of his plate and exhaled before looking up at first me, then Gage, and last Henry. "They have a right to their queries. One man is dead and another injured, after all."

I appreciated his good grace and his restraint. Had our situations been reversed, I hoped I would have been able to respond with as much goodwill. Though Mrs. Barker appeared less certain this was such a wise course.

"Go on," he prodded. "What else did you wish to know?"

From the manner in which his pale eyes locked with mine, I knew he was giving me permission to ask about last night when I'd seen him in the corridor. But now I was even less certain that had anything to do with the inquiry rather than his awkwardness at encountering me under such circumstances. In any case, it was not a query to subject him to at the dinner table.

"Lord Gage's appetite still seems rather diminished," I said instead. "Is it because of the laudanum?"

His pupils dilated in surprise, probably because he'd been expecting a much different question. But he recovered quickly. "Yes. It's been difficult to figure out the precise dose that will manage his pain while not blunting his appetite." He sighed. "I've been gradually trying to lessen his dose, to wean him off of it, so to speak. But he overexerted himself today." He offered Gage a commiserating look. "Insisted on descending the stairs mostly himself, didn't he?"

Gage responded with a sardonic look. "You know my father well."

"So I had to give him a larger dose this afternoon."

His answer reassured me that he had matters well in hand when it came to Lord Gage's continued recovery. I knew from experience how little care some physicians gave to regulating their patients' use of laudanum, and how difficult it could become over time to stop. But Dr. Barker appeared determined for that not to happen.

"Do you know anything about the meetings that are happening at the Blue Bell?" Henry asked as he speared a few of the beans with his fork. "They seem to be political in nature."

Mrs. Barker looked to her husband in some alarm, but Dr. Barker appeared unruffled by the question except for a slight furrowing of his brow.

"You must be referring to the local union society. I've been invited to join them from time to time, but I find it best to keep my thoughts to myself, lest those who most need my help refuse to call on me because of it." He looked at each of us quellingly. "I *can* tell you that they are all talk. There have been no marches or disturbances like those that occurred a decade ago."

"Like at Grange Moor?" Gage asked.

Dr. Barker risked a concerned glance at his wife, whose eyes had dropped to her plate. "Aye."

I could feel Gage and Henry both darting looks toward me, clearly hoping I would be the one, as a fellow woman, to address our hostess.

"Mrs. Barker, I believe you told me you grew up just south of here. Near Wakefield."

Her brown eyes flashed upward, tentatively meeting mine. "Aye." She smoothed her napkin over her lap, where it covered the saffron silk of her skirts. "And I know what thee are goin' to ask next. Aye, I remember the uprisings." Her words were somewhat halting as they came. "'Twas a tense, awful time. My father forbid me from leaving their house for days. 'Til it was all over."

Dr. Barker watched his wife in concern. It was evident there was more.

"Did you know any of the men who were wrapped up in it?"

"A few," she answered softly. I couldn't tell if it was shame or grief that made her lower her eyes again.

"Were they protestors or militia?"

"Both."

I nodded. In a smaller community, one's acquaintances were bound to be. "Were you ever privy to any details of what happened?"

She shook her head.

"Her father would have kept that from her," Dr. Barker interjected. "But why the interest in Grange Moor? Surely it can have no bearing on the attack on his lordship."

"The subject of it has arisen more than once," Gage explained, scrutinizing both of our hosts. "And it's come to our attention that one of our suspects took part in the Grange Moor Rising. That he was arrested and released."

These words appeared to jolt Mrs. Barker, and her eyes widened with what I would have described as alarm. Dr. Barker saw it, too, for he began to rise from his chair to go to her.

She stayed him with a raised hand. "Please, no. It's just . . ." She swallowed, summoning her composure. "It's a shock to hear, that's all. I thought that dreadful incident was long behind me." Her hand shook as she reached for her glass, taking a long drink before continuing. "I know almost nothing about it. Nothing pertinent anyway. I'm sure almost any of the men living between here and Barnsley could tell you more."

I nodded slowly. And yet she knew enough to be scared. But perhaps she simply didn't wish to recall all the details. Perhaps this was deflection rather than avoidance.

Dr. Barker shrugged. "And I did not live here at that time. I'm afraid I'm no help either."

We couldn't argue that point. Though I still felt certain the Barkers were keeping something from us. Maybe it wasn't about Grange Moor, but it was reflected in their eyes as they met and held. I turned to Gage, and I could tell I wasn't the only one who suspected it. The trouble was convincing them to share it with us.

Gage and Henry set off on horseback early the next morning, hoping to reach Bramham Park to speak to Mr. Lane-Fox and return before sunset. Meanwhile I allowed myself to loll in bed longer than usual, snuggling and playing with Emma before taking her for a brief visit to see her grandfather. Given the manner in which he'd exhausted himself the day before, brevity seemed in his best interest. Though I also admitted, notwithstanding the guidance I'd given Gage then, his father had riled me greatly with his behavior toward his sons. As such, I decided the least amount of time I spent with him until my temper had cooled, the better.

I was just returning from delivering Emma to Mrs. Mackay in the nursery when I spied Anderley and Bree in hushed conversation at the end of the corridor. I slowed my steps, uncertain whether their discussion was personal or related to the inquiry. It seemed rather too furtive and intense to be any sort of flirtation. So when I caught a glimpse of a folded paper Anderley appeared to be attempting to conceal in his coat, I decided to risk approaching.

Anderley was the first to see me, straightening from his hunched position.

"M'lady," Bree gasped as she turned to discover who had caught the valet's eye. "We need your advice."

I glanced significantly at the door behind them leading to the servants' stair. "Then come into my chamber."

They both followed, though Anderley was noticeably more hesitant. Bree might have said they both needed my advice, but it was clear Anderley was less enthusiastic about that.

"What is it?" I asked after he had shut the door.

Bree looked to Anderley. "Show her," she urged with arched eyebrows. When his efforts to do so were too slow for her liking, she attempted to snatch the missive from his hand, earning herself a ferocious scowl when he lifted it out of her reach.

Reluctantly, he passed it to me. "Mr. Gage asked me to monitor Lembus's movements. To be crafty if necessary."

"I see," I replied, not entirely surprised Gage had resorted to such methods. After all, his father was not averse to underhanded behavior. He must have decided to employ a bit more cunning himself. "Do you know what he hoped to find?" I flipped over the paper, which appeared to be a letter.

"No, but . . ." He broke off, reading my surprise. "I believe I found it."

"How did you get this?" I asked. It was a letter addressed to Lord Sidmouth. One likely penned by Lembus's hand on behalf of Lord Gage. I recognized the handwriting from the letter Gage had received at Barbreck informing us of his father's injuries. Gage had read it dozens of times over, so the appearance of Lembus's loops and scratches were well familiar to me.

"Lembus dropped it."

I arched a single eyebrow in disbelief, but Anderley didn't even bat an eyelid.

That is, until Bree scoffed. "Och, she kens ye nabbed it as well as I do."

Then he looked as if he wanted to box her ears, but he restrained himself.

I shook my head but said nothing while the pair of them glared at each other. I supposed I shouldn't have been surprised that pickpocketing was yet another skill my husband's valet had acquired in his youth during his time living on the streets of London and later Cambridge. Given the fact his circumstances could hardly be blamed on him, and he'd used the ability to our advantage, I decided it was best to overlook it. In any case, it would be rather like the pot calling the kettle black since I was about to open the letter, which was fortunately still unsealed. Ignoring the flush of guilt I felt at perusing pilfered correspondence, I began reading.

The missive was, indeed, from Lord Gage to the former home secretary, Lord Sidmouth, and it made it quite clear the two men were well acquainted. It was also rather brief and to the point. Lord Gage wanted to ensure that all pertinent correspondence and records from his time working at Sidmouth's direction for the Home Office had been destroyed, and to compel

Sidmouth not to share any details with his son should Sebastian ask.

I looked up—still struggling to digest these revelations—to find both Anderley and Bree watching me. It was no wonder Lord Gage hadn't dictated this letter to his son when he'd forced him to pen all those other missives for him three days prior. Not that Gage and I hadn't already realized what a ploy that was, a way to force his son to cultivate relationships with the men he wanted him to. But it was still shocking to see.

"You've both read this?" It was more of a statement than a question, for their reticent expressions made it clear they had, but they answered anyway.

"Yes," Anderley confirmed. "And now I don't know what to do with it."

I could appreciate his dilemma. Did he somehow return it to Lembus and allow it to be mailed, or did he hang on to it to possibly prevent such a thing? Of course, if Lembus realized the letter was missing, he could always write another one, as long as he could remember what Lord Gage had dictated, and given its brevity, that would not be difficult. If Gage were here, he could direct him, but he wasn't. And he wouldn't return until nightfall.

I paused for a moment to consider our options before deciding, hoping it was what my husband would wish. "First of all, we're going to make a copy of this." I crossed the room to sit at my writing desk and swiftly duplicate the letter. Then I refolded the original and held it out to Anderley, only to withdraw it as a thought struck me.

I narrowed my eyes at Bree's pretty face. Her strawberry blond ringlets looked particularly fetching today, swept up high on her head. "Why don't *you* return this to Lembus." A sly smile quirked my lips. "Tell him you found it lying in the corridor and suggest he take better care in the future."

"What do I say if he accuses me o' readin' it?" she countered, judging Lembus's character correctly. He would undoubtedly try to turn the blame back on her.

"Tell him you took it to your mistress, and *I* read the signature. If he wants to take issue with my doing so and saving him from Lord Gage's displeasure, then he can take that up with me."

Bree grinned, accepting the letter from me. "Aye, m'lady."

They both turned to go, but I halted Bree. Anderley looked back but said nothing as he exited through the dressing room door.

"Were you able to uncover anything about any bloody garments or linens?" I wanted to believe that what Dr. Barker had told us over dinner was truthful, but it was best to be certain.

"Aye, m'lady. So far as I can tell, nothin' has shown up in the laundry or the rubbish." Her lips pursed. "But I did learn somethin' curious."

"Go on," I coaxed, crossing my feet at the ankles as I sat forward in my chair to listen.

"Kitty, the laundry maid, told me that Mrs. Barker . . ." She hesitated, as if debating how to communicate what she needed to. "Well . . . Kitty said she soils more cloths during her courses each month than a normal woman. A lot more," she emphasized, but then frowned as if she wasn't certain whether she believed this. "She claimed her mistress has some sort o' condition. One that makes her bleed more."

"Every month?" I clarified.

She nodded.

I supposed this was possible. Though the loss of too much blood would make one weak and short of breath. But Kitty's quantification was also hardly scientific. Surely some women bled more than others. Perhaps Mrs. Barker had a condition which made her shed just a little bit more than average. Whatever average was.

In any case, I didn't see how this was pertinent to our investigation. It certainly didn't suggest Dr. Barker had assisted the injured highwaymen. But I made a note of it nonetheless and sent Bree on her way.

Once she'd gone, I moved toward the window, peering out at the cloud-strewn sky. For Gage's and Henry's sakes, I was glad the clouds didn't appear to threaten rain. I turned toward the woods where I'd seen the men disappear the night before last, wondering if there was a visible trail leading into the trees. My gaze slid toward the left. And what of the summerhouse? I'd yet to visit it. Plucking my ivory shawl from where it lay draped over a chair, I set off to do a bit of exploring.

But I hadn't ventured far before my attention was diverted by the sight of Dr. Barker entering his study. His head was bent over a book he was reading, his attention riveted to the page, for he didn't see me farther along the corridor. Even when I stood just inside the doorway, waiting for him to acknowledge me, he failed to notice me.

His study was much like those of other gentlemen—lined with bookshelves and decorated in deep masculine tones. The walls were papered in a deep green forest print, and the artwork reflected that theme. Heavy leather tomes filled most of the shelves except a glass cabinet of curiosities through which I could see various rocks and natural materials, as well as what appeared to be bones and specimens in jars. While married to Sir Anthony, I'd discovered that many scientific-minded gentlemen possessed such a collection—whether big or small—so this did not surprise me as it might others. A pair of interesting-looking stuffed birds—one with colorful plumage and one without—were displayed on stands on opposite ends of the fireplace mantel. They were species I couldn't identify, making me suspect he'd acquired them during his time in South Africa.

I was still scrutinizing them when he finally looked up and

saw me. "Lady Darby," he gasped, pressing a hand to his chest. His thick cinnamon brown hair stood nearly on end, as usual, adding to his impression of shock. "My apologies. I didn't see you there." He glanced behind him to see what I'd been examining. "Ah, yes. Have you ever seen a button quail?"

"No, I have not," I admitted, advancing into the room to get a closer look. "Are they much like our common quails?"

"Only superficially."

I studied first the bird with the mottled brown coat and then the one with the smoky blue feathers along its head and sides and deep crimson underneath. "Female, male?" I guessed pointing at them each in turn.

Dr. Barker's eyes lit with intellect. "You would think, since male birds most often boast the brighter plumage. But in button quails the opposite is true."

"Really?" I remarked in interest, giving the birds another examination.

He nodded, pushing to his feet. "The males also incubate the eggs and tend to the young, which likely accounts for the variance."

"Because they wouldn't want to attract the attention of predators."

His eyes narrowed on the female button quail. "It's rather fascinating, isn't it, how the natural world can just as easily demonstrate how wrong our perceived notions are of what is proper or improper, male or female, as it can reinforce them? And yet we're all God's creation."

This seemed to be a topic he ruminated on frequently. One that, given my history with characteristically unfeminine pursuits, I couldn't help but also find interesting. But perhaps that's why he'd shared it with me.

He turned his head to look at me, and once again I was overcome by the feeling that we shared a deep understanding of certain things that others did not. It was an affinity I couldn't exactly explain. One that—while I was grappling to comprehend it—Dr. Barker appeared intent to continue to confound me.

"I really must see to Lord Gage," he declared as he gathered up a few items and stuffed them into his black medical bag where it rested on a table beneath one of the windows. "Did he appear more rested this morning?"

"Yes . . ."

"Good, good," he murmured before I could say more. "Then I daresay he should be in better spirits." He snapped his bag shut and hastened toward the door. "Enjoy the sunshine," he offered in closing, leaving me standing in the doorway staring openmouthed after him.

CHAPTER 22

I shook my head in bemusement, for honestly, I didn't know what to make of Dr. Barker. The man had just spoken to me for several minutes about button quails, made a rather insightful comment about the manner in which things were perceived to be masculine and feminine, and then practically run away from me. Were his actions normally so erratic, or was he deliberately avoiding some sort of conversation with me? The previous night at dinner, I'd thought he was giving me permission to ask about his presence in the corridor the night before, but just now when we were alone, he'd rushed off before I could broach it. It baffled me.

But it was a bafflement that apparently others shared, for when I turned to find his wife approaching from the morning room, her lips were creased with a commiserating smile. "Thee would think that with his bein' a surgeon with a wife of his own, Dr. Barker would be quite comfortable conversin' with our fairer sex, but I'm afraid that's not the case." She tipped her head so that I could see her warm brown eyes beneath the wide brim of her bonnet. "Thou should have heard him when he courted me."

Judging from her attire and the basket she carried, she was bound for the garden like I was, so I turned my steps in that direction, assuming she would join me. Though sincerely expressed, her remark somehow smacked of disingenuousness. She might claim he was uneasy speaking with females, but our past interactions did not bear that out to be true.

"Is that why he joined the army?" I asked, curious how far she would carry this excuse. "Because he would be treating men."

"Perhaps partly. But he also needed the position. At that time, he didn't have his full inheritance, and he needed to establish himself somewhere."

And the British military had certainly needed able surgeons at that time. At the Royal Military Hospital outside Plymouth he would have treated wounded soldiers, and even in his position in South Africa his purview would have been mostly men. Though apparently he'd treated at least one woman, if the story about his performing a successful cesarean surgery was true. But I still felt somehow that Mrs. Barker was doing it up much too brown. What I didn't know was whether she was doing this out of a sense of duty as hostess and wife—eager to smooth any tension in the household—or for some ulterior reason.

"You seem to have a keen understanding," I said as we stepped out onto the terrace, intentionally hoping to mislead her. "But you didn't know him while he was still an officer, did you?"

"No, he'd only just resigned his commission."

"Was your first husband a military man?"

"Nathaniel?" Her breath caught slightly as she inhaled. "He was, actually. He fought at Waterloo and a number o' other battles before it."

I nodded, hesitating out of guilt before I asked my next question, for I could sense the pain she still felt talking about him. But perhaps, also the relief? I didn't imagine she was given cause to speak of him very often.

"Did he get mired in the Grange Moor Rising?"

"No," she answered with a breathless laugh. "No, he'd long since been demobilized."

But I didn't ask if he'd been part of the militia, only if he'd become mired in the matter. She paused next to a bed of flowers. Her cheeks were flushed with color. "I'm goin' to cut some flowers to refresh those in the house. His lordship told me how much he favors the dahlias."

He'd said much the same to us the day before, telling us how Gage's mother had grown dahlias in her garden.

"I'll leave you to it, then," I said. "I've been admiring your summerhouse from my bedchamber window since I arrived but haven't yet taken the opportunity to explore it."

She straightened, her mouth opening as if to say something more. I waited for her to speak.

"'Tis a delightful vantage," she murmured, a tight smile on her lips, though I was almost certain that wasn't what she'd intended to say. "The murals on the ceiling were inspired by the stained-glass windows at the church in nearby Campsall." She looked up from pulling on her gardening gloves. "Where Robin Hood allegedly wed Maid Marian."

I remembered Mr. Robinson mentioning such a place. Of course, the connection would be to the merry thief.

I turned away, treading down the narrow trail between the flower beds and out across the lawn beyond. The sky remained choked with clouds, but the wind blew dry, tenderly rippling the grass. As I neared the summerhouse, I could see that the white walls were in need of a fresh coat of paint. Not that the structure was dilapidated in any way. Just worn from the normal pattern of the seasons here in Yorkshire.

I climbed the steps to the door of the hexagonal structure, and then allowed myself to look back toward the house as I'd been itching to do since I'd left the garden behind. However, contrary to expectation, Mrs. Barker was no longer there. If she'd been watching me before, she wasn't now.

Though only several hundred feet from the garden, this structure at the edge of the estate seemed more isolated than it had at first glance. Perhaps it was the gusts of wind, which smothered any sounds farther than a few feet from me, or the overcast skies casting a pall over everything. Regardless of the reason, I suddenly felt exposed, and hastened inside the summerhouse.

The building was empty save for a pair of benches built along two of the walls. It smelled musty inside, so I left the door opened a crack as I crossed toward the seat from which I might have the best view of the house and the woods. The air was very still compared with that outside, and I found myself inhaling a breath deeper than the ones that had come before, trying to shake the uneasiness that had settled over me. My head seemed to naturally wish to tip backward so that my eyes were drawn to the murals above.

If they were based on the windows at the church in Campsall, the interior of that building must be extraordinarily reverent and lovely. It also must be dedicated to Mary Magdalene. Her saintly image was depicted at the center of the mural, complete with becomingly restrained strawberry blond locks. In truth, her portrayal here reminded me a bit of Bree, including her pert nose and bright eyes.

I tilted my head left and right, analyzing each of the figures, studying the techniques and brushstrokes of the artist as best as I could from such a distance. Their talent wasn't exceptional, but it was more than adequate. I wondered what had made them wish to duplicate the Campsall church windows here. Had they felt a particular connection with the subject, or had they purely been interested in the church's connection to the Robin Hood legend? I supposed there was no way to know, but if I knew how faithful they'd been in their recreation it might tell me something.

The skin along my arms began to prickle, and I lowered my gaze, allowing it to trail over the edge of the woods that bordered the property. The leaves on the trees fluttered in the late-morning breeze, the shadows beneath their boughs deep and all but impenetrable to sight because of the gloomy skies—all factors which made it easy for anyone who might be concealed within to hide. Unwilling to sit cowering, I pushed to my feet and exited the summerhouse, closing the door behind me.

To any prying eyes from within the trees or the house, I appeared to be doing nothing more than strolling down the property line, but I remained vigilant. Out of the corner of my eye, I scoured my surroundings for any sign of movement, any hint of a trail leading into the trees. I was rewarded when I came upon a patch of trampled grass. It seemed as though someone might have stood there for some time and then carried on into the woods. Though their path across the lawn toward the house was less obvious.

I continued a few more paces southward before veering off toward the front drive. A chill swept down my neck, but a glimpse behind me proved I was still alone. Clutching my shawl tighter around my shoulders, I lengthened my stride, hoping it was only the breeze playing havoc with my nerves and not some foe I had sensed but could not see.

Gage and Henry returned shortly after nightfall, tired and dusty from their long day of riding, but hale and hearty and untroubled by any highwaymen I'd feared might be waiting to ambush them. As the Barkers and I were already seated at dinner, they merely sent in their regards courtesy of the butler, and their assurance that they'd already eaten and intended to retire for the evening. Knowing Gage would wish to bathe, I did not rush through the remainder of the meal, but I also didn't dawdle in the drawing room after. In truth, I suspected the Barkers were rather glad to escape my company for the rest of the evening.

I entered our bedchamber to find my husband already seated before the hearth, nursing a glass of whisky. He stared into the crackling flames of the fire that had been laid against the sudden chill of the evening. His mouth was tight, and the corners of his eyes seemed to droop with fatigue.

I crossed toward him, lifting my skirts to crawl into his lap rather than sitting in the perfectly acceptable chair adjacent to his. He said nothing but adjusted his posture to accommodate me.

Burrowing into his neck, I inhaled the clean scent of his skin. "I missed you."

I could hear the smile in his voice. "I was gone for less than sixteen hours."

"Still."

He bent his head, pressing his lips to the skin of my forehead just below my hairline. "I hope you had an uneventful day."

"For the most part," I replied. "But what of you?"

He sighed wearily. "I can tell you unequivocally that our trip was a complete and utter waste of time."

I lifted my head to look at him. "Oh, no."

"Oh, yes." His expression was a mixture of jaded discouragement and exasperated frustration. "I appreciate that the duchess was trying to help us, but I almost wish she hadn't."

I cringed. "That bad, huh?"

His brow furrowed. "Lane-Fox is one of the most thoroughly unpleasant and disagreeable men I have ever met. The things he had to say about his wife . . ." He broke off, shaking his head. "Suffice it to say, they are separated, and expected to remain so. And if he treated her in an even remotely similar manner to the way he spoke about her, I do not blame her for leaving him."

"But you don't think he was angry enough to try to get revenge?"

"He claimed she'd slept with so many men that any attempt to defend her honor would be futile. But all of that is secondary to the fact that the man can barely afford the three-person staff who cares for his small cottage, let alone pay for repairs to the burned-out rubble of his manor house, or hire a gang of blackguards to attack my father."

"Then he is not our culprit."

"He is not our culprit," he confirmed. He drained the last finger of his whisky before setting the glass on the table next to his elbow. His head lolled to the side as he turned back to me. "Anderley told me about the letter he intercepted from my father to Lord Sidmouth."

I couldn't help but arch my eyebrows at his use of the word *intercepted*. "Yes, apparently, you knew your valet was light-fingered."

"Anderley has a range of wide and varied talents."

"So I'm discovering," I murmured in good humor.

"But back to the letter." His hand smoothed up and down the silk on my back as he turned to stare into the hearth. "Clearly my father is worried I *have* written or *will* write to Lord Sidmouth for information about something that happened while he was working at Sidmouth's direction. The obvious solution to that is to ask Sidmouth, but he's either in London or at his estate in Devon. And being my father's friend, he's unlikely to share what my father doesn't wish me to know."

"Yes, but what could that be? And how does it connect to his attack?"

Gage's gaze shifted to meet mine.

"That *is* what we're thinking, isn't it? Or else why would your father be so anxious to write to Sidmouth now and reassure himself that all 'pertinent correspondence and records' were destroyed." I frowned, another troubling thought occurring to me. "Unless Lembus was carrying it because your father had dictated it when he was at his gravest."

"And feared he was dying?" Gage finished the thought. "But my father dictated it yesterday. Did you not note the date?"

"Yes, you're right. Then that makes little sense, for your father is recovering well." I plucked a piece of lint from the lapel of his dressing gown. "Then how do the contents of the letter connect with his attack?"

His jaw hardened. "My father knows."

And yet he'd not shared it with us. Why? There had to be a reason.

My eyes drifted idly over my husband's profile as I ruminated on this. "Darling, what do you know of your father's life after the war? What did he do with himself?"

"He sold his commission about six months after Waterloo and settled down with all the money he earned from the war prizes his ships captured during the conflict."

"Yes, but how did he become a gentleman inquiry agent?" I pressed a hand to his chest over his heart, recognizing what I said next would pain him. "I know you said he sort of stumbled into it after he investigated your mother's death. But how did he go from that to conducting investigations on behalf of royalty and the highest members of nobility?" I'd always assumed I knew most of the specifics of my father-in-law's history as an inquiry agent, but since arriving here in Wentbridge, I'd begun to suspect I was wrong. That there were far larger holes in his story than I, and perhaps even his son, had realized.

A deep vee formed between Gage's brows. "I'm not sure. I

was still at Cambridge, and then away on my Grand Tour. My father and I had never had much of a relationship, and after Mother's death I wanted little to do with him, even though his now being home in England would have actually made it possible. We corresponded when necessary, and I saw him at holidays, of course, as obligated, but that was essentially it."

My heart ached at hearing this, for I'd known that his mother's passing, and the discovery that she'd been slowly poisoned to death by her longtime maid, had devastated him. His mother's relatives—whom he should have been able to rely on—had been all but estranged from him at that time, and he'd barely spoken to his father's family. This left Gage effectively alone.

"Oh, Sebastian," I whispered brokenly, wrapping my arms around his neck and pressing my forehead to his cheek.

Thank heavens Anderley had happened upon him not long after and saved him from a group of street thieves, attaching himself to him as a sort of boy-of-all-work trained up to be his valet. I felt an even greater pulse of affection for the rascal now, suspecting he had saved Gage as much, if not more, than Gage had saved him. And thank heavens Gage had befriended my future brother-in-law, Philip Matheson, who was soon to be the Earl of Cromarty, and Michael Dalmay. Both men were honorable and true, and just the sort of people Gage would have needed most.

Gage embraced me quickly with one arm before he continued. "So I don't have any idea precisely how my father went from retired naval captain and acquaintance of the then regent's brother to trusted adviser to the current sovereign and most sought-after gentleman inquiry agent in all of Britain."

I sat back so that I could see him. "He's never spoken to you about it?"

He shook his head. "All he's ever said is that to become powerful one must be useful. He's always tried to hammer that into my skull."

I bit my lower lip, contemplating everything we'd learned up until this point. "It seems to me that whatever he was doing during that missing time has to do with Lord Sidmouth. And since he was home secretary for much of that time, then it stands to reason it has to do with the Home Office."

"That does seem logical. A political affiliation with Sidmouth would have gained him entry into levels of society he'd previously been unable to touch." His face contorted into a wry scowl. "Unless one was a duchess charmed into a dalliance by a war hero."

Given all the things I'd heard about Lord Gage's renowned good looks—good looks he still retained—and the evidence of his sons' attractiveness, it was not difficult to imagine what had drawn the Duchess of Bowmont to him, regardless of his rank. *Golden like an angel, but with the devil in his eyes* was I believe how someone had phrased it. That sort of gentleman always fascinated women like the duchess.

Though I was one to talk. Gage had fascinated me as well, even though I had been loath to admit it at first.

I brushed the twist of golden curls that was so prone to fall across his forehead back from his eyes. "Then the quandary is, what did your father do for the Home Office that he doesn't wish us—or anyone—to know about?"

It was an interesting conundrum. It had to be scandalous, perhaps even disgraceful. Something that would reflect poorly on him if it was revealed. What work for the Home Office would fit those parameters?

"There were rumors," Gage began slowly, his expression troubled. "Rumors that the government sent agents to infiltrate some of the radical societies and sects sprouting up across the country."

"Spies?"

He nodded. "That they didn't just report on their activities, but in some instances provoked their actions."

"Do you think the rumors were true?" I asked in a hushed voice as a dawning realization began inside me.

"I don't know. But at least one fellow, a man named William Oliver, was exposed as a government spy some years back, following the Pentrich Rising, and there was a general reaction of public disgust. It happened even before Grange Moor, and it was revealed in the press that Sidmouth was the one to sanction Oliver."

"Then . . ." I hesitated to speak the words. "You think your father could have been a government spy as well?"

"That or the man tasked with organizing them. But if he was somehow involved with the Grange Moor Rising, it might explain why we keep encountering that event."

"So he was recognized at the Blue Bell by someone who had been at Grange Moor. Someone like Tom Hutchinson. And that's why he was attacked. In retribution."

"If he *was* at Grange Moor, he wouldn't have presented himself as Stephen Gage, former Royal Navy captain and son of a baronet. He would have adopted a humbler identity."

We both fell silent as the ramifications of this being the answer to our riddle settled over us. If true, it would explain why Lord Gage didn't want it revealed. Spying was considered a shameful act, certainly not something a gentleman participated in, and certainly not among his own countrymen. It would also explain any hold he might have over Lord Sidmouth, for he undoubtedly knew things the other would not wish revealed. I could easily imagine Lord Gage making the step from agent of the Home Office to private inquiry agent should one of Sidmouth's high-placed friends have required some delicate assistance. From there his repute must have only grown. And yet he still had this dishonorable undertaking in his past he would have to keep concealed or else his character would be tattered to shreds.

"We have no proof," I said. "At this point, it's nothing but speculation. *Educated* speculation. But speculation all the same." I turned to search his features, finding them conflicted. "If we ask your father about it, he'll only deny it."

"And castigate us for reading his mail," Gage added dully.

I was at a loss as to how to proceed. We could write to Sidmouth, but it would take days to receive a response, *if* he would even provide us one, given his presumed loyalty to Lord Gage. We *might* be able to get answers from Tom Hutchinson and his crew—presuming they were the culprits behind the attack—but we had to find them first, and Constable Robinson had the best chance of doing that. So what was our next best step forward?

Gage suddenly grimaced and lowered his head, rubbing his temples in circles with the thumb and middle finger of his right hand.

"Here, allow me," I said, brushing his hand aside.

He willingly submitted, allowing his head to fall back against the chair.

"You are spent," I told him in concern. I dropped my hands to his jaw and then his shoulders, feeling the tension he was carrying there. "I know none of this has been easy for you."

He blinked open his bleary eyes as I kneaded his shoulders and upper arms, but he didn't speak.

Ceasing my ministrations, I cupped his jaw gently. He was driving himself to utter exhaustion, and I feared if he did not take care he might collapse.

"Tomorrow we are all taking a respite," I declared with finality. "We need some time to reassess the situation anyway." I glanced about me. "Somewhere where we won't be overheard through walls or windows. And I think I know just the place." I shifted, lowering my feet. "But first, to bed with you. Though . . . I would prefer not to have to call for Bree." I turned my back toward him. "So will you unfasten these buttons." I peered over my shoulder at him, unable to keep the flirtation from my voice. "And then . . . to bed."

He stared back at me through half-lidded eyes. "As you command."

CHAPTER 23

The village of Campsall stood just five miles to the south-east. However, we took a leisurely route there, pausing to view the slopes of Brockadale covered with purple flowers and follow the winding course of the River Went for a short distance. Emma took well to the adventure, trying to capture the butterflies and lulled to sleep by the gurgling sound of the river. Henry, Bree, and Mrs. Mackay also seemed to be enjoying themselves, though I was sorry we'd had to leave Anderley behind to keep watch over Lord Gage. But Bree gathered bellflowers for him into a bouquet and Mrs. Mackay filled an empty flask in the river so that he could taste the crispness of the water if he wished. I had to smile at their kind and rather whimsical endeavor to include him in the day.

For Gage's part, he appeared to breathe easier as the day went on. His shoulders lowered from the vicinity they'd taken up by his ears, and his chest seemed to rise to its normal posture.

The taut smiles he wore in the morning transformed to genuine laughter by early afternoon when we reached Campsall.

We drew our carriage and Gage's and Henry's horses to a stop near the church of St. Mary Magdalene, a massive Norman church whose stone edifice revealed its age. While the others clambered out to view the building, I settled down to nurse Emma. Once she was satisfied, we joined them. Tall trees surrounded the church, trying and failing to compete with the height of the west tower, providing cool shade to the lush grass and gravestones covering the churchyard.

Gage exited as I was approaching, a broad grin on his face as he reached for Emma. "You and I shall explore out here," he told her. "So your mother can indulge to her heart's content in studying the artwork and sculptures inside."

"You know me too well," I conceded with a light laugh.

He pressed a kiss to my cheek before striding off under the trees, chattering amiably to our daughter.

I paused before entering, examining the doorway with its eight slim columns—four to each side—fashioned stone arches, and wooden door with intricate tracery. Stepping inside there was more beautifully carved wood and etched stone—some of which was in desperate need of restoration. The scent of the passage of centuries surrounded me—of dust and cold stone, of long-extinguished candles and the prayers of thousands still lingering in the air above us. I steadily made my way down the aisle, attempting to take in everything from the vaulted ceiling to the flagstone floor. I noticed abstractly that Henry was engaged in conversation with the rector near the stone baptismal font, and that Mrs. Mackay and Bree were investigating some of the memorials built into the far wall, but most of my attention was riveted to the architecture.

There was much to see—from the lovingly carved alter and rood screen to the sculpted stone capitals and corbels to the soaring stained-glass windows. I was soon absorbed in my study of them to the exclusion of all else. Including the presence of another person lurking in the shadows of the south transept.

I was kneeling at the rail, leaning forward to see the five figures whittled into the wood around the base of a secondary altar, when I heard footsteps shift against the stone floor behind me.

"Don't move," someone ordered me in a low voice barely louder than a whisper.

I lifted my head and froze, my gaze seemingly transfixed on the altar crucifix, though I was really trying to see the figure who stood just over my right shoulder out of the corner of my eye. He was male, that much was certain, and not small in stature, but I couldn't tell anything more than that. I tried to hear where the others now stood in relation to me, but I couldn't detect the sound of any voices. For all I knew, they might have left the building some time ago.

"And don't try to alert the others to my presence," the figure said, as if reading my thoughts. He was now closer, just behind me, and my heart kicked in my chest, uncertain what the man intended.

"I don't want to hurt you or any of the people outside waiting for you, and I give you my word that I won't, as long as you do as I say."

I swallowed, nodding my head tentatively. What else could I do? He had me at a disadvantage.

"Rise to your feet."

I did so slowly, keeping my eyes fixed forward. Now I could clearly appreciate his superior height towering over me, and while he never touched me, I could sense his strength.

"You shouldn't have come here."

I tried to speak and failed, having to stop and clear my throat before attempting it again. "Why not?"

"Because now I must stay away. It has always been a place of solitude for me, but it will now no longer be safe for me here."

I knew then who stood behind me, and my head jerked to the side in a vain attempt to glimpse the man currently masquerading as Robin Hood. However, the wide brim of my bonnet prevented me from seeing anything more than a portion of his woolen hood. Now I understood why he'd forced me to stand.

"I would have thought this church would have proven unsafe for you long before today, given it's the place where you are rumored to have married Maid Marian," I remarked dryly, letting him know I had understood his cryptic comment.

"Nay, I've never wed. Though my namesake is rumored to have built this chapel."

I didn't dispute this argument, figuring he was referring to contradictory accounts of the Robin Hood legend. In any case, it didn't matter whether Robin Hood sponsored the construction of this church or wed his ladylove inside it. Knowing those facts was not going to help me out of my current predicament.

"What do you want from me?" I demanded, the hairs across my body standing on end, alert to any indication of movement from him.

"To warn you that you're looking in the wrong place."

"Is that right? Then you're going to tell me you and your band of merry men didn't attack my father-in-law or murder his footman?"

"We didn't." He paused, and the air thickened inside my lungs as I felt the brush of his cloak against my back as he moved half a step nearer. "But you already know that."

The pitch of his voice sounded unnatural—rough and gravelly. The type some stage villain might use. In annoyance, I tipped my head backward to look up at the three-light stained-glass window above with Mary Magdalene at the center—the same image duplicated on the ceiling of the summerhouse at the Barkers' residence. I hoped the feathers decorating the crown of my bonnet would smack Robin Hood in his face.

He chuckled, as if amused rather than irritated by this ploy, but he did retreat that half step he'd just taken.

"Then who attacked Lord Gage's carriage?" I challenged.

"That I do not know. Not for sure."

I huffed in aggravation.

"But there are members of the community who are trying to help. I . . . asked them to." He seemed almost hesitant to admit it. "They should be able to tell you more."

There was a faint click in the distance, and he paused. Both of us strained to hear. Had it been a door opening? Or perhaps simply the sound of the building settling? Whatever the case, he crowded closer again, his words taking on new urgency.

"My men and I only meant to do good. We never intended any harm. But harm has been done in our image all the same. So we intend to retire from the field. But only after doing all we can to make right the wrong that has been done."

"How?" I asked, growing impatient.

"Start with Robert Butler. He has information for you."

Considering that we'd already intended to speak to him again and had in fact already tried, this was not a great deal of assistance. "What information?"

But even as I spoke, I realized he was no longer standing behind me. Whirling around, I searched the transept, trying to figure out where in heaven he'd gone. I looked behind a table and lifted aside a tapestry before stepping out into the nave. I gave a little shriek at the sight of Gage striding toward me. I pressed a hand to my pounding heart, and he smiled.

He grinned in return. "Did I startle you?" His lifted his eyes to search the architecture around us. "What were you absorbed in studying this time?"

"No," I gasped. "Robin Hood." I felt a bit ridiculous using the name, but what else could I call him? "He was just here."

Gage's entire demeanor changed, shifting to alertness. "Where?"

I pointed toward the south transept. "He snuck up behind me. But he must have heard you coming."

He inspected me. "Are you injured?"

"No. No, he didn't harm me. He only talked."

There was a world of questions in his gaze, but he didn't ask them. Not then. "He must have slipped out through one of the side doors." He grasped my elbow, hustling me down the aisle even as he craned his neck to peer between the arcades. "I'll have Henry and Joe help me search while you join the others near the carriage."

The man in question was likely long gone, but I didn't argue, knowing it would do no good. A blanket had been spread out beneath the branches of one of the tall beech trees, and Bree sat playing with Emma while Mrs. Mackay stood watching indulgently. They looked to me in concern when Gage suddenly barked at Henry to accompany him.

"Robin Hood was inside," I explained, trusting they would understand what I meant.

Bree's head snapped around to look toward the church, causing the ragdoll she'd been tossing upward for Emma's amusement to sail to the opposite side of the blanket. "But no' his merry men?"

I leaned over to collect the toy. "Not that I saw."

We waited quietly for the men to return, which they did in relatively short order.

"What did he say?" Gage asked without preamble, propping his foot on a random stone nearby—likely a piece of rubble from some of the church's crumbling features.

"That we were looking in the wrong place." I inhaled past the knot of anxiety that had lodged in my chest. "That he and his men were not responsible, and we should speak with Robert Butler again. That he would have further information for us."

Gage scowled. "That's it?"

"Perhaps he meant to say more, but I believe he heard you coming."

He turned to the side, battling his rising frustration. So much for our respite. The tension that had slid gradually from his shoulders all day had retaken residence throughout his frame. "Then maybe we should return so we can venture forth to do that."

The others didn't quibble about our cutting short our holiday. But I could tell by the glint in Bree's eyes that she had something to ask me, though she waited until we were on the road driving north out of Campsall.

"What did he look like?" she finally burst forth with.

I shared a look with Mrs. Mackay, who was seated across from us holding Emma. Gage and Henry were in front of us on horseback.

"He snuck up behind me and wouldn't allow me to turn around, so all I could tell was that he was tall and strong." I frowned, thinking of the other things he had either intentionally or unintentionally revealed. "He also pitched his voice in a lower register than normal. Maybe because he feared I would recognize him?"

"That would explain why he didna want ye to look at him," Mrs. Mackay concurred.

I sank back, latching on to the idea as I peered out the window at the passing countryside. "His tone was crisp and clear, and he didn't use any cant."

"So someone from polite society," Bree summarized.

"And he spoke of his gang of fellow robbers as his men and talked about retiring from the field."

"Haven't you been speculatin' for some time that both sets o' highwaymen must have been part o' the military at one point?"

"Yes, and he spoke of them rather possessively. *His men,*" I reiterated. "Maybe that was part of his Robin Hood persona, but maybe not."

My mind conjured the outriders Butler had sent to accompany us home to the Barkers', and how well they'd acquitted themselves on horseback. I also remembered them telling us they could make their way back to Skelbrooke without trouble using the back trails. Back trails that Robin Hood and his men would have used to ambush carriages and escape without being caught.

I stifled a curse. Butler *was* Robin Hood. I would have staked my reputation as an investigator on it, though I didn't have definitive proof, and he would, of course, deny it. *Start with Butler. He has information for you.* Of course he did. Because he *was* Butler.

So why hadn't he sought us out himself? Why these games? Or had we forced his hand, nearly catching him out at Campsall? Maybe he'd been retrieving ill-gotten loot or destroying evidence.

Whatever the case, he'd distracted us long enough to get away with it. Now the only question that remained was whether he actually had pertinent information to share, or if it was all a diversion. And the only way to find that out was to ask him.

I exhaled through my nostrils, disliking the feeling of being manipulated. As well as the idea that I might have been wrong about Butler, and Gage was right.

By the time we returned to Bowcliffe House, Emma had long since fallen asleep. Some miles earlier I'd had Mrs. Mackay pass her to me in order to give her arms a rest. Plus, I enjoyed the feel of my sweet infant daughter slumbering in my arms. As long as it wasn't the middle of the night.

Having begun to doze myself, I opened my eyes as we rounded the carriage yard, catching sight of Anderley standing just outside the door. Gage had leapt from his horse to confer with him, and Henry was following suit. I could tell from their postures that something was wrong. When all three men hurried inside, I leaned forward to pass Emma back to Mrs. Mackay.

The carriage stopped, and I waited impatiently for the footman to lower the step before disembarking and following them, almost tripping over my skirts in my haste. I paused inside the entrance, looking to the butler for guidance.

"His lordship. I believe he's taken a turn for the worse," he pronounced, but I was already on my way up the stairs, having heard anxious voices coming from above.

I stumbled past a wide-eyed Mrs. Barker into Lord Gage's chamber to find Gage kneeling on one side of the bed, demanding answers from Dr. Barker, who was ministering to Lord Gage on the other side. Lembus stood in the corner, cradling a bowl from which the foul odor of vomit must be emanating, while Henry and Anderley hovered in the background. Meanwhile, my father-in-law lay in the middle of the bed looking ghastly pale and sweating.

"I am doing all I can," Dr. Barker was telling Gage. "He has finished purging, and now we must get his heart palpitations under control."

At the mention of purging, my gaze darted around the room, searching for a food tray. For surely Dr. Barker hadn't purposely induced vomiting. But whatever Lord Gage had most recently eaten, it had since been whisked away.

"Why . . . are all these people . . . in my room?" Lord Gage gasped.

"We're all concerned, Father," Gage replied, clasping one of his hands between his own. "When did this . . ."

"I don't care . . ." Lord Gage interrupted, raising his voice and trying to push to a sitting position despite Dr. Barker's and his son's protests. "If I'm standing . . . at death's door. I don't want *him* here." He pulled his hand from Gage's grasp to flip it at Henry. "Or your manservant. Or your *wife*. Good God, woman, can't you ever recognize your place!"

Gage voiced his objection to his father's offensive words, but Dr. Barker merely cast us a look of pleading. Realizing that my presence was not making anything better, I backed out of the room, followed by Anderley and Henry. I glanced about to ask Mrs. Barker a question, but she had since disappeared, perhaps into her sitting room.

Leading them a short distance down the corridor, I turned to Anderley. "What happened?"

"About a quarter hour before your return, his lordship became violently ill."

"From something he ate?"

"Maybe. But Dr. Barker seems more concerned it's from an injury to his organs inside. One he can't see." His brow was etched with deep furrows. "He said those can be the most dangerous injuries because a person often doesn't know they have them until it's too late."

I did not want to consider that possibility, or what it meant for my father-in-law's future.

Henry was looking back over his shoulder toward Lord Gage's doorway. His hands were clenched at his sides, and I could all too easily guess at the direction of his thoughts.

"Stay here," I directed Anderley. "Find out from Lembus when and what Lord Gage last ate. Then see if you can locate it in the kitchen."

Henry turned to me in surprise while Anderley's dark eyes expressed his skepticism.

"You think Dr. Barker is wrong?"

"I think it's best to gather as much information as we can, and not to rush to any conclusions. We need to be certain his food wasn't tampered with."

Given recent events at Barbreck, when Bree was nearly poisoned to death from eating tainted chutney, I trusted Anderley would take my orders seriously.

Before Henry could melt away as I could tell he wanted to, I threaded my arm through his and dragged him down the corridor toward Gage's bedchamber. It was inappropriate to enter the room alone with him and would spark salacious speculation among the Barkers' staff if we were seen, but in that moment I was beyond caring.

Henry stared at me guardedly when I turned to face him, leaning back against the closed door. I knew I was overstepping, but what I was about to say still needed to be said.

"What will you do if Lord Gage dies?"

His silvery gray eyes blinked back at me, but he did not answer.

I pushed away from the door. "What will you do if your natural father dies without accepting you, without speaking to you?"

He opened his mouth, but no sound emerged, either because he'd stopped himself from replying or because he didn't know what to say.

"I'm not asking this to be cruel, but when you set out on this journey with us, you must have recognized it was a possibility." I stopped a foot from him, my heart aching for the pain I knew he was masking behind his blank expression.

"Yes. Yes, I knew it was a possibility." His Adam's apple moved up and down as he worked to swallow. "I just hoped . . ." He shrugged one shoulder futilely.

I turned to look at the wall, searching for the right words. "Henry, I don't know why Lord Gage is the way he is. Why he rejects you, and treats Sebastian so poorly, and disdains me. Heaven knows, I've asked myself enough times." I offered him a commiserating smile. "I suspect it's partly to do with something in his past, though I doubt we'll ever know what. But I also think it's simply something inside him. I don't know if he has the capacity within him to be different." I lifted my hand to grasp his elbow. "So if you're searching for something from him, if *any* of us are searching for something from him . . ." I shook my head. "He just may not be capable of giving it to us."

Henry's shoulders drooped and he closed his eyes. He nodded.

Tears burned the back of my eyes. "I know it's not all you hoped for, but Gage and I are tremendously fond of you." I dashed away a tear. "And our lives would be the worst for not having you in them."

"Come now, Kiera. None of that," he mumbled, despite the fact his own eyes looked suspiciously moist. He pulled me into his embrace, and I rested my head against his shoulder, both giving and receiving comfort.

That was how Gage found us a moment later, his face fixed in a rigid scowl. "No weeping. The blighter's not dead yet."

CHAPTER 24

I didn't bother to correct Gage about the reason for our tears. In any case, I knew he didn't mean what he'd said. He was simply trying to shroud his own fear and grief with anger. He was rather like his father in that regard.

I stepped back from Henry, swiping the remaining tears from the corners of my eyes. "Was Dr. Barker able to steady his pulse?"

"Yes, though he says it's still too rapid for his liking." He pulled his riding gloves from where they draped out of his coat pocket and threw them down onto the bed.

"That's only to be expected," I tried to reassure him. "After all, he lost a lot of blood two weeks ago, and his body is still compensating for that loss. Add to that his gastric distress, and his pulse is bound to be quicker than normal."

Gage nodded distractedly, his hands planted on his hips. I wasn't certain he was even listening to me until his head perked up and he turned it to look at me. "Anderley said you wanted him to find out what my father last ate and examine it if possible. Do you suspect poison?"

"I don't suspect anything. Not yet. But . . ." I moved toward the window, crossing my arms over my chest as I tried to put my misgivings into words. "I can't help but find the timing suspicious." I squinted at Gage before continuing my scrutiny of the drive below. "We've been here for nearly a week, but your father doesn't suddenly fall ill until the day most of us happen to be away from the cottage?" I allowed my cynicism to show. "That must give you both pause."

Gage exchanged a look with his brother. "It does. And I also can't help but note that our Robin Hood conveniently places himself in a different location—five miles away—when it happens. Yet his men could be anywhere." His eyebrows arched as if he expected me to dispute him.

"That's true," I acceded. "And it very well might have been a ploy." I couldn't deny that I'd already wondered why Robin Hood had confronted me at all. He'd not had anything of note to tell me. Unless he believed we'd given up on paying another call on Butler. It had been two days since our last attempt. "But I also firmly believe Tom Hutchinson and Haigh—the man with two different-colored eyes—are involved, and I don't see them fitting with the rest of Robin Hood's gang."

"We haven't met the rest of Robin Hood's gang yet," Gage countered, and then relented somewhat grudgingly. "But I understand what you mean."

His reluctance not to see Robin Hood and his gang as the villains made me wonder if he also suspected Butler of being the man masquerading as the myth. Or perhaps he merely saw too much of our uneasy ally, Bonnie Brock Kincaid, in the figure. After all, Bonnie Brock was the head of one of Edinburgh's largest criminal gangs, and the lower denizens of the city often equated him with Robin Hood. He and Gage had a contentious relationship—one that I had long suspected would have resulted in serious injury or death for one or both of them if I hadn't been standing between them. However, I kept these thoughts to myself, knowing my husband would not welcome them.

"Whatever the case," he declared, "until the culprits are apprehended, I don't want my father left alone. Someone being on the property at all times may not have proven to be enough of a deterrent. So one of us will be posted to my father's room at all hours of the day and night—be it Lembus, Anderley, or one of the three of us." He looked to us both in turn, his bravado unequal at the moment to masking his fear. "I don't trust anyone else to have my father's best interests at heart."

I also privately intended to have a word with Mrs. Mackay and Bree, to ask them to be extra vigilant with Emma. No threats had been made toward our daughter, and there was no real indication she was in any danger, but it would reassure me to know they were alert to the potential for it and taking additional precautions.

I noticed then the strain on Henry's face and realized he must be anticipating the verbal abuse his natural father would likely heap on him. Gage seemed to recognize this at almost the same time, for he reached out to clasp his brother on the shoulder.

"Are you equal to the task? If not, there is no shame in it. The man has treated you unconscionably. I would not blame you if you washed your hands of him."

He swallowed and gave a little nod. "I'm willing."

Gage searched his features, either expecting more or because he was uncertain whether to believe him, but that was all Henry said. He nodded in return. "But if he becomes too much, take up your post outside his door. You'll be able to monitor who comes and goes, and the items brought to him, just as easily from that position." He swiveled his head to look at me. "The same goes for you."

"Yes, I'll be certain to mind my place," I quipped wryly.

Gage winced. "I should apologize for my father . . ."

I held up my hand to halt his words. "No, you shouldn't. His words are his own." I moved closer, gentling my voice. "And if I'm being generous, I know he must have been hurting and scared. So he lashed out at his easiest and most familiar targets. But none of that is your fault. You must know that as well as I."

He blinked down at me, and I could see that he was perilously close to cracking under all of the strain.

"Henry, would you mind checking with Anderley?" I asked, without removing my eyes from my husband.

"Of course," he murmured, and a moment later I heard the door open and close.

I wrapped my arms around Gage, resting my head against his heart as his own arms lifted to embrace me. For a moment he squeezed me so tight, I felt I might need to protest, but his grip loosened before it became necessary. "It will be well, and it *will* be well," I crooned, trying to comfort him. "You'll see."

His only response was the rise and fall of his chest and the steady beat of his heart against my ear.

The weather the following day wasn't precisely auspicious, but we set out for Skelbrooke Hall through the driving rain as early as Emma's feeding schedule allowed. Gage even forwent the bacon, sausage, and black pudding he'd enjoyed for breakfast the previous mornings in our haste to find answers. Or perhaps he'd lost his appetite for the food from the Barkers' kitchens since Anderley had been unable to recover the remnants of the beef consommé and stewed vegetables Lord Gage had last eaten before he'd cast up his accounts, even among the rubbish. It might have been irrelevant, but without examining the food, we couldn't dismiss the suspicion it had been tainted.

For this visit, we elected to take Anderley with us as well, leaving Henry behind to mind the others. We offered the valet a seat inside the conveyance, but he insisted on sitting up on the box with the coachman, a rifle covered in a blanket propped between his legs no doubt. Truth be told, I didn't know whether to feel comforted or unnerved by his watchfulness. Did they truly expect trouble today of all days, in the blustery rain? I was afraid to ask Gage.

Having been at Skelbrooke Hall before, and now suspicious about who Butler was, I knew better what to look for and this time was not so easily fooled. The gatehouse was not as deserted as it seemed. Though no one came out to question our arrival, I caught a glimpse of someone peering at us through a window—the light of their lantern giving them away. Just as I caught fleeting glimpses of men positioned among the dripping trees like sentries as we traveled down the long, narrow drive leading to the house. Should they wish it, an ambush of our coach could have been easily accomplished, for there was no room to turn around and little space to even swing a sword or lift a rifle to defend ourselves. But no attack occurred.

Butler was once again waiting for us as we rounded the drive, but this time I wasn't surprised. I'd already deduced how he was being alerted to the arrival of guests, and it involved the strategic angle of mirrors, like the one hanging in his drawing room. Holding an umbrella aloft, he hurried down the steps to open our carriage door as we drew to a stop.

"Mr. and Mrs. Gage, I understand you've been looking for me," he said as he took hold of my hand to help me out of the coach. "Come inside out of the damp and we shall have a long chat."

Considering the fact that was exactly the reason we'd come, neither Gage nor I ventured a comment. The rain was falling now in earnest, and Butler drew my arm through his and swept me into the house. A more appropriate-looking butler held the door for us and then took the umbrella and our hats and coats. It all happened so quickly and efficiently that before I knew it, I was seated on the same Hepplewhite sofa I'd inhabited during our last visit with a warm cup of tea cradled in my hands.

I found my gaze drawn to our host, evaluating his appearance for any indication my suspicions were correct, analyzing the timbre of his voice to discover if it might match, though Robin Hood had attempted to disguise it. His height and physique were about right, but I'd been given no real glimpse of the fellow's features. Even so, I thought I detected a glint of amusement at my intent scrutiny in his green eyes. Although, to be fair, he seemed to enjoy moments of personal amusement often.

"Given how dreary the weather is, you must have something important, indeed, to speak to me about," he said.

"I've been making inquiries about you, Mr. Butler," Gage declared, after taking a sip of his tea and setting it aside.

I turned to my husband in surprise, but our host looked thoroughly unconcerned.

"Have you?"

"You were a cavalry officer. You served for many years with distinction."

I could easily see this. Despite his informal appearance and the almost careless manner in which he wore his clothes, the relaxed way in which he presented himself was almost too calculated, and his bearing was still flawlessly correct.

"And when you sold your commission," Gage continued, "word is that a number of subalterns and former soldiers in your company entered your employ."

His merry men?

Butler sat back, arching his eyebrows in studied unconcern. "They served me well in the field, so I knew they would serve me well here. You can hardly fault me for wishing to employ trustworthy men."

We couldn't argue with that. It even spoke well of him, given the difficulty returning soldiers had in finding work during the lean decade or more following the wars with France. However, Butler didn't seem old enough to have commanded a company of soldiers during the Napoleonic conflict. He must have served somewhere farther afield, perhaps in India or South Africa.

"Are you and Dr. Barker acquainted?" I asked, suddenly curious if the two men had a connection.

"Only vaguely." He tilted his head to the side. "We did not serve together, if that's what you're asking. Though, I am aware of his . . . reputation."

What that meant I didn't know, and Gage seemed uninterested.

"I imagine having trustworthy former soldiers in your employ comes in handy," he remarked a trifle waspishly.

"Yes." He cast us both a knowing look. "As I'm sure does your own staff."

Handy didn't even begin to describe our staff. Anderley; Bree; Mrs. Mackay; Joe the coachman; Jeffers, our butler; and many of the others were indispensable. But just how indispensable *he* was implying them to be was unclear. Though he'd made his point. Or perhaps made ours.

"This *cannot* be what you've come to speak to me about," he leaned forward to say, revealing his impatience. "But even if it is, *I* have far more important things to share with you."

"We know you were at the political meeting at the Blue Bell four nights past," Gage stated before Butler could say more.

This appeared to take the wind out of his sails. At least slightly. "Yes, I was there," he admitted. "And yes, for all intents and purposes, the meeting was political in nature, despite its being described as a 'union society.' But the vast majority of the members are peaceful. Their central aims are merely better representation in government to listen to their needs and grievances and continuing to expand the franchise to more men."

"And do these peaceable members include Haigh?" Gage pressed.

Butler sat back again, struggling to stifle his aggravation at Gage's antagonistic behavior. "He is one of the reasons in particular I attended that meeting some nights past. I'd seen a fellow with two different-colored eyes there before, but we'd never been introduced." His gaze shifted to me, perhaps sensing an ally. "I know what you're thinking, and you would be correct. I believe Haigh is one of the men who attacked Lord Gage and killed his footman. Haigh and a few other men, likely Hutchinson, Wood, and Jackson."

I shared a look of anticipation with Gage, for this was the first we'd heard the last two names.

"And I'm not the only one who suspects it," Butler added. "A number of the members are furious with them. There's been a lot of private discussion about what should be done."

"Seems straightforward to me," Gage quipped dryly.

Butler's lips quirked upward at one corner. "You would think. But all four men have gone into hiding, and no one seems to know precisely where. Obviously, they realized the tide was turning against them."

"But I still don't understand *why*?" I interjected. "Why did they attack Lord Gage?" I looked Butler directly in the eye. "I take it you don't believe Hutchinson and his crew are the same highwaymen who have been robbing carriages along the Great North Road and emulating Robin Hood?"

His green eyes didn't waver for even a fraction of a second. "I know they're not."

"How do you know?"

Amusement flickered again in his eyes. "I can't tell you that. But let's just say, I'm acquainted with someone who's acquainted with the crew."

Of course, he was. They were *his* men.

"But as to why," he hastened to say before we could argue, "I believe it's retribution for something that happened many years ago."

"At Grange Moor?"

His head reared back slightly, and he assessed me with new eyes. "It sounds like you already know more than I realized."

"Maybe." I glanced at Gage, whose tight features communicated his growing impatience. "But tell us anyway." Everything we thought we knew was mostly inference and speculation. And those inferences and speculations were not something we wanted to repeat to an outsider.

He nodded slowly, seeming to construe some of this from our silent communication. "You may already know Hutchinson took part in the Grange Moor Rising. He was even arrested, though later released. What you might not know was that three of his brothers also took part."

My eyes widened. "What happened to them?"

"Two were transported to Van Diemen's Land and, from what I understand, chose to remain there. The third was injured attempting to flee and later died from his injuries."

My gaze locked with Gage's as he asked, "How was he injured?"

"Shot in the right thigh."

That's why Lord Gage had been shot in the leg and not "his black heart." Hutchinson had most likely been the shooter, and he had been avenging his brother.

"But why do they blame my father?" Gage asked. His face was a mask of stunned incredulity, making me realize that despite all our rampant conjecture, he'd still not wanted to believe it. "Did he think my father shot him?"

"Probably not. I gather it was one of the militiamen called in to round them up, though they were supposed to do so peacefully."

"Then . . . ?"

Butler leaned forward, propping his elbows on his knees. "Hutchinson and at least one of the other men—Wood or Jackson—claim that Lord Gage was an informant for the Home Office." His lips pressed together, plainly aware this was not easy to hear. "Worse, they claim he instigated the march from Monk Bretton, that he stirred them up to join the contingents from Barnsley and Dodworth marching out to Grange Moor. Stirred them up to rout them out. Something it's doubtful they can prove. The three contingents were clearly affiliated and had all been part of the planning for the larger Huddersfield uprising which they were supposed to be joining. Grange Moor was merely the meeting place. But that's the justification they're using."

Gage stared blankly at the rug before him. I wanted to reach for his hand, but he seemed locked inside himself, and I suspected he would not wish for such a gesture of empathy at the moment.

"Then they must claim that when they saw Lord Gage at the Blue Bell they recognized him. Or perhaps they'd already known who he was for some time." After all, my father-in-law wasn't exactly an inconspicuous figure. Caricatures and illustrations of him had graced the pages of any number of newspapers and gossip sheets over the years. "So all they needed to do was recognize his name. Whatever the case, they saw their chance for revenge and took it."

"But this is just ludicrous!" Gage exclaimed, pushing to his feet. "My father, an informant? A spy?" he turned to demand. "I've never heard anything so ridiculous in all my life."

Except it wasn't. And he knew it. We'd just ruminated on

the possibility two nights prior. But hushed speculation in the dark of night was not the same as facing such unsettling allegations in the stark light of day. Particularly in front of a stranger.

"Darling, please," I urged. "Come sit down. True or not, in this instance, it doesn't matter. All that matters is what Hutchinson and his conspirators believed, because it explains why they waylaid your father's carriage and tried to kill him. We already know their shooting Gregory probably wasn't intentional."

Gage reluctantly resumed his seat next to me, and I grasped his upper arm between my hands, anxious to offer him some reassurance. "Except Father didn't die from his wound," he stated bluntly.

I looked up at him, realizing what he was saying. Did that mean they would try again? Was that what yesterday's relapse had been about?

I turned to Butler, who had been quietly observing us. "You said no one knows where Hutchinson and the others are hiding?"

"So they say." He straightened. "But if anyone knows, it's Fryston at the Blue Bell." His eyes narrowed. "I would exert some pressure on him if I were you. Remind him of all he has to lose should the authorities from London start taking a closer look at his establishment."

Gage's voice hardened and his eyes glittered like ice. "Then that's what we'll do."

I was suddenly glad I wasn't in Fryston's shoes, even if the innkeeper deserved it.

He pushed to his feet, offering Butler his hand. "Thank you."

Butler rose to accept it, but after a brief shake, Gage tightened his grip, pulling the other man toward him. "As for the rest, I suggest you inform your acquaintance of an acquaintance that it would be best if he found a new line of occupation." His scrutiny flickered over the other man's features. "And a new way to help."

Rather than take offense as I feared, Butler gave him the respect of almost a direct response. "I imagine he's already re-thinking matters."

A look passed between them then, one in which they took each other's measure, and then appeared to come to some sort of understanding.

We reclaimed our coats and hats and hustled back out to our carriage, with Butler escorting me once again, shielding me as best he could from the rain with his umbrella. He didn't speak to me directly, not until I was seated in our carriage. "Mrs. Gage," he pronounced solemnly with a bow of his head. "It has been a genuine pleasure."

"Likewise," I responded politely.

Then with another of his private smiles, he closed the door and we were on our way. I peered back through the window as the coach rounded the drive, finding him still watching us, and I pondered if I would ever see him again. When he was swallowed up by a curtain of rain, I wondered if I had my answer.

Turning to Gage, I found him staring straight ahead, his jaw locked in fury.

I reached out to touch the sleeve of his coat. "I know that could not have been easy . . ."

"Not now, Kiera," he cut me off by saying.

I closed my mouth and withdrew my hand, trying not to feel hurt by his rejection. Clearly, he'd chosen to take refuge in anger once again. But knowing that intellectually and accepting it emotionally were two different things.

I clasped my hands together awkwardly in my lap, keeping my eyes averted.

But then Gage touched my knee, and I turned to find him looking at me. "Not yet." The depths of his pale blue eyes shimmered with a hundred unsaid things, but swimming amid the pain and discomfort and frustration and rage I spotted the affection I was most anxious to see.

As we swept past the gatehouse, I saw a figure standing next to the door, watching us. He had presumably been the man inside who had signaled our approach to Butler using the reflection of mirrors. But I also realized I recognized him. He was the fellow Fryston had been chuckling with on our first visit to the Blue Bell. The one with a red birthmark on his neck. Yet he was employed by Butler. Did that mean Butler had sent him there to keep an eye on the inn? Or could it mean Buter was sending us into a trap?

CHAPTER 25

It took a considerable amount of persuasion, but I managed to convince Gage that a visit to the parish constable was in order before he confronted the Blue Bell's proprietor. Though had Robinson not been home, I wouldn't have wagered on my ability to prevent him from carrying through with whatever he intended for Fryston.

When we arrived at the Blue Bell, we found the carriage yard about half-full. Given the time of day, the wayside inn should be filled with mainly travelers, but considering the high rate of unemployment in the area, any such assumptions were of little use. We pulled to a halt and Gage clambered out, but when I moved to join him, he stopped me.

"Stay in the carriage."

When he would have shut the coach door, I stopped him with my hand. "You cannot be serious?" I retorted in angry disbelief.

"Kiera, this is not the type of conversation I want you privy to," he growled impatiently. "Stay in the . . ."

"Why?" I spied Anderley over his shoulder, water dripping from his greatcoat and the brim of his hat. Alarm tightened my gut. "What are you going to do?"

I'd seen Gage and Anderley stand shoulder to shoulder, working in accord as they interrogated a suspect. Their impressive physiques coupled with their fierce countenances made for an intimidating sight. Given their unspoken rapport, one that could have been born only from past experience, I'd long wondered how often they'd resorted to such tactics in the past and just how physical they'd become. But I'd never dared to ask. Probably because I'd not wanted to know. But confronted with their obvious intentions, I couldn't remain silent.

"Whatever we need to do to get some answers once and for all," Gage answered in a hard voice.

"Gage! Sebastian, please," I pleaded. "Don't do what I think you mean to."

For a moment he almost seemed to relent, but then his mouth firmed. "Don't worry, Kiera. Robinson will prevent us from going too far." With this he slammed the carriage door before I could halt him a second time.

I gave a shriek of aggravation as I watched through the window while Gage turned to order Joe to make sure I stayed put. Then he and Anderley joined Robinson near the entrance to the inn. Struggling to contain my ire, I hurled myself back against the squabs, crossing my arms over my chest.

Gage knew how much I disliked being told to mind my place, as his father had done the previous afternoon. He knew how much his high-handed attempts to protect me in the past had infuriated me—and how often they'd backfired, placing me in even more danger. When we'd wed, he'd promised to be rational, and to not insist on wrapping me in cotton swaddling. Just as I'd promised to listen when his requests were reasonable. However, this smacked more of imperious demand than sensible precaution. Except in this case I feared his aim wasn't shielding me from physical harm but rather the sight of him resorting to violence.

I stared anxiously through the rain-streaked glass, praying he didn't allow his darker emotions to overrule his good sense. I knew he didn't know what to do with all the grief and rage bottled inside him. If he couldn't heal his father or secure his approval and affection, then maybe at least he could apprehend and punish his attackers. Those were the thoughts that would be running through his head, whether he was entirely conscious of them or not. And I was terrified how far he might go to make them reality.

At least if I'd been present, I might have acted as some sort of deterrent. My physical being, if not my words, might have kept his anger restrained. I didn't know if Anderley or Mr. Robinson would have the same effect. If they would even *try* to hold him back.

I sat stewing for what felt like hours, my chest tight and my stomach twisted in knots. When they finally emerged from the inn, I exhaled in relief, even as they stood under the overhang conferring briefly with Robinson. It was obvious from the determined set of their jaws they'd learned something.

"What is it?" I asked as Gage climbed inside the carriage and sat across from me, presumably to keep me from getting wet. I scoured his features as he shook out his coat to remove some of the rain, reassured not to see any blood or abrasions. Though that didn't mean Fryston was similarly unblemished. My gaze dipped to his gloved hands. "Did he talk?"

"Once we'd persuaded him it was in his best interest." He

arched a single eyebrow. "Though I can't promise the Excise Office won't receive a letter from my father in due time."

I couldn't tell if this meant their threats to expose Fryston's smuggling operation had been enough to persuade him to talk or not, but I chose to believe it. "Then what did he say?"

He fidgeted with his cuffs before settling down to peer out the window as we exited the inn's carriage yard. "Hutchinson and the others are hiding in the forest near Sayles Plantation. Which, interestingly enough, stands about a half a mile to the east of Bowcliffe House."

"Beyond the woods I saw those men disappearing into in the middle of the night?"

"Yes."

Then they'd been close all along. Close enough to attempt to strike at Lord Gage again. And close enough that Dr. Barker might have gone to *them* to attend their injuries.

"Robinson is gathering a few more men and meeting me, Anderley, and Henry—if he wishes to come—at the end of the Barkers' drive so that we can ambush them before someone alerts them that we're aware of their hiding place. But I need you . . ."

"To remain at the Barkers'," I finished for him brusquely. "Yes, I gathered." I wasn't actually upset at being left behind for this undertaking. I knew I would only be a hindrance and a distraction. And I had no desire to go traipsing about in the forest in the rain, potentially dodging bullets. That last thought made my heart lodge in my throat. But I was still miffed by his treatment of me before they went into the inn.

"Kiera, I need to know you're safe."

"Yes, I understand."

He appeared cross with me for not being more appreciative of his situation, and I ignored him, too cross at him for his failure to apprehend his imperious demeanor.

We continued the short drive to Bowcliffe House in silence, and upon our arrival I nearly climbed from the coach without saying another word. Only the realization that he might literally be forced to dodge bullets made me pause to look at him. His pale blue eyes still accused, and his mouth was still clamped in a tight line, but that didn't make his features any less beloved.

I leaned forward so that our faces were inches apart. "Be careful," I murmured, pressing my lips to his warm cheek before turning to go.

But his hands pulled me back, and his mouth settled over mine in a brief but intense kiss. His eyes, when we separated, were serious. "Keep to the house."

I nodded.

As I dashed through the rain toward the house, I heard Anderley ordering their horses to be brought around. I passed through the entry hall, pausing long enough to pass my wet outer garments to the butler before heading toward the stairs. Dr. Barker emerged from his study, and Mrs. Barker peered out from the morning room, but I didn't address either of them. I didn't want to believe that either of them had any sort of connection to the highwaymen who'd attacked Lord Gage and killed his footman, but the proximity of the attackers' encampment and the glimpse I'd caught of two men in the middle of the night—one of them moving away from their cottage—were too suspicious to ignore. So I deemed it best not to say anything, lest they attempt to alert those men to the impending raid or take some other action against us. Best to let them assume I was in a hurry to tend to my daughter.

I found Mrs. Mackay and Bree in the nursery with Emma and swiftly informed them of our discoveries. We said a prayer for the men before I sent Bree belowstairs to monitor the staff for any questionable behavior. Mrs. Mackay volunteered to alert Lembus while I settled in to feed and snuggle Emma.

It took all my resolve not to dwell on the events that might be unfolding on the opposite side of those woods. My fretting wouldn't change the outcome. But it might make Emma fussy. So I did my best to push my worries aside and focus on my daughter.

She grew drowsy shortly after eating and fell asleep in my arms. I brushed her downy golden curls back from her soft, round cheeks. Her lips puckered for a moment and then relaxed as she settled deeper into sleep. Cradling her so and gazing down into her sweet little face, an intense feeling of contentment flooded me. It was almost enough to counteract the panic still battering at the back of my brain. Almost.

When I looked up, I found Mrs. Mackay standing in the doorway with a look of regret. "His lordship is askin' for you," she said.

"Did he hear what you told Lembus?" I murmured.

"I'm afraid so."

I sighed, gazing down at my slumbering daughter one last time before nodding. I transferred her to the cradle before slipping out, knowing she was in good hands with her nanny. But that didn't mean I was any happier to leave her company for that of my surly, demanding father-in-law.

I'd not changed out of my rose and blue striped carriage dress and decided I could remain in it for a little longer. Turning the corner, I met Mrs. Barker approaching from the direction of Lord Gage's bedchamber and her private parlor. She worried her hands before her and seemed lost in deep thought, not seeing me until I was already in front of her.

She gave a little gasp of apology. "Is it true? They've located the men who attacked his lordship?"

"We believe so," I replied, curious how she'd found out. Had she been listening through the wall? Or had she overheard Mrs. Mackay in the corridor speaking to Lembus?

She nodded nervously, seeming to search the floor. "And . . . and they were staying so very close to here?" She glanced vaguely over her shoulder. "Just beyond the eastern woods."

"Yes, it is rather a disconcerting discovery," I said, softening toward her.

"Aye."

I touched her on the arm in reassurance, and she lifted her gaze to mine. "It will all be over soon."

She licked her lips. "Aye."

But she didn't sound very certain, and I supposed I couldn't blame her. The ball of dread knotted in my own stomach even agreed with her.

"Please, excuse me," she mumbled before hurrying down the corridor, I supposed to inform her husband.

I considered following her, curious what Dr. Barker's reaction would be to the news, but then decided such a move might be viewed as suspicious. If our host was in some way involved, I didn't want to alert him to the possibility we might know while my husband, Henry, and Anderley were all away, with little idea when they would return.

Instead, I turned my steps resolutely back toward Lord Gage's bedchamber door, rapping lightly. His voice bid me to enter, and I slipped inside to find him sitting upright in bed. Lembus rose to his feet, and I nodded to the valet.

"I can sit with him for a time."

He bowed and absented himself from the room. How long he'd been confined with his employer, I didn't know, but it had been long enough that he didn't bother to hide his eagerness to be away.

I turned to scrutinize my father-in-law, glad to see his color had improved and the same defiant spark lit his eyes, no matter how aggravating. Lord Gage was not the sort of man to go down without a fight. Something that proved to be both a blessing and a curse.

"Well, don't just stand there gawking at me," he groused. "Have a seat."

I arched a single eyebrow at his bullying before complying. "You seem to be improved."

"Yes, yes," he remarked impatiently. "But what of my attackers? Sebastian and . . . and the others have gone to apprehend them?" Had he been about to say Henry?

"Yes, but they haven't yet returned."

He sat back, resting his head against the oak headboard and closing his eyes. "Then it's almost over," he murmured in an unconscious echo of my words to Mrs. Barker, his voice so quiet I almost couldn't hear him. I was as surprised by the admission as I was by the haggard relief which seemed to momentarily overwhelm him. Plainly this entire episode had troubled him far more greatly than he'd let on.

I waited for him to gather himself, curious if he would say more. No matter his protests, I wondered if he'd known more about his attackers than he'd admitted. If Butler's allegations and our own suspicions were true, then he'd not only been at Grange Moor—or at least been a part of it—but he also knew who Tom Hutchinson was. His earlier protests to the contrary had seemed a little too vehement, and now his sense of relief was all too palpable. But was that because he was relieved the culprits wouldn't attempt to harm him again, or because he thought we wouldn't need to ask any further questions?

If it was the latter, his anticipated reprieve was premature.

I was sorely tempted to begin interrogating him now, when his defenses were down, but I hesitated for two reasons. The first being that I knew Gage would not thank me for depriving him of the privilege, and given the fact Lord Gage was his father, that seemed only fair. And secondly, because Lord Gage already had a distinct aversion to any display of weakness—in others but most notably in himself. I didn't yet know why, but it likely stemmed from something that had happened to him earlier in his life, before Gage was even born. If so, my attempt to capitalize on his moment of vulnerability would merely result in greater anger and resistance.

"How long have they been gone?" Lord Gage queried, glancing toward the bedside table. I wondered if his pocket watch rested in its drawer.

I looked at the watch pinned to my bodice. "Less than an hour."

"And how far away was the attackers' encampment?"

"About a half a mile."

His eyes lifted toward the ceiling, and I was surprised to see that he appeared at a loss for words. Was he actually worried? I'd never imagined my father-in-law as an apprehensive sort of man. After all, he had sent his son into danger countless times during the course of their inquiries over the years. Shortly after my and Gage's marriage, he'd sent us haring off to Ireland with little information and little thought to our safety. But here he was, by all appearances, fretting.

"They know what they're doing," I found myself assuring him.

He cleared his throat before replying gruffly. "Of course. After all, I trained him. And I suppose he wouldn't let his valet and that brother of his take part if they couldn't handle themselves properly."

I chose to view the fact that he'd nearly said Henry's name a few minutes before, and he was now referring to him as Gage's brother, as an encouraging sign.

"Where is my granddaughter?"

"Napping," I said, and then we discussed her for a time before lapsing back into silence. I noticed a book lying on the bed-side table and reached for it, discovering it was a copy of *Gulliver's Travels*. It was not the sort of book I would have imagined my father-in-law enjoying, but maybe I was wrong. "Shall I read to you?"

He turned to me, but it took him several moments to respond, his thoughts having been far away. "Yes. Better than the alternative."

I wasn't sure if the alternative was our sitting in silence or his having to converse with me, but rather than take offense, I simply shook my head and opened the novel to the page marked.

For a time, our thoughts were faraway in fictional Brobdingnag, until the sound of raised voices suddenly jerked us back to the present. Alarmingly, they sounded as if they were coming closer, and I pushed to my feet, exchanging an anxious look with Lord Gage. What I intended to do if it was someone intent on harming him, I didn't know, for my lone weapon was the book clutched before me, but I placed myself in their path anyway.

When the door burst open, I lifted the hefty book like a shield. Only to drop it on the end of the bed behind me when I caught sight of Gage.

"Oh, thank heavens," I exclaimed, flinging my arms around him, heedless of his damp hair and garments.

He embraced me before setting me aside. I saw then that Henry and Dr. Barker were following in his wake, the latter still protesting Gage's insistence on barging into his father's chamber in such a manner.

"He must not be riled or unsettled," he insisted.

But Gage ignored him, and so, too, this time did Henry. His scowl equaled if not exceeded Gage's in ferocity.

"Have you apprehended the attackers?" I interjected while I still had the chance.

"Yes." My husband flicked a look at me. "Robinson took them to his home. Says he has a room in his cellar where he can secure them until arrangements can be made to transfer them to York."

A long breath whooshed from my lungs, but my respite was short-lived.

"You knew at least one of your attackers," Gage accused his father. "Don't bother denying it," he added when his father opened his mouth to argue. "What I don't know is when you realized it. Did you recognize him the night of your attack? Or was it only later, when we mentioned his name?"

CHAPTER 26

Lord Gage's lip curled. "If you're speaking of Tom Hutchinson . . ."

Gage's voice cracked like a whip. "Of course, I'm speaking of Tom Hutchinson! You knew him. You knew his brother. You met them twelve years ago in Monk Bretton and Barnsley."

That name. Monk Bretton. It nagged at my brain again, just as it had done when Butler had mentioned it. But I couldn't recall where else I'd heard it. And before I could contemplate it further, Lord Gage spoke.

"I have never been to Monk Bretton or Barnsley, least of all twelve years ago," he sneered with such contempt I might have believed him had it not been for his hands. They gripped and knotted the bedsheets where they rested at his sides, channeling all the tension from the rest of his body.

Gage shook his head. "I'm not going to bother to question Lord Sidmouth about it. He wouldn't share what he knew anyway."

Lord Gage's eyes narrowed in suspicion, likely thinking of his letter. I wondered if Lembus had dared to tell him it had gone missing for a short time, or that my maid had been the one to return it.

"But we're all perfectly aware that you worked for the Home Office at one time. And that at least two days ago you became aware of the motive behind the attack made on you. The attack that resulted in Gregory Reed's *death*. And yet, you denied and refused to share what you knew, placing us *all* in further danger simply to salvage your pride!" Gage turned away in disgust.

He had been all but screaming at his father, but Dr. Barker was apparently too stunned to oppose it, staring at him with wide eyes.

"If we hadn't wounded two of the men in their subsequent attack on *us*," Gage turned back to say, "then who knows what else they might have attempted. When we caught up with them, they were still intent on vengeance."

I wanted to ask about those injuries. Whether they had been tended by someone. Whether they would survive. I deeply did not want one of their deaths on my conscience, even though I had shot them to protect Gage. But now was not the time.

"I don't know what you're talking about," Lord Gage scoffed, though his face was pale. "I don't know those men. I still don't understand why they attacked me. They must have confused me with someone else."

Until this point, Gage had been very careful not to speak the accusation out loud in front of Dr. Barker and his brother, but I could tell by the glint in his eyes that he'd been driven beyond that. "I see. So you weren't a spy, an informant, an instigator working on behalf of our government?"

The ripple of shock from this revelation was almost tangible. Lord Gage's face flushed fiery red. "How dare you! I have served this country with honor and distinction. I would never sully it by engaging in such disgraceful conduct."

"Now, why don't I believe you," Gage drawled, tapping his chin in feigned ignorance. "Oh, yes. That's right. Because you've had no trouble denying disgraceful conduct in the past. In continuing to deny it!"

Lord Gage's mouth clamped shut in impotent rage and perhaps humiliation. Had he been able to storm out of the room, I'm certain he would have. But he was trapped in his bed, unable yet to do much more than hobble. I felt a pulse of discomfort and unwanted compassion for him at this realization. Despite all the pain and injury he'd caused and the fact he'd brought this on himself, this confrontation was beginning to feel more like an attack. There must be a better way.

"Sebastian," I murmured, moving toward him.

"Don't you have anything to say to me?" he demanded of his father. He gestured behind him. "Don't you have anything to say to Henry?"

But I could tell Henry was no longer in accord with him, and that he wished he would leave him out of whatever point he was trying to make.

"Sebastian," I tried again, touching his arm.

"Yes, I have something say." Lord Gage straightened as best he could while reclining in bed, arching his chin upward. "I am your father. And as such you owe me your respect. Had I treated your grandfather as you're treating me, a backhand across the face would have been the least of the consequences. You did not question him *or* his actions. He did as he saw fit. And I expect the same filial respect from you, Sebastian."

"Except I'm no longer a child, Father. And I cannot respect a man I cannot trust."

Lord Gage flinched as if he'd been slapped, but his son wasn't finished.

He stabbed his finger at him. "You dishonored my mother, and you put my family in danger when you placed your pride above our safety." He made a sound of disgust at the back of his throat. "I wash my hands of you." He turned to go, glancing back at me and then Henry as if he expected us to follow.

Henry shook his head, and Gage's glare sharpened before he strode away. Evidently, he'd expected his brother to follow his lead, but he'd forgotten Henry's words several days ago. Just because there were things Gage wasn't willing to accept from his father didn't mean Henry was of the same opinion. Lord Gage and Henry's relationship—or lack of one—was different from that of Gage and his father. And as such, it would, by necessity, be forged differently.

But Lord Gage still seemed unwilling to build anything with his second son.

"I don't know why you're still here," he told him coldly.

Henry's hurt and frustration were evident even if he did not respond, instead turning and walking away.

The silence that reigned after his departure was thick and fraught.

Dr. Barker's troubled gaze met mine, and I mutely urged him to give me a moment alone with Lord Gage.

"If you'll excuse me," he murmured, closing the door as he slipped away.

I crossed toward the bed, smoothing the covers which had become rumpled and passing him a glass of water unasked so that he could take a drink.

"Aren't you going to follow your husband?" he queried with a nasty sneer.

"In a moment," I answered, refusing to be riled.

"I see. You intend to speak your mind first. Is that it?" He passed me back the glass. "Well, let me save you the bother. You would be wasting your time."

For a moment I struggled with the impulse to dump the remainder of the water over his head. "Quit behaving like an infant," I snapped instead, thumping the glass down. "Do you not understand all you have to lose with your pigheadedness? Both of your sons *and* your granddaughter."

He scowled. "Sebastian will relent."

"Will he?"

When he didn't have a retort ready, I realized he wasn't utterly oblivious to the seriousness of the situation.

I sank down on the edge of the bed with an exasperated sigh as I searched for the right words to penetrate his thick skull. "You may have lost control of this situation." A fact that I knew must terrify a man who ruled his world with an iron fist covered in a velvet glove—one he could don or remove at his whim. I leaned closer. "But you ultimately have control over what happens next. Only *you* have the power to decide whether you will keep or lose your sons, whether you will pursue a mutually respectful relationship with them or watch them walk away and forever keep their distance."

He scoffed. "If I cower at their feet."

I shook my head. "No. Sebastian only wants the truth. And your acknowledgment that what you did to his mother was wrong." I pressed a hand to my chest. "That what you did, placing us in danger, was wrong."

"I didn't place you in danger . . ."

I glared at him, cutting off the rest of his protest. "You did."

He grumbled under his breath but at least had the grace not to persist in his argument.

"If you want our respect, you need to respect us in return. And that includes recognizing that what Sebastian wants from his life is not the same as what you want."

"But I only want the best for him."

"Maybe. But that doesn't mean it's what Gage believes is best."

I could tell from the return of the stubborn glint in his eye that I wasn't getting through. "Is what you've accomplished in your life what your father wanted for you?"

His brow furrowed, and I knew I had him there.

"My father expected nothing from me." There was a world of pain behind those words—one I was certain he hadn't intended to reveal.

"And yet you still defied him." I tilted my head, studying his features. "You told Gage you didn't question your father or his actions. That he did as he saw fit. Is that true?"

"Aye," he stated defiantly before relenting. "At least, not to his face. Not more than once anyway."

I scoured his granite eyes, trying to peel back the layers of lies. Lies he'd been told or shown by others, and lies he'd told himself.

"You do realize that admitting you're wrong, that recognizing your fallibility, doesn't make you weak. When you were a ship's captain, did your officers and midshipman not sometimes make miscalculations? Calculations that had perhaps been made with good intentions and the best information at hand that later proved to be faulty. Would you not have rather they confessed those errors and corrected their course rather than blunder forward obstinately and sailed you to the wrong coordinates?" I arched my eyebrows. "Insisting you *intended* to sail for the Falklands rather than Shetland?"

The corner of Lord Gage's mouth quirked. "I should hope I would have noticed the many thousand miles difference in the length of that journey before reaching port, but . . . I accede your point."

I pressed my hand to his. "We all must make course corrections from time to time. Or we're bound to strike a rocky shore or underwater reef. Or flounder out on the stormy sea."

"Aye."

"Then will you give the rest of what I've said consideration as well?"

He didn't agree openly, but I felt hopeful when he didn't outright refuse.

"And . . . at least have a conversation with Henry."

His mouth flattened, but I silenced his protest by tightening my grip on his hand.

"*Just* a genuine conversation. You owe him that much. He *is* your son, after all. No amount of dissembling will change that."

I stared expectantly at him, unwilling to accept failure to argue as an answer this time.

He muttered something under his breath again, but then agreed.

I smiled, patting his hand before releasing it.

"I see now why Sebastian married you," he groused with what sounded like reluctant approval. "Had the Whigs sent you to speak to His Majesty, they wouldn't have needed to employ such underhanded tactics. He would have agreed to endorse the Reform Act then and there."

"Perhaps, but then I wouldn't have been minding my place, would I?" I couldn't help but retort.

His silver eyes gleamed. "Touché."

I entered Gage's bedchamber to find him stripped to the waist and toweling off.

"Calmed Henry's ruffled feathers, have you?" Fury still flashed in his eyes as he lifted the cloth to his head to scrub his wet curls, a move which showed the muscles of his torso quite favorably. "Now come to chide me?"

"I was talking to your father actually."

This made him pause, a furrow ruffling his brow. "You were

the one who told me to lay it all open for him and tell him to choose," he stated almost accusatorily.

I frowned. "Sebastian, you don't sincerely believe that's what you did?"

"Of course it is."

I huffed a humorless laugh. "Darling, you weren't calm and collected at all. You stood over him shouting loud enough for the whole house to hear. You were positively enraged."

He threw his towel down. "He placed all of us in danger!"

I held up my hands, my heart rate accelerating in the face of his ferocity. "I know he did. And you have every right to be angry with him for that. But, darling, you've been angry since the moment we arrived in Wentbridge and directing that anger at everyone and everything to no effect."

He stood staring at me, his chest rising and falling with each outraged breath.

I lowered my arms. "Don't you think it's time to try a different approach?"

He turned away, raking his hands back through his hair. "But I don't know how to do that! I can't just stop!" He struggled with his words. "There's so much . . . *rage* inside me."

"Are you certain it's all rage, or is it maybe something else? Something that's more difficult to confront."

I don't know whether it was my words or the calmness of my voice, but his head swiveled so he could look at me. His eyes flickered with the emotions he'd been carrying for months, since he learned Henry was his brother. Or perhaps years, since his first memories of his father and his tangible disapproval. His arms dropped to his sides.

I went to him, sensing the walls he'd tried to build around that pain beginning to crumble. Walls he'd tried to shore up with his anger. I coaxed him to sit on the edge of the bed beside me and wrapped my arms around his torso. I rested my head against his chest, heedless of the dampness that still clung to his chest hair and the way it tickled my face, breathing in the musk of his skin.

He embraced me back, gently at first and then more tightly. His shoulders bowed and his breath grew ragged. I could sense he wanted to weep, but he would not let himself.

"Let it out, my love," I whispered. "You are safe with me."

And he did then. He wept as I'd only ever seen him weep once before. I laid back and gathered him in my arms, cradling his head against my chest as his body shook with great racking sobs, letting him know I wasn't going anywhere. That I would be there to help him put himself back together.

Witnessing his anguish, it was impossible to remain unaffected, and my own fair share of tears slipped down my cheeks to drip into his hair. Even when his sobs subsided, we lay quietly tangled in each other's arms, consoling each other. Such was the solace that I almost regretted the need to speak.

It had been a trying few weeks, and we were all exhausted. The men who'd attacked Lord Gage's carriage had been caught, but that had not brought a happy resolution. Not when there were still so many underlying problems to be contended with.

"I know your father betrayed your mother," I murmured. "I know he's not been the supportive, loving father one might wish for. But that doesn't mean he doesn't care."

Gage shifted his head so that he could look up at me, his eyes rimmed in red and shimmering a brilliant almost crystalline blue shade from his recent tears.

"He *does* care. I've seen it in his face. He just doesn't know how to express it. Or perhaps he feels he shouldn't express it because of the way he was raised. Whatever the case, it's still there. Just as I believe he genuinely cared for your mother."

A pucker formed between his brows before he admitted in a raspy voice, "I believe so, too. *Not* as she deserved to be loved. But he did care."

"You may not wish to hear this, but . . . you really do need to forgive him for that moral failing, darling. Even without his apologizing or admitting he's done any wrong."

Gage frowned.

"Yes, he betrayed your mother and he's horrendously stubborn, but what's done is done. And continuing to harp on about it only hurts Henry." I arched my eyebrows. "You may not have realized it, but your continuing to berate your father about his infidelity is wounding Henry. After all, had your father not been unfaithful with the duchess, he would not be here."

"Henry knows I don't resent him. That I'm happy to have him as a brother."

"Maybe so. But it wounds him all the same." I brushed my thumb over his jaw, his bristles lightly abrading it. "Place yourself in his shoes. How would you feel?"

He appeared to give this some thought, and he didn't like the conclusion he came to.

"In that same vein, what do you think your mother would want you to do? Would she want you to hold on to your anger at him on her behalf, to grow further estranged? Or would she want you to forgive him?"

He exhaled a long, disgruntled breath. "Yes, I take your point." His fingers absently combed back the hair that had fallen from my hairpins to straggle around my face. "She *was* always encouraging Father to take me on outings while she rested during the middle of the day when he was home on leave. Fishing and such. That's how I learned to swim the summer I turned five." A note of longing had entered his voice, telling me this was a good memory.

We lay quietly for a few moments, Gage presumably absorbed

in those recollections while my thoughts drifted to the things I'd learned about Lord Gage this week—both by his admission and my inference.

"I think there is much more to your father's behavior than what it appears to be at the surface."

Gage's gaze met mine, and I could see him working out some of what I already had. "Something to do with why I barely knew his parents. Why he didn't want me to attend his brother's funeral."

"Yes." I bit my lip, wondering if I was venturing too far into speculation. "I think something happened when he was young. Something that goes a long way to explaining at least a little bit of why he is the way he is." I searched his face for understanding. "You do realize that beneath all of his bravado he's terrified of admitting he's wrong, of seeming weak. Contending with this injury has not been easy for him."

"Because it has actually physically weakened him and practically rendered him immobile."

"Yes." I fanned my fingers over the strong tendons of Gage's throat, which were so often covered by his cravats and neckcloths. "I'm still angry at him for denying all knowledge of Grange Moor and Tom Hutchinson, but . . . I understand why he did it. He's obviously ashamed of the role he played as a government informant. Even if it got him to where he is now. If such a thing became public knowledge, he would be disgraced and lose all credibility."

"Yes, it's clear he was looking out for his own best interest," Gage remarked, taking a dimmer view of his motivations than I did.

"I know spying seems rather . . . dishonest and deceitful, but the government *is* tasked with keeping the peace and keeping the public safe. Undoubtedly, matters can be taken too far. If your father purposely manipulated events and incited them to riot, then that is unconscionable. But if he was merely reporting to his superiors on what was occurring, then I feel torn about how faulty his actions were. At least, in that regard."

His expression was unsettled, and I knew that Gage, with his keen sense of honorability, would have more difficulty accepting the necessity of such an act. Although, at times, our own actions as inquiry agents could sometimes skirt the edge of artifice.

"Maybe," he said. "But it also doesn't stop me from empathizing with those he misled about his identity. Especially men like Tom Hutchinson, who lost one brother to an injury and two others to transportation. Though that doesn't give them the right to enact revenge and kill an innocent young man in the process."

"Did they put up much of a fight?" I asked, not having heard anything about their raid on the highwaymen's encampment.

"Minimal. We snuck up on them from all sides, and once they realized they were surrounded and we'd taken control of their horses, they surrendered with little fuss."

"What of their injuries?"

His expression turned cynical. "I'm glad you asked. Because they seemed to have been tended to. Albeit not with regularity."

I pushed up on my elbow. "What do you mean?"

"At some point someone had skillfully bandaged the furrow your bullet tore out of Hutchinson's arm and dug the bullet out of Wood's chest, but they were ragged and dirty and had not been seen to in many days."

I felt almost dizzy with relief to hear that my shot had not seriously injured anyone.

"Robinson asked me to send Dr. Barker to his home to see to their wounds. Which is presumably where he is now, unless you left him tending my father."

"He departed soon after you."

He nodded. "Wood was in a bad way. He wanted me to know

they weren't intending to kill us when they ambushed our coach. They simply wanted to scare us away."

Except I'd seen the way Hutchinson had taken careful aim at Gage. Either their leader had changed his mind and decided killing one Gage was as good as killing another, or Wood was lying. But it seemed pointless to belabor the point now. All four men were either facing execution or transportation.

Gage's expression turned grim. "I'm not sure there's much that can be done for Wood at this point."

I felt a pulse of compassion for the man despite what they'd done and offered up a silent prayer for his comfort. "Do you think Dr. Barker lied? That he tended their wounds and then denied it."

"I honestly don't know." He flopped over onto his back, pressing a hand to his forehead. "But they might have just as easily been tended by someone with a rudimentary knowledge of physic. A soldier or a midwife or even a farmer's wife who tends to the farmhands' injuries."

"It does seem counter to Dr. Barker's oath as a surgeon to take the risk to care for their wounds but then leave them to fester. It seems more likely he would have done just as he claimed. Bind their wounds and then report them to the authorities so they could be cared for properly."

"I harbored a similar thought," he admitted.

"Barker also seemed shocked by the revelation your father was an informant."

Gage grimaced. "He was in the room when I threw that in my father's face, wasn't he?"

"I'm afraid so. And until that moment, I don't think he knew anything about it."

Yet there were so many instances of odd, unexplained behavior from him, I didn't know what to think. Was the man simply a sensitive eccentric, or was there something more to it? Something far more nefarious?

CHAPTER 27

It is never pleasant to be awakened in the middle of the night by pounding on one's bedchamber door. But it's even less pleasant to wake in the morning to discover you should have been.

I was seated in the chair near the windows, tending Emma as the sun was just beginning to peek over the horizon, sending soft, probing rays of light through the gap in the drapes, when an urgent rap sounded on our door. Emma broke off her nursing at the intrusion, and I turned toward the bed to see Gage slowly sitting up.

"Will you see who that is?" I grumbled, trying to settle our daughter again.

He clambered out of bed, stumbling in his haste as his foot tangled in the sheets.

Because he cracked the door to preserve my modesty, I couldn't see who was on the other side, but I could tell from the lower tone of the voice that it was a man. In any case, they didn't converse for long.

"What is it?" I asked as Gage closed the door and hastened toward the dressing room.

"My father. He's taken another turn for the worse. This time even more serious."

It took all my effort to still my suddenly racing heart and remain in my chair with Emma as he dashed through the dressing room door, remembering almost too late to close it softly. If I could have communicated my sense of urgency to my daughter without upsetting her, I would have, but she seemed determined to take her time.

When she finally finished, I lifted her to my shoulder, patting her on the back while I hurried toward the bell-pull to summon Bree. But my maid must have been waiting in the dressing room, listening for me to do just that, for she rapped once before sweeping through the door with my cerulean blue morning dress already draped over her arm. Mrs. Mackay soon followed, taking Emma from my arms to continue burping her.

"What has happened?" I demanded to know as Bree whisked my nightdress from my frame and replaced it with a lace-trimmed shift followed by my stays.

"Apparently, his lordship began vomitin' again in the middle o' the night."

"The middle of the night?" I gasped in horror. "Why did no one wake us?"

"I dinna ken, m'lady," Bree replied, exchanging a glance with the nanny. "But none o' us was awakened. I was the first to realize somethin' was wrong when I went belowstairs to break my fast. Anderley joined me soon after and went off to discover from Lembus what had occurred, and *he* told him he'd been askin' for hours for Mr. Gage to be sent for."

"Why on earth wasn't he?" I ruminated in horror, knowing neither of them held the answer.

Bree shook her head in disapproval as she gave one last tug to the ribbons of my stays before settling my gown into place.

"Maybe Dr. Barker didna believe it serious enough to disturb your slumber," Mrs. Mackay suggested more charitably.

"They still should have woken us," I insisted angrily.

She nodded. "Aye."

My suspicions were aroused even as my stomach sickened with dread. "Do you know if he's still retching? Are there any other symptoms?"

"We dinna ken," Bree said, her face taut with concern. "Anderley ran straight to summon Mr. Gage, and we followed after."

I forced myself to inhale and then exhale, steadying my breath. "Has Lord Henry been awakened?"

"If he's no', I'll make certain he is," Mrs. Mackay assured me, heading toward the door with Emma.

Bree finished buttoning up my gown and fastening the belt, and then seated me before the mirror of the dressing table to take out my braid and begin brushing my hair. All the while, I struggled to rein in my racing thoughts. Why *hadn't* we been sent for? Dr. Barker *must* have known we would want to be. And according to Lembus, he'd been asking that someone be sent for us, taking his directive to stay with Lord Gage seriously.

But by that account, if Lembus had remained with Lord Gage all night, then what had happened to make Lord Gage so ill? Was he actually injured internally where we couldn't see? Was he slowly dying? Or had someone snuck something past Lembus?

My head swirled with so many questions I didn't know what to think. But I knew one place I might be able to get some answers.

I lifted my gaze to Bree's reflection in the mirror as she began pinning my hair in place. "I need you to do me a favor."

Her eyes met mine, sensing the seriousness of my intent. "O' course."

"I need you to keep Dr. Barker away from the ground floor as long as possible. If he's not attending Lord Gage, I need you to keep him occupied some other way."

She didn't ask me what I intended or caution me against it, but merely nodded her head in solidarity. "Done."

I descended the stairs as if on my way to the breakfast room, mindful of any servants that might be posted in the entry hall. When none appeared, I turned down the corridor leading toward the back of the house instead, treading with soft feet toward Dr. Barker's study. Then with one last peek over my shoulder, I slipped inside and quietly shut the door. I turned first toward the glass-fronted cabinet I'd nearly missed seeing upon my first visit, tucked into a niche in the wall next to the door as it was. It was filled with glass vials and porcelain jars, each labeled with its contents. My eyes slid over the array of herbs, tinctures, and extracts in various colors and preparations, but if the surgeon kept his supply of laudanum here, it was missing.

I turned to scrutinize the contents of the room—the bookshelves and cabinet of curiosities, the parted drapes and fireplace mantel displaying the stuffed button quails, the chairs and desk. Striding forward, I rounded the oak desk, deciding it was the likeliest place for a locked compartment. There, the bottom left drawer boasted a lock. After tugging on it to ensure it wasn't already open, I sat down in the chair and began searching the other drawers on the chance one of them would carelessly hold the key. It was astonishing how many people locked things away in drawers only to leave the key in an adjacent one.

But Dr. Barker was shrewder than that. I found little of interest—and no key—except a small portrait fashioned in watercolors. It captured my attention not only because I was a portrait artist myself, but also because it appeared to be a depiction of Dr. Barker. Or someone who looked similar to Dr. Barker.

An older brother perhaps? But why was it hidden away in a drawer?

Despite the time I knew was ticking away, I couldn't help but scrutinize it more closely, feeling a prodding at the back of my skull. Why did this intrigue me? Why did it seem important?

I forced myself to try to step back from the subject and analyze it as I would any portrait, starting with the technique. All artists who had received any amount of training would begin in the same way, building the picture from the internal foundation of a person outward in layers, first with charcoal or graphite and then layer after layer of paint. They would start with the skull and underlying facial structure, working from a tried-and-true template which experience had shown to be crucial in constructing an accurate framework. For failure to capture the bone structure correctly hindered the precision of everything that came after. This was an area of portraiture I happened to have more familiarity with than most, courtesy of my late anatomist husband, but the technique remained the same for all artists, regardless of the depth of their knowledge of anatomy.

My practiced eye detected that this artist, whoever they were, must have received some sort of instruction, for they appeared to have at least begun with the accepted process. Since the figure of their portrait was a male, they had rendered the underlying facial structure with a broad, high forehead and pronounced brow; large orbits for the eyes; a prominent nose with a wider nasal base; and lips separated farther from the nose than was typical on a female template. Then the artist had moved on to the next stage to alter his sketch to account for the wide variance in human features, fleshing out the portrait by making the necessary adjustments to portray the unique characteristics of the individual before him.

In Dr. Barker's case, the artist had narrowed and elongated the face and nose, among other things, to reflect the surgeon's appearance. However, these alterations had been awkwardly implemented. The proportions were at times too large but at other times too small, and the effect was not entirely pleasing or accurate. Yet I could see the intention behind the artist's choices. They had certainly tried to utilize proper technique to paint their subject. Had the execution of it simply been beyond their abilities, or had something else hindered their efforts?

I shook my head. Why had they done such an expert job depicting his small lips yet made little adjustment to the prominent forehead and marked brow? It gave the face an odd triangular shape. If only they'd softened the brow and lowered the hairline, if they'd made it more tempered, more feminine even, then . . .

I stilled. The thought that had been needling at my brain, trying to make itself known, prodded more insistently, urging me to probe further. Mentally, I adjusted the facial structure, beginning with a female template, and swiftly made the alterations, imagining the brushstrokes until I sat back with a jolt. *That* was what was wrong. The artist hadn't been able to capture Dr. Barker's features accurately because he'd started with the wrong underlying bone structure and been unable to compensate.

A dozen thoughts flitted through my head. Impressions I'd captured throughout the week—Dr. Barker's smaller stature, his higher voice, even the manner in which his cravats and collars were starched high to conceal his neck—merged with other more tangible clues. Chief among them the large amount of laundry supposedly generated from Mrs. Barker's courses alone, purportedly from a medical condition. But there was another explanation. One that also went far to explain the affinity I'd felt toward Dr. Barker, the natural understanding that seemed to exist between us. For Dr. Barker wasn't a man.

I looked up at the subject in question as he suddenly strode into the room, still in shock. "You're . . ." I stammered, breaking off as Dr. Barker quickly shut the door and stood staring down at me warily. I thought for a moment the surgeon meant to deny it, but the doctor had the grace not to insult my intellect.

"Yes, your deductions are correct."

"But why . . ." I began, but then stopped. Didn't I already know why?

Dr. Barker nodded as if I'd spoken the words out loud, advancing toward me. "Because I could never have become a surgeon. I would have been denied entry to Edinburgh Medical School. Denied admission to the Royal College of Surgeons. Denied the opportunity to serve in the army at the Royal Military Hospital and so on." The doctor paused to plead with me. "All I've ever wanted to do was be a doctor. But as a woman, I couldn't. As a man, I could. Surely you can understand that."

I could. Society denied women of gentility the right to pursue anything outside the home. Only lower-class women worked in menial jobs or assisted their husbands. Genteel, well-bred ladies were wives and mothers. Nothing more. We certainly weren't doctors, or attorneys, or merchants. And those of us who *did* wish to pursue such things were thought to be unnatural or stepping out of our place. Those pursuing the arts were given some leniency, but there was a reason polite ladies who wrote books often used male pen names. A reason female artists usually acted in conjunction with a father or husband. Even before the scandal erupted involving my work sketching Sir Anthony's dissections for his anatomy textbook, as a female portrait artist I was seen as an oddity.

So yes, I could understand why Dr. Barker had chosen to become a man in order to attend medical school and beyond.

"But how on earth did you manage it?" I asked. "For twenty-odd years?"

"I was fortunate in having the patronage of an uncle, and my mother had some rather highly placed, open-minded friends," the surgeon admitted. "It wasn't easy at first. When I entered medical school, the administration was convinced I was twelve, not eighteen, and I feared at any moment I might be found out. But the longer I remained undetected, the easier it became. And I had my service record to commend me. Yet I never stopped worrying completely. So when I fell ill, I decided it was time to stop taking chances and retire from the army to set up a small, rural practice."

"That's why you've been so erratic around me. One moment happily conversing with me and the next unable to escape my presence quickly enough. You were anxious I would figure it out."

Dr. Barker shifted uncomfortably. "Yes, well, I figured you are rather more perceptive about such things than others. And I was right." His gaze dipped to the portrait I still held in my hands. "Is that what finally gave me away?"

"Yes. In a way." I set the portrait on the desk. "Though I've been noting things all along without realizing it."

"Such as my smaller stature, my less prominent Adam's apple."

I tilted my head to the side. "Is that why you were so nervous when you encountered me in the corridor that night?" I recalled how Dr. Barker had clutched the top of his banyan closed around his throat. "You were afraid I would notice?"

"Partly," the surgeon conceded, seeming to withdraw slightly.

I narrowed my eyes. "Is that why you didn't send for us in the middle of the night?"

He didn't respond immediately, but I could tell I'd hit the nail on the head.

"Is that the *only* reason?"

His brow furrowed. "What do you mean?"

"You didn't help his lordship to this relapse?"

Dr. Barker drew himself up in affront. "Absolutely not. And

I'm insulted you should think so. I have genuinely been caring for his lordship to the best of my ability. But there are some elements that are beyond my control, even as a surgeon."

I scrutinized the doctor's features, finding that I was inclined to believe him. "And this locked drawer? Is this where you keep your laudanum?"

"Yes. I lock away any substances which can be particularly dangerous and subject to abuse or theft."

I rose from the chair. "Is any missing?"

Dr. Barker's eyes widened as if he'd not even considered the prospect, but then he rounded the desk, removing a small ring of keys from his pocket, and unlocked the drawer. I watched over the surgeon's shoulder as he sorted through the bottles, examining the contents of a few of them.

"No. Everything is as I last left it when I gave his lordship his most recent dose." The doctor looked up to find me puzzling over the matter. "You suspect poison?"

"I suspect something," I conceded. "The timing of his lordship's moments of decline are simply too convenient. While we're away for the day. After we've captured his attackers, when our guard is down."

Dr. Barker frowned, not seeming to like the implication.

"And you didn't treat the attackers' wounds?" I pressed.

"Before yesterday? No." His scowl turned troubled. "But someone had."

"Do you know who?"

It was clear from his expression that the surgeon suspected someone.

"Who? Who tended them?" I leaned over the desk to demand.

"I . . . I don't know for certain. But . . ." The words crowded into Dr. Barker's throat, making the pitch of his voice rise. I could tell he didn't want to utter them. "My . . . my wife. She would know how to tend to such wounds."

I straightened in surprise, but then certain things began to fall into place. Certain things that Dr. Barker further elaborated on.

"She . . . she didn't want me to treat his lordship at first. Told me it would be unseemly to have him in our home. I didn't realize the connection at the time, but . . ." The surgeon swallowed. "Her first husband was wounded at Grange Moor and later died. So she may . . ."

"She blames Lord Gage," I gasped, whirling toward the door. "Where is she now?"

"I don't know," our host confessed, following me.

I dashed up the stairs, anxious to find Mrs. Barker. Anxious to discover Lord Gage was safe. Surely Gage was sitting with him. He would not be left undefended.

"M'lady," Bree exclaimed breathlessly as I gained the next floor. Her eyes widened at the sight of Dr. Barker following me, and then she flushed, perhaps because she knew she had been tasked with keeping him away from the ground floor.

My heart surged into my throat at the evidence of her urgency. "What is it?" I asked, not breaking my stride and ignoring the rest.

She hurried alongside me. "That maid I befriended. She . . ." She glanced distractedly over her shoulder at Dr. Barker. "She said that Mrs. Barker insisted on takin' his lordship his tea yesterday evenin'. That that wasna normal."

I stopped midstride to turn to her, before exchanging a look with Dr. Barker. "Thank you for telling me that. Where is Mr. Gage? Is he with his father?"

"Nay."

My gaze jerked back to her in alarm.

"He's belowstairs questionin' the cook."

"Tell him he's needed in his father's room. Tell him now!"

She raced off, and I hurried even faster down the corridor.

As we neared the door, I could hear raised voices. My stomach tightened, for one sounded distinctly like a woman's.

I paused before opening it, concerned that if we startled Mrs. Barker she might do something drastic. However, Dr. Barker was not of a similar mind, throwing open the door before I could stop him. Mrs. Barker pivoted, swinging the barrel of the pistol she held in her hand toward us. By instinct, we both ducked, raising our hands to our heads, as if that could stop a bullet.

"What are thee doing here?" Mrs. Barker shrieked. "No! Go!"

"Prudence, please," Dr. Barker begged as we straightened. "Don't do this."

"I have to," she replied, steadying her aim and redirecting the pistol at Lord Gage where he reclined pale-faced in the bed. But he did not cower. That was not his way. "He killed Nathaniel. He killed him. And he as good as killed our baby as well."

I remembered then that she'd said she'd lost the child she was carrying within a month of her husband's death. That she'd blamed it on her grief, though there were any number of reasons why she might have miscarried. But now was not the time to reason with her about that.

I noted Lembus in the far corner, beyond Lord Gage—too far away from the door or Mrs. Barker to be of any use in stopping her. She had chosen her moment well.

"Mrs. Barker, please," I said, recognizing the only way out of this situation without anyone being injured was to convince her to relinquish her weapon. "This is not the way."

"There is no other way!" Her eyes were wild. "Not for the likes of *him*. He'll never face justice for what he's done." She arched her chin. "That's why Tom and the others decided to ambush him when they were given the chance."

"Tom is your brother-in-law," I deduced. Nathaniel Hutchinson was the brother who'd been shot in the leg at Grange Moor and later died of his wounds. They were all from Monk Bretton. That was why that name kept poking at me. She had lied when I'd asked if her first husband had gotten mired in the uprising. She'd tried to muddy the issue by saying he'd long since been demobilized, but I'd not asked if he was in the militia, simply if he'd been involved at Grange Moor, and she'd lied.

"Aye," she confirmed. "But Tom had to get clever. An eye for an eye. A leg for a leg," she sneered. Her angry glare swung toward Dr. Barker. "And then *you* had to save him. Shoulda let him bleed to death. Shoulda let the infection take him."

"And Gregory Reed? The footman," I prodded.

The corners of her eyes twitched. "That wasn't part of the plan. No one else was supposed to get hurt."

"And that's why you relented," I deduced, holding up my hand to halt the owners of the footsteps pounding down the corridor toward us. There wasn't room for one more person to crowd into the room. Not if we didn't want Mrs. Barker to be pushed into acting. "When we arrived, your feelings began to change." I was certain of it.

Her arms wavered and the gun began to dip. "Aye. Thee were his family. I'd known the pain of loss. I never wanted to inflict it on others. Especially not a child." She nodded toward the window. "Tom's ambushin' your carriage was just supposed to scare you away."

Or at least that was the plan as she'd known it. It seemed like Tom Hutchinson and his men had more of a vindictive streak and far fewer qualms about innocent bystanders than she realized.

She inhaled, appearing to steady herself and her aim. "But then I heard the way his lordship treated thee. I heard the way he spoke to his own sons and the terrible things he'd done." Her voice hardened. "Thou are better off without him."

"So you put poison in his tea," I sputtered, anxious to keep her talking.

"Not poison." Her gaze darted briefly to Dr. Barker. "I couldn't risk my husband noticin'. Nay, 'tis just some ashes and a bit of curdled cream."

I cringed.

"'Twas supposed to weaken him, to purge him dry. To finish him off as his fever should have done. But it didn't work as I hoped." She narrowed her eyes, appearing to harden her resolve. "So it's come to this."

"But we *aren't* better off without him," Gage interjected, crowding into the room close behind me. "We aren't."

Mrs. Barker's expression turned suspicious. "I heard thee say thee washed thou hands of him."

"Because I was angry. Angry because he'd lied—outright and by omission." His hands clasped my upper arms as he pleaded with her, either because he needed the comfort and support or because he was preparing to thrust me out of the way. Perhaps both. "But lies shouldn't condemn a person outright. Not to death. And not to banishment. Even those told in bad faith."

Lord Gage stared at his son in a way I'd never seen before. It was a look of astonishment mingled with regret. I could only imagine how his son returned it.

"Though it certainly helps if the person in question shows remorse," Gage prodded. Given the uncertainty now stamped across Mrs. Barker's features, it was clear he meant for this remorse to be aimed toward her.

Taking his cue, Lord Gage cleared his throat before speaking with a sincereness I'd rarely heard. "My good woman, I did not shoot your husband, nor did I incite those men to march. *But . . .*" He lifted his hand as anger surged in her features. "I am sorry if my presence or any intelligence I may have passed on in any way caused the events to unfold as they did. I believed I was simply discharging my duty. And I am most heartily sorry you lost your husband and later your child." His voice wavered, causing him to clear it again as his eyes shifted first to Gage and then a spot behind his shoulder where I presumed Henry stood. "A child is a precious thing. Something one should not take for granted."

We all stood in silence for a moment, each of us, perhaps, coming to terms with those words in our own way. For my part, I was forced to blink away a stinging wetness, refusing to give way to tears at a time like this. Then Gage nudged me to the side, squeezing between me and Dr. Barker as he slowly crossed the room toward Mrs. Barker.

She turned to him, her face wreathed with misgiving. For all her anger and grief, it was clear she didn't truly wish to shoot anyone. She simply believed it was the only way.

"Please. Give me the gun," Gage appealed, holding out his hand. "For my sake."

She resisted for a few seconds longer, but his last words seemed to penetrate through her haze. She glanced at everyone in the room watching her and then lowered her eyes and the pistol, willingly relinquishing it to him.

My shoulders collapsed in relief, and I moved toward the bed as Dr. Barker joined Gage in coaxing Mrs. Barker from the room.

"I . . . I couldn't . . ." Lembus stammered as I drew near, and I held out a hand to touch his arm, finding that he was shaking.

"I know," I told him. "She surprised you." I glanced down at Lord Gage. "She surprised us all. Why don't you go splash some water on your face. I'll stay with his lordship."

He nodded and hurried from the room, so agitated he forgot to even ask for his employer's approval.

I sank down beside Lord Gage, gently taking his hand. I realized it was covered in age spots I'd never noticed before. "Are you well?"

"As well as can be," he admitted, still seeming a bit stunned himself. "It's . . . been some time . . . since I faced down a person intent on killing me." He looked over at the other side of the bed as Henry joined us.

"A prospect I have never found enjoyable," I conceded.

He huffed a laugh. "Yes."

"A few weeks ago, Kiera faced down a knife-throwing opponent," Henry supplied.

Lord Gage turned to me in interest. "Really?"

I shuddered. "Yes. Don't remind me."

"But Emma wasn't nearby, was she?"

"No," I assured him, giving his hand a squeeze. "But speaking of Emma, I should look in on her."

This wasn't strictly true. Emma was probably already having her morning nap under Mrs. Mackay's watchful eye, so there was no real need to check on her. However, I was not above using a bit of connivance to see that Lord Gage conversed with Henry as he promised. Especially while he was in such a humble mood.

I pushed to my feet. "Will you sit with him until Lembus returns?"

"Of course," Henry replied.

I nodded, turning to go before Lord Gage could detain me. But even so, I couldn't resist pausing at the door, glancing back to see Henry seated on the chair pulled close, leaning forward as they talked.

CHAPTER 28

After peeking my head into the nursery to look in on my slumbering daughter, I returned to Dr. Barker's study to wait. Gage joined me a few minutes later, his face still haggard with shock. Rather than speak, I simply offered him my hand as he settled into the chair next to mine before the desk. Sometimes words were unnecessary. Sometimes they only got in the way.

A quarter of an hour passed before Dr. Barker closed the door to the study and then sank into the chair behind the desk. The surgeon exhaled a long, weary breath.

"First, I must apologize," Dr. Barker said after taking a moment to gather his composure. "Had I any idea she would attempt to harm his lordship, I would have stopped her."

"You didn't know, then?" Gage asked.

"I admit I had my suspicions she knew something. Particularly when you kept mentioning Grange Moor. But I had no idea she was acquainted with or assisting those men who attacked his

lordship, or that she would take it upon herself to finish the deed."
Dr. Barker reached out to straighten the implements and papers
littering his desk as if the very act would straighten his thoughts
and his life. "I have sedated her. And I will keep her thus until
you have all departed. But please, I beg of you. Please do not press
charges."

The doctor's eyes pleaded with us. "Prudence loved Nathaniel
with all her heart and soul. Truth told, she still does," he stated
with brutal honesty. "And she had a rough life after he died. Her
family essentially cast her out because of her husband's role in
the rising. She scraped together a living for a few years from her
stitching, but she was in rather desperate circumstances when I
met her while walking here in Wentbridge. I had intended only
to be passing through, but we struck up a friendship, and, well . . .
I decided there were worse ways to begin a marriage than with
simple companionship and protection."

For them both.

Dr. Barker's gaze bored into mine, asking whether I'd told
Gage his secret. Whether I intended to. "I do not believe she will
ever harm anyone. In all honesty, I don't believe she would have
actually shot his lordship, but thank heavens we needn't find
out." He leaned forward, stretching a hand out to us. "I give you
my word that I will look after her and ensure she is never a threat
to anyone ever again."

Gage turned to confer with me. "I am amenable to that. But
the decision will ultimately be my father's. Though I believe he
can be persuaded this would be in her best interest." His lips
curled upward solemnly. "Despite any evidence to the contrary,
he is not truly heartless."

And seeing Mrs. Barker thrown into prison or transported
to the other side of the world would certainly be that. Particularly when she was acting out of grief.

Dr. Barker nodded.

Gage pushed to his feet. "I will go speak with him now." He looked down at me when I didn't follow. "Aren't you coming?"

"In a moment," I assured him.

His eyes searched mine briefly before he gave a little shrug and carried on.

I waited for the door to close behind him before speaking. "You said you didn't suspect Mrs. Barker of assisting the attackers, but that isn't strictly true, is it?"

Dr. Barker stared back at me warily.

"The night I met you in the corridor. You said you were only partly anxious because you worried I would uncover your secret. But the reason you were out there in the first place wasn't because you heard a noise, was it? I found it a flimsy enough excuse at the time. It was because your wife was missing."

The surgeon turned away, breathing shallowly. "I *did* wake because I heard a noise. It wasn't coming from down the corridor, but from the room next door. I was worried something was wrong, so I went to look in on her. That's when I discovered she wasn't in her bedchamber."

"And where did you think she'd gone?"

Dr. Barker scowled. "I didn't know. I was simply concerned for her health."

I arched my eyebrows, not believing for a moment that he was telling me everything, but as I had no way to prove it, I allowed the matter to drop. We stared at each other silently for a moment, and his demeanor softened. I recognized again why I'd felt such an affinity between us before. Why I'd sensed we both understood certain things others did not.

My eyes lifted to the stuffed button quails on the mantel— the drab brown male and the smoky blue and crimson female.

"Do you intend to tell Mr. Gage?" Dr. Barker asked, drawing my eyes back to the doctor's anxious face. "Do you intend to tell anyone?"

I knew what Dr. Barker was speaking of, and I understood his anxiety. This had not been an easy secret for him to carry. It never would be. Perhaps one day it would prove unnecessary, but for now, the surgeon had no choice. Not if he wished to continue to treat patients and avoid possible prosecution.

Some might have felt angry or affronted at his actions, but now that my initial shock had worn off, I felt only mild intrigue. Dr. Barker had wished to practice medicine, and this had been the only way. And he had proved to be an excellent surgeon, receiving promotions and commendations, and doubtless saving countless numbers of soldiers' and civilians' lives, including Lord Gage's. As far as I could tell, his choices had hurt no one and, in fact, had done others a great deal of good. Even his wife.

So rather than dance around the issue, I gave Dr. Barker the respect of speaking to it directly. "You are an experienced, well-trained surgeon, a member of the Royal College of Surgeons. Your wife knows exactly who you are. You can attest to these truths?"

"Yes," the doctor stated unequivocally, arching his chin as if suddenly facing a jury of his peers, which I suppose I was.

"Then the rest is none of my business."

The day being a fine one, we gathered in the garden during the late afternoon. Lord Gage had mercifully regained much of his strength after his illness during the night, though he was prudent enough to allow his sons to carry him down the stairs rather than try to manage them himself. If actual apologies had been exchanged, I had not been made party to them, but nevertheless there was an ease and acceptance that had not been present between Gage, his father, and his brother during their previous encounters.

The three of them sat side by side in chairs at the edge of the terrace, chatting and even venturing a few good-natured teases, while I sat on the blanket with Emma, coaxing her to roll over and even helping her to sit upright. I expected nothing more from them as they tentatively began to build and rebuild the bonds between them. I certainly didn't expect Lord Gage to offer any sort of explanation for his past behavior. But apparently something had shifted within him.

There was no telling whether it would last. Truth be told, I anticipated that my father-in-law would always be a difficult man to contend with. A leopard doesn't exactly change his spots. But it was impossible not to be encouraged.

Our conversation had lapsed, the song of a blackcap warbler and the drone of a passing bee filling the silence, when Lord Gage suddenly announced, "I didn't join the Royal Navy by choice. Though I came to be grateful I did."

His words almost caused me to let Emma topple backward, but I steadied her in time before looking up at him. His gray hair had grown overlong in the days of his convalescence, and lay slicked back from his forehead, revealing wrinkles and spots it had previously hid.

"You've heard me refer to my mother's family, the Roscar-rocks, as smugglers and rogues." His mouth hardened. "Well, that's because they are." His eyes lowered to his lap, where he smoothed out the striped banyan draped over his shirt, waistcoat, and pants. "When I was young, I thought it a great lark, what they did. I was forever begging to be sent to visit them so that I could take part."

I could well imagine the excitement such wiles would hold for a young, adventurous lad. One who didn't know better, particularly when the adults around him turned a blind eye to what was right.

"My father had little use for me anyway. I was the second son, the spare. Much of the time I was merely in the way."

Henry flinched, and I could tell this comment had struck

home, though I didn't believe Lord Gage had intended it to. He was speaking of his past, not Henry's status as his second son, and an illegitimate one at that. But I also wondered if some of the memories of how his father had treated him had also colored his perception of Henry.

"So I spent as much time with the Roscarrocks as at my father's estate. The distance between them was not very great." He sighed. "I thought life there was idyllic." His lips firmed. "Until my friend was shot by a customs officer and I . . . I was arrested."

I struggled not to react. We all did. For none of us wanted Lord Gage to stop speaking. But this was a shock. Based on the avid look on Gage's face, I could tell he'd never heard any of this, and he was listening as intently as Henry and I were to every word his father uttered. But the revelation his father had once been arrested seemed to almost knock the wind from his lungs.

"It's shocking. Yes, I know." His face revealed the shame he still felt at this admission. "London's premier gentleman inquiry agent was, in fact, once a criminal."

"What happened?" I murmured.

"The magistrate gave me leniency." He frowned. "Of a sort. I could pay a hefty fine, I could go to prison, or I could join the navy."

"So your father bought you a commission?" Gage surmised, for officers were not promoted out of the general crew. They were gentlemen who bought such a commission, starting in the lower ranks before they earned or bought their way up.

"My father couldn't afford to buy me a commission, or to pay the fine. If it had been up to him, I would have gone to prison." His voice had turned dry and mocking, but I could tell it was meant to hide a world of pain.

"How old were you?" I asked.

"Eleven."

I couldn't withhold a gasp. My gaze met Gage's. The same

age Lord Gage had wanted his own son to join the Royal Navy. And had it not been for his ill mother begging his father not to take her son away, Gage would have gone.

"Then how . . . ?" Henry began to ask.

"My Grandfather Roscarrock bought me my commission. Out of guilt. After all, if not for him, I would never have been involved with their smuggling, and I never would have been arrested.

"And that's how I came to be in the Royal Navy. And that's why I don't talk about my family. Why I rarely visit them. In one instance, they wanted nothing to do with me, and in the other, I wanted nothing to do with them." He turned to look at Gage and then Henry, stating with finality, "You are better off not knowing them."

It was clear he believed this, and I wasn't about to argue. Not when the repairs to his relationships with his own sons were so tender and untried. But I wasn't so certain this was true. At least, I wasn't so certain spurning them had been in Lord Gage's best interest. Perhaps if he'd confronted them about what had happened, he might have made some peace with it. Perhaps at age eleven, there were things he hadn't known or even been able to fathom.

But there was time yet to confront that now that relations with Gage's father were no longer severed. Time yet for a great deal of things.

Gage leaned forward to retrieve Emma's silver rattle from where it had rolled toward him across the blanket, passing it back to her. "Why have you never told me any of this before?"

Lord Gage's face folded into a scowl, but not of anger, rather of embarrassment. "Because I was ashamed. Just like I was ashamed of the work I'd done for Sidmouth and the Home Office after the war. And the way I treated your mother." He peered at Gage out of the corner of his eye. "She deserved better."

"She did," he agreed evenly. "But . . . she loved you anyway. To the bitter end."

"She loved us both."

I lowered my eyes, lest either man spot the tears lurking there. Fortunately, Emma abetted me, choosing that moment to topple sideways onto my arm and emit a loud string of babbles. Soon she had all four of us cooing and fussing over her. A sight that made me laugh. If the criminals these men had helped apprehend could only see them now, they wouldn't be the least intimidated.

Later that night, I lay in Gage's arms, the sweat from our most recent efforts cooling on our skin. "Happy?" I asked him, pressing my thumb to the cleft in his chin.

He realized I wasn't speaking about our amorous attentions to each other.

He considered the question, humming as he exhaled. "Contented." His fingers brushed up and down my arm. "At least we're leaving here *with* my father and not without him."

"Yes." That was definitely an improvement. Dr. Barker had told us Lord Gage should be well enough to travel in short stretches in just a few days' time. We were all eager to be on our way. "Though I admit I am a bit anxious about spending so much time in close proximity."

It was true; his father could not be left to travel alone. Particularly not the distance of several hundred miles we would be journeying to Lord Gage's country estate—the manor he'd been awarded by the Crown, not the childhood home he'd inherited upon his elder brother's death. I admitted to a touch of curiosity about the place. After all, the estate would be my husband's one day. But I was mostly concerned about familiarity breeding contempt.

"We shall simply have to hope for the best." He inhaled

deeply. "And be grateful we prepared for the worst by bringing our mounts with us."

I smiled. "Now let's hope the weather remains fair."

"That, too."

I pressed my lips to his before snuggling my head into the junction between his neck and shoulder. "I will miss Henry, though," I confessed after a few moments of silence.

He had received word from his acknowledged father, the Duke of Bowmont, that his presence was needed at Sunlaws, and given the fact that his other brothers and their families were all gathered there, I couldn't begrudge his going to be with them.

"I'm sure we'll see him again soon enough," Gage replied, though I knew he would also miss him.

As good as it was to see Gage restoring his relationship with his father, I couldn't help but feel a bit melancholy that we seemed to be moving farther away from the rest of our family. My brother, my sister, and much of my extended family and closest friends were in Scotland, and now Henry would be there also. It was true, my friend Lorna and Gage's cousin Alfie were in England, but all the way in Dartmoor. It was a somewhat unsatisfactory discovery that we might not see any of our other loved ones for months.

But I had learned there were many different types of family—those you were born with, those you conceived, and those you created. They could love and bolster you or infuriate and drive you to distraction. And unfortunately, as I soon discovered, they could each equally betray you and stab you in the back.

HISTORICAL NOTE

While researching these books I stumbled upon a plethora of fascinating discoveries, some of which I utilized straight from fact and some which I twisted to my own purposes. One historical feature I highlighted in this book was the Great North Road, which was the main route from London to Edinburgh before the advent of the railroads. It was utilized by mail coaches, stage-coaches, and private coaches alike to swiftly travel from the north to the south and vice versa and was lined with an assortment of interesting wayside inns and attractions. The industries of many smaller villages along its route were centered around the road.

Wentbridge was one such place. It stood at a crucial point along the road because it boasted the only bridge over the Went River for many miles. The Blue Bell and Bay Horse Inns were real establishments. In fact, you can still visit the Blue Bell today, though it has undergone many changes since 1832. You can also visit Brockadale, which is now a nature reserve, and the

Norman church of St. Mary Magdalene in the village of Campsall. Most of the other buildings I utilized either no longer exist or were made up out of whole cloth.

Robin Hood has long been associated with the medieval vale of Barnsdale, within which Wentbridge lies. Indeed, the earliest surviving manuscript of a Robin Hood ballad mentions the village, and other early ballads refer to several sights nearby. In one of these ballads, Robin Hood builds a chapel in Barnsdale dedicated to Mary Magdalene, which has led to his connection with the Norman church built in Campsall.

An entire genre of stories and "urban legends" sprang up around the macabre possibilities of what might occur at some of the more remote wayside inns along the coaching roads. Trapdoors, bone pits, and turning human fat into candles featured in several of them.

The tale of Gervase Thompson, the tapster from the White Swan in Ferrybridge, being shot by Vanburgh as he was attempting to return his purse is both sad and true. You can visit his grave at the St. Andrew's Church in Ferry Fryston.

The Grange Moor Rising, as I've depicted it, is a real historical event, as are all the risings surrounding it. It is an often-overlooked event in a time of great struggle between the general populace and the government in Britain.

Lord Sidmouth and his Home Office did utilize government informants to gather information about these union societies. Some were given the task of infiltrating them, such as the infamous William Oliver, and there were often accusations that these spies acted as agent provocateurs, provoking them into action. These charges are difficult to prove, though that didn't silence the allegations at the time. All of which only fueled more anger at the government.

Dr. Barker was loosely based on the real historical figure Dr. James Barry. Dr. Barry was a renowned surgeon who received his degree from the Edinburgh Medical School and served at the Royal Military Hospital in Plymouth, and then South Africa and various other locations throughout the British Empire. He eventually rose to the rank of inspector general of all military hospitals, the second-highest medical office in the British Army. He served with distinction for more than forty-five years, beginning in 1813, and upon his death in 1865 was discovered physically to be a woman. Dr. Barry is an intriguing figure. Historical research has all but confirmed he began his life as Margaret Bulkley and with the help of his mother and highly placed friends was able to conceal his physical sex for more than fifty years.

ACKNOWLEDGMENTS

The creation and publication of my books is never a solo endeavor. Many thanks go to my editor, Michelle Vega, who helped me navigate some tricky elements in this book. As always, her keen insight enables me to make the story better. My thanks also go to the rest of the stellar staff at Berkley, including but not limited to Yazmine Hassan, Jenn Snyder, Jessica Mangicaro, and Annie Odders.

My gratitude goes to my amazing agent, Kevan Lyon, for her support and guidance.

A list of acknowledgments is definitely incomplete without thanking my husband and daughters for their love and care, and for bolstering me when my confidence is low. I'm also grateful for the rest of my family and friends, whose support means the world.

I want to give a special shout-out to Jackie Musser and Stacie Roth Miller—my dear friends and writing group partners for their always impeccable advice.

Ready to find
your next great read?

Let us help.

Visit prh.com/nextread

Penguin
Random
House